I0565120

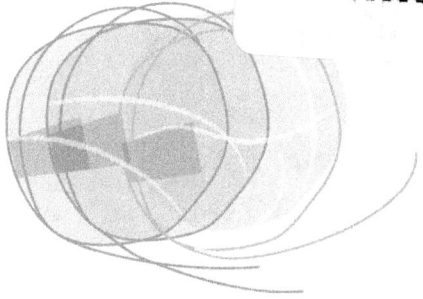

Threads

A novel by Edie Ayala

Happiness runs in a circular motion,
Thought is a little boat upon the sea.
Everybody is a part of everything anyway.
You can have everything if you let yourself be.
Happiness runs. Happiness runs.

—Donovan (released 1969)

Print 978-0-9880032-0-0

Ebook 978-0-9880032-1-7

Publisher: Stories with Character
www.storieswithcharacter.com

Publication Date: September 30, 2022

FIC000000 FICTION / General
FIC051000 FICTION / Cultural Heritage
SOC015000 SOCIAL SCIENCE / Human Geography

Book and cover design: berthaclark.com

www.edieayala.com

CHAPTER 1

IRENE

When you look back on it, it's hard to believe that in those early spring days of 1987 Irene was happy-go-lucky. Although she'd had her share of ups and downs, in the grand scheme of things any weight that threatened to bear down on her was easily lifted. Sometimes she even felt she might float away.

At this moment, Irene was giggling her way across the meadow, tall grass tickling her legs beneath her favorite circle skirt. The wind, with the taste of wild roses and yarrow still on its lips, tugged and finally freed one end of the sash from around her waist and whisked it upwards in swirls that practically wrote her name. I-r-e-n-e.

She had loosened her ponytail and a few fine blonde hairs swept across her cheeks, some catching in the corners of her mouth. Her peaches and cream complexion was rosy with delight. She glanced back at Chuck, her new husband, tossing her hair and batting those long eyelashes around those big blue eyes. She was taller than most women, almost 178 centimeters and she was voluptuous. She was Chuck's large angel.

That afternoon, the hills around the valley watched, amused, as a panting puppy-man (one of your smaller breeds) cavorted in pursuit of his lovely goddess of nature, whose full, flower-print skirt and satin sash rippled against her frolicking form.

Irene turned and tittered at Chuck. He was hopping about a short distance behind, reaching for and finally grasping the end of her sash. Just at his moment of victory, his black-framed Dior eyeglasses bounced and slipped right off his nose. As he dropped to his knees and fumbled around for the spectacles, she sighed and pretended he had captured her. She flounced and fluttered on the spot until he finally got to his feet and urgently waved the black frames in the air before replacing them on the bridge of his thin nose and pushing them tight up in front of his eyes. He blinked hard twice and grinned boyishly.

Chuck was a man of all the same color, inside and out – monotone mousy, a mousy brown crew cut, thin colorless lips, hazel-brown eyes and a pasty complexion with feathered ghosts of teenaged acne. He blended into himself. Although he tried to be cool (the most obvious sign being that he called himself Chuck rather than Charles), it was impossible for him to appear spontaneous and impossible to imagine him sexy. You could always see him planning his next move, a robot lover.

Just then he shouted something Irene couldn't hear but she laughed along with him when he gripped the sash between his teeth in a fake small-dog struggle.

She'd learn to love him.

The two of them were a good team. He was the brains and she was the brawn. He gave the orders and she carried them out. She didn't object to this arrangement (at least not in those early days) because she knew he was the intelligent one. He was the one who knew how to play the stock market and invest their profits. He owned a thriving grocery store, and he built her a sprawling four-bedroom house situated in a cul-de-sac of a sought-after neighborhood in Grant Falls, British Columbia. Chuck would take care of her. All she had to do was put in a few hours a day at the store, keep the house clean, and allow him make love to her on Tuesdays, Thursdays and Saturdays (with the odd Thursday off if things at the store had been crazy busy). Easy-peasy.

Irene was a realist but even realists dream. Right now, though, the two of them were focused on Chuck's dream. And her role in this dream was to bear and raise children, and they were going to start right away. In spite of their regular Tuesdays, Thursdays and Saturdays there wasn't a baby in the making yet, but her doctor said all the pipes were in working order and it was just a matter of time.

In preparation for a child, and when she wasn't dusting off the shelves at Chuck's East End Grocery, Irene frequented the wool department at The Bay. She'd saunter in and pull at strands of yarn, caressing exquisite English wools and twisting bulky fat fleece between her fingers to find the grit in it. Sometimes, after glancing around, she bent in to lick the threads like a baby, and savored them.

Irene was also a nature-lover. Not a wilderness adventure type, though. Heaven forbid that she'd be caught snowshoeing through a blizzard or that she'd have to survive on wild mushrooms or build her own shelter under spruce trees. She wasn't even the fair-weather kind of nature-lover where she'd have to get her feet wet crossing a stream. No, she preferred the gentle side of nature in the semi-tame countryside near town. She loved fresh mountain air, rolling meadows that were dotted with wild flowers, open fields where cows grazed lazily and where deer leapt over and disappeared behind thickets. She picked berries, wild roses, black-eyed daisies, even dogwood and fire weeds. She took her time and examined everything closely before plucking blossoms and dropping them into her reed basket for potpourri.

But the nature outings came second to knitting. Knitting was the best. Plus it fit perfectly into Chuck's well-laid plans to start a family. She would knit for babies of course. It was part of the reason she'd married Chuck. Because he could plan these things. And although she wasn't just dying to be a mother any more than she was head over heels for Chuck, he would make her life come true.

Chuck, on the other hand, well he was madly in love with Irene and he was kind to her. He sometimes blurted to total strangers, "I fell for her. I mean I really fell hard." He'd grin his boyish grin and he'd sniff and push up his glasses and inform anyone within earshot about how lucky he was to have found his Irene. He always punctuated this by removing the Diors (as he referred to them) to huff on the lenses and rub them with the patch of microfiber he kept in his pocket, as though this proved the veracity of his statement.

Chuck never raised his hand nor his voice but Irene soon realized that he was pragmatic to the point of being almost dictatorial. He expected Irene to apply the same dedication, drive and military-style self-discipline that he applied to everything that he did. As a result, there were early tell-tale signs of a life that might become too rigid for Irene, who was more impetuous.

Her mother had accused Irene of being reckless in marrying Chuck. "He's not your type, Irene. You'll be sorry you married for money instead of love." This of course, was purely a cultural deficit on the part of her mother. "Plus," her mother had insisted, "You're too young. Eighteen is too young to know what you want. You're still growing up."

But Irene had always known what she wanted. She didn't need more time to figure it out. She replied, "Mom, I see what happens when you marry for love. Look at you. Seven kids and you've never had enough to feed us. And what does Dad do? He wanders up and down the fields, hoping to harvest enough hay to feed the horses each winter. I, for one, don't want that."

But her mother's words rang in her ears years afterwards when things changed for the worst.

CHAPTER 2
COLUMBA

Columba marched in to the beat of her navy-blue platform shoes, the ones she'd pilfered from the Bata store when the clerk wasn't looking. Her stout figure was backlit by the mid-afternoon desert sun whose rays grinned through the frame of the front door that her friend Juana always had propped open with a rock, on which was joyfully graffitied *"Aquí hay amigos"*. Columba had arrived early for lunch.

Sunlight peered through her crepe dress, outlining her spindly thighs. Her knees, like rusty hinges, seemed that they would collapse under the weight of the oversized pear that was her torso. Thin fingers of sunlight raked through the spaces of her carefully backcombed, peroxide nest.

As she progressed down the hallway, the sun, who could never keep secrets, hollered out Columba's shape to the group that was seated at the kitchen table at the far end of the house. They all stopped talking to watch her approach. Her lips stretched into a broad grin in front of slightly stained teeth and the one gold-filled one at the top. The wrinkles on her sun dried cheeks deepened as she beamed out, 'I have arrived.' The makeup around her eyes was heavy and smudged from the heat. The extra set of eyebrows that she had hurriedly pencilled in above the original ones, which had been tweezed into oblivion in her youth, resulted in a perplexing combination of surprise and whatever else she was actually feeling. This morning her expression transmitted a surprised devil-may-care contentment.

The faded flowers on the dress got sucked in between her thighs as she thundered across the ceramic floor. At one point she slipped and was forced to crouch and touch the ground with her fingertips to regain her balance and the people at the table sharply drew in a collective breath. The large leopard-print plastic purse that was slung across Columba's shoulder slipped off and its contents were sent clattering across the floor – an oversized almond chocolate bar, a pair of sewing scissors, a florescent pink mirror, a faded woven wallet, four half-rolls of gauze bandages, two red BIC pens, a small plastic dinosaur, a ceramic saint icon and several hair pins tipped with happy blue and yellow flowers. Columba didn't carry money in her purse.

"Miguel, I'm here to take care of those callouses," she jokingly brandished the scissors, her face was red from the exertion of raising herself back to a standing position." And here, I brought you a treat." She marched forward and crouched to hand a chocolate bar (the one that everyone knew had been pilfered out of the goodness of Columba's big, generous heart) to the little neighbor girl who was in the corner chewing the ear of a small plastic pony.

Columba arrived at the table in time for lunch, which was always served no later than two o'clock because Juana wasn't going to miss her Turkish soap opera. Either you watched it with her or you left. "We Chileans have lots in common with the Turks," Juana liked to say. No one disagreed. Both nations topped the global list for having the lowest trust level among neighbors and friends. You have to be careful who you put your confidence in. That partly explained the country's excessive bureaucracy, long queues and abundance of notary publics.

Columba plopped down opposite Miguel, her chair squeaking backwards across the ceramic tiles. It was her usual place at the table. Although she was always welcome, her presence was never taken for granted.

Juana's steady stream of friends changed with the seasons. More mindless banter had been exchanged across that table than any other in Progreso, the small port town at the Pacific shores of Chile's Atacama Desert. Sometimes the banter was replaced by tales of hardship – of slow starvation, or stories about a relative who was 'disappeared' during Pinochet's regime, or the frustration and impotence over the senseless ruin of a family tomb by delinquents who slept in the cemetery. Sometimes there were tales of victory – how someone had finally gotten through to a malicious, low-minded, bureaucrat, or how someone had forced a lazy good-for-nothing bum to finally get out of bed and find a job. Life in small-town northern Chile was gritty. You couldn't really call it anarchy but when lax and lazy authorities turned a blind eye, you had to take things into your own hands and sometimes this led to circumstances that fell outside the purview of the law. And sometimes this happened often.

This afternoon, this particular kitchen in this house in the row of cinderblock side-by-sides halfway up the narrow slope between the Pacific and the Andes was filled with mindless banter between friends. The barren cordillera loomed high over the scene, its magnificence simply taken for granted. Brightly colored fishing boats bobbed near the rocky shore. Waves rolled in. Piles of saltpetre, white as snow, were piled high on the docks. One or two heavy vessels waited there to be loaded.

Vultures perched on the broken wall of a grimy auto repair shop on the corner near Juana's as the wind formed mini-tornados at the far end of the street, sucking in paper wrappers and empty styrofoam cartons and then scattering them as it wound down. Most houses had iron security grills but many preferred to keep panels of rusted corrugated metal nailed to their walls, a testament to their hardship, insecurity, neglect, or all three. Tropical music blared onto the streets from everywhere, mangy dogs sprawled across sidewalks and tough cats with crooked tails and torn ears paused on their paths over hot tin roofs. These details were eternal and went unnoticed. They were just part of home.

Miguel, the toothless gentlemen (who in true gentleman form wore a meticulous white shirt tucked into a pair of well-pressed charcoal trousers) laughed with everyone else when they served him corn on the cob. He just pushed it aside. "You know I can't eat that. I have no teeth."

"Columba," Juana said, "Why don't you get together with Miguel? You're both single. You could keep each other company."

"Are you kidding? Look at him."

Miguel smiled with his lips closed.

Light prattle and laughter echoed off the walls until the soap opera came on. Juana got up to turn up the volume, the theme music streaming down the hallway and beyond. The house slowly emptied itself of her guests.

Columba was the last to rise from her chair.

"Gracias, Juana. See you next week." She crouched, gave her a half-hug and a peck in the air and she made her exit, conscious of how the crepe fabric felt so sensuous between her thighs. Juana's eyes remained glued to the TV but she mumbled "Okay, you're in my prayers."

CHAPTER 3

GAVIN

Gavin hobbled down the hill and fell into the grass near the sewer-filled creek because he simply didn't have the stamina to carry on. It was an unpleasant spot and he wouldn't rest there long. No sir. He'd push back onto his feet and pick up the chase in a matter of minutes.

His new life as a private detective was nothing like what he had learned in the long-distance correspondence course. Not nearly as romantic. Nope, not what he had expected at all. It was hard work. And maybe the hardest part so far was finding a client.

Since completing his course a month ago, he had not been able to find one single person in need of his services. Not one client so far. And not for lack of trying either. This afternoon's jaunt had been a dry run in the event that he would need to chase some degenerate scoundrel through the bush.

He collapsed and rolled onto his back, breathing in the shit smell that bubbled up from the bog at his feet. He closed his eyes. He hated to admit defeat but maybe he'd need to think of something else. It was nearing winter, the leaves had already fallen, there was heavy frost on the ground each morning and he needed better winter clothing, especially if he was going to be pursuing 'subjects' day and night.

Part of Gavin's problem is that he lived in Burgeon, a quiet town just west of Grant Falls, British Columbia. Not much happened in Burgeon. Sure, it was a Peyton Place in terms of extra-marital affairs, which is why he thought being a private-eye was the perfect career choice. However, what he hadn't taken into account was that everyone already knew everyone's business so there were no secrets that hadn't, by hook or by crook, already come to light. All the husbands played around in the same circles with the wives who played around and they all had their own means of pay-back. No one wanted a divorce and as a result no one needed proof of the kind a private dick could provide.

The town's population of 18,720 was an established one, you could maybe even call it stagnant. Not many people moved in or out of Burgeon. Supported by its relatively prosperous mining and logging sectors, the spin-off service and retail businesses had been founded at least five decades earlier, and not much changed. People were comfortable here. Families appreciated the fresh mountain air. They bragged, "We're in the foothills of the Rockies. What more do you need?" The surrounding forest had ample wildlife – moose, deer, beavers, black bears, to name just the big ones. There was a lake at the west edge of town, good enough for swimming if you didn't mind freezing to death, and it was always great for fishing no matter what. The town of Burgeon boasted a small curling rink, a ski hill, lots of ski-doo trails and frozen lakes for skating and ice fishing. During the summer, people hiked and rode bicycles in paths that were probably, once upon a time, deer paths at the edge of the forested areas. The town celebrated its history with gold panning contests and fishing derbies and every so often, they hosted outdoor concerts, during which performers and audience alike, fought off hordes of mosquitos. It was a good place to grow up. Good clean fun, a single movie theater, a multi-purpose community center, where the essential but thank-fully rarely called-upon (and never in Gavin's lifetime) volunteer fire rescue service parked their truck and held annual fund-raisers. The town had four churches of different Christian denominations. So far, no mosques or tem-ples had sprung up here. Most guys in town drove a pickup truck and wore ball caps. Most women were stay-at-home moms. It was a cozy, relatively iso-lated community. If people were bored with the town's facilities they did their own thing – pickup games at the decaying baseball diamond whose rusty-red surface was tinged with potassium cyanide mine tailings; guys went hunting and fishing in any of the dozen nearby lakes; women formed book clubs; the Catholic Women's League organized semi-annual bazaars; kids ran wild through the bushes playing 'Cowboys and Indians.' What more could anyone need?

In 1987, Gavin turned 20. This reminded him that his whole life lay ahead of him and he had no idea what to do with it. Up to now, he didn't particu-larly feel in control of his situation and today he was trying to figure out how to do things right because lately he'd really blown it. Some weeks ago, his Dad kicked him out of the house for 'slothfulness' and in his despera-tion, Gavin had gone to live with his friend James Miner. James pumped gas at the Esso station. He was also a self-styled musician who played at the Pentecostal church where everyone met three times a week to worship and talk in tongues. Gavin had briefly lost his head and joined James' band (as a percussionist – he half-heartedly shook one of two tambourines), mostly to be friendly but also to enjoy some of the social benefits, which, as it turned out, were non-existent if you didn't like to drink freshie and eat sugar cookies and praise the Lord – which Gavin didn't. That's why his membership in the band was so short-lived.

Luckily, though, James had an extra bed and was generous with his food, so Gavin took advantage of the situation and it was during that first week at James' that he signed up for the private dick course that he had seen advertised at the back of a two-year-old True Detective magazine from Los Angeles, USA that James had tucked under his mattress. The advertisement shouted, "You Can't Fail! Order Today."

Gavin borrowed enough from James to purchase the money order and he sent away for the course. The entire course arrived all in one batch inside a flimsy kraft envelope. Surprisingly and much to his delight, he didn't even need to write exams. The bundle consisted of four thin booklets (Courses 1, 2, 3 and 4), each one folded and bound with staples. The last page of the fourth booklet was a certificate (with a smudged scissors icon on a dotted line right near the center fold) and a space to print your own name and the date when you completed the course. It had a black seal in the shape of multi-pointed star and underneath was a scrawled signature from the correspondence school executive, George Elwin McCallister, President. Gavin completed it all within two weeks. He printed his name and the date with a black fountain pen and he framed it in an 8 x 10 varnished wooden frame (placed neatly over top of the photo of James' dead grandmother).

Anyway, the point now was that Gavin was tired and unsuccessful and he was pretty sure that his Dad still wouldn't let him return home.

"Until you can get up in the morning with some purpose – and that purpose better be to make some money so you can support yourself (God knows what happens if you ever need to support a family) – you're on your own, Buster."

CHAPTER 4
IRENE

Life has a way of teaching you what you'd rather not have to learn. Some people become bitter with the experience, some people become ill, others insist there is no lesson to be learned at all and yet others look for the wisdom in it and move forward, healthy and happy to the extent they have not been irreparably damaged, and maybe even (as they see it) having improved.

For Irene the damage was huge. It was insurmountable. Deep down, she knew there was wisdom to be discovered but the discovery switch had been turned off and the microscopic seeds of aforesaid wisdom were scattered like fine dust in the waning light of an empty corner of her brain. She tried and failed to grasp them but in the end she simply became expert at compensating for their elusiveness and eventual absence. This turning point was still three years down the road.

It would take more than two years for Irene to get pregnant. The doctor repeatedly assured her that there was nothing physically wrong. "Sometimes getting pregnant just takes time. No need to blame yourselves," he told her, "You're both healthy."

She prepared each month, and each month that she wasn't pregnant, she consoled herself with her favorite things and Chuck, although becoming impatient, tried to keep their minds off the goal. "They say if you just relax and stop trying so hard, you'll be surprised… in a good way." He busied himself at his store and with phone calls to his stock broker.

In those two years, they worked hard, and played hard, scheduled a few holidays – the most far-flung was a trip to Hawaii and one to Arizona where they rented condos with other Canadian Snowbirds. They partied with friends abroad, all laughing their boisterous laughs, heads thrown back, jaws wagging, whiskey and beer glasses raised in exaggerated merriment. In their small circle, jokes were never off-color, there was no couples-swinging and no one displayed their dirty laundry in public. They were all model citizens with perfect lives back home, equally balanced between hard work and leisure. When it was time to return home, they all politely said goodbye to holiday neighbors and exchanged calling cards, which were usually left on the night table under the tip for the maid on the morning of their departure. Most really had no intention of staying in touch. And once, when one couple dropped them a line, Chuck and Irene found themselves too busy to respond and it died there.

Correction. They didn't both work hard. Chuck worked hard and Irene pretended to work hard. In reality she day-dreamed a lot. Hers were not ambitious dreams of achievement. No, Irene's dreams were the fluffy kind, often memory-based but more in the present and quite ethereal. She envisioned the sensual – flowers she had identified at the base of moss-covered tree trunks and bees that buzzed from one flower to the other. She dreamed about making jam and drying flowers. She dreamed of knitting. She imagined the feel of the oversized multi-colored sweater she'd seen in the Vogue magazine and then, in sharp contrast, the sequined backless evening gown of the woman at the swanky club in Hawaii. She played romantic songs over and over in her head. And she sang too. She had a beautiful, warbling voice, clear as crystal. Often when she was strapped up in her store apron (the one with the dull green East End Grocery logo on the top right corner of the bib), she sang as she dusted cans of broad beans and boxes of powdered milk and as she handled, one by one, the convenient plastic cases with emergency sewing essentials in the non-food aisle, the items that were slow movers, as Chuck called them. She felt sorry for the slow movers and gave them extra time.

"You have to keep them looking new or chances of them ever moving off these shelves is zero." He formed a circle with his thumb and forefinger and winked. Light glinted off his Diors. She could follow instructions okay – it was just that she took her time to complete tasks. Chuck had to crack the whip. The best way, he found, was to promise rewards. Things like a drive out to Dupont Lake or a trip up to the old lookout near the ski hill, promising to stop along the way so she could pick berries and wild flowers. "Just say the word," he'd say. "But you have to finish stacking the cereal aisle by three pm."

On these outings, she sang unself-consciously as they cruised along the country roads, her eyes bright, alert for deer or foxes or even bears, should they appear from an opening in the forest. Chuck turned off the radio and listened. Her voice was beautiful. It briefly occurred to him to make her a recording star. But he was possessive of her voice. No, he'd make up for it with photographs. He considered himself a good amateur photographer and he showed off his Irene shots. "Here was one of Irene posed with a basket full of berries. And here she is on her knees in front of a wild orchid. Notice how the light filters through the leaves onto her cheek. Doesn't she have the most perfect complexion? Here she's flipping her hair over her shoulder. That's so characteristic of her. Oh, and here, she's shielding her eyes from the sun as she gazes over at a hummingbird that's hovering near an unusual stand of foxgloves. What an afternoon that was."

Chuck allowed Irene to indulge in her own private outings to wool shops. What husband in his right mind would want to be there? Anyway, a woman had to have some time to herself. He was an understanding, reasonable husband who had absolutely zero interest in wool.

But she accused him of being unreasonable at the store. "I'm not your puppet, Chuck. you can't just expect me to lift up my arms and do everything you ask, in exactly the way that you imagine it to be done." She would raise her arms and let them drop, as if boneless, down to her sides.

"No, my dear. You're not my puppet. And you have freedom to come and go but we need to keep things on track, right darling?"

CHAPTER 5

COLUMBA

Consider being contracted for an underpaid part-time job without benefits in addition to an already underpaid part-time job without benefits. Of course, it equals two underpaid jobs without benefits, the sum of which is something.

It all began with waste from the gringos. Well, they didn't consider it waste. It was good stuff that was simply unwanted, discarded, tossed aside, better used by someone else. What was that word? Oh yes, 'recycled.' The gringos 'recycled' their clothing. Over time, Columba came to recognize their brands. It seemed that gringos wore their clothes with labels sewn on the outside. She could never see the logic in that. She would come to learn that gringos regularly purged their closets in order to fill them again with new outfits from the likes of Walmart and Sears and Zellers while others needed to make room for expanded wardrobes from The Gap or Le Chateau or Club Monaco, sometimes Lacoste and Roots, adidas or Nike. These names she became familiar with. When the garments arrived, fresh off the boat, the bloated plastic bundles were sliced open with carpet knives, and the shirts, trousers, shoes, dresses, sweaters, pajamas, and nightgowns slipped like an awesome animal that had just been gutted; they bloomed – large colorful flower innards appeared as if in a series of stop-action photographs. Some garments were still like new, others slightly worn and scant others heading towards threadbare. Perfectly good all the same to be re-sold and re-used and appreciated in a developing country like Chile.

The gringo recycling trend opened up new businesses in both hemispheres and Columba was among the first wave of employees to jump on the bandwagon in South America. She heard about it one morning while eavesdropping on the bank manager. At the time, she was cleaning at the State Bank. This is where she loitered and puttered and mopped over the same narrow stretch of floor, pocketing the odd ashtray, pen, pencil and notepad and anything else that wasn't nailed down, her auditory faculty stretching around corners and under doors. She tucked snippets of conversation behind her ears like cigarettes, that she might pluck them out later and leisurely draw on them.

One particularly crisp blue morning as she knelt down to scrape gum off the floor just outside the manager's office, an imposing businessman (at least he seemed so from her floor-level perspective) marched past her and almost crushed her baby finger with the heel of his impeccable black brogue. He continued without a backward glance, the heavy odor of Brut cologne filtering down to the hands-and-knees level where Columba was cringing in pain. He failed to notice her and he failed to latch the office door. Here's what she remembered of his conversation with the bank manager:

"I'm seeking capital to cover start-up costs. And an increase to my line of credit..." His booming businessman voice carried easily. "We're getting into a new import business. It's called recycled clothing. The gringos are preparing to send huge garment shipments and this is only the beginning. Some do-gooders up there want to donate re-conditioned garments (and whatever comes along with that) to our less than fortunate population." He paused and she heard him chortle. "But it's a great business opportunity, not a charitable venture. We pay by the kilo. I'm not going to get into the details at this point, and I'm sure you don't want to either. Let's just say, it's beneficial to all involved, including the less fortunates in our community." She imagined the eyes of the bank manager holding steady as he counted the social benefits in dollar signs. The businessman continued, "I see spin-offs and growth in the market both here and in North America. Of course, my recycling plant will be at the dock. I'm expanding my facilities there. And I'll sell to my own outlets in Santiago, on the street that is gaining a reputation for this kind of thing. You know Calle Bandera in downtown Santiago.... well, you probably don't. But the point is that I plan to open a few stores under different names and I'll market the clothing as '*Ropa Norteamericana*'. I mean, who doesn't want a bit of North American clothing, right? Initially, we'll attract young kids but it won't be long – mark my words – before it'll gain popularity with everyone. We'll offer very competitive prices. The wheels are already in motion. And we are expecting the first shipments within the next month or so."

The bank manager responded. "I agree it sounds like an interesting venture and I'm not surprised to hear that you're the one who got in on the ground floor." He sniffed. "Well, of course you know that these decisions aren't all made by me alone but because you and I are long time amigos, I won't need much. Just as a formality, can you see your way to sending me a basic plan? Something I can wave under my boss' noses... you know what they need... again just a formality." Columba knew that the bank manager was rubbing his thumb against his index forefinger as he said, "And you know what I need."

The businessman replied, "Yes, of course. I brought something with me today." There was a brief pause during which she heard the unmistakable rustle of *billetes* (no doubt of larger denomination). "But it's urgent and you'll need to push it through for me because I have to start hiring people to sort through the bales that'll land on the dock. The transport logistics are worked out and I don't need you for that but I'd appreciate you getting an early approval from higher up the food chain, partly to cover initial wages. If not, well, the workers will have to wait. But you know, it's good to at least start off on the right foot, show good faith for the first month or two."

"Of course. And just so I can pass it on, where will the laborers be working?"

"I'm dividing up my main plant. Everyone will be at the dock. No need for big changes. This whole thing is very opportune. Extremely encouraging to see how easily it all just kind of fell into my lap. The business will grow itself."

And that's how Columba came to be the first in line to apply and be accepted for a part-time job without benefits at Progreso's first clothing recycling depot called simply 'The Recycling Plant'. The businessman beamed, "It has an environmentally-friendly ring to it."

In her interview, she said the three things the imposing businessman needed to hear. "I'm a hard-worker. You can rely on me. And I'm honest." The first was, of course, absolutely true.

What, if not hope, drives us? A change in rhythm, a quickening of pace, the marching forward into a multi-colored life to a different tune, following the piper up the road towards the river of better times, even if such a river gasps its way through the shallow underground caverns of the driest desert on earth.

CHAPTER 6

GAVIN

The river of better times in the interior of British Columbia has no need to hide itself underground or to be shy or pretend to be humble. It gushes joyously through lush green valleys and abundant fields, it meanders through forests replete with trees whose leaves you might mistake for the green of money. The global disparity is so obvious that perhaps it need not be stated. But the point has to be brought forward.

With Gavin giving it some thought and James praying about it, the two of them reached the same conclusion one night over pizza. And this conclusion was that Gavin's Dad wasn't a dick at all (and we're not talking about the private kind) but rather he was just a parent trying to educate a 20-year-old son in the ways of the world.

James said between bites, "Well, the old man isn't all that bad. And I figger you have to realize that you're not a teenager anymore, Gavin. As a man, you have responsibilities."

"Yeah, I guess. What responsibilities do you mean?"

"Well, I mean... there's lots. I mean, I guess the most obvious is that you gotta be able to support yourself."

"Are you trying to tell me something James? Are you tired of having me around here? Do you think I'm not pulling my weight? Do you think I'm freeloading? 'Cause if that's the case, I don't know why I've been sweeping your floor and doing your dishes and taking out your garbage. Like, I've been your maid, man."

"Hey, no, I'm not insinuatin' that, Gavin. That's not what I mean."

Gavin dug in. "Cause if you do, I'm outta here right now, buddy. I mean you know I've been trying to get some skills and stuff. It's not like I'm just sitting around on your couch all day long, man."

"Hey, I didn't say that."

Insisting, Gavin slapped the slice of pizza onto the table and stood up. "I mean it, James, if you don't want me, I'm gone. I don't stick around where

I'm not wanted."

"Relax. That's not where I was goin'. What I meant is that your Dad has a responsibility, like any father, to see that his son gets on in life. Okay? And that's all he's doin'." James' face was red. Gavin noticed the veins punch out on his neck and realized he'd pushed it too far. Pretty soon he'd bring God into it.

Gavin sat back down and stuffed the rest of his pizza into his mouth to chew over where James was going with this.

"Yeah. Okay. So, I see your point." Gavin was bobbing his head non-stop, like one of those fuzz-covered plastic dogs in the back of a car that assents to your passing. James watched and figured Gavin was really thinking it through.

"So, Gavin.... so maybe you gotta go over to your old man and talk to him. Tell him where you're comin' from. Tell him you've been studyin' and stuff. Make him see that you're makin' an effort here."

James' face lit up and he continued, "Besides, the corner outside your old man's store is a perfect spot. You'll be killin' two birds with one stone. Eventually everyone crosses that intersection on the way to the post office and more often than not, there's conversation on the way over, and it's gonna be more than just gossip. You see, man? If you identify a crisis or hear about some kinda conflict that needs clearin' up, you'll be in the right spot to offer your services." He didn't wait for Gavin to agree with the logic. His eyes were shiny because he was so right. "You know I'm right, man. That corner," he was pointing hard to the ground with his index finger, "That corner is the crux of opportunity."

The next day, Gavin headed over to the town's crux of opportunity, which was, as James had pointed out, right in front of 'Stan's Men's and Boys' Wear.

Luckily there was an old electric pole that some genius had planted right in the middle of the sidewalk decades ago. Electric poles on sidewalks were perfect for being nonchalant. He'd seen secret agents use them in movies. Probably more than a dozen people had written letters to the The Weekly Post over the years complaining about how they had to maneuver baby carriages onto the street to get around this particular post and how it was dangerous and how, anyway, electric poles weren't supposed to be right in the middle of sidewalks. He sauntered over and leaned into it, casual-like. He played with a book of matches, lighting them and watching the flames snuff themselves out one by one as the matches dropped to the ground. Although it didn't appear to be a difficult thing to pull off, it wasn't easy standing out there in plain view looking disinterested or better yet, like some kind of urban chameleon who could just blend into the landscape. He considered it good practice, though.

His Dad appeared at exactly 11am, the usual time for his morning break. Gavin watched as Stan Reid extracted a package of Du Maurier Light King Size from the breast pocket of his light blue Arrow shirt before the door had even finished closing and he moseyed over to the corner of the building. Gavin couldn't tell if his Dad had spotted him. If so, he didn't let on.

Stan leaned lightly into the vertical beam at the corner of the store, eyes closed, taking his time, and he blew a few smoke rings. What did he think about during these intermissions from his 'precise work of fine alterations'? Gavin kept his head lowered and observed from under his nonchalant eyebrows. He was chipping away at the dirt with his right foot, the metal tip on his cowboy boot disappearing under the dust. He fidgeted. He couldn't think of a casual way to approach his Dad.

Stan's Men's and Boys' Wear had been situated on that spot for more than 30 years. It was the only men's clothing store in town and right across from it was the only pool hall in town. With its beige stucco façade and royal blue wooden trim, Stan's Men's and Boys' Wear was one of the town's most familiar landmarks. "Turn right on Main Street and pass Stan's and then...." Stan had the paint freshened every two years but he never changed the colors. The condensed serif typeface on the sign was the same beige as the stucco. The sign, with its royal blue background ran the width of the main window and there were two spot lights on the top of each corner that focused on 'Stan's' and 'Wear'. The lights came on automatically at night.

A signal that he was finishing his break, his Dad ground his cigarette butt into the old tomato can filled with sand that sat on a disused concrete curb. Both the can and the curb had been in those exact same spots for as long as Gavin could remember. The can's label had peeled off years ago. Gavin remembered it had been an old tomato can that Stan had asked his Mom for one Saturday afternoon when Gavin was only about three years old and playing with the pots and pans at his Mom's feet. The tin was really rusty now but his Dad never changed it. His Dad didn't change much, come of think of it.

Gavin had to make his move now. He sauntered over.

After butting out the cigarette Stan always looked up at the sky as though the meteorological conditions would have an impact on business inside the store, like his alterations depended on good weather or something.

Gavin raised his hand in a half-salute, trying to look surprised. "What a co-incidence," he said as he reached Stan's side of the street. He wasn't sure how to begin but as it turned out, he didn't have to. Without smiling or asking how Gavin had been or how things were going, or even offering his hand in a friendly gesture, his Dad just nodded and got right to the point.

"Ernie, from the pool hall came over the other day to buy a new pair of trousers and we got to chatting. He said that things've been really busy over there lately and he's short-handed on the evening shift on account of Gus cut out without giving any notice. He said he needs someone who knows how to handle himself. I don't know if you're the guy, but I told him you were looking for work."

Gavin glanced over at the pool hall. Yeah, this just might be right up his alley. Like a bouncer. Sure, he could put his people-watching skills to work too. It was an unexpected opportunity. He glanced up at the sky (like father, like son, a little tell-tale mannerism) for who-knows-what... maybe a full moon or something magic like a shooting star in the middle of the day. Then he prodded the ground with his boot, pretending such a proposition needed a lot of thought, as though he'd have to adjust a heavy schedule. Finally, furrowing his brows he looked up at his Dad, conjuring up his most pensive expression, and he nodded affirmatively. He tried not to sound too eager, "Actually, yeah, I could probably be his guy."

Gavin could see that his Dad was hopeful. "Well, son, boot it over there then and talk to him before he finds someone else for the job."

"Yeah, thanks Dad." Gavin started off and then he turned around. "I've actually picked up a course since I've been over at James'. This job'll be a good fit."

Why did he have to blurt that out? Now his Dad would think he was trying to impress him.

Stan just gave him a blank look, reached down to shake the can of sand and ashes and headed back to resume the precise job of fine alterations.

CHAPTER 7

IRENE

Win or lose, you think you've reached the finish line, your chest bursts past the ribbon signaling that you ran a good race. But the end is just the beginning.

It was June when Irene realized she was pregnant. The early part of the month had been rainy but the sun was out this week. Flowers blossomed. She had planted the vegetable garden early this year but instead of tiptoeing around it and bending down and fingering lumps of soil, checking for new sprouts and annoying Chuck because he would have to wait for her, this year she felt too tired and she neglected it. Her excuse was that it was too early for sprouts or weeds. Why bother yet?

"Just a flu," she told Chuck when she woke up feeling a little queasy and she begged him to let her sleep in. "You go and I'll meet you there before noon. I promise." She wasn't sure why she hadn't told him that her period had been late. She suspected she was pregnant but it had not been confirmed. Maybe she just needed to keep something to herself. Maybe she just needed a little secret or two. Maybe she just needed a life.

It was well after lunch when the little bell above the store entrance rang in her arrival. Chuck looked up, frowning. "That took you long enough. You don't look ill. You look fine."

He walked around the counter, glanced over his shoulder and in a low voice, "Look Irene. This is supposed to be a partnership. You know the inventory is already overdue. I need your help around here."

It was true. She felt fine. In fact, she felt great now. She smiled. "It must have been something I ate. I'm good now."

She ignored his foul mood and in a tone that exaggerated her vigor, she said, "Okay, where should we start? Well, wait. First things first. How about a cup of coffee?"

Chuck rolled his eyes, "Irene, didn't you have breakfast before you came in? Now you need to eat too?"

"No, Chuck, just a coffee. Would you mind?"

He always made the coffee because he said hers was too strong or too weak... whichever – it was never right.

"Alright." He smiled too sweetly when he glanced at Maureen, Wednesday's assistant, as he hurried Irene along, hand under her elbow, "Can you get me the inventory lists please?"

It was the way he ordered everyone around all the time, – do this, do that, don't waste time. She was bored with it. But suddenly (and at first, inexplicably), she felt omnipotent and she straightened her back and drew herself up, stiff, and very tall.

She deliberately sauntered across the floor like a super model – hips out, shoulders back, toe, heel, toe, heel slowly, slowly. She paused to turn and lean in, taking her time to align a can of peaches on the shelf and then she gracefully dipped to adjust the angle of a box of Cheerios. She back-stepped and tilted her head to examine the new design on a shampoo bottle. Not that she cared but just because she could. She felt much taller than Chuck.

The significance of her pregnancy had dawned on her. She was the queen bee, the vessel, the keeper of the cargo. She possessed and controlled what Chuck wanted. She touched her belly, nothing to see or feel yet but she knew it was there, the fetus that would be Chuck's baby. And for now, it was just hers. She was the one in possession, she owned it, she alone knew about it. She didn't feel maternal, she felt industrial-strength.

Carrying the baby was the thing, the prize, the treasure, the ultimate source of all power. And this secret – this one about its existence – was an early spinoff bonus prize. This secret was 100% hers. Chuck could order her around to kingdom-come and she could do just as she wished. He was helpless against what he didn't know. His own precious seed had weakened him, given her the leverage.

When she finally reached the coffee room, Chuck had his back to her, his rigid posture a sign of his annoyance. A moment ago, on her pedestal of omnipotence, she would have been unimpressed by his childish behavior. Who was he to be annoyed with her? She, who was the guardian of the gold. But just then, she was overcome by a wave of nausea. "Chuck, don't worry about the coffee. I'll just get to work."

It was the smell of coffee. Fleeting as it was, it nauseated her, depleted her strength. She felt like Superman up against kryptonite. She had to escape.

Her mother didn't seem surprised to hear from her. Irene pictured her standing beside the kitchen cupboard where the old beige phone was attached to the wall, the string knotted around a pencil, which hung from a nail that had been there for decades. Her Mom would be twisting the phone cord between her fingers, scanning the view of the fields outside the kitchen window as she always did when she talked on the phone. Her voice was soothing, as though there had never been a rift between them, as though she had been poised, waiting for Irene's call. "Hello, Irene. How are you?"

"I'm fine, thank you." She didn't ask how her Mom was. "Well, or maybe I'm not fine. I don't know, Mom." She blurted it out, "Mom, I'm pretty sure I'm pregnant."

Her mom was quiet for a second. "What makes you think so?"

"Well, first, I'm about two weeks late. And I feel sick sometimes."

"Are you tired, bothered by smells? Can you drink coffee?" Her Mom was an expert on pregnancy.

"Well, yeah, I've been more tired than usual and I felt nauseous when I got up this morning but it went away, and then when Chuck made coffee at the store, I had to leave the room. So yeah, I guess smells bother me."

"You're pregnant my dear." She knew her Mom was smiling. "You're pregnant. Best make an appointment."

A week had passed since her doctor's appointment and Irene still didn't feel like breaking the news to Chuck.

She was annoyed that her own body had weakened her with nausea, and just when she had reached the summit of control, just when she was on top of the world with the power button under her thumb.

Another reason for keeping her pregnancy a secret was that Chuck would shift into turbo-control and, for as little as her life was hers now, it would never be her own again. He'd want to protect her, he'd make her walk on the inside of the sidewalk, maybe he'd even insist that she ride in the back seat of the car, buckle her up with a pillow and cover her with a blanket, like a crystal vase. What next? Would he put her in a box? He'd send her to bed early, he'd make her eat beets and kale, he'd wave off cravings for ice cream and pickles. But isn't that what pregnant women are supposed to eat?

Irene made an effort to hide the waves of nausea. As long as Chuck left the house promptly in the morning, it was manageable. As it turned out, the real challenge was hiding her overwhelming urge to sleep. She would fall into irresistible, drug-induced-like states of heavy drowsiness in the middle of the day. She knew she wouldn't be able to continue running to the bathroom, to fold forward on the toilet and doze. Maureen knocked on the door more than once, "Will you be much longer?" Chuck accused her of avoiding her job, he tightened his upper lip and berated her through his teeth, complaining that as usual, she wasn't pulling her weight.

Thus, three weeks after the doctor had confirmed the pregnancy, it was the simple desire for blissful, uninterrupted sleep that toppled her from her secret pedestal. She couldn't hold out any longer, and she finally walked up to Chuck, swaying her hips, smiling coyly, "Chuck, what do you say we go to our little Italian place for dinner tonight?"

"It's not one of our scheduled nights." He sighed and let his shoulders drop. "You just want to get out of cooking again."

She stepped up, wrapped her arms loosely around his neck and looked down into his eyes. He was wearing his low shoes again, which made her even more aware of her higher status. "No. Well, maybe. But it's not the only reason." She tried not to look too bright.

"What's up?" He said, more curious than annoyed now.

"Nothing. What do you say?"

His hesitated and softened his voice. "Of course. If it's for a good reason. I'll make the exception."

She knew he could guess. What else were they waiting for? "It's not busy today. Everything is in order here." She suggested, "Let me go home early this afternoon and you can meet me there after you lock up." She'd squeeze in a few hours of sleep.

Although she could have slept until the next morning, she managed to rouse herself in time to shower and be ready just before he walked in the door. His mood was buoyant. Her mood was not as light but she made an effort to hide it. She was relinquishing something, surrendering. He would usurp her power. All along, she'd known her power would be fleeting and she'd eventually have to give in. Nevertheless, that hadn't prevented crazy scenarios running through her head. Scenarios like how she could run off and have the baby on her own, maybe she could go and live at her Mom's or maybe she could move far away, live under a new name. Chuck would never find her. But where? Plus, she'd have to get a job or ask for help from Social Services. And she'd live in some kind of dumpy basement apartment with second-hand baby furniture. She knew she wasn't capable of supporting herself, let alone a child. And certainly not to the standard to which she was accustomed with Chuck. Maybe she could even have an abortion. She didn't know where to start with that one. She chalked such thoughts up to an influx of crazy hormones.

The waiter directed them to a private table at the back. Chuck said, "Let's order first and talk second." He had a twinkle in his eye, something Irene hadn't seen for more than a year. She knew he was just playing along.

She took her time scanning the menu. Chuck had closed his and sat in silent expectation, hands folded politely on the table. The waiter stood a short distance away, waiting for a signal. She could make them both suffer longer but she was hungry. First sleep and now food, her body letting her down again, forcing her to rush things.

Finally, when the business of what to eat was out of the way (she ordered lasagna and a side salad and fresh juice instead of her preferred glass of Merlot), Irene made the announcement without ceremony. It wasn't how she had intended. She wanted to prolong it, make him sweat a little, watch as he bit his tongue and knitted his fingers, anxious for the words he knew she was going to utter.

But she went and blew it. "Chuck, the doctor told me that I'm pregnant. It's more than eight weeks now."

He dropped his arms to his sides, lowered his head and, nudging his black Diors above his nose, he dabbed his eyes with his napkin. She watched his shoulders shake with joy.

CHAPTER 8

COLUMBA

At first its arid landscape appears harsh and lifeless and you're almost dying for a touch of color. But you must become accustomed to it because here life is a chameleon of monotony – it scampers undetected across rocks and disappears into caves, burrows beneath the sand, flies past you in the wind. However, if you study it, you will begin to see that the desert glitters, its minerals reflect the stars so brightly by night that you could mistake it for daylight but during the day, its waves of hot color make a fool of you. You will soon discover that the color of the desert is far and beyond the range of monotony, it is far more than your eyes will ever see.

The grey, hobbled-together hodgepodge population of Santa Rita that hung on the high ridges overlooking the Pacific port city of Progreso was preparing for an upset and Columba was going to take advantage of it.

For more than twenty years, Santa Rita had been a conglomeration without status. It did not constitute an official community but rather a *'toma'*, a slum, a hovel, a shanty-town. And its residents were growing restless.

Santa Rita's humble existence began when several families of *pirquineros* set up shelters between Progreso and their small mining stakes. These shelters were the beginnings of Santa Rita. Its location was a steep, uphill climb from Progreso and still a few kilometers from any of the small mines. Somehow that spot was chosen and nobody remembered exactly why. Or at least, all of the stories differed. The most likely reason was because it was a sort of level shelf, a pause part way up the craggy mountainside, like an empty hand held out, waiting for someone to put something in it.

But the story of how the place got its name had one version and one version only.

It was said that a young woman called Rita was rushing back from her husband's stake to their home on the ridge of the future Santa Rita pueblo. She was returning after having delivered his hot lunch. Her husband satisfied, and the thin metal pot now empty, she headed back home with the pot swinging from a leather strap that was slung over her arm. She was tramping hurriedly across the rocky, sloping plain in her thin-soled shoes when a tremendous gust of wind caught her off-guard and sent her reeling across the desert like a tumbleweed. Her empty pot was found the next day, tilted on its side, still slightly pitching in the wind, squeaking and clattering eerily against the very rock that saved it from rolling down towards the sea.

But it would be two days before an old miner would find Rita's remains. He was on his way back from work one evening, slogging along, head down as usual, alert for signs of a seismic shift that could have concealed a deep cavern just beneath the sandy surface, a stealthy trap ready to swallow a man and leave his bones to rot forever in its belly. It was well past dusk, the sun had dropped behind the slow curve of the Pacific and the blue-purple heavens shimmered, bringing the sky so close to the earth, you could almost gather the stars into your hands and let them spill out between your fingers, like magic. A half-moon peered down and the minerals lit up the high plains like millions of lanterns.

The old man's eyes caught what looked like a red flag waving from the other side of a rock. Curious, he trudged over to take a closer look. And that's when he found what remained of Rita. Her thin red sweater had snagged on a craggy butte off the beaten track and her small body, bent at the waist, arms dangling, was swinging ever so slightly, "Just like a broken door hanging on one hinge," the old man reported. She had a long gash in her forehead and blood had dripped and dried on the rocks beneath.

As is the tradition, her husband erected a small chapel for her spirit in the place her body was found. In this case, the chapel was made of smooth white-washed rocks piled up to make a hollow dome that was topped with a small wooden cross. It covered the dark bloody rocks over which her body had been suspended. A photo of Rita was pushed back under the protection of the dome along with a miniature pot and a bowl and spoon. After that, people claimed to hear her calling to them, offering to feed them if they would stop to visit. Some locals made regular pilgrimages to her chapel, lighting candles, leaving bottles of water planted in the sand (what more precious a gift than water?), and often breaking bread with her in exchange for an intercession. They whispered prayers and stuffed little notes between the rocks of the dome. Mostly they were pleas. "If you help me with rice, then I promise I'll come and visit you every month." But sometimes the pleas were more serious. "Please heal my son's back," "Make my husband stop cheating." And when she granted their wishes, they tucked new notes between her white stones, "Thank you for curing my daughter's headaches." "Thank you for keeping my children safe." Before long they declared Rita a saint and without ceremony, they named the desolate hodgepodge community that huddled in the palm of the outstretched hand on the side of the mountain, Santa Rita.

The original dwellings of Santa Rita were made of wine crates and slats of warped lumber. Old advertising placards (with faded smiling faces of happy housewives feeding their blond-haired child a candy proclaiming 'a flavor you'll never forget') leaned beside corroded and warped metal road signs, cracked plastic sheets and cinder blocks conjoined to make walls. Ripped and oil-stained nylon tarps were knotted and strung end-to-end, and where possible, sheets of rusty corrugated metal were anchored by heavy rocks on top of corner posts to make a roof. The shelters were no match for the night-time desert cold and the searing mid-day heat but they mostly stood up to regular afternoon dust storms. Occasionally, however, if the wind wailed and battered long enough, walls twisted and bits broke away and somersaulted along the flats. And during extremely fierce winds the rocks that anchored the metal roofing sheets thudded to the ground, releasing the sheets. They careened across the desert like the giant lethal blades they were, sometimes cutting the life out of someone.

Since the early days, the community had expanded to well beyond 700 families and the dwellings had evolved to small side-by-side houses, some with wooden façades, some partially painted in bright pinks and greens and yellows (stopping abruptly when the paint ran out). Wooden and wire fences joined one house with another to corral chickens and children. Cables stretched from a noisy generator that chugged for three hours each evening to high points on the constructs. Clothes swung from ropes, fences and posts. Old-fashioned TV antennas bent into the wind. Tropical music burst forth with a vengeance and TV announcers shouted out the news from amidst the domiciles that folded and blended one into another.

After nearly twenty years, it was time to grant official status to the community of Santa Rita so its inhabitants could live with dignity. They wanted development and infrastructure. They wanted running water and electricity and garbage collection. They wanted a mayor and a town council. Mostly, they wanted law and order. Because of its isolation, the community had become a haven for thieves and drug dealers who stealthed back and forth along the long unmarked borders of the open desert.

Finally, after their umpteenth appeal, someone behind a desk in a regional government office paid attention and appealed to someone else in the Capital who paid attention because it just happened to play into a new political agenda. After much to-ing and fro-ing between the state and a businessman who claimed ownership of part of the land (with several dog-eared documents that he dug out of his tin box behind the old steamer trunk), the state eventually informed the assemblage from the shanty-town that before the government would buy the land from said businessman and grant official status to the community, Santa Rita would require a greater population. So, the leaders of Santa Rita announced that they were taking applications from anyone who wanted a bit of free land on which to construct a dwelling. The bar for acceptance was set extremely low and successful applicants would be allocated just enough money to build a small house of up to 45 square meters. Columba was among those who considered it the offer of a lifetime, even though it meant moving away from Progreso and its public transport and up the hill into unknown territory where taxis refused to go because of its lawlessness and its frequent crazy bullets that sometimes pierced flimsy walls to penetrate the skull of a sleeping child.

Columba qualified because she was of age, she had a job and she really, really needed her own abode. Living with two children in her aunt's garage had its drawbacks. Besides, was not owning your own house on a bit of land the ultimate aspiration?

This unexpected housing opportunity and the new job at the dock opened up a new era for Columba, her first steps towards staving off the constant threat of hunger. For the first time in years, she felt that the sky was truly blue, the sea was really clear and that the desert really was painted with minerals. She felt vital, the world needed her.

These were the days previous to her learning the meaning of the word 'budget'. Budget. What's a budget when you live hand-to-mouth, when your next coin is spent before it has a chance to warm itself in your palm? No, here you buy in quotas. You buy to pay later, small amounts, bit by bit. Always later. Time passes so quickly sometimes and you don't stop to think about all the quotas that are adding up to something you can't ever afford to pay. First, you pay the local grocer at the end of each month and if you don't have enough, and if he is patient, he waits until the next month. But finally, he won't sell to you anymore. And then you're in trouble. That's when you have to finagle dinner invitations for you and your kids from every friend you have, no matter how remote. "Oh, we thought we'd just drop in. It's been an elephant's age."

Columba announced to Anita, her ten-year-old daughter and José, her young son of seven, "*Cabros*, we're moving. We're building our own house. You'll make new friends and it'll all be great."

But the new era didn't arrive without sacrifice. Change was harsh because lack of security up in the high ridges of Santa Rita was a problem. They had to watch their backs... and their roof and their walls and their windows and their gate. Columba thought it was essential to have someone at the house at all times to discourage thieves who might forage through her scant treasures. Thus, her chair at Juana's sat empty at lunch time more often than not. When she wasn't cleaning the floor at the bank or working at the garment depot or selling pilfered items from her spot around the plaza, she was at home, protecting their space.

Money for the construction of the house trickled in from the authorities at a much slower pace than promised but after three years, the dwelling finally came together. By the time it was finished, Anita was 13 and José 10, their possessions filling the space with their personalities.

Columba's home had been built in slow increments and she was proud of each completed step. The walls were perfectly straight rows of cinderblocks, the floors were finished in giant squares of ceramic tile (no more hard-packed, oil-stained earth), the roof was a series of corrugated metal sheets. The house had zero insulation against the scorching midday sun and cold desert nights but it was a house and it was their home. One tried to avoid thinking about the freak event of rain, which if it occurred at all would surely arrive as drizzle, a scant millimeter or two. However everyone knew that scant millimeters pelting the steep slopes of the arid Andes would wreak havoc. A mudslide, if and when it might occur – would be nothing less than a tsunami pitching and rolling and roaring down the bald mountains, the houses and anyone in them being be swept along. Outside of such an event, although the roof was not impermeable, Columba was satisfied with it.

Columba was most proud of the bathroom with its flushing toilet and small enamel hand basin. No hot water but running water just the same. By the time they managed to cover the front patio with rows of bamboo canes to prevent thieves jumping in over the fence, safety in the sector as a whole had improved. The community had achieved its official status and now had its own mayor and counselors. Public transportation joined Santa Rita to Progreso, microbuses rattled and wheezed their diesel fumes up the steep hills, and there was a bus top right on her corner. Collector taxis had also begun to make regular runs because the drug dealers and thieves had slowly migrated to the outskirts of the settlement, making Santa Rita proper feel safer. Columba was becoming legitimate in every sense. She had her salary from the clothing depot and the cleaning job at the bank and up to now she had avoided stealing from her boss at the depot and she was proud of that.

She had never attempted to smuggle anything out. Not yet. Plenty of other workers had gotten away with it and although she couldn't say why for sure, she'd never gone that route. Instead she used her light fingers to pick up objects at the edge of a park bench when someone's back was turned or she lifted the odd hair brush or perfume bottle from an unattended street seller's table. And she still made the occasional trek to check around the edges of garbage piles at various unauthorized dump sites (always increasing in number) beyond the once pristine but now litter-strewn children's park in Santa Rita.

Eventually, in light of her self-proclaimed stellar performance that she based solely on the assumption that she must the only sorter who wasn't stealing, she mustered courage to ask for a raise.

She approached with confidence and tapped lightly on the door of Señor Alfonso Rodriguez's office. She had rehearsed her appeal during the 45-minute jostle on the microbus down the hills of Santa Rita to the dock in Progreso. And now she was using time from her own lunch break. Surely, he would appreciate how conscientious she was.

El Señor glanced up briefly before waving her in and returning his attention to documents on his desk. "I'm all ears. What's your name again?"

"I'm Columba, Señor." She would get to it after a polite preamble. "Señor, you know that I've worked in this illustrious depot for almost four years. From the first day you opened as a matter of fact. And you know I'm loyal and I work hard. No one appreciates this job more than I do." She took a breath. He didn't appear to be paying attention. "I've come to ask for a raise, Señor. You know I never remove any garments from the premises and I'm the best sorter you've got. Everyone comments that my selections are always the best."

He fingered the corner of one of the papers in his hand and responded without looking up. Did he even know what she looked like? "Look... Columba, you said, right?" He waved off his own question and mumbled as though he was addressing the papers. "Right. Columba, I have to pay a lot of workers. You know that. I can't afford to give anyone a raise. This is a small business. If you want more money, you'll have to go and work up in a mine."

Still without lifting his eyes, he shooed her out of his office with the back of his hand like she was a housefly.

Humiliated and disheartened, she retreated, head down, listening to the sound of her soft soles flatly slap the floor until she reached the opposite end of the plant. How could she have overestimated him? He was no different than any other greedy businessman. He was as tight as a bullfighter's suit. In her mind he morphed into a cartoon figure, a tall man with a moustache, hair greased back under the oblong hat of a matador who poured himself into his too-small suit every morning, forcing flabby thighs through spandex tights, squeaking his arms through taut, sequined sleeves. He was the Bullfighter who glittered with evil, he was a despicable antagonist with an unfair advantage, who, with the help of friends in high places, beat down and even killed defenceless beings with all the weapons at his disposal. He was nothing more than a character from the pages of a cheap comic book.

Another long, hot day in the depot without air conditioning was made worse by the Bullfighter's off-hand rejection of her request. All at once her steady part-time employment lost its enchantment. Her lunch break had been cut short by the snarky new security guard and at the end of the day the same new guard was eager to do the most thorough employee bag check in the history of the company. As a result, she was ushered out the door 45 minutes later than usual. All summed, it put her in the mood for a little revenge. She slipped out the door, deviating from her usual path. She approached the peacock blue BMW that was parked just inside the gates. She pulled out her house key and dragged it slowly, and with great satisfaction, leaving a deep gouge across the front fender of the driver's side. And then, in order to keep the symmetry, she bustled around and dragged the key along the passenger side, making a nice, matching groove. She watched as the metallic blue flecks peeled and dropped to the ground.

She slept well that night.

CHAPTER 9
GAVIN

Youth laughs at adult ritual and the narrow spectrum of courteous behavior that adults assign themselves. Then one day, youth wakes up, seeing it all through a pair of adult eyes and it moans that it has come of age.

Steady work for nearly three years had taught Gavin a few things. The first thing it taught him was that he wasn't really a steady employee kind of guy. The second thing it taught him was that he was capable of persevering, and thirdly it taught him that he was capable of doing things he didn't know he could do and that he didn't even like to do. And that he could do them all very well. He surprised himself with – what did his Dad call it? – good work ethic.

Over the course of these three years, Ernie had given Gavin three pay rises and more responsibility. In fact, now Gavin was in charge of the pool hall between four pm and midnight. Ernie trusted him not to give freebies to friends and to draw the line at horseplay that might lead to damage. "This is a fun place but not out-of-control rowdy. You know the difference, right? You're a chip off the ol' block, Gavin." Ernie gave a couple of quick nods in the direction of Stan's Men's and Boys' Wear.

The fourth thing Gavin learned was that his Dad respected him for holding down a job.

"You've developed some healthy work habits, son. I don't envy you that job (he nodded towards Ernie's Pool Hall) but you've stuck it out. I have to say that I underestimated you and I'm sorry for that. Either that or you've really changed, son. And for the better."

"No big deal, Dad. It just took a while to get going, I guess."

Every afternoon before starting his shift at Ernie's, Gavin wandered over to Stan's Men's and Boys' Wear. He waited for Stan to step outside as he routinely did, to rest his eyes from the precise work of alterations, and to luxuriate in his third cigarette of the day.

Gavin accommodated himself, leaning against the building, knee bent with his foot pushed into the wall, forming a triangle, and he waited. Stan nodded at him as he approached, drawing heavily on his smoke as he dropped the cigarette package back into his breast pocket. Although he knew Gavin smoked, Stan never offered him one and Gavin never would have accepted. "I don't smoke in front of my Dad," he'd told James, who shrugged and shook his head.

"So, Dad. How's business?" With his own experience in service retail (as Ernie referred to the pool hall), Gavin felt qualified to ask the question and understand the answer.

The usual response was, "Not bad, son. But it can always be better."

Then they'd stand in silence scanning the street, their heads turning in unison first in one direction and then the other as Stan dragged leisurely on his cigarette. When Stan glanced up at the sky, it was a signal that his break was over. He'd grind the butt into the old tomato can and Gavin would say, "Well, I better get going then. See you tomorrow." And they would both shove off.

This was Gavin's experience of a father-son relationship, a closeness built on male instinct and a lot of things unsaid. He never would have expected or asked for more. He thought about the things he and his Dad had in common and quite honestly didn't think there were many. They looked alike though, him being a younger, slimmer version of Stan. They both had strong backs and stood straight and tall, something that Gavin thought might have been trained into both of them by his Mom. "Come on you guys, no slouches at my table." So maybe it wasn't a physical trait as much as a learned posture. Unlike his contemporaries, Gavin never went in for the sloppy look, the long hair, loose jeans and baggy shirts. He was Mr. Clean, a preppy. His deep-set blue eyes were sharp and discerning above well-defined cheek bones and a thin, straight nose. His chin was not Superman square but it was carved out like someone determined lived behind it. His Mom had insisted on good dental hygiene so he had a perfect set of teeth and his smile, when he decided to flash one, made him disarmingly handsome. He was not unaware of this but he didn't play on it.

These days, Gavin was still living at James' place and he had pretty much taken charge. Now it was James who slept on the sofa and Gavin who got the double bed in the back bedroom. Neither of them was certain how that had happened but it probably had something to do with the fact that Gavin did the laundry and kept the place tidy and maybe he was just a natural leader. James got up early to pump gas at the truck stop and he returned late most nights because he was playing music over at the church or jamming with friends until well into the wee small hours.

"No point in waking you up, man. Why don't you take the bed for tonight? I'll crash on the couch when I get back."

It happened so often that it became the norm.

Gavin hadn't slept in his old room at his Dad's house since the morning Stan had kicked him out but he knew the bed was still there for him. These days, he went to his Dad's place pretty much every Sunday for dinner and he noticed that his bedroom was just the same as when he left, except the bed was made up military-style and there was no dust anywhere.

Gavin's Mom, Marianne had died more than twelve years ago and Gavin and his Dad had been fending for themselves ever since. His Dad paid a neighbor lady to come and clean up at irregular intervals but mostly he handled the household chores on his own. Tidiness. That must have been one of the other things Gavin inherited from his Dad.

As much as he tried to avoid it, sometimes Gavin thought about his Mom and he wondered how she would have felt about him working at Ernie's. Mostly he tried not to dwell on memories of his Mom because sometimes they'd take over and lead to a melancholy that would hang in for a week or more. Maybe he wasn't lazy, like his Dad thought. Maybe he was just really sad sometimes. During those episodes, he couldn't make himself get out of bed and he couldn't find a reason to do anything all day long. He had once admitted to James, over a pizza and beer, that since his Mom died, his heart was an empty cavern.

"Cavern. What do you mean?" James asked.

"It's just like a big empty hole, James."

"Oh." And James gently patted Gavin's shoulder three times. How was a guy supposed to respond to that? He looked at Gavin sideways and mumbled something before guzzling the rest of his beer. James' parents were both still alive and living at the end of the street. Now he felt guilty for wishing that they'd sometimes take a little trip somewhere, disappear for a while, stop interfering in his life. He peered over at Gavin who must have regretted mentioning his Mom and he could tell that Gavin was sort of in a funk.

Gavin's Mom, Mrs. Marianne Reid, had taught school, grades five to seven right up until the day she collapsed at the chalkboard. No one knew she was sick. Not even Stan. Five weeks after her collapse she was gone. She had protected Stan and Gavin from the inevitable. Maybe they wouldn't really have wanted to know anyway. About the pool hall – Gavin figured his Mom would have told him to keep looking, that the pool hall wasn't a place for a young man like himself. She was straight-laced and strict and she didn't mince words. She had a reputation and the kids at school called her Dragon Lady behind her back. "A pool hall is a place for rats and good-for-nothings," she used to say. "I don't ever want to see you wasting your time in that place."

But he wasn't wasting his time there now. He was being useful. He knew she would have told him that he had set his sights too low, that he could do more, make more of himself. His Dad never pushed him, though. All this time at Ernie's pool hall, it seemed that Stan was just relieved that Gavin had a job and he didn't want to jinx it by suggesting he move on to something else. Who knows if Marianne would've agreed? Probably not. But she would've been tough on Gavin, same as his Dad had been. No loafing around when you're finished school. Either get a job or get an education. No time for idleness or freeloading at Marianne's and Stan's place.

CHAPTER 10

IRENE

Being pregnant had its advantages. Chuck served her tea in bed in the morning and encouraged her to take her time coming to work.

"You need to conserve your energy, darling. We don't want you to tire yourself out." She knew he was talking about the energy that needed to be channeled to the baby. Her own well-being took a back seat.

No matter. She took full advantage of it. She lounged in bed and listened to the radio, dawdled around the kitchen, puttered in the back garden and usually waddled into the store just after noon. The bell hanging above the glass door chimed her arrival and Chuck looked up with a smile. Even if he was serving a customer, he politely excused himself and rushed to her side, raised up on his tiptoes and greeted her with a peck on the cheek.

"My wife is pregnant, you know." As if everyone was interested. "It's our first."

"Well, congratulations, Chuck. Good for you."

He beamed and basked in the attention, chatting and grinning some more, and once in a while he turned and winked at Irene (something she tried to ignore).

Since the morning sickness subsided, she be better than healthy. Her complexion was radiant and her eyes were bright. Her 'condition' began to reveal itself. She was proud of it and could sense that everyone around her, even strangers, made way for her, treated her like she was really something special. She soaked it all in.

Her Mom called regularly to check on her. Her sisters, Amber and Jocelyn swung by to take her baby clothes shopping. They also bought cakes, ice cream and pickles and loaded them into her pantry. "We know this is cliché but who knows what you might crave."

"How will you decorate the room? We'll help." Everything was handed to her. All she had to do was sit there and nod. Her younger brother, Chris, made a huge toy box and a wooden rocking horse with a green saddle and blonde mane and tail. They were certain the baby would be a girl but because Chuck insisted it was a boy, they compromised with yellow and green.

Chuck signed them up for prenatal classes and he was determined to help her through the birthing process. "I'll be at your side, Irene. You won't have to do it alone. Besides, I want to participate."

"Thank you, Chuck." She soaked it all in and feigned helplessness with an added bit of fake terror so that he would be reminded of all the work and pain she would have to endure when the time came.

Surrendering the secret of her pregnancy to Chuck didn't have the negative effect she had anticipated. In fact, sharing the knowledge with him had turned out to be advantageous. She observed from her pedestal (the one he had put her on) and all she had to do was raise her baby finger for him to come running.

So precious was her cargo.

The fact that he wasn't taking care of her so much as whoever was inside, was not lost on Irene. No matter, because the benefits were abundant. She was aware of how she was changing too. Not just physically but emotionally. "They're just hormones," Chuck said. But Irene felt it was more than that and she wholly surrendered herself to the natural process of becoming a mother. She was conscious of her maternal feelings. She now knew what a mother bear must feel – fierce protection, profound intimacy, a growing and incomparable love for the helpless creature, her baby, this tiny, cooing extension of herself – baby – the word was now so much more than just a word. Just pronouncing it sometimes brought tears to her eyes.

She found herself crying happy tears at the most inopportune moments and for no apparent reason. Her eyes glistened as she stepped along the cold December sidewalks, slowly, carefully, lest she trip and bump into something that could jar or harm the baby. Christmas lights twinkled and she hummed along to the same carols that only last year she had hated. She used to complain to Chuck. "I'm tired of those songs, I hate Christmas carols. It's always the same old thing. And it doesn't do anything for me." But this year Christmas was different. The night light in the baby's room glowed and she even asked Chuck to string some colorful bulbs around the edges of the baby's window. "It should be festive," she said.

As her belly expanded, she adopted the posture that pregnant women tend to adopt – she cupped her hands under the bulge, and unconsciously massaged it, feeling the bumps and the kicks. When Irene sang to the baby, Chuck almost cried in delight. They grew closer during her pregnancy, although their love-making routines disappeared because Chuck was afraid of causing damage. "It's all in your head, silly. You're not going to disturb anything." But he insisted that 'cuddling' was as much as he could, in all good conscience, manage. Quite prematurely, he began to talk about 'the next time' and how, by then he would be well-educated and more at ease with her pregnant condition. Irene didn't discourage him or attempt to curb such ideas. Who knew? Maybe in a couple of more years, she'd be planning another surprise announcement. She curled up (somewhat clumsily) in the big chair by the fireplace, dropped her head back and smiled at the ceiling.

At the end of January, when the time came, in spite of his preparation and best intentions, the pain and the blood was too much for him and Chuck passed out on the delivery room floor several minutes before their daughter was born. The hospital staff left him where he fell (they had warned him, hadn't they?) as they went about their birthing business and when he re-gained consciousness, they were preparing to take Irene and their baby to the ward.

"What did we have? Is it a boy?"

"We have a daughter, Chuck. She's beautiful."

He forgot to kiss Irene and he forgot to thank her as he had rehearsed so many times in his head. He forgot to count the baby's toes and fingers and forgot to check her ears and gums. He forgot to ask how much she weighed and how long she was. He forgot that he was going to cradle her ever so care-fully and snuggle the back of her little neck (how many times had he dreamed about that?). Instead he climbed, exhausted, into the first chair he saw and covered his face with his hands while he cried.

Irene looked down at him as the orderly wheeled her past and she never knew if Chuck was crying from joy over the new baby girl or from disap-pointment that she wasn't a boy.

They called her Alicia Linda because Irene said the combination was like a bird song. Chuck didn't object.

Alicia was a good baby. She slept when she was expected to sleep and she ate when she was expected to eat. She took easily to Irene's breast and she never had colic.

"Look Chuck, she's smiling. She gurgles too."

Chuck returned from work just after seven o'clock every evening. He wanted to get home earlier, he really did but he had to lock up, you know – the usual stuff. "I'd much rather be home with Alicia." Then he looked at Irene over his shoulder and added, "And you, too, of course, darling."

Every day, as soon as he walked in the front door, he absentmindedly pecked Irene on the cheek and went to wash his hands before lifting Alicia from Irene's arms. Or if Alicia was sleeping, he bent into her crib and, ignoring Irene's pleas to let her sleep, he gently raised her from her bed. Then he walked her around the house, rocking her in the curve of his elbow. He cooed and chatted, "Alicia, my girl, I would like to hold you more, to cuddle and carry you all hours of the day but I have to run the store and get the groceries and put gas in the car and pay the bills and do house repairs. One day, you'll understand all of that. I'll teach you."

"Chuck, you're getting ahead of yourself," Irene laughed at him.

"Alicia, let's dance." Irene had always been surprised that Chuck was a such a great dancer. With Alicia in his arms, he stepped in and around, the catchy rhythms in his head taking them in small loops, slick easy glides. If Alicia had an uncharacteristically bad day, he whisked her up and danced with her. They waltzed, they did the fox trot, they even stepped to the cha-cha-cha. They wound into the living room, through the kitchen, down the hall, in and out of the bedrooms and back again. When spring arrived and if it was a warm evening, he danced Alicia out onto the back patio.

"Don't take her outside, Chuck. She'll catch a cold."

Chuck ignored that and, cradling Alicia, he dipped, showing off the little angel in his arms. Alicia smiled, even tilted her little angel face and laughed her little crystal chimes, the most delightful sound in the world. They pranced down the sidewalk and meandered along the perimeter of the fence. He bent and nuzzled his nose in her hair and hummed into her ears, "You are my destiny, you share my reverie, you are my happiness, that's what you are...". She grasped at his nose and poked her small fingers into his mouth. He buzzed around her forehead and breathed circles around her cheeks. She shivered and giggled her baby chimes.

Alicia was a gem, a star, a miracle.

Already at five months old, Alicia looked forward to dancing in the back yard. When Chuck got home, she held out her chubby arms and smiled.

Well before Canada Day, the black-eyed Susans, phlox and cabbage roses in Irene's garden were in full bloom. The azaleas had opened ages ago and the bleeding hearts hung elegantly (Irene would always remember those bleeding hearts) and they combined in glorious explosions of color against the fence. The evening of July 1st, the sky was saturated with the mauve happiness of a perfect sunset – Chuck cradled Alicia tenderly in his arms, danced her to sleep and finally tucked her in. The day had been a perfect story, a fairy tale come true.

Then, without a breath, without a warning, someone ripped out the pages from the heart of the book. The tale could have no ending.

The next day Alicia was gone.

Irene's screams pierced the early morning air of July 2nd, 1992. Then there was a searing silence, followed by soft moans like those of a wounded animal. Tormented bellows pushed up from her bowels and through her throat, exhaling as thick, voluminous sounds that roared through the house. Savage groans flooded the hallway, the air became thick and muddy. They summoned Chuck and engulfed him in a powerful tsunami of terror. He leapt from bed, the security of familiar boundaries eluding him – there was no ceiling, there were no walls, there was no floor. Everything was destroyed by the sound of Irene's interminable agony. He panicked in circles before finding his bearings and he finally reached Alicia's room. Irene was leaning into the crib and pumping on Alicia's chest. She was screaming and crying, pushing and prodding the still child.

She felt Chuck's presence and without turning away from Alicia, "Chuck! Chuck! Chuck!" Her voice, ragged, was crushed under her sobs. "My baby! My baby! Alicia! Alicia!" The words, hardly recognizable, guttural, gushed into the icy blue air around them.

Chuck shoved Irene aside and she tripped on her own feet, collapsing in a heap on the floor. She stayed there and curled into a ball. Head between her elbows and, convulsing in pain, she rocked in the empty, twisted space and she was silent, almost not breathing. Chuck ignored her.

Alicia's lips were blue. She was cold. He bent down and thumped the heel of his hand into her little chest in a steady rhythm. His whole body trembled with effort, with will. Tears streamed down his face. He saw them fall one by one, a stupid slow-motion playback of someone else's tears onto Alicia's white cheeks. He could hear the tears as they landed. They were hollow, and loud, like thunder. Then he began giving her his breath, carefully releasing it into her mouth, through the purple wilted petals that should have been her lips. "Take my life. Take mine. Take mine. Take mine."

They didn't know how long they'd been there like that, torn and exhausted from trying.

Finally, Chuck collapsed onto the floor beside Irene. This wasn't happening. He was dreaming. He was desperate to wake up.

Irene was shaking violently now. She tried to raise herself on all fours but couldn't balance and she fell back and, desperate to erase the silence (or desperate to have it gather her into its calm), she began to wail, the sound of her pain drilling through Chuck like bullets ricocheting inside his painfully hollow chest, finally exploded in his head. He couldn't tolerate any more. But he was helpless and he rolled onto the floor, clawing over the carpet, away from Irene, he folded up, trying to bury his head. He cupped his ears with his trembling hands. He didn't know how long he'd lain there, eyes squeezed shut, ears covered, empty-headed, nothing real. Then he was deafened by silence when Irene passed out.

Maybe it was all a nightmare and they'd wake up. But little Alicia, still and quiet as a perfect, frozen little blue angel, insisted on being gone. She had left them to go somewhere else, somewhere very distant.

The coroner said, "If it's any comfort, it wasn't your fault. You didn't do anything wrong. It's not uncommon in infants of this age. She just stopped breathing, unfortunately like many others before her have done. I'm so sorry for your loss."

The doctor suggested counseling and group therapy.

CHAPTER 11

COLUMBA

No matter how hard you might try during your lifetime, your little spot on the planet will always rotate into the light after the little spot of someone else who lives to the east of you. You will never catch up to them. Never. Little lives, fastened to the earth as it turns, are carried from the dark side to the light, and around again, in time with the planet's predictable rhythm. Paradoxically, within it, unpredictable circumstances are the norm. Go with the flow.

If there was money to be made from the gringos' discarded clothing then Columba wasn't going to allow a cretin in a bullfighter's suit who cruised around town in a scratched, late model BMW convertible take it all.

On the third morning after her boss had dismissed her with nothing more than a lazy wave of his heavily-ringed, manicured fingers, she woke up with renewed purpose and confidence. She marched her way into the kitchen and settled at the table, craning her neck to check on Anita and José, who were still fast asleep on their mattresses.

The loose fragments of creativity in her brain shook themselves out of the dregs where they had fallen dormant, they rinsed themselves off, cleaned themselves up and made themselves presentable. She was thinking straight for the first time in years.

If heists there ever were going to be, then she would be the one to pull them off, plain and simple. She would get hers. She filled the kettle, wrenched the sticky knob on the stove, waited to hear the hiss of gas and scratched and broke two matches before a flame curved fitfully around the burner. It flickered and died as the small gas cylinder surrendered its last fumes. She kicked the iron bottle several times, sighed and glanced at the old Nescafe can up on the shelf. The can was supposed to be her salvation, her fountain in times of need. But mostly it sat there on its high altar, dry and empty, between two small holy relics.

To its left was the plastic statue of San Expedito, his sandaled foot stomping on a crow, a wooden cross raised victoriously in his right hand. Truth be told, in her whole life, San Expedito hadn't expedited anything in her favor.

At least not that she'd noticed. But as the story goes, he had surrendered himself in the name of Jesus, which gave him a lot of sway with the Virgin, making him a saint not to be ignored. So, she prayed to him. On the other side of the Nescafe can was a somewhat taller statue of the Virgin Mary herself. To date, the Virgin's intercessions, like those of San Expedito, had gone unheeded, causing Columba to question the veracity of the Virgin's influence. Did she truly have the ear of her son? The Virgin's eyes were droopy in her innocent sort of way, her lips were thin and chipped, her face colorless. Maybe Columba should have paid attention to the tell-tale signs of the Virgin's exhaustion (after all, she was a mother too). Her exhaustion, like that of most mothers, Columba would remind herself, could explain the Virgin's ineffectiveness. She was too tired to appeal again and again to Jesus to perform miracles. She probably quit harping on him centuries ago.

As Columba reached for the Nescafe can, her eyes beseeched San Expedito, and she whispered, "Dear San Expedito, you, our saint of urgent causes, please intervene for me in this difficult time." And then, just to cover all the bases (not wanting to expose her lack of faith in the Virgin), she looked to the right and breathed, "Dear Mother of Jesus, queen of the universe, please help me, a most miserable of sinners, in my hour of need." She pulled down the Nescafe can, hoping, as the crack on its brittle plastic lid elongated when she folded it back, that this morning there would be a miracle. Her fingers, nails bitten to the quick, burned into the can's empty bottom. Of course, she hadn't forgotten it was empty but with a saint and the Virgin on either side, she held out hope. Only yesterday afternoon she had scratched into the can, rummaging for coins to buy rice. Even if there were some coins there now, without a miracle there would not be enough to refill the propane tank. Reaching into the can was a compulsion. One must have hope. One day there will be enough money to take the kids to a movie. People sometimes win bingo games.

She'd have to tell the kids there would be no tea again this morning. She extracted a day-old bun, tore off a third of it and returned the rest to the plastic bag. She bit into the dry bread, chewing absentmindedly as she settled down to the task at hand – stitching four big pockets to the inside of her heavy cotton skirt. It was part of her two-pronged plan.

When Anita saw the cold kettle and raised her eyebrows, Columba waved her off. "Never mind. I'm making some changes, starting today. And you're going to help me." She pointed at the plastic bag. "You can have a piece of that bun but leave some for José. You two will have to eat breakfast at school."

Anita sat down and fingered the bun, her mouth moving in silent prayer. Columba glanced over at her.

"I've been praying too, Anita but so far, my prayers have fallen on deaf ears. Sometimes we have to help ourselves. And that's just what I'm doing. So, if you're going to pray for anything, just pray that you'll do exactly as I say."

Anita tilted to the right a little as she listened to Columba's instructions. "You're going to run down to the dock today. Here's where I want you to be at 1.30." She handed her a map that she'd scribbled onto a corner of an old newspaper. "And no later. You have to be on this exact spot or we'll miss a big opportunity. Don't bring any friends. And don't forget your packsack."

"Mom, I don't think Father Cortés would approve of this. Stealing is a sin."

"Yes, maybe for people like Father Cortés, for people who have everything they need, it's a sin. But for people like us, well, Jesus looks the other way. In fact, sometimes he even helps us."

"And anyway, after school, I have to go to the young people's group at the church."

"Okay, then you can take your packsack to the church but keep an eye on it." Anita was spending too much time at the church lately. Young people's programs, they called them. Well, better the Church than a plaza full of druggies. Besides, Columba was confident that a mother's influence was greater than that of a priest, especially since Anita had only met him a few months ago.

That morning, Columba arrived at the depot wearing her drive and purpose. She stashed her purse in her locker, stood in front of the time clock and waited until it clicked over to 9 am. Never again would the Bullfighter squeeze so much as an extra second of her time. She made an effort to greet the other workers but she was in no mood to be sidetracked by idle gossip. She worked at a steady but slow pace all morning, aware of the hawkish eye of the new jobsworth security guard who was still out to prove himself. His enthusiasm would wear off soon enough. She had already stuffed some women's t-shirts into her big skirt pockets, a couple with flowers and glitter, one with script text that yelled, 'I'm the light of your life' with bright yellow circles over the breasts and another that said 'Let the good times roll', with arrows that pointed down. She picked out men's t-shirts that said, 'I'm the Second-Coming' and 'Run for Epilepsy, Minnesota 1982'. Never mind that no one understood English, the t-shirts would sell because of their color and good condition. Besides, she would be the first on her side of the sidewalk to sell *ropa Americana*. Even here in Progreso it was becoming all the rage. No matter what she displayed, she knew it would sell at the right price.

Columba watched as the hands on the big clock finally jittered around to 1:20 and she sidled up to Jessica, the new employee who was rifling through the pockets of a pair of oversized jeans. "Jessica, I can tell you that those pockets are empty. I already checked. But you can be first to that section over there." Columba pointed to the wide doors where the 'Restricted Zone' sign had fallen sideways and was all but invisible behind two fiberglass bins on wheels. A couple of men with the shaggiest hair she'd ever seen were outside the door laughing and spitting as they cut thick nylon ties from around huge spongy bundles. The contents spilled like they had been gutted, and faded colors gushed across the wooden dock. "No one has gotten near those yet."

Jessica nodded and winked, gave her the thumbs up, and hustled towards the scraggly men who stood near the outpouring of new garments, her own bulk bouncing around her waist, running shoes squeaking across the oil-spattered concrete. Columba waited until the new security guard was distracted by Jessica. Columba had nicknamed him Hawkeye. He was standing tall, arms akimbo, his head pivoting slowly (he could be Chucky's twin with a moustache), tracking Jessica like she was prey. Jessica quipped something to the shaggy men and then she began picking through the garments on the floor, undoubtedly planning to slip something beneath her oversized sweater.

Hawkeye pounded over there, planting himself between her and the pile of new garments. Legs astride, hands on hips and chest inflated he rocked on his heels and Columba watched him point to the 'Restricted Zone' sign that dangled behind the bin. Columba couldn't hear what he said but she could tell by the gestures that Chucky the Jobsworth, aka Hawkeye was delivering a firm upbraiding. Jessica, fearful of losing her job in her first week, stood in silence, head down. She grovelled, probably apologizing, pleading ignorance but not daring to point out the ineffective signage, nor mentioning who had sent her there.

Before Hawkeye's tirade came to an end, Columba slinked across the floor and disappeared into the bathroom. The door of the end cubicle doddered on its hinges and she took a moment to secure the broken latch before stepping up onto the chipped toilet bowl, the toes of her shoes covering the holes for the bolts of a toilet seat that had never been installed, and she called out the window. "Anita! You there?"

"Yeah, Mom," in a soft voice, "I've been here for ages. Just waiting... praying for our souls."

"Good girl. Keep it up. Just wait a second." Columba tied shirts, two and three at a time into knots, small enough to slide through the bars of the window and she shoved them hard so that they landed on the other side of the fence that hugged the building.

"I got them, Mom."

"How many?"

"Wait. Let me count." There was a pause and then she said, "Eight. Is that right?"

"Yes, that's all of them. Good job, my little heart. Now don't let anyone look in your packsack and don't tell anyone where you've been." She blew her a kiss. Anita ignored the kiss, turned on her heel and trudged away, pleated skirt tapping saucily against the back of her skinny knees. Columba smiled.

She jumped off the toilet and sat down on its edge. She lit the half-cigarette she'd saved to celebrate this moment. Leaning forward, elbows on knees, she squinted into the future. This was just the beginning. Content that the whole operation had been a real breeze, she grinned into the smoke. Her heart wasn't racing and she hadn't broken into a sweat. She was game for more. And tonight, even if she had to dawdle to find the right moment, she'd give the precious BMW one more good, long scratch. No harm, no foul.

CHAPTER 12

GAVIN

The evening sun sets over a coastal mountain range in the west of a northern territory well-known for peace and tolerance. Watch the sky as its wispy tranquility quivers through pink clouds in its orchestra of miracles. After a drawn-out hush, blood-red flames suddenly arise in crescendo from the horizon and scorch upwards and outwards. Finally, exhausted they shift and disperse into a calm violet haze that relaxes across the distant tree-covered mountains.

Up to now, fall was Gavin's favorite season. Today was a beautiful day, the trees had turned color, the air was fresh. You could feel the change of season – bears preparing to hibernate, squirrels working overtime. Everything in full vigor.

In his whole life, he'd never seen a dead body. Not even when his Mom died. When Marianne died, Stan had sent Gavin over to James's parents' place while he made the funeral arrangements.

"This is no place for a 10-year-old kid." Stan told James's Mom. She nodded and, crouching, she guided little Gavin to sit on the sofa and she served him a big bowl of chocolate ice cream. To this day, Gavin refuses to eat chocolate ice cream.

Marianne's days had been numbered since the doctor told her about the cancer. She had hidden it from Gavin and Stan until she was admitted to the hospital, never to return. She had tried to make it as simple as possible. "No fuss, Stan. We know what's coming. We're as prepared as we can be and I don't want to prolong it."

Her instructions were simple. "Have me cremated, Stan. And don't go arranging a big service. You know I'm not like that and if you do it, I swear I'll haunt you until you wish it was you in that urn." By now her voice betrayed her weakness but her resolve was still evident and Stan would obey.

"But Marianne, we have to do something so Gavin has closure." He meant himself but he didn't dare talk about how he felt. No way. He couldn't trust himself to open that floodgate because he'd be flushing himself into a current so strong, so unpredictable that he'd wash away in thin strings that would disintegrate entirely in its turbulent waters.

"Okay, maybe you're right, Stan. Then how about this? Get a pastor from a church... I don't care which church as long as it's not a Catholic one. I don't want a priest. This is just for Gavin's sake, mind you, so not loads of scripture. None, if you can get away with it, although fat chance if you're talking to a preacher. I know, I know..." She coughed weakly and spit into the bowl. "But you know I don't believe in all that. Maybe a little ritual will be good for Gavin, maybe it'll help ground him. Ask whoever you want to attend but keep it simple."

Stan remained stoic in the face of her instructions. When the time came, he'd see how he felt about adding some words of his own.

"And Stan." She was looking at him, brow furrowed, the closest to pleading that she'd ever get. "Keep me with you, okay? Don't go scattering me to kingdom come. Just put me on the mantle under the clock and give me a pat once in a while."

That's when Stan broke down. Gavin was watching through the crack of the door. The nurse had been called to an emergency so Gavin slid off the bench and sidled towards his Mom's room and leaned in. He watched as Stan cried without a sound, head falling to his chest, shoulders shaking, and he saw his Mom reach over and rest her tired hand on his shoulder.

That was the last time Gavin saw his Mom. Only minutes before he'd been in there with both of them and his Mom had told him, "Now Gavin, you're old enough to understand what's going on. You know how sick I am and you understand there's nothing we can do about it so you have to accept it." He hardly recognized her voice. It was cracked and broken and when she coughed he thought she would shatter. But she insisted, "You're a big boy and you and your Dad know how to take care of yourselves but I'll always have your back. Remember that. I love you very much, son. And I'll keep on loving you even if you don't see me. You be a big, strong boy for Dad."

His Mom was the strong one. She had always made the decisions and she was always the one who laid down the law. Gavin had always known she was wise. Unlike some of his friends, who at ten years old, had outgrown their admiration for their mothers, he never questioned Marianne's judgment or authority. No sir. She was always at the top of his respect list. She always knew best. His Mom always hugged anyone who needed a hug, and she always told off anyone who needed to be told off. She marched forward too, without blinders. His Mom's arms were always open. She never bypassed anyone in need. And soon she was going to be gone and he didn't know who would do the hugging and he was really worried about that.

Now, at 23 years old, Gavin would be faced with encountering his first dead body. Because last night Stan died.

Apparently, he went quietly. Like with Marianne, no one saw it coming, or maybe also like Marianne, he just didn't reveal it. Anyway, as a good man (if you believe good is rewarded with good), he was allowed a peaceful exit in his sleep. It's what he would have wanted. When he thought about it later, Gavin figured maybe Stan had seen Marianne in his sleep. Maybe she had beckoned him, telling him that this was the time at last, assuring him that Gavin could stand on his own two feet. "He's a grown man now, Stan. You can't keep him under your wing much longer. Don't you think it's time we were together again? I know you. You're tired. I don't mean to be selfish but I do miss you, Stan. And I know you miss me too."

The day that Stan died, Gavin had wandered up to the crux of opportunity at Stan's Men's and Boys' Wear (he now simply referred to it as 'the crux,' a private joke between him and James) to hang out with Stan who, at any moment should have appeared with his third cigarette of the day. But Stan didn't wander out. In fact, the door of Stan's Men's and Boys' Wear was still locked, the sign still showed its 'Closed' face through the glass.

Gavin's first thought was that Stan had a meeting at the bank or something and since it was Wednesday and his assistant Mark didn't work on Wednesdays, he'd have had to lock up for an hour or so. From time to time, Gavin pushed his nose up to the smudged window at the pool hall watching for Stan to step out and look up at the sky. It wasn't until late afternoon, when Stan didn't answer the phone at the store or at home, that the alarm bells went off.

Against his own better judgment, Gavin recruited one of the pool hall regulars. "Watch the fort, will you? I have to take care of something important. I won't be long. No funny business, you got it? 'Cause if you do something stupid, I'll find out and this will be the last day you set foot in here." He thought better of that. "No, I mean, you know... I trust you. I do. Just play it straight."

He quickened his pace, urgency increasing with each step. By the time he arrived at Stan's house he was at a full gallop. He ran down a mental list of the reasons his Dad wouldn't be where he was supposed to be. Maybe there was a gas leak at the house, or maybe he discovered a mouse in the basement and decided to have the place fumigated, maybe old lady Margaret across the street had some kind of health issue and his Dad had rushed her into Grant Falls and maybe Mark just wasn't around to take over the store. If he tried hard enough, he could think of a dozen reasons why Stan wouldn't be there today but in his gut Gavin knew that none of his reasons was the right one.

Except for the grandfather clock ticking off the seconds at the far corner of the living room, the house was quiet. Before the first stair creaked on his way up, Gavin knew that he was approaching the thing he had tried to deny all day. He was filled with dread.

He found Stan in his bed. Stan was facing the door, his eyes closed and he was curled up towards the outside of the bed, arms folded, hands praying under his left cheek. He looked as though he had just laid down to close his eyes for a quick nap. "Just give me 15 minutes and I'll be as good as new. A cat nap is all I need." But he was wearing his pajamas. He never cat napped in his pajamas. That was the thing. Gavin knelt down, his face only inches from Stan's, already knowing that he wouldn't feel a breath.

"Dad. Dad." His own low voice sounded like it had come from someone else, someone who was whispering, pretending to be him. He rested his cheek on his Dad's shoulder and was startled at the cold of it. He stayed, squatted on his heels staring at this Dad's face. Nothing.

He didn't know how much time had passed before he stood up and creaked his way down the stairs. Maybe if he started again. Maybe if he did this over. He paused at the base of the stairs and looked over at the clock. It hadn't stopped ticking. He turned and walked into the kitchen and rinsed out the coffee pot, gathered the old filter and dumped it into the garbage bin under the sink, rinsed the pot again, filled the machine with water, fumbled in the cupboard for the coffee tin, spooned grounds into a new filter and switched it on. The coffee machine gurgled and chugged, puffs of steam wetting his face. He inhaled the aroma as the first brown drops splashed into the carafe. When the machine stopped, he poured two cups of coffee. He added milk to Stan's and walked upstairs again. "Dad, how about some coffee?" He stood, a mug in each hand, looking down at Stan.

Then downstairs again, mugs still in hand, and he did circles around the kitchen table, not questioning, not thinking at all. Finally, he set down the coffee and reached for the phone on the wall and called the RCMP.

"My Dad is dead."

"Who's speaking, please? Where are you?"

A young constable arrived with Dr. Wilson. "Where is he?"

Gavin pointed up the stairs. He waited, one foot on the lowest stair, dropping his head so that his cheek rested on the square post of the bannister and he listened to their muffled voices and the creaking of the floor as someone walked around the bed. There was silence for several seconds. Someone took a few steps towards the window and walked back to the bed. More muffled voices. More creaking floorboards.

Finally, they were clomping back down the stairs towards him, the doctor was squeezing his shoulder, "I'm sorry son." The constable was asking him something, the words didn't register, the constable's face was out of focus.

Gavin's head was suddenly very heavy, like a boulder weighing into his shoulders, crushing his spine.

"What time did you find him?"

Gavin's back couldn't sustain the weight, his knees buckled.

The constable repeated, "Gavin, what time did you find him?"

Gavin drew a blank. "I don't know... I mean, this afternoon. I mean, I don't know what time." He looked around in a daze. "What time is it now?" The doctor gripped Gavin's shoulders and braced him against his own chest. Gavin knew he needed to sit down but he didn't know how. He tried to lift his feet but they were numb, just like the rest of him. He couldn't respond. The officer grabbed his elbow and dragged him over and sat him on the sofa. They sat there, the officer on one side, the doctor on the other, sandwiching Gavin between their shoulders.

The doctor said, "It looks like he died of a tired heart, son. It was probably quick and I don't think he even woke up. He would've just stopped breathing. Simple and painless. I'd say he passed away between midnight and six this morning."

Gavin didn't recall much after that. There was something about the funeral director and documents for the government. He was told that his Dad had taken care of all eventualities, that Gavin was lucky – no need to worry about a thing. There was something about a will. There was something about the business. There was something about his Mom. There were people coming and going. There was food, lots of it – lasagna, sandwiches, salads, casseroles in disposal tin receptacles carried in by the neighbors. There were lots of voices buzzing, blending into one another, people's faces getting close, soft words in his ears, sympathetic eyes peering into his, arms gently around his shoulders, hands patting him on the back, fingers softly squeezing his wrists.

James was the last one to leave. "Do you want me to stay with you, Gavin?" Gavin shook his head. The air was so still and he couldn't seem to find oxygen. He noticed how silent the house was. The only sound was the ticking of the clocks, the grandfather one and the one over the mantlepiece, with the long metal spokes that splayed out like sun rays from around its face.

Gavin picked up the brushed silver urn, trying not to think about what his Dad had been reduced to, and placed it carefully under the clock and he slid his Mom's so that it was right next to Stan's, no space between their cold metal exteriors. The longest vertical ray of the clock pointed exactly to the center of the two urns and it twitched slightly each time the long hand clicked into place. It was counting back through the couple's lives in minutes. None of it made sense.

CHAPTER 13

IRENE

There is an abrupt turning point that some feel more acutely than others – it's as though, against all the laws of the universe, the planet abruptly stops (almost imperceptibly, mind) just for a mere fraction of a second. Then slowly, very slowly, it revs its engines and begins to grind around again. But as far as Irene is concerned it might as well be rotating in the opposite direction. East and west are meaningless. Seasons pass unnoticed. The heavens, clouded or clear are dark voids all the same. Worse than being without purpose, life for Irene makes no sense.

For her, the planet and the universe it hangs in, have ceased to exist. Imagine, if you can – nothing. Impossible. But maybe you can imagine floating around in an abyss and, of course, the abyss has no point of reference. This is where we find Irene.

The doctor said it was absolutely normal for Irene to be depressed for the first several months. But they were well past one year now and this was too long. Another summer had come and gone.

"Now." the doctor said matter-of-factly, "Well… now it's beyond a healthy period of time." He patted her knee and looked her straight in the eye and she looked back at him blankly.

"Now," he said, "You have to make an effort to pull yourself together."

He was worried not only about her mental health but also about her physical well-being because Chuck said that most days he almost had to force-feed her. But anyway, Chuck decided to quit the grievance counseling because, just like the group therapy, it was getting them nowhere. To say Irene was lethargic was putting it mildly. Although she was deep down in her own troubles Chuck just couldn't see her in a psych ward where she'd 'get the care she needs' because he also feared she'd get the drugs she didn't need. And who knew where that would lead? Maybe he'd end up visiting her in a psych hospital for the rest of his life. No, he'd rather take care of her. He'd love and coddle her as much as she'd allow and things would run their course.

Chuck, too, had suffered greatly, perhaps even more deeply than Irene, although it was not only impossible but unjust to compare or measure their

pain. Having a child had been Chuck's desire for many years – since long before he knew Irene. But until Alicia was born, he could not have conceived of
the joy their little girl would bring, of the love that would wash over him, con-
verting who he was, overshadowing any other purpose in life, past, present or
future. The concept of fatherhood was one thing but the extraordinary reality
of being a father to his beautiful baby girl was beyond description.

At first, and although she thought she hid it well, Chuck knew that Irene
hadn't been 100% into having children. But no matter. Because he also knew
that after a woman carries a life into the world, and once she knows the magic
of the little creature, nothing can compare to their bond, or to the all-consuming love and attention, the fierce protection (to the point of paranoia), to
the unique, intimate relationship that reigns supreme and will forever change
her life.

In spite of his grief, Chuck was forced to move on, to take care of business, to
attend to customers, consider his employees, generate income for the family.
Maybe he was fortunate in this, lucky to have responsibilities that, for brief
seconds and then minutes and then hours, and finally days, forced him to
compartmentalize his sorrow, somehow even schedule it. And perhaps this
made it more difficult for him to understand Irene's grief. Her grief immobi-
lized her. She sat for hours at the edge of her chair, staring at a point on the
floor across the room. She didn't acknowledge him when he spoke. She was
a body with no soul.

Finally, in August, he took her, against her will, for a leisurely drive out to the
edge of the Nazko Valley. She used to love going there at this time of year.
She'd raise her arms and open herself to the turning of the leaves. She'd gently peer through bushes for the last of the season's berries and bend down to
examine agates at the edges of a stream.

So that day, he had encouraged her to pick flowers, to look for berries. He
had prepared a picnic lunch of ham sandwiches, boiled eggs, apples, and
grapes, her favorite carrot cake with cream cheese icing and a bottle of white
wine. He remembered how she used to laugh and rummage into the basket
looking for the dessert, offering to top up his wine, the pure joy of being out
there reflected in her eyes.

Now her eyes were empty, she rested the ham sandwich on her lap, did not
even raise it to her lips but she obediently accepted the cake he offered, and
she bit into it, mechanically chewing a small morsel and leaving the rest. He
faked frivolity, pulling at her arm with a forced laugh, and he made her walk

with him through the tall grass. But she didn't take notice of the flowers or the bees or the berries. It was all useless.

One Sunday morning, Chuck was in the kitchen as usual with a cup of coffee and the newspaper. Irene, as was her habit since Alicia died, would probably sleep until noon. Finally, he heard the shower running and after awhile she padded out to the kitchen. Her eyes were puffy, her hair hanging limp around her shoulders, her dressing gown, which was in need of a wash, was tied loosely at her waist. She shuffled over and without a word, she poured a cup of coffee.

Chuck had come up with a new plan. Something to get them out in public. Maybe it was the company of other people that she needed. "Let's go see a movie this afternoon," he suggested. "They're playing 'When Harry Met Sally.' Remember we wanted to see last year? Well, they're playing it again at the Roxy." He dared to feel excited about it.

They'd heard good reviews and Irene had been especially enthusiastic.

She was slouched on the chair opposite him, seemingly lifeless. But at his suggestion, she slapped both hands so loudly on the table that it reverberated across the room. Then slowly but deliberately she raised her eyes, glaring at him. She was stiff with rage. "How dare you suggest we go and see a movie that came out last year!" She pushed herself up. The chair scraped and fell back on the floor, and she yelled. "Last year we had everything. But we can't go back to last year, can we? We're supposed to move past last year, remember? It's you who keeps trying to move away from last year and now you're bringing it up and throwing it in my face." She was shrieking now. She was crazy. "We lost last year, Chuck. And nothing is going to bring it back, especially a movie you want to see. A movie. A movie! You're a fool." She spat the words from between her quivering lips. Her face was contorted, almost purple. "You want to do something that will be fun? Do you? How about you get my baby back? Huh? How about you wave your magic wand and wake her up? Huh? How about you buy her back? You can buy anything can't you? You bought me after all. You know that, right? You bought me. You bought me and you controlled me. I got you what you wanted and then she left. What did you do about it? Nothing. I hate you. I hate this house, I hate this town, I hate this life. I want out! Do you hear me? I want out!"

She hurled her cup at the floor and it smashed it into a million bits. Furious, she lost her balance and stumbled over the mess and then she began yanking at her robe, pulling at her hair and punching the air, grunts and sobs caught in her throat. Chuck watched in horror as she turned and kicked dents into the bottom of the fridge before she raged towards him. He managed to raise himself but only barely, his fingers snatching at the edge of the table. She glared and slapped him hard across the face. It burned into him. They stood staring at one another. Finally, he grabbed her arms, forcing them to her sides, and then, bracing her from behind, he wrestled her to the floor, slipping across the spilled coffee and cutting his hands on the broken porcelain. He dragged her away from the shards to the base of the cupboard. They fell back into it, chests heaving, heads jerked back. She struggled and screamed, tried to bite him and threatened to kill him. But he held her, surprised by his own strength against hers. His glasses dangled unnoticed from one ear. Finally, she dropped her head and fell limp, and twisting towards him, she sobbed into his chest. Chuck held on and cried into the top of her head.

CHAPTER 14

COLUMBA

This place of earthquakes and mudslides and constant delays towards endless tomorrows breeds a different culture. But its cycles of fortune behave just like everywhere else. One day the world is good and the next it's bad. While some lie low in their valley of bad luck, others celebrate their fortune on the summit. As some fade away, others begin to prosper. But Columba is not one to philosophize.

Sunday mornings called for Sunday dress.

After a quick fumble through the mounds that now defined her bedroom – clothes heaped on the floor, garments spilling off the small bureau and piles reaching for the sunlight that was burning its way through the polka-dotted curtains – she found what she was looking for. It was a pink linen skirt. It would go with the flowered chiffon blouse with ruffled sleeves. She imagined the gringa who wore it before her. Possibly a famous country singer or perhaps the wife of a wealthy Texas rancher. The skirt and blouse would be perfect with the new pair of salmon-colored three-inch platforms that she'd worn out of the depot on her very own two feet the night before.

Now that she had accumulated a wide selection of garments, Columba was beginning to discover her true style. Not all of the clothes fit her as she had imagined. Most were tight around the midriff and called attention to the rolls there. Sometimes buttons popped off right after she fastened them or else the buttonholes couldn't be stretched around the buttons at all. Occasionally, zippers burst. Recently she had chosen garments with wide elastic that she could easily slip around her waist. Luckily she could count on today's pink skirt's extra-long, industrial-strength zipper.

Columba reserved some of the best dresses for herself and when she tired of them, she washed them (or not) and displayed them on the sidewalk just off Progreso's main plaza on Tuesday and Thursday afternoons. She had acquired a small metal clothes rack (not the kind with wheels – this one she had to scrape across the concrete) that made her appear more bona fide than sellers who displayed their wares on blankets.

It's not that Columba was a pack rat, it's just that her house was crowded because it was small. Her living room and kitchen, which were one undivided space, doubled as a bedroom for the kids. During the day they stood their single mattresses on end between the back of the sofa and the outside wall. At night, they pushed the sofa aside and flopped the mattresses, side by side, onto the floor.

The kitchen area was a short row of cupboards with doors on the bottom and open shelves on the top. A sink fit snugly into the corner and a light weight stove was connected to a portable propane tank at the other end. The two pots and one frying pan didn't fit anywhere and were constantly moved from side to side to make space while cooking.

The kitchen table had a wide hollow pedestal in which she stored two thick blankets for the cold desert nights. Everyday belongings could be found on one of several shelves that were fastened wherever there was the least danger of bumping your head on them. Cords were knotted around screws underneath the shelves to hang school uniforms.

The bathroom occupied a corner of Columba's bedroom, separated by a wall but no door. In addition to the narrow chest of drawers, Columba's bedroom had a tottery shelf that was cluttered with her collection of Avon bottles, hair spray cans, and outdated makeup. Most of these, at one time or another, had wobbled and crashed to the floor during even the lightest of seismic events but she couldn't find a solution for that.

Three nylon cords were strung across the enclosed front patio and one of them was always occupied with at least a towel or a pair of trousers or a t-shirt, and Columba and the kids expertly navigated them to reach the front door. Several months ago, José and Anita, pink-cheeked and proud, had dragged in an empty cable spool from the side of the road and presented the patio table. José said his friend had given him the three plastic milk crates that completed the spool patio set but Columba wasn't born yesterday. The crates belonged to the corner shop.

Life was largely defined by luck and happenstance. They made the most of what they saw as opportunities. Columba had never asked for support from Anita's father nor from José's. Both men had been ships in the night and she preferred to keep them that way. She never stopped to consider if their absence – not only their absence, but their anonymity – had an impact on the psyche of the kids. There had been questions from time to time but Columba was consistent in her response. "What father? You were both born of a virgin mother. The two of you are little miracles." She'd pinch their cheeks and break into a broad smile, her single gold tooth shimmering. The gold, by the way, had been an offering from a miner who had occupied a few brief months of her life. Anyway, the kids used to believe Columba's virgin story and they proudly spread the word around school.

One day Anita's friend Lucia told her, "My Mom says that you and José are no more miracles than a dog on the corner. All born of a bitch. And it was no virgin one either. My Mom says your Mom is a whore."

Columba was not one to leave this type of slander unanswered so she marched over to Lucia's Mom's place, pausing only to pick up a rock to bang loudly on her door. "What's this about your daughter calling my daughter the daughter of a whore? That she's no better than a stray dog?"

"Lucia wasn't supposed to repeat that."

"Well, but you said it!" Columba pushed her way inside the little house, which was not unlike her own. She marched to the kitchen and picked up a wooden spoon. "And you're lucky this isn't a knife. Do you know what I can do with this?"

Lucia's Mom cowered against the wall, preparing to make a run for the door.

Columba shook the spoon in front of her nose. "If I ever hear another word about me or my kids' fathers – ever! – you know where I'll shove the wide end of this spoon. And don't think I won't!"

With that, she broke it over her knee, stomped out the door and down the street where several snoopy neighbors were disappointed by the quick end to it. Scant though it seemed at the time, it ended up being fodder for about a week's gossip.

When she reached her own house, she shooed the kids inside with a swift swat across their behinds, slammed the door and bent forward to look them in the eyes, and in a soft voice, "You two are miracles. Do you hear me? Miracles!"

But they never repeated it again.

Although everyone in the neighborhood proclaimed themselves Catholics, very few attended Sunday mass. Rather, Sunday mornings began like every other, except they were delayed by a couple of hours. The smell of freshly baked bread drew neighbors like flies to the bakery. The bakery was a social hangout, and they stood in the queue gossiping. The sun warmed the streets, children with cow-licked hair and loose t-shirts straggled out of their houses to kick balls down the road, dogs stretched awake and sidled up to passersby, sniffing for a handout. Cats scrapped and stretched out on tin roofs.

Since Columba had recently more or less established herself as a merchant of quality second-hand clothing, she took advantage of Sundays to model some of the nicer outfits as she queued for bread. For those who rarely found themselves down at the plaza in Progreso on Tuesday and Thursday afternoons, she arranged exclusive opportunities at her house so they could try something on. For this reason, every Sunday she chose her favorite new outfit, herself the living, walking proof of what her neighbors could be.

If she was lucky, two or three clients followed her home from the bakery for a private showing.

"You'll be the first. I haven't even shown this down in Progreso yet." Columba would gush, garments hanging over her arms as she bustled back and forth between her living room and her bedroom. If she was lucky, one of the clients bought something. And if she was extremely lucky, they paid immediately.

CHAPTER 15

GAVIN

Prosperity: from the Latin prosperitas, from prosperus 'doing well.' It's all relative.

Judgment and keeping up appearances, a time-honored practice. Identities and cliché phrases. Is it possible to avoid putting others into neatly labeled boxes? Does it prevent us from understanding each other better? Or does it help?

Gavin was not a suit-and-tie guy so he was relieved when Mark, his Dad's assistant told him that a suit and tie was not necessary – at least not every single day – but it would probably be a good idea to wear conventional, casual slacks and a sweater or vest. After all, if he was going to be taken seriously as the new owner of Stan's Men's and Boys' Wear, he had to dress the part. People were watching.

Gavin decided that he could live with the image that slacks and a vest created, which was one of a businessman and not some fly-by-night greaser. To his dread, his new position included a membership at the local Chamber of Commerce and a seat at the table of the Rotary Club. For the most part he would sit silently during the meetings, head tilted at an attentive angle, listening and nodding so that he would be seen as a well-dressed, positive and serious guy, someone with whom they could all get along.

Gavin, the formerly unsuccessful private dick, turned somewhat useful assistant at Ernie's Pool Hall, was now expected to fill the shoes of one of Burgeon's most respected businessmen. He felt that all eyes were on him. Stanley Moore Reid had his name on several plaques around town and now it was up to Gavin not only to ensure that the Reid name remained untarnished by things from his past, such as an unsuccessful P.I. career (zero – count them – zero clients to his name) but also that somehow, he would be able to amplify the Reid family stature and prestige. He owed his parents at least that much. After he passed what he considered his first test of peer approval at the Chamber of Commerce he tasted, for the first time, the flavor of personal ambition.

Before stepping into Stan's shoes, Gavin had not regularly ventured into his Dad's store. But after a week under Mark's tutelage, he realized that it included far more than shortening the hems on a pair of trousers and other 'highly precise alterations' tasks. While he always had, and always would shy away from the measuring tape, the sewing machine and the thread and buttons that were neatly organized in the back room, and while he had been ignorant of his Dad's account ledgers and thought he'd steer clear of the cash register, he now considered the business an exciting challenge.

"Mark, I'm not cut out for the actual hands-on sewing stuff. You'll have to help me here." Mark said that until he could find a seamstress to do piece-meal jobs, he was willing to pick up on that. Mark's strongpoint, he felt compelled to inform Gavin, was in the buying end of things. He had always accompanied Stan to the seasonal shows and, as a matter of fact – he said, in-flating his chest like a pigeon – in the last few years, he had been the one who bought the best-selling lines. He would appreciate being able to continue with that part – that is, if it was okay with Gavin.

"Hey, man, do what you do. At least for now, you're the brains behind the operation."

Mark was unreservedly enthusiastic. He surpassed himself by guiding Gavin through the world of men's fashion, instructing him in the latest trends and even recommending suits and casuals for Gavin's own wardrobe, which Gavin was surprised to find himself liking. "That Mark can really read some-one's style, man."

Stan's old friend and part-time accountant picked up on the books and taught Gavin the basics. Gavin appreciated that.

He moved back into the Reid home. At first, he was uncomfortable with the idea of making major changes. He slept in his old room. He kept his parents' room intact with its lace doilies on night tables under bronze lamps with heavily-tasselled shades. His Dad's cologne bottles were still lined up in a neat row on the tall bureau. Not that the bedroom was a shrine but, well, almost. It would be several months before Gavin would see his way to emp-tying his Dad's closets and drawers. Being a 'big and tall' man, none of Stan's clothes fit Gavin and when the time came, Gavin donated them to a local charity, who advertised them as 'Original Stanley's', which demanded and received a higher than normal price. Anyway, as Mark pointed out, Gavin was not the right kind of guy to wear what Stan used to wear. "Your body and personality cry out for a different style," he said with an exaggerated waving of the arms through some invisible billowy fabric.

It wasn't until after the first anniversary of 'the thing that happened to his Dad' (Gavin couldn't quite bring himself to say that his Dad 'died') that he made a few bold changes. He donated his parents' bedroom furniture to James's church bizarre (but James got first pick) and he ordered a sleek, modern bedroom set and allowed the saleswoman to sell him three sets of fine Egyptian cotton bed sheets and a quality goose-down quilt. He had the old wallpaper removed and the room painted a demure slate grey with white trim. But he let it stand as it was, no matter how tempting, for more than two months. During that time, every night on his way to his own room, he pushed open the door, standing for several minutes on the threshold to survey his Dad's old bed chamber.

On the night that it finally looked like a different room – when the memories faded enough, so that as he peered into the room and he could no longer see his Dad standing at the foot of the bed winding his watch and when he couldn't picture him stretching his arms above his head before drawing back the curtains to look out the window, or see him perched on the edge of the corduroy bench at the foot of the bed to push his feet into his shoes with the help of a long shoe horn – Gavin was comfortable enough to move in.

Mark helped Gavin fill the closet with the new clothes he had selected. Mark even organized his closet and bureau, arranging garments in order of color, with suits at one end, slacks and shirts at the other and at the far end, shelves for several pairs of shoes. The new bureau drawers were populated with linen handkerchiefs and several choices of the brand-name men's bikini briefs and boxers that Mark recommended. Mark had arranged boxes for rings and tie clips and designer cologne (for which Mark himself admitted a weakness) in the narrow top drawer of the bureau.

Rumors about Mark and Gavin were starting to spread around town. "They make such a snappy couple."

Mark was amused and flattered by them but Gavin wasn't his type and he told him so – rather apologetically (in order to let Gavin down gently, just in case).

"You know what they're saying, right? And of course, it's very flattering." Mark batted his eyelids rapidly as he looked down. "But, you know, Gavin, I go for a different kind of guy. You're very handsome and everything. Of course, you are…. But, well, you know."

"Say no more, Mark. Or you'll put your foot in it."

They were both relieved to bring that conversation to an end.

Initially, it occurred to Gavin that it might be fun to play the role but he didn't want Mark to get the wrong idea or, worse yet, give him the upper hand by allowing Mark to believe he was capable of breaking his heart. Also, he didn't want to fuel gossip. So, he remained quiet. He reasoned that an outright denial might be construed as a 'no' that means 'yes.'

For as long as he could remember, Gavin had not been sexually attracted to girls. The last time he had a girlfriend was when he was about sixteen. He knew that he was supposed to be preoccupied by sex. All his friends sure were. But he wasn't. This worried him a little but mostly he chalked it up to not having run across the right girl yet. He'd gone out with a few because he liked them, not because he wanted to persuade them to jump into the sack. It was probably for that reason that they all dumped him, come to think of it. Maybe he'd find that he was attracted to men. But he felt nothing in that direction either. He remembered back then, that he'd once slyly given Mark the once-over when his Dad wasn't looking. He was alert in case he might notice a quickening of the pulse and blood rising where it wasn't supposed to. But no. Nothing. He wasn't attracted to Mark any more than he'd been attracted to Lucy, the last girl to dump him for, what was it that she had said? – 'lack of energy.'

Maybe he could have used this adolescent confusion as an excuse for what his Dad had called 'slothfulness.' Being in sexual limbo could really bog a guy down. And maybe, just maybe, he had been in the midst of a legitimate identity crisis and this is what had caused his inertia. But how was he to know that? He didn't necessarily feel that he was in a crisis. No one talked about such things. And there was no reason that something like this should ever cross Stan's mind either. And if it did, wouldn't it just have caused unnecessary turmoil? And besides, Stan never would have talked about it.

When Gavin was about 17 years old, the question weighed on him to the point where he had to investigate. So he discreetly carried out a bit of research into the nature of sexual attraction.

At the time, it was extremely difficult to find books on the subject of sexual anything because of Burgeon's limited and conservative downtown library. So one day, he made a trip to Grant Falls, telling Stan he had a doctor's appointment for a sprained ankle (that he had begun faking several days earlier). He limped his way into the college library like any other student on a mission, and browsed the shelves for material on sexuality. It was a small section and he was discouraged as he pulled out and browsed one title after another. The book covers had been creaked open so carefully that the spines were still stiff. They'd had obviously been of clandestine interest. When a library assistant excused herself with a polite whisper, pointing her index finger to a shelf and indicating she needed to re-shelf an armful of books, Gavin meandered off, slightly embarrassed, to hide in the philosophy section so he could keep an eye on what she was re-shelving. As soon as she bustled away, he returned to scan the titles.

Unexpectedly (and quite miraculously), he found what he was looking for when he extracted, just for curiosity, the follow-up Kinsey Report, 'Sexual Behavior in the Human Female,' which stated that while between one and nineteen percent of women had no sexual contact or reaction to either men or women, between one and four percent of men had the same lack of reaction. These individuals, whom Kinsey had paid no special attention to in the famous 1948 report, and whom he categorized as 'X', were called asexual. Gavin re-read the section at least five times while he was standing there. And then he squatted down right there on the floor between the shelves and read it five more times until the words on the page were burned into his memory. When he slipped the book back into place he felt like a new man. He whistled himself out of the library, ignoring the annoyed glares of students at the tables.

He was in a light mood, maybe even jubilant all the way home on the bus. It was a kind of victory, maybe something like an adopted child finding his birth parent, a feeling of self, and legitimacy, a certain validity. Now, rather than wonder (at best) and torment himself (at worst), he realized that he fit into a known, albeit minor, category of human beings who probably got along well, thank you very much. This knowledge was sure to make his life less complicated. There was, indeed, comfort in fitting into a small box.

So for the people who were gossiping about him and Mark, well, let them speculate. He could be whatever they thought he was.

Gavin quietly walked the line. And James just prayed.

Chameleon is as chameleon does.

IRENE

Heartbreak, too, is a chameleon. Its dark shadows skirt behind the flash of an image or hang onto the brief whiff of a scent or whisper in the breath of a few bars from a song. You may be caught unawares when it presents itself in one of its many guises. Your heart constricts and hardens like a fist and you must resist as it punches away at the pain.

The week after Irene's terrible rage, Chuck went alone to The Roxy to see the final Sunday matinee re-running of When Harry Met Sally. He settled into a seat at the back of the narrow theater, balancing a box of popcorn on his knees. He sat through the previews and the animated message about etiquette – remember not to talk aloud during the film and to remove tall hats. Who even wore tall hats anymore?

The film opened to a scene on a university campus and zoomed in on the couple who were kissing like there was no tomorrow. The image of the two young lovers, wrapped in their youthful passion, stabbed into Chuck's heart and from that point on he saw nothing but pain. He sobbed silently into the darkness of the theater when everyone around him was howling with laughter.

He ached to be held and he longed to laugh, to find something funny, to enjoy Irene's attention, to feel her closeness. They used to dance. They were so good together. They really enjoyed some good times. Didn't they? Did they not love each other like crazy? Did they love each other at all now? Or did the love really trail out behind Alicia, like air from a slow leak in a balloon? A balloon that you thought you'd tied up so securely that it would stay inflated forever? Or maybe the balloon itself, fully or partially inflated (it didn't really matter) simply floated away behind Alicia because the string was tied around her little life.

Chuck knew he still loved Irene and that he would always love her, no matter how long it took her to return to him.

That Sunday afternoon as Chuck was crying into his popcorn, Irene was rocking idly in the armchair beside the front window. She would never return to Chuck. She had never fully been with him in the first place. It was all a ploy, a survival strategy, something to lift her out of the poverty of her childhood and into an easy life. Sure, they'd had some laughs but she had never been in love with him. At first, she'd hoped that she'd grow to love him but now she was certain that would never happen. What they had was cordial and mostly tolerable. At least it used to be. In spite of that, she never had eyes for anyone else. No, Chuck didn't have to worry about her leaving him on that account. Such an eventuality would be like jumping from the frying pan into the fire. She knew what she had. God knows it would never change, not with a man like Chuck. She could count on it.

Irene stopped dreaming her Irene dreams after Alicia left. Her life had become one big boundless nightmare. She had lost her bearings because the only one she'd cared about, the one that had grounded her and had given her purpose, was gone. That Sunday afternoon as she sat rocking back and forth for hours in front of the plate glass window, she was like a useless pendulum who couldn't even count off the empty seconds. Her rocking went deeper and farther, seemingly out of control, towards the void, ready for her to plunge in face first.

Suddenly – and why it suddenly became clear at that moment she could not say – she stopped rocking and slammed both feet flat on the ground. It occurred to her that she had two choices – either she would have to die or she would have to fill this void with something. She stood up, and then she sat back down, stood up, sat down – up, down – like a stupid toy with an up-down repertoire, trying to decide whether to lay down in the bathtub with a razorblade or go outside and look for something meaningful.

CHAPTER 17

COLUMBA

Hawkeye had become a weight around Columba's neck. He was everywhere she didn't want him to be when she didn't want him to be there. He was a curse in an ill-fitting blue uniform. She had had to become more and more creative in order to evade his hawkish eye. Her afternoon drops (as she had come to refer to them) to Anita had to be staggered and less frequent, each opportunity riskier as she tried to smuggle more garments at once.

After her initial caper in which she had used Jessica as a decoy, she had to give up on the idea of creating distractions because Jessica had approached her afterwards, cannons at the ready. She accused Columba of endangering her job. "You're not funny, you big sack of shit. It took me more than a year it to get this job. You almost ruined everything. Do you think you're dealing with someone who was born yesterday? And what's more, Fatso, my family is not afraid to take on the likes of you in a dark alley. So, from now on, if you know what's good for you, you won't come within ten paces of me. If you do, you'll find out what happens when someone messes with the likes of Jessica López." Images of cartel-signature dismembered bodies and corpses hanging upside down from poles on the beach flashed before Columba's eyes. It was true, she didn't know who she was dealing with.

Columba waited stone-faced until Jessica finished listing off the various dangers of crossing her on a bad day. It was true she'd burned her. But she could avoid her now. The bigger hurdle was that Columba had no allies on the warehouse floor. Without collaborators, it was very difficult to pull off regular heists. When Jessica finally finished her tirade, Columba glanced past the mounds of worn-out Levis, limp North Face vests, balled-up Esprit t-shirts and Joe Fresh flannel pajamas to see that Hawkeye had been observing them from the other end of the warehouse.

She pretended not to notice him as she applied herself to sorting through the hodgepodge of stretch nylon and polyester dance costumes. Experience told her right away that this pile wasn't going to make the cut and she wouldn't be able to sell anything from here herself either. She quickly turfed the whole lot into the discard bin and stepped sideways to the next mound.

There was now something afoot at the depot. Occasionally, over the last couple of months, at the end of Wednesday shifts the Bullfighter stood at his office door and, as though there was a generous side to him, he bellowed that workers could rifle through the discard bin and take what they wanted. This was a good thing for Columba, who had a nose for potential where others failed to see it. More often than not she spied a few beauties amidst the discarded beasts and she returned home with surprises for Anita and José as well as with more possibilities for her plaza sales.

One Wednesday bin nights, Hawkeye, lording it over the circling vultures, framed himself in the corner near the Bullfighter's office, legs astride as though bracing for an earthquake. Alternately stroking his moustache and patting his comb-over, he casually surveyed his small crowd of minions, as he liked to think of them. When he was bored, he stretched his arms straight out and spread his fingers, admiring his home-done manicure. Sometimes he cracked his knuckles, anything to keep him awake and on the ball. Columba noticed his small vanities. Did he think he was god's gift to women, a real Don Juan? She recognized an easy mark for coquetry and she decided to test that angle for her benefit.

The next day, because of a better than expected haul from bin night, Columba was in a light mood. At the end of her shift, as the employees queued for inspection on the way out the door, she watched Hawkeye as he stood stiffly by the exit, eyes darting in all directions, conscious of his own manicured hands deftly feeling around inside backpacks and purses. "These hands are expensive to insure," she'd heard him joke more than once. From the end of the line, when she caught his eye, she coyly cupped and lifted both breasts and gave him a deliberately long, unwavering look, batting her eyelashes and lightly running her tongue around her lips. He lowered his eyes and nervously tucked his hands into his pockets, withdrew them and tucked them in again. His already dark complexion took on a slightly red undertone.

Columba's body was like a ripe pear balanced on a couple of black lace toothpicks. Surprisingly she was very light on her feet and was a great dancer (although it had been eons since she'd gone to a club or even danced at a house party). Today she had exchanged her skirt of many pockets for the tight fake leather mini-skirt she'd pulled out of last week's discard bin, cleverly coordinated with a mauve three-quarter length, drop-off-one-shoulder knit pullover to which she had attached a heavy wooden pin that bounced double time on her ample bosom. She was not unaware of the effect this had on Hawkeye. Fortunately, she wore the spongy-soled, striped adidas that assisted with her spring. As she pranced her way along the queue towards Hawkeye, swinging her hips to the tropical music that played in her head, she winked at him. Boldly. And again.

When it was her turn, she pushed her bag towards him and casually yet sensuously rubbed her collar bone and let her hand dip into her cleavage.

Hawkeye was totally undone and he said, without removing his eyes from her chest, "None of that, Columba. You think you can flirt with company security?"

She winked and grinned and Hawkeye noted that a dob of freshly applied lipstick was stuck on one of her front teeth. He'd always found that kind of thing rather appealing.

Noticeably flustered, he ushered her past without dipping into her bag. "Next. Hurry up. We don't have all night."

And that's how you overcome a little problem like lack of collaborators in the warehouse. From then on, Hawkeye was in her proverbial pocket and they both knew it. They had an understanding. She teased and he squirmed in obvious delight (although he would swear his enthusiasm was well-hidden) while performing a negligible search, his hands just brushing the top of her backpack. Although he fantasized about entering her other forbidden places, they both knew he would never get there and they settled on an unconventional partnership – that of teaser and teasee, with plenty of sparks but no fire.

When the Bullfighter was absent, which was most of the time, Columba managed to sneak outside the big doors that faced the sea to steal a quick smoke once or twice during her shift. Finally one afternoon she invited him, with a wink and a nod, to join her. Straddling the exit, he rolled his back around the door frame to occasionally glance back into the warehouse but there was no doubt that Columba was where it was at. At first, they just watched the waves roll in in a comfortable silence. Hawkeye lit a cigarette, drew on it with an exaggerated Keanu Reeves style 'puh', and handed it to Columba for a drag. After a while, they got talking.

Hawkeye started. "So, do you know why the boss is allowing more and more Wednesday bin nights?" He arched one eyebrow, James Bond style.

"No. I just thought that since he's too cheap to pay a living wage, maybe it actually niggles at him and so he came up with this idea to ease his conscience. If he has one, that is. Why? Does it matter?"

He stepped back and grinned. "Well, maybe yes, maybe no." Columba was surprised to find that she was attracted by Hawkeye's fleeting, almost rakish grin that made his oversized brush of a moustache extend to tickle his cheeks.

"Don't be a tease." she said. "What's the reason?"

"Truth is that it saves him money."

"How can that be? I mean if he's giving stuff away... And you know that I've found more than a few good things on bin night that shouldn't have been turfed out. He should train people better, is what he should do."

"Yeah, well, training people costs money too."

"Then, how does giving stuff away save him money?"

"Well, think about it. What happens to all the stuff in the discard bin?"

"I don't know. I never thought about it. I guess it gets sent back or dumped in the garbage."

"Bingo!" His moustache twitched twice. Columba had a hard time concentrating. In spite of herself, she was becoming more attracted to this man in uniform.

"What?"

"Well, you can sure as hell bet that it doesn't get sent back to where it came from. That's a given." Hawkeye scoffed and passed the cigarette back to Columba for a final puff.

She nodded. "Okay, you got me. So, what does he do with it?"

"I'll explain." He paused for the drama of it, squinting towards the sea. "He has to pay for trucks to take it to the dump, right? On top of that, the trucks have to pay a dumping fee. So they charge that back to him."

"So, he's giving the stuff to us instead of paying to dump it?"

He winked and clicked his tongue, and pointed at her like he'd just pulled the trigger. "You got it. And every bit you take off his hands saves him money. I won't be surprised if he has bin night more often. And this year he'll probably tell us there won't be any bonuses for National Day or Christmas because he's been so generous all year long. And some people will be grateful and we'll all stand and applaud. Just wait and see."

Columba knew better than to trust someone after only a few friendly conversations and a shared cigarette or two. But upon closer study, if not trustworthy, at least Hawkeye was informed and informative.

CHAPTER 18

GAVIN

"I've been so busy lately. Seems I'm in demand." It was Mark, his voice raised a pitch or two, in his effort to be heard from the back office. "Seriously. I don't know what it is, Gavin but everyone seems to think I'm a teddy bear or something. They all want to hug me."

"It's all that charity work, Mark. You've gone soft."

"I don't know. Maybe. But a lot of people want to bend my ear, well, more it's like they want advice, and well, it's really just the married ladies. I can't tell you how many dinners I've been invited to lately. And it's always with three or four women, no husbands around. I see all the same faces, it's just we're at different houses. Food is always good though. I had some crab the other night. Delicious."

"So, it's a good problem to have then?"

"I don't know. Do you think the husbands are going to have it in for me?"

"Should they?"

"Well, no. I mean... I'm innocent."

Gavin had heard from James that Mark had become the town's new sex therapist.

"I don't know what you guys have goin' on," James said, "But whatever, he's popular, man. I heard that all the young married ones are goin' to him for advice about how to please their husbands..." James blushed. "Sexually I mean. And it's ever since he started buyin' your clothes and takin' over Stan's, basically. He's become a gem around these parts. A real shining star."

James leaned back and waited eagerly for Gavin's response. They were having a cold one over at the bar beside Ernie's pool hall.

Mark had worked for Gavin's Dad for about a decade before Gavin took over and rumors about Mark's sexual preference had been rife from the get-go, blossoming each year until one year (no one could remember exactly when) it simply became a fact that, yes, he was a blooming gay. Stan had never uttered a word about it to Gavin or anyone else. As far as Gavin knew, for Stan it was neither here nor there. Some guys (like James) steered clear of Mark, while others didn't pay any mind. Whatever the case, everyone now took Mark's gay 'condition' for granted and because he now carried a lot of sway with Gavin, Gavin had also become the target of many gay rumors. Everyone saw the change in Gavin and they could see Mark's hand in it. Mark had style. Mark had control. Some said Mark even had Gavin. "You bet, clear as a mountain stream."

Gavin didn't feel inclined to discuss how Mark, the town teddy bear, doled out advice to married women much less how Mark enlightened Gavin about fashion. And he certainly wasn't going to be rooked into answering veiled questions about his own sexual preference.

No need to go where James wanted to go with this. But he set him straight on who was in charge at Stan's. "I'm the one running the store now," he said flatly. And without so much as an extra blink of an eye, he changed the subject. "Have you been spending much time at Ernie's lately?"

Disappointed that Gavin didn't take the bait, James slumped down noticeably and he sighed before picking up on Gavin's thread. "No, not much. I mean you know I have lots to do at the church. We're practicing for a big retreat. It's comin' up in two weeks. It's gonna be at the community center. Mayor Hall got us permission 'cause his daughter joined our church about a month ago. Really helps who you know, right?"

"Yeah, so I've discovered. Mark introduced me to a few people down at the buying show in Vancouver. It's a whole different ball game, James. You'd be amazed. And we plan to go to the big one in Toronto next season."

James wanted to say, "So, it's about Mark again..." but he bit his tongue.

Horizons were being broadened. Gavin learned quickly about all aspects of the retail clothing business and Mark said he was 'astute'. Gavin thought the astuteness was a result, at least in part, of his private investigator training. Maybe it was a good thing that he never got clients as a P. I. That way no one could gossip about it. Still, though, maybe things do happen for a reason and maybe the correspondence course wasn't a total waste of time.

Gavin discovered that he had a natural talent for sales and marketing. The day after someone broke into the store on a Sunday night, shattering the main window and damaging the frame (and luckily getting away with only a few pairs of Wrangler jeans before the RCMP showed up), Gavin advertised a 'Break 'n Enter' Sale. He got the handyman to paint a huge sign that said,

"Prices so low, it's robbery." Everyone in town wanted to see the broken window too, so Gavin left it boarded up for a while. Mark said it was brilliant and he began to see Gavin in a new light.

Since Mark updated Gavin's wardrobe, Gavin was a walking advertisement, even better than Stan had been. One morning as he admired himself in the mirror, he admitted that in a slightly more rugged way, he was more attractive than Mark. So, he owned it. He lengthened his stride and added a bounce. As much as the clothes, he decided, it was the way a man carried himself – with an air of confidence and you could even say, yes, grace – that really made the cut. Sure, his casual dockers and preppy cotton knit, V-neck sweater with the two forest green stripes were symbols of a certain success but the icing on the cake was how he carried it all.

CHAPTER 19

IRENE

Solace is like the generous great-aunt who sits in the back, poised and mostly unnoticed. She has a voluminous body – good material for hugging, she has big ears and a tiny discreet mouth, her eyes are watchful. She is intuitive. She receives a spark from somewhere at exactly the right moment, perhaps you could liken it to a friendly electric shock and it spurs her to step up and encircle you in one of her warm, woolly hugs. You sink into her comfort, and you taste tiny shots of bittersweet joy that you should (if only you were capable) graciously sample. But instead you find yourself gulping them back like a thirsty child.

"Chuck, I'm going for a walk."

The announcement startled him. He hesitated, at first afraid to believe it (because what did it mean?), and then he cleared this throat and managed, "Do you want company?"

"No. I'm just going out. Maybe I'll wander over to the mall."

"But it's too early." She was dressed in casual trousers, a sweater, sensible shoes, and she was buttoning her coat. It was her summer coat, too light for this time of year.

"What time is it?"

"It's only 8:00." He was alarmed by Irene's presence in the kitchen, who, for nearly two years had not even opened one eye by this time of the morning, and he wasn't sure if he should be rejoicing or bracing himself for the worst.

"Oh." She turned around and walked directly towards the bedroom, her coat bustling around her.

"But," he called after her, "Stay and have a coffee with me before I go in this morning. And if you want, I can drive you to the mall. Maybe you can pop into the store afterwards. I've made a few changes over the last few months. I think you'll like them."

Irene didn't care to see the store, and she wouldn't notice the changes anyway. She recalled the smell of East End Grocery, its industrial floor cleaner (combination of bleach and lavender), the aroma of ripe bananas, the out-dated, sickly sweet strawberry candies at the till, the damp cardboard in the back room. The little bell above the door. She hated that bell. Chuck would direct her, hand under her elbow, probably to a display nearest the checkout counter. He'd expect her to stand there while he explained the rationale for each detail on the stand and then he'd describe how they had managed to accomplish the final display, who he hired, where they bought the supplies, how much it cost and how much impulse-buying revenue it had already generated. She'd be bored out of her mind. She didn't want to ride in the car with Chuck or make small talk en route, she didn't want to hear that stupid bell or stand there and pretend to be interested in his store.

She stopped halfway down the hall and turned. "No, it's okay. I really need the fresh air." Maybe she should pretend to be more kind. So as an after-thought, she said softly, "Don't you think?"

"Yes, my dear. If that's what you want." He had risen to his feet and was moving towards her. She wanted to back away. She didn't want him groping her and she didn't want to feel his coffee breath on her cheek. But she saw tears in his eyes. He was hopeful, maybe even happy. She allowed him to put his arms around her but surely, he must realize that it was simply too much to expect her to hug him back. It was more than she was capable of. She stood, arms hanging at her side, and let him lean into her, let him rub her back and kiss her neck.

He was humming when he went out the door ten minutes later.

Keeping her head down, Irene wound her way towards the town center, hands in her pockets, ignoring the cold that penetrated her coat. She was grateful for the thick scarf she'd tied around her neck at the last minute.

She'd apparently arrived at Grant Falls' main street before anyone else. Except for four men in quilted jackets and toques who were brushing away the light skiff of snow in front of their storefronts, it was quiet. Irene had always loved waking up in the morning to the silence of an overnight snow-fall. It was heaven's gift to the valley. Snowflakes softly drifted down, quietly chasing one another with their gentle white breath, unifying the whole town under crystal tranquility. The mere presence of fresh snow was a promise that everything was alright.

All but a few stores had removed their Christmas decorations. They had switched gears to embrace the spirit of a new year, kicking it off with renewed energy and determination. What year was it now – 1994? Yes, of course. This was the year she would make her a new start too.

The wool shop's door was an old-fashioned one, the top half was a window with six panes, the bottom half was weathered wood, its routed panels eroded, edges worn away.

A beige needlework sign with bright letters hung for dear life to a colorful braid of embroidery thread in the middle of the glass. The sign had been flipped over to "We are Open" and it tapped the glass as Irene clicked open the latch. She stood transfixed, inhaling deeply and forgetting to close the door. She had entered, as magically and silently as the overnight snow, into the bosom of solace.

"Good morning," the elderly lady at the back counter looked up. Her green cat-eye glasses with gemstones at the corners hung on a chain around her neck. Her lips curved in a smile, showing top and bottom rows of teeth that seemed to be too short, and her eyes crinkled to the point of almost closing. People in this town were always cheery, even early in the morning. Chuck had reminded Irene of that when she served customers at the store. "Irene, they expect us to be happy to serve them, no matter how early it is. Come on. Put your game face on," he'd say before clicking his tongue and smiling a hard smile.

Irene nodded at the lady. "Morning."

"Can I help you with anything?"

"No thanks. I just want to look around."

"By all means. Take your time." The lady brushed her way past Irene to close the door. "Gotta keep the heat in," she said with another smile that made her face squish like a lemon.

Irene took the lady at her word, and she casually browsed and poked around. The store was warm and rustic, you could even say fecund and lush. It was more comfortable than any place Irene had experienced in a very long time. It welcomed her. It was better than home. "Home," she sighed and looked around, "where there is soul." Briefly, she reflected on the emptiness of her and Chuck's place, the way their house echoed and clicked, the hard surfaces that Chuck took such care to dust, where his things were placed in orderly Chuck fashion, lined up according to categories he had devised, angled at 90 degrees, 180 degrees.

Here, she could breathe. Here she could feel her heart beat, she was aware of the blood circulating into her fingers now, warming her hands and filling her face with pink. She suddenly felt alive, even content. Maybe. The huge variety of blended and pure strands that were rolled into balls and wound into skeins were shoved into wooden cubby holes that covered the walls from floor to ceiling. There was everything from fat woolen strands, to thin and elegant, subtle and bold; everything from earthy and bright to pastel and natural, undyed. They were of infinite textures. "We're here," they whispered to her. "We're here." That was all she needed.

After about an hour, the store lady offered Irene a cup of tea. "I'm having one myself. How about a cup of Earl Grey?"

"Yes, that would be really nice. Thank you." By now Irene had piled more than 20 skeins on the counter. "I'm still looking." Two hours later she was still circling around, the old wooden floor creaking and groaning as she fondled hundreds of different yarns. She drank four cups of tea and had to use the staff washroom. She carried on, ignoring the few customers who came and went, gently pulling at the wool, rubbing it against her cheek and inhaling, savoring the scents. Finally, she said she was ready to purchase and she swung out of the store carrying oversized "Spin a Yarn" kraft paper bags with string handles. Much more, so much more than three bags full.

CHAPTER 20
COLUMBA

Justice. Has that been mentioned? Certainly, we all hope it is meted out fairly. But it, too, is relative and of course, depends on the judge. We all hope the good guy will win and we all know who the good guy is.

Lately Columba had studied Hawkeye from all possible angles and she decided he was a useful acquaintance and she would squeeze that for all it was worth. But she would treat him with caution. Whichever way she looked at him, Hawkeye should not be trusted. No matter what she might feel from time to time, he still worked for the enemy and she had no choice but to peg him a few notches lower than a friend.

She remembered that at first sight, and from a distance, he had passed as a taller than average man because he stood erect and seemed to expand into the space around himself. However, as he approached, his stature diminished, his shoulders slumped and his uniform folded into the cavity of his chest, his shirts were ill-fitting, his trousers too short and his shoes too big. Thick brown socks rumpled down in the space between the shoes and bottom of the trousers.

Columba blinked several times when she saw that his belt, which was cinched high up on his waist, yanked at his trousers to reveal soft details at his crotch that she wished she hadn't noticed. She looked away but her eyes returned more than once and she couldn't decide if it was because this mystery detail sheathed behind the folds of blue gabardine attracted or disgusted her.

One afternoon when they met outside the back door of the depot for a quick smoke break, Hawkeye confided that he had once been a private detective. "It was another lifetime ago but I still have the certificate to prove it, signed by George Elwin McCallister, President of an American Academy," he bragged. "Of course, that was when I was younger and more fit, faster on my feet. I do have to admit that I'm still pretty spry, though." And without so much as a 'Mother may I', he jumped up to sprint twenty meters for no other reason than to prove that he could. He returned out of breath and flopped down on the cracked plastic lawn chair. It bent under his weight and slumped heavily to one side as he leaned closer to say, "And believe it or not, I also took a business course. Got pretty high marks too."

Columba wondered why he had chosen to work as a security guard but she never asked. His versatility was striking and she made a mental note about his athleticism in case it would be necessary to reassess her stance on their friendship. Still, all good points considered, she could not erase the niggling mistrust that hovered somewhere in the back of her brain.

He was right about one thing, though. The Bullfighter announced there would be regular bin nights – one on Wednesdays and, out of sheer big heartedness, he declared an additional one on Fridays. Workers would be assigned to one night or the other. Minor scuffles broke out next to the washrooms when there was a scramble to sign up for the best night, with passionate reasons for needing one night over the other. When the skirmishes flared up out on the floor, Hawkeye's heavy shoes stomped to the scene, his authority measured by how far he could stretch his arms. In the end, it was Hawkeye who made the decisions, and he assigned Columba to both Wednesdays and Fridays. When Jessica noticed, he said it was an oversight and that he'd change it. But he never did.

By now, even though his private detective certification had not helped him find the culprit who had damaged the paint on the boss's BMW, Hawkeye had earned the Bullfighter's trust and was the unofficial commander of the warehouse floor. This served Columba's purposes just fine and gave her more reason to keep Hawkeye close.

She overheard the Bullfighter referring to something he called vintage clothing. "I don't understand them but the teenagers are crazy for retro stuff. It sells faster and at higher prices than anything else. We'll be opening two new vintage stores in the Capital."

So Columba fell in line with the trend and promoted her retro-vintage collection at the Sunday morning exclusives and on Tuesdays and Thursdays on the sidewalk. Her hand-printed sign that she propped at the front of her table announced "Retro North American clothes, sought-after in the Capital."

In addition to Hawkeye looking the other way at the end of shifts, Columba still managed two or three weekly heists with Anita's help because one should never put all their eggs in one basket. But it seemed that just as one thing got easier, something else got in the way. This time it was Anita.

Anita whined that her days were not her own anymore and one morning she flatly refused to do her afternoon pick-up at the depot.

"Mom, I'm missing out on all the fun at school and the youth group at the Church. Father Cortés is going to let some of us work on special projects.

You have to stop dragging me to the depot all the time. Besides, it's wrong Mom and it has to stop, okay?"

"And when did you wake up on the right side of right and wrong?"

"Mom, no, I mean, I don't want to be stuck in this life. Father Cortés said I have potential. I can get an education and I won't have to steal for a living."

Columba huffed back, "I don't want to hear any talk about you joining the convent. I'm not stopping you from going to the youth group but if I ever hear anything about you even thinking – even if it's the tiniest seed of a thought passing anywhere even close to your brain – about you becoming a nun, you'll be sorry. That kind of foolishness better not be on the horizon. Or you'll have to deal with me. And you don't want that."

And then in a deeper, more threatening tone, "And don't let me find out that you've told Father what you're helping me with."

Anita shook her head but lowered her eyes, not a sign of absolute honesty.

Columba squinted at her. "Well, and Señorita Too-Good-for-Us, how do you think you're getting your education? Do you think your uniform is free, your books are free? Do you think that the time you spend in school and with Father Cortés might not be better spent helping me make ends meet? Who are you to get an education when the rest of us struggle to get by?"

"I'm not ungrateful Mom. I appreciate what you're doing. It's just that I don't want to be part of it anymore."

And that was the end of the mid-day smuggling.

What with her own long hours and Anita's commitments to Father Cortés, Columba saw less and less of Anita.

Without Anita's company, Columba felt the need for camaraderie. She hadn't been down to Juana's for months so after a long interlude, she let her feet march her body down to Juana's front gate, where her shadow stretched into the front patio and she was greeted with open arms.

CHAPTER 21

GAVIN

Tinsel and bling, a trip through a subculture, swinging under skirts and diving into pockets, ducking under lapels and staring up at the stone-cold, disinterested faces that are meant to portray beauty and glam. The infatuation will die quickly. What percentage of garments, do you think, will be nothing but clutter, discarded like so many forgotten memories at the back of a closet?

Gavin was not enamored of Toronto Fashion Week. For one thing, it was an enormous affair. Not like anything he was used to. He felt crowded and pushed. The pace was fast, the glitz was in your face. Whispered conversations amongst those in the know and vendors aggressively plying their trendy garments – "In fashion, you have to tell a story. What's ours? Well, let me tell you... see this...?" A gauzy overskirt would be flaunted, a flushed face peering between flounces, a semi-smile on haughty lips. Spindly, manicured fingers pointing to perfectly blended rows of wool and polyester, salesmen declaring the best styles of the season, crafted to perfection. And it went on. He hoped to disguise his naiveté with a nonchalant exterior, and in his first few encounters, he walked away without uttering more than a greeting.

Mark, on the other hand, bounced in and about the multitude with a permanent smile, nodding non-stop. He was awash in the clamor, the lights, the persistent drone of voices broken by loud salutations that ricocheted across the aisles and between bursts of music that shuddered out of one locale and the next. His eyes darted, his cheeks flushed. "This is my milieu. Gavin, we've got three glorious days. Feel the energy. Go with the flow."

"Three days isn't enough time. And it's too much time," said Gavin. "I'm new at this. And we have a responsibility. We make it or break it on all of these trips, right? Isn't that what you told me? Anyway, I think it's more like a zoo or a stampede."

Although Mark should have taken the lead because of his experience in these events, Gavin decided that he needed to lay down the law in order to curb the wild truant that Mark would undoubtedly become. "Okay, listen. Let's spread out. See if we can make progress." Gavin handed Mark a program on which he had circled the 'must-sees'. You take this side, the east end. And I'll check out the west side. I'll see you at the runway at 4pm, okay? Will I know how to find you?"

"Yeah, I brought my red feather." Mark raised a dyed ostrich plume, and made it quiver above his head.

Gavin tried to walk the walk of an experienced buyer but the closest he'd been to a show like this was leafing through the Business of Fashion that he'd subscribed to. He was intimidated. The noise, the bustle, the sideways glances and one-on-ones, the private conversations, the heads that nodded in unison, the little fingers that were poised assuredly on tiny handles of espresso cups, knowing, knowing, knowing what he had yet to learn.

Yet, he was able to call up an underlying confidence. From where, he wasn't sure, but probably his Mom. He could hear her voice in his self-talk. 'Gavin, don't get caught up in yourself. Don't get carried away. You're the owner of a successful men's wear shop. You're Stan Reid's boy. You have prestige and you are credible.'

By the time he saw Mark's red plume fluttering several rows back from the runway, he felt almost comfortable in his shoes. He sipped coffee, little finger held high, with several vendors, he responded to their nods with nods of his own and he took notes. "I'll be back," he said. "Remind me again of your minimum order for these," or "You'll have to agree to more friendly terms. I'm open to making an initial order, a lot bigger than your minimum but your price is too high. Think about it and I'll be back." and "Listen, we're located in a small town in western Canada but I serve an expanding market area. We have to agree on shipping." Where he learned to use this sort of language he had no idea. Perhaps he watched the right TV programs or maybe it was urgent osmosis. Anyway, here, he was bigger than himself.

He settled down beside Mark who was on the edge of his seat, a silly crooked grin on his flushed face, enchanted by the engaging male voice that was projected above the music of the catwalk.

Gavin prepared to be critical as the models pranced and bounced past them, skillfully showing off extra-large pockets and wide lapels, expertly flipping wide panels to expose patterned lining, hips cutting through the air to pounding Eurodance. He was Gavin, owner of Stan's Men's and Boys' Wear. He couldn't afford to be taken in. No sir.

"Look at the lines on that one," Mark flashed a rakish smile as a male model whisked himself to the end of the runway. "And I'm not talking about the suit either."

Gavin ignored him. He was looking at the designs for this year. The trend was loose and baggy, pleated trousers, long sweaters, shirts hanging out. Gavin wasn't sure how well it would sell in their shop, given their mostly conservative market. He whispered "It's bland, colorless. At least we can sell that."

"Our clients are not totally unsophisticated, you know." Mark said. "They demand the latest. I mean as long as we don't take it too far. Looks to me like it's all about comfort."

"Yeah. We're apparently looking for something that tells a story. I guess relaxed and comfortable is a place to start."

For an instant, Gavin pulled himself above the rabble, and he looked down on the buzz and commotion of the fashion show, the constant prancing, sashaying, skinny arms, skinny legs, bony faces with blank, black-rimmed, drugged-out-looking eyes that stared beyond the heads in the audience. And the heads in the audience, necks craned as they tracked all the prancing, pretending to know it all, to be critical, to express their opinions with upturned lips or nods of approval or whispered tsk-tsks of distaste, demonstrating their power of selection.

He tried to imagine his father at a buying show. Did Stan fawn over the fashions – or the models – on the catwalk? Did he stare up at the flesh and bone that clacked past him in the flowing clouds of fabric, rebounding jewels, clopping shoes and billowing feathers? Was he taken in by it? No, probably, he avoided the catwalk. Probably he let Mark sit there while he went about the business of negotiating for the conservative lines that were the bread and butter of Stan's Men's and Boys' Wear. Had he, Gavin, turned into his father?

He hadn't seen it coming. Stan used to spread fabric swatches across the kitchen table, flipping them over, rearranging them, sometimes looking at the fibers through a magnifying glass, muttering to himself. In those days, Gavin could whiff it as soon as he walked into the house. Although at the time he couldn't identify it, now he knew it was the lingering smell of Italian wool and herringbone tweed. Panels of heavy linen and rounds of raw silk filled the air with fancy. He had imagined the fabrics taking shape across mechanical looms, workers bending over it, and then giant shears cutting the life out of it, section by section.

Now Gavin found himself interested in fabric. Granted, he didn't yet grasp all the subtleties and intricacies of quality but he was fascinated by weaves and prints. He was hoping to find something irresistible, something entirely unusual that he could really blow away the customers with, heck, blow away the town. He wanted to challenge the status quo. Just a bit. There was a lot of plaid in the lines this year and he assumed rather naively, with Burgeon being a mostly forestry crowd, it would be an easy sell. Outside of a few bold but traditional Scandinavian knits, he was secretly disappointed. He made a mental note to look for long sweaters and cardigans with daring motifs, albeit with the subdued colors of the upcoming season.

He and Mark stayed three full days, walking the aisles and comparing notes each evening over dinner. They met at showrooms to discuss possibilities. They handled the fabrics, checked the craftsmanship and haggled over price, delivery schedules and shipping.

There was another surprise at the end of it all. Gavin found himself attracted to the teen's lines. Capricious is the word he heard and adopted. Perfect for children who were going to outgrow the clothes on their skinny little backs by the end of every season. The teen market was something to look into. On the third day, he sent Mark to do the rest of the buying so he could wander through showrooms that featured garments for youth and he even returned to the catwalk to watch cocky teenage models swagger and flash their made-up faces with frozen stares as they looped and bobbed one after the other up and down the ramp. Something for the future, he thought.

CHAPTER 22

IRENE

Habitual comfort zones offer no refuge from torturous memories. The zones are slowly expropriated and fall into ruin. Therefore, they must be transformed, they must be filled to the brim with insulating physical mani-festations that are capable of keeping bad memories at bay.

It didn't take long for Chuck to realize he had been replaced by yarn. Rolls and balls of wool on shelves, skeins in baskets (reed and wicker baskets had begun to appear here and there in the living room – two large ones at either side of the fireplace, another three underneath the low living room window) and he knew there were more at the foot of her bed.

At first, Irene didn't make anything with the wool, she luxuriated in it – un-raveled it and drew it between and around her fingers, sniffing at it, and a few times he even saw her licking it. She was like a little kitten. Then she wound the balls back up, tucked the ends snugly inside, and gently set them back in the baskets. Her hands tilling through the soft mounds, she whispered and clucked to herself, sometimes smiling and nodding. Should he start to worry? No, not yet.

Irene had also resurrected the Wilson Silver Shadow baby carriage from its place in Alicia's room – the museum, as Chuck had come to think of it (much better than to liken it to a mausoleum). It must have been the first time she had entered Alicia's room since that harrowing morning three years ago. For that, she must have screwed up all her courage. Chuck re-membered how, a week after Alicia had left them, he had, in his state of disbelief, tiptoed into her room with a thin string of hope that the previous days had just been a horrible nightmare. The smell of his baby girl was still there, mingling with her powder and cream. Her soft hairbrush with a few fine hairs, was upturned on the dresser, barrettes with their yellow and pink flowers, an elastic headband with the floppy velvet rose on the side, her favorite plush bunnies and oversized (for her age) Winnie the Pooh bear, all bowing on the dresser beside the bright rattles that she had already outgrown. The closet was full of the little sweaters and hats and booties that Irene had made, and the shelves were packed with crocheted and knit-ted baby blankets, also Irene's handiwork. He knew the room would stand empty for who-knows-how-long, an unholy grotto in which nobody would go to pray, and as he stood there, he felt its desolation – the air spiked with acrid remnants of disaster. It was like Grant Falls had suffered a tornado or an earthquake or something of that nature, something that smothered the world of yesterday under a dark, smoky blanket, making it difficult to breath, and forcing you to wade through it.

On that day when he had re-entered the room, somewhere in the back of his artificially tranquilized mind, he conjured a spark of hope that the room would one day be occupied by another baby. Immediately struck with guilt for such a heartless, selfish thought, such an utter betrayal, he knelt before Alicia's crib and kissed the floor three times 'mea culpa, mea culpa, mea maxima culpa' and then he turned around and walked out, closing the door softly behind himself. Since then he hadn't walked back through that door. After three years, it must have taken enormous courage (and an unimaginable amount of motivation) for Irene to walk in there and retrieve the carriage. Why had she done that?

The Silver Shadow was now parked just inside the front foyer. The carriage had been a whimsical indulgence. Chuck remembered the day they bought it. It was three months before Alicia was born and they'd decided to splurge on a trip to the coast. They were wandering through a shopping district in west Burnaby. Irene was laughing, always laughing in those days, fingers happily tapping across her swollen belly. It was drizzling and narrow streams glistened across the sidewalk. Rain was so innocent back then. A few rays of sun pierced the clouds and everything was washed in golden fairness. Life sparkled. They even saw a rainbow, and they both turned their faces to follow it, one end dipped down behind the high-rises and the other washed out into the sea. And he remembered that they had looked at each other, and without saying a word, they shared a smile that spoke their perfect pleasure because the pot of gold at the end belonged to them. Chuck smiled now as he remembered how good he felt that day. Maybe it was the enchantment of the rainbow or maybe it was the golden afternoon light that teased them into the antique shop, arm in arm, with Chuck pointing to Irene's belly and him saying to the clerk, "We need something special for this one."

They had no way to transport the Silver Shadow back home so they arranged for it to be shipped to East End Grocery. It arrived a couple of weeks later in the middle of the day. The buzzer at the delivery entrance summoned just as Irene was serving old Mrs. Mangus.

Thinking back on it, Chuck would say later that he had thrown caution to the wind. He actually encouraged Irene to abandon a customer, one of their 'usuals' in order that they could uncrate the carriage. He couldn't wait for old Mrs. Mangus to leave. She was a harmless but chatty busy-body and could quite easily detain Irene forever by going on and on about the weather or her cat or Mrs. Milne's bad back. Chuck couldn't remember himself ever being so undisciplined.

"Excuse us, Mrs. Mangus, do you mind?" He motioned for Irene to put aside Mrs. Mangus' milk and bread. In hindsight, it was a good thing that Irene had the presence of mind to invite the old lady to join them for the unveiling.

"You have to see this." Irene took her by the elbow. "We must have been crazy when we bought it."

Old Mrs. Mangus waddled to the back of the store, delighted to be included. "My, what have we got here?"

Chuck used a screwdriver to pry open the thin boards, he swiped at the shredded packing and carefully slit open the plastic wrap and then he stood back so they could marvel at its engineering, its beauty and its promise. It stood there, glinting and winking at its new owners.

When Mrs. Mangus saw it, she leaned forward. "My goodness, it looks like something for royalty."

Chuck was beaming. "Yes, it does, doesn't it? And it'll be carrying royalty too."

"Oh, yes, my dears. Of course, it will.... a little prince or princess. So, remind me again, when is the royalty scheduled to arrive?"

And now here it was, after more than three long, lonely years, the royal carriage was parked once again in their front foyer. And Irene had begun to fill it with wool. She changed the wool every day or two, switching the yellow angora for a pink virgin and adding skeins of rustic Icelandic topped with some of her recently purchased heavy cotton threads and precious lavender lamb's wool. No matter the daily combination, it was an eclectic mix that didn't fail to catch Chuck's attention. But the yarns were dormant, they weren't taking shape.

He frowned when the Visa bill arrived, but he bit his tongue because it brought Irene a certain strange comfort that he was obviously unable to provide. After a month or so, signs of her former self began to emerge. She even suggested a Sunday drive out to Emerald lake and she got out of the car and wandered ahead of him, face turned up to the sky.

Granted there was still no intimacy and not yet a lot of laughter but he thought that would come. "Just give her time," the doctor had said. "If you notice a positive change, then we're all doing something right. She's on the path to wellness."

One evening as they sat opposite each other in the living room, both pretending to be absorbed in the latest episode of L.A. Law, he dared suggest that she should make something with the wool.

Irene snapped, "Mind your own business, Chuck."

He bit his lip. And she repented, "Yes, I know I should make something but I don't see the point."

"Well, what's the point of collecting all the wool if you're not planning to make something with it? I mean..." and he couldn't help himself, "Irene these piles of yarn are costing me a fortune."

Her eyes turned icy.

He was obliged to say something, so he repeated, "I mean, I'm sorry but I don't see the point."

"Well, I do. I know what I'm doing, okay?"

But she didn't. She didn't have a clue. All she knew was that the wool, such as it was – soft, warm, innocent – was, apart from Alicia, all she wanted. She couldn't help herself. And she didn't want to. It filled the space. End of story.

Her love of yarn was mostly connected to Alicia but also to the happy years of her early childhood, way back when she was one of only three children and she used to sit beside her Mom on the sofa, radio buzzing, a cup of tea with milk cooling on the end table beside the driftwood lamp. Her Mom didn't talk much. She didn't have to. Young Irene snuggled into her shoulder, caught in the rhythmic motion of her Mom's arm as she cast one stitch after another, making a baby blanket for the 'new arrival.' Her Mom gently guided Irene's hand to her growing belly and Irene jumped and giggled when she felt a kick.

By the time the fifth baby was on its way, Irene had learned how to pick apart big old sweaters that old Mrs. Greeson from down the road had given them. They smelled heavy and full, like someone had lived a lifetime in them and Mrs. Greeson, try as she might, couldn't wash that smell away.

Irene unraveled the sweaters and wound the yarn into balls, separating colors, preparing for its rebirth as mittens and hats and patchwork sweaters. The art of reincarnation, the redirection of past life energies. She almost floated in the luxury of it.

By the time her youngest brother was born, Irene was the one doing the knitting. She had long since graduated from the novice stage, during which knitting needles felt foreign – too long, too wieldy, too thick – and she had had the urge to toss them aside in frustration. Now she manipulated them with ease. She had learned to control the tension as she knitted and crocheted. She transformed wool and cotton into little garments. Her Mom taught her how to reverse, to slip stitch, yarn-round-needle, cast and turn, and don't forget to count. She sat beside her Mom on the sofa. Now rather than shoulder touching shoulder, there was a short distance so that her elbow didn't interfere with her Mom's, and she tried to keep time. They sat in silent communion, winding the wool deftly around, pulling it through, letting it glide between their fingers and along the needles, little balls of wool unwinding and shrinking. And they crocheted – treble crochet, chain stitch, cluster. Count, count. Music crackled from the radio and she could hear bees at the flowers just outside the screen door and horses whinnied from the pasture behind the house. Those were the quiet days of comfort and belonging. Those were the days before she noticed the lack of – lack of food, lack of boots, no skates, no skis, no money to go to the movies.

"Why don't you make some sweaters and mittens and scarves? You could donate some to charity? Or something." But she ignored Chuck's pestering.

The next day, Irene did something better. She marched into the convenience store just before noon. The bell made its usual announcement, "someone's walking in," all faces lifted and turned. Oh, how she hated that bell. She stopped two paces in front of Chuck, her gloved hand stiffly offering an envelope.

"What's this?"

"My resignation."

"What? What do you mean? You haven't been working here for ages anyway. What're you doing, Irene?"

"Well, it's final. I'm quitting." She saw dark worry wipe across his face as he turned a half turn, head down. Maybe she was quitting him. Was she quitting him? He pulled her (too roughly, she thought) by the elbow and made her walk to the back of the store.

"Are you quitting me?" His whisper was hoarse and urgent and she could see fear in his eyes.

"No, Chuck, I'm just officially quitting the store."

"I don't get it."

"It's simple. I don't want to work here anymore and I don't want you to think that I ever will. I want to do other things."

"Well, okay but are you still going to work at home? I mean, do you plan to cook dinner? Do you plan to do laundry and clean the house?"

"Well, I don't know."

"What are you talking about? Irene, this isn't fair. You're not making sense. Are you leaving me?"

"No, Chuck. No, not that."

His shoulders dropped and he sighed. "What then?"

"I just got a job at the wool shop!" And for the first time in more than three years the whole world lit up with her smile.

CHAPTER 23

COLUMBA

Hold your breath and cover your face if you must as we trek over the black dust that has settled on the sandy shore through decades of pollution, oil spills and petcoke fallout. Scramble quickly uphill. The world here is noisy, cracked and unruly. But you must endure the unpleasant aspects in order to harvest the experience.

This afternoon, the crew in Juana's kitchen down in Progreso watched as, for the first time in months, the unmistakable shape of Columba declared itself behind the tall iron fence at the front patio. She leaned in, her nose poking through the grill, and yelled, "Juana. It's me."

"Columba." Her name was whispered around the table.

Even though there had been a partial changeover of regulars at Juana's, everyone knew Columba. These days, the regulars included Susana, aka the Devil's Doll (named because of her often evil, Chucky-like temperament), the Brother without Pain (named for the fact that after his house burned down, his wife left him and his dog died, he seemed oblivious to the pain and he rose up and got on with it), and of course, Miguel, who was there with his son Carlos, both of them breaking into an identical toothless grin at the sound of Columba's voice. As she began her strut down the long hallway in her three-inch platforms, the house filled with her funky perfume. Her big personality hijacked the assembly around the table, like they suddenly realized that this was exactly who they had all been waiting for. In anticipation of the real conversation, they began with polite, rote greetings, "Hi Columba, it's been ages," "How have you been?" "What've you been up to?" Juana nudged Susana to move her chair to make space for Columba, who would sit at her usual place at the table.

"It's been a long time." Columba plopped down, her oversized bag thudding to the floor.

"Sí, it's been ages," they all nodded to one another around the table.

Without further adieu, Columba did what came naturally and she took command. Even though it was only three days a week, work at the depot was grueling. And don't forget she still put in two mornings a week cleaning the bank. And of course, her sidewalk sales were booming. She inserted a little self-promo, "Should anyone be interested in a trip up to Santa Rita for a Sunday morning exclusive, you know where to find the best vintage clothing, all the rage today. Your kids will love it."

"Columba. Look at you. You've become a bigshot business woman."

"I get by." She beamed her smile around the table. "I have a good system for acquisitions." She'd heard the Bullfighter use that term and she loved the way it rolled off the tongue – so 'big business' – she used it at every opportunity. "And I can't complain about sales."

She bent down to reach into her bag. "Speaking of that. I have a little something if anyone is interested." And she pulled out several sample bottles of pungent perfume that had just arrived. "It's Cuban," she said, without really knowing (but it smelled like it might be Cuban and the bottles were shaped like cigars). "They're even sending this down to us now. I brought enough samples for everyone."

Hands reached across the table with murmurs of thanks and how these would be perfect for Christmas and how Columba continued to be the gift that just keeps on giving.

The Devil's Doll straightened and leaned back, cocky and expectant, her bad left eye twitching and seeping inconvenient tears. She covered it behind her hand. She turned her good eye towards Columba. "So, what does your boss have to say for himself?" Her voice was partly muffled by her wrist.

"What? That jerk. Probably nothing. He says as little as possible to us. The only time we see him is when he strides across the floor with the bags of money that he carries from his safe to his car."

"Taking a chance, isn't he?" Miguel said. "It's a wonder he hasn't been robbed already. Doesn't he believe in armored carriers?"

"Oh, the bastard is too cheap." And she proceeded to tell them what Hawkeye had told her about bin night.

The Devil's Doll was smug. She'd been waiting for her moment. "Well, his bin nights aren't enough. You know what he's doing? And I heard it on good authority from Frozen, 'cause he's in the trucking business and he sees things on the road. In fact, I think he's even one of them."

"One of them-what?"

The banter stopped and all eyes were tuned in to the Devil's Doll. She squinted and leaned in, elbows on the table, removing her hand from the bad eye, which was now twitching at a rate of three times per second, which was a great distraction.

"He's dumping."

"What?"

"He's dumping."

Columba leaned into the Devil's Doll, shoulder rubbing shoulder. Cocking her head but without turning to look at her because she wasn't sure what to do about that jumping eye, she asked, "What do you mean?"

The Devil's Doll wallowed in the attention. She was in the know. She held the ace in this conversation. Taking her time, she looked up at the ceiling and slowly inhaled before surveying the faces around the table, the twitch settling to a slower pace. "So, Columba, your boss, Tight Pants, or I've heard they call him 'The Bullfighter' - good one! - is not paying the truckers enough to cover the fee at the garbage dump. So of course, the truckers are hauling their loads into the interior and dumping them all at the side of the road."

"But how can they do that? Does he know?"

"Sure. And he doesn't care. Why should he be bothered about a few hundred tons of garbage on the side of the road? It's just desert. Nothing there. (You know his fancy house is on a beachfront at the south end of town, right?) Far away. He doesn't have to see the dumping and he probably never will."

"But what about the authorities?"

"Authorities!" She snorted. "None of them bothers. And even if someone told them about it, which they probably already have, they're too lazy to drive out there and see what's happening for themselves. Because then it would mean they might have to do something about it."

Carlos added. "Yeah, but anyway, you know that greasing the palm of an inspector is going to cost less than landfill fees. So, it could be that too."

"Yeah, probably more likely. But what's more," the Devil's Doll leaned in, one eye bright and her bad one still stubbornly twitching. "And what's more... some of the immigrants from southern Chile, you know the ones who settled up above Santa Rita, well, they've started to make their way out to the desert. They're vultures. They're picking through the stuff and selling it on the sidewalk." She was quick to clarify, "Not the established market, like where you are, Columba. They've started another one over near the hospital. They move around though. I heard there are even more travelling markets up in Santa Rita now."

"Oh, I bought a pair of jogging pants from there last week," said Carlos. "Look, they're perfectly good." He stood up and turned around to show them off, stubby fingers lining up along the white stripes at the sides. "Pockets without holes, great find."

"Pose like the model you are. Or maybe the skunk... Smile Carlos."

He waved them off. "A man with no teeth doesn't smile."

The conversation turned to shameful politicians and lazy bureaucrats. "They're all good for nothing. If they'd stop throwing us in jail for not voting, I wouldn't bother casting a ballot," said Brother Without Pain.

"There's talk of them making the vote voluntary. And if everyone is like you, it means our president will be elected with something like three votes."

"Well, not voting is a form of protest."

"Maybe so but some guy will still end up being president. And how? With three votes? And he can do whatever he wants because of three votes?"

"No, thanks, I'll exercise my right."

"A lot of good that'll do. They stomp all over your rights anyway."

"And with this misery we earn compared to what they pay themselves? Old man Riveros told me our congressmen earn more than the American congressmen or the British Loros, Parrots, or whatever they call themselves. We have to at least do something, use what little power we've got, those *corruptos*, lazy, good-for-nothing, shameless bastards."

"Hey, but there's more!" The Devil's Doll raised her hand, palm out to signal a stop, and she turned to Columba and said almost accusingly, "Your no-good boss is planning to run for mayor."

"What? I never heard that. How do you know? Are you sure?"

"There are rumors all over town. Where've you been, Columba?"

"Obviously not with my ear to the ground. But this is crazy. That guy can't be trusted."

"Exactly. So, what're you going to do about it?"

"Me? Why me?"

"'Cause he's your boss."

"Well, it's not like I have any influence over him. He won't give me the time of day."

The Devil's Doll's eye twitched hard a few times.

Columba was serious. "Anyway, tell me how to find Frozen so he can take me up to the desert. I'm gonna see this for myself."

CHAPTER 24

GAVIN

It's hardly worth the time to tour James' closet. Suffice to say that he stores a set of metaphorical building blocks that he's had since childhood. Theoretically speaking, he stuffs every single person he knows into one of these blocks, adjusting their bodies as necessary, cutting off an appendage if need be or binding a torso, whatever it takes to make them fit into what he thinks he knows. It's the importance of identity. Perhaps the need to categorize people is a hard-wired survival instinct, enabling better protection for oneself – predictable behavior being the key to getting a jump on the enemy, as James might say.

Gavin and Mark used their own trim bodies to showcase the new line of pleated trousers and wide-lapel shirts, with the top three buttons always open. They became known as Walking Mannequin One and Walking Mannequin Two – WM 1 and WM 2, for short. Gavin had a sign made for the main window 'Wear the Bear – Minimum!' and he followed it up with a half page ad in The Weekly Post.

"What's that about?" Mark asked.

"Exactly." said Gavin. "It will attract the curious." And it did.

The buying trip had been a success. Sales were good enough to hire Sherri, a part-time seamstress and Gavin advertised free hems on new trousers. Sherri, a buxom young woman with big blue eyes and a smile as big as her breasts, was as much of an attraction as the free hems. She provided stellar service, especially when she was allowed to measure the inseam. Mark preferred not to comment on that. He simply blinked quickly several times and prodded her out of the way so he could take over.

Mark continued to proffer advice to young women but word around town was that it had gotten tired and repetitive. So he turned his full attention to the store, generating great ideas that would make Gavin happy. He was the one who instituted regular business meetings over dinner at Whispering Pines Fine Dining and he also arranged Sunday morning tee times at the local nine-hole golf course, where the pair appeared in their impeccable Ralph Lauren golf wear, pulling impeccable, matching sets of Titleist clubs.

Gavin bought himself a new 1994 Volvo, metallic blue sports model, and Mark bought a red 750 Kawasaki motorbike, which they exchanged depending on the need.

They were invited to all the best parties in town and their calendar was always full but Gavin made a point of dropping by James' place for take-out pizza at least once a month. James, being a conservative Christian who didn't approve of the homosexual lifestyle, didn't like to think of Gavin as a gay man. But the talk around town definitely put him in that category so what was he supposed to think? He confessed at one of the church meetings that he and Gavin had been best friends since childhood and Gavin had never displayed homosexual tendencies. What could have happened to him? Did Mark corrupt him? Who knew about these things? No one at the church could say anything definitive but they all kind of leaned in the same direction – caution. Of course, no one admitted to having had homosexual tendencies or experiences themselves (God forbid!), so how would they know anything about homos? In their naivety and consternation, they advised James to stay clear of his friend. It stands to reason that if Gavin could be corrupted by Mark, then, who knows? maybe James could be corrupted by Gavin.

Consequently, Gavin's visits with James were more or less clandestine, which, in itself, made the relationship suspect and made James feel doubly vulnerable. In spite of that, he remained loyal to their lifelong friendship while keeping his physical distance from Gavin at all times. He was also careful to remember to disinfect the bathroom after Gavin left. The church people had told him that he should leave nothing to chance. Better safe than sorry.

Gavin was amused by James's dicey situation and he did nothing to relieve it. But for James's sake, he never told anyone about their regular pizza night get-togethers.

One pizza night he presented James with a gift-wrapped box.

"Oh, uh... no Gavin," James feared it might be some kind of fairy outfit that Mark would have recommended. "I can't accept anything. I mean it's not even my birthday." He took a long swig of beer and he looked at the gift box that Gavin had placed on the table, wondering if it really could be a queer outfit? James had to be doubly cautious about what he wore around town. He didn't want to give the church crowd the wrong idea, and especially since he thought he had something finally going on with Christie, Mayor Hall's daughter. He was movin' and shakin' with an important crowd now and he didn't want to do anything stupid like walkin' in and lookin' like a fairy.

"Go on. Open it." Gavin was grinning.

James approached the box, tugged at the ribbon, careful not to wrinkle it. It was a nice one and he was already thinking about recycling it for when he got a gift for Christie, maybe... if this friendship with Gavin didn't ruin it all first.

It was bulky – a sweater maybe– and it was wrapped in lavender-scented powder blue tissue paper (warning bells started ringing in James's head) with a round gold seal, embossed with 'Stan's Men's and Boys' Wear. Gavin had gone all out, man.

James was pretty dazzled with the presentation. They say that homos are good with details and decoration and you gotta give it to 'em for that. He glanced up at Gavin who stood back, hands in his pockets, grinning the whole time.

He unstuck the seal and gingerly unfolded the layers of tissue paper, one light leaf at a time, to finally reveal a heavy plaid jack shirt. Red and black brushed cotton. Big lapels, wooden toggle buttons, heavy stitching, the works. And just his size. He held it up and turned it around. He didn't know what to say. This wasn't gay at all. This was impressive, man. Christie would want to jump him in a minute when she saw him in this. Sorry Jesus. He didn't mean that. She's a good Christian girl and she's still a virgin. Probably. Well, yeah, of course she is.

"Like it?" Gavin was still grinning.

"Yeah, man. This is great."

"Put it on."

"Right. Yeah. Of course." He plunged one arm in and felt the soft cotton brush against his neck and then he slid his other arm in and shrugged it around his shoulders. He walked to the bathroom and stood a short distance from the mirror so he could get the full effect. It hung comfortably past his hips. He lifted the collar around his ears and turned sideways. Every way he looked at himself, he was a rugged masculine specimen. This was right up with the times, man.

James forgot himself and stepped across to give Gavin a hug. Realizing his indiscretion, he withdrew to a safe distance and patted Gavin hard on the shoulder. He might be his best friend but he didn't want to ruin a good thing with sex. No way.

Gavin had just created another walking mannequin and this one was a born-again lumberjack.

CHAPTER 25

IRENE

One's absence can have more impact than one's presence.

The wonderful world of wool. Irene could play in it all day but her boss Matilda, who as it turns out was also the owner of the shop, had her limits. "I've been in this business for more than 30 years, my dear, and I have never seen anyone so enchanted by yarns as you. But you have to tend to the customers first please." She removed the glasses from the end of her nose and let them drop on the chain so that the spectacles dangled to her flat bosom. Irene was distracted as they hung at an uncomfortable angle, the left spectacle falling down at the center of Matilda's sagging left breast.

Irene had come to recognize the removal of the glasses as a warning sign, a no-nonsense, listen-to-me-because-I'm-serious-and-I-can-fire-you signal. Matilda deserved respect because she was the keeper of the wool, queen of the fibers, commander of the threads. Because of this, Irene put in a much greater effort than she had at Chuck's convenience store. His jaw would have dropped had he seen the energy she invested in her job at Spin a Yarn.

However, she had one major shortcoming and it revealed itself when asked how a particular worsted or a fine merino or the raw alpaca performed under the stress of a fast-moving knitting needle or the staccato perforations of a crochet hook. Although Irene handled the wool (and what an expert handler she was), she was either unable to answer, or she had forgotten how certain yarns performed under the stress of creation. In those instances, Matilda jumped in to save the sale but she was tired of coming to Irene's rescue, and Irene could feel it. The truth was that Irene used to be expert in all the various yarns but it was painful to think back on it. It gave her an Alicia migraine.

Matilda has a solution. Matilda dressed the window of Spin a Yarn with hand-made sweaters, embroidered handbags, and crocheted doilies, complementing the finished items with balls of wool, placed just so, some slightly unraveled in order to tease passersby as they slowed to admire the display.

"Do you know who made these things?" She asked Irene one day, her hand sweeping across the display, Vanna White style.

"I thought you probably did."

"Yes, you're right. I did. And actually, they're years old. I just change them out. But I have to admit that I worry someone might recognize them from one display to the next, that they'll see I'm repeating myself. Truth be told, I haven't made anything new for more than five years." She held out both hands and Irene noticed they trembled ever so slightly.

"No one knows this except you now." Although there was no one else in the shop, Matilda leaned in, looked at Irene over her glasses and whispered, "I have a bit of Parkinson's."

A bit of Parkinson's. How does someone have a bit of a disease? Irene waited.

Matilda continued, "That, coupled with a bit of arthritis, has made it hard for me to work with needles. I mean, I carry on, you know, giving classes and what-not. But apart from that, I do very little actual knitting and crocheting, to say nothing of needlepoint. Sometimes I miss it but anyway, I'm so busy with everything else." She gestured towards the color-coded file boxes and trade magazines on the shelf behind the counter.

The logical next step, according to Matilda would be to have Irene display some of her own work. "Of course, the shop'll provide the yarn. It's a promotion after all, a write-off." Certainly an opportunity to take advantage of, and it would satisfy both of them. "I don't know why I didn't think of this earlier." She was grinning from ear to ear, her eyes crinkling to slits as she studied Irene.

Irene clasped her hands, knuckles turning white, and she could feel sweat beginning to roll down from her armpits. Matilda didn't know what she was asking. She would play the humble card. "I don't think my work is good enough to put on display."

Matilda waved her off. "Nonsense. Of course, it is." Quite naturally, because of the amount of wool that Irene had bought over the past year, she must be not only prolific but very accomplished. She ignored the protest and pointed to the newly arrived selection of worsted wool. It was the easiest to work with, tiny imperfections would be less visible, and if lack of confidence was the problem, then this would help build it. "Choose a few skeins from here and make whatever you think will look good for the window. I'm thinking we need some items that would appeal to mothers of toddlers." She clomped across the floor in her old wooden clogs to the pattern rack, pulled out a booklet, and flipped to a page with the picture of a curly-haired child in a yellow striped cardigan who had been posed (to the point of possibly toppling over) on a matching yellow tricycle. "What do you think?"

Irene didn't think. Matilda would never comprehend the impossible. Matilda had three grown children. Not one had died in the middle of the night. Not one had a face that had turned blue by morning. Not one had converted from one moment to the next from a smiling, gurgling, soft warm bundle into a cold, empty package. Irene shuddered and turned away.

She walked towards the wool and stared at it in silence. She had never mentioned Alicia to Matilda. In fact, since the morning that Alicia had left them, she had not uttered the child's name at all. There was no need to name her because she was always there. She was both the constant cause and witness to her torment. And yet she didn't want to let her go. She longed for her to forgive her for she-didn't-know-what... somehow it had to have been her fault, hadn't it? She sought to inhale a modicum of comfort whenever she plunged her face into the woolen skeins that she'd stuffed into baskets and cedar-lined closets. The yarn, although an inadequate substitute for a child, was at least something she could feel. It made her skin tingle.

The wool would never disappear from one day to the next as Alicia had. But the problem was that her hunger for it only grew. No matter how many baskets and shelves she filled, there could never be enough.

Yet, all of Alicia's blankets, sweaters, mittens and scarves, little dresses and hats were still untouched in her room, some still wrapped in tissue and packed into a chest in the bedroom closet, the key for which hung around Irene's neck. The key weighed more some days than others. But she couldn't bring herself to unlock the chest lest she disturb how things had been before, lest the memories distort and disappear. Matilda would never understand any of these things.

Matilda said, "Well, okay. Take your time to choose the ones that speak to you."

It was simply expected that Irene would take on the task. "A delight," is what Matilda had called it. "I wish someone had given me free yarn to work with," she said as though she was doing Irene a favor. Irene took the wool home and worried about it.

CHAPTER 26
COLUMBA

The earth creaks and rotates under human clutter. It brings you the sun each morning and the stars each night. Multitudes of discarded foreign memories in the form of polyester and spandex and Indian cotton, and rubber-soled shoes and plastic buttons and worn-out woven handbags (and lately also plastic cases of makeup and outdated creams and little glass jars of cheap perfume in the shapes of high heels and hats) go up in smoke at the edges of the world's driest desert – the Atacama. This happens after those faraway closets can no longer contain the sheer volume, when disenchantment that begins by hiding in pockets and under collars finally leaks out and gasps for air. The clothes are then gathered up and shipped off, posing as gifts of hope. And they often are.

When asked, Frozen said he was going to haul fresh seafood to a restaurant in the high plains next Saturday and he agreed that Columba could ride along if she would bring sandwiches and a thermos of tea. But, he said, she'd have to be prepared to go all the way and back with him. No long stops along the way and no noisy chatter and no complaints.

"What's the point if I can't stop and see what I want to see?"

"Well, but on the way back then… and in that case, you'll have to give me a few pesos for gas."

"Why should I pay for gas? You're going anyway and you're getting paid for it. No, Frozen. Sandwiches and tea are as far as I go. Anyway, how often do you get someone to talk to on the road? You should be paying for my company."

He considered for a few seconds. "Okay, no gas money then. But tea and sandwiches and don't forget who's in charge."

The highway was practically deserted that morning. Columba didn't feel much like making small talk but Frozen was chatty. She opened the thermos and poured some tea and passed him a sandwich, hoping he'd shut up if he had something in his mouth. But he talked with his mouth full, crumbs spraying from between his fat lips to the dashboard. She shifted as far from him as possible but some crumbs still made it to her lap. She brushed them off.

"We truckers are probably the earliest risers in town. Look what time it is and we're on the road already. Do you think anyone sees the sun rise as often as I do?" He lowered his sun visor. "It's blinding already and it's only eight in the morning. See what I mean?"

Columba was going to say that the fishermen see the sun rise far more often than Frozen but there was no reason to remind him. The fishermen were, after all, the ones who supplied him with the sea bass and albacore. He said he also had some octopus and sea anemones on ice in the back of the truck.

From the corner where she had agreed to wait for Frozen, she watched the fishing boats bob over the waves. They were already anchored near the dock, having returned hours earlier with the morning's catch. The fishermen had it tough lately, what with the new law that allotted big industrial boats an unfair quota. And there were always numerous small boats out of commission and at the dock for repair. They had the usual maintenance tasks – filling cracks, cleaning barnacles, retouching paint. And there were the eternal net repairs. God forbid an outboard motor might fail. Not to mention the days when the sea was too bad to go out in a small boat or those times when the water was red with bacteria, and fishing was prohibited. But she wouldn't bring that up to Frozen. He preferred to think of himself as the hardest-working and least rewarded individual on the planet.

They were nearly 30 kilometers out of town when Frozen pointed ahead.

"See that?"

She squinted towards the horizon. At first, she thought the mounds were huge boulders that had gotten in the way of some lunatic artist with extra cans of paint. But as they approached, she could see that the piles weren't static. They shape-shifted. The wind was tugging at them, biting out pieces of color and spitting them a few meters beyond, where they landed and flip-flopped over the desert floor like frenzied fish. Some of the garments sailed away, their sleeves waving over the cold morning sand until the wind dropped them and they rested like wounded birds, occasionally lifting a cuff in one last goodbye before the sun burned down on them. The vultures circled.

Frozen slowed as they passed the first dump site. If you could call it a site. The piles weren't contained in any way. They were scattered haphazardly on both sides of the highway, helter-skelter, thinning out as she and Frozen raced away from town, heading further east, up into the high plains. Someone had also dumped loads of rubber tires and it looked like household garbage had been added alongside.

Although it was hard to tell from the windblown dispersion, Columba calculated that at present there were more than 300 truckloads – left-overs from bin night, and more. Some of the piles were still wrapped in plastic, not even opened or sorted. And a dozen people were already foraging. Further off the highway, there were low mounds that had been set alight (on orders of the Bullfighter?) and left to smolder – the charred remains of peoples' lives (someone wore that sweater on her first date, he bought that suit for his father's funeral, those sandals cut into her feet that week in Hawaii). They were outcasts in a new reality, their muffled stories hustled off by the wind before the scavengers had a chance to hear.

Columba's turned her thoughts to the scavengers. How did they get out here?

"See these people? You know how they get here?"

She waited because Frozen was going to tell her.

"They jump onto the rear bumpers of tanker trucks and trucks with trailers. They're crazy. They do it even though it's against the law. It's dangerous, especially when they jump off. I've seen them rolling along the side of the road and once I thought one of them died when he landed because he laid there for a long time without moving."

"Was he dead?"

He dismissed the question with a wave of his hand. "I don't know. I didn't stop. The scavengers can take care of themselves."

Columba watched as a large, bumbling woman with thinning grey hair lost her balance and teetered over, sinking sideways into a soft pile. A young girl yelled and hiked over in jerky strides until she reached the sunken woman and she yanked her up by the arm. When the woman resurfaced, she was triumphantly waving a bright orange jacket. A lucky accident, it seemed. At the base of a different pile, a child was stuffing a green polyester dress into a big black plastic bag. Another woman slipped her hands into a man's shoe, turning it over to examine the sole and then she dove to search for its mate. Others tossed clothing over their shoulders as they stomped through the mounds, eyes down, scanning for a good find.

Frozen said, "We're not stopping here until the way back." It wasn't a question.

"Okay but you can't take all day up there." She motioned towards the eastern horizon that stretched off in the distance. Would they never get there?

At least the trip with Frozen was without incident – no flat tires, no break-downs. They trundled along the paved highway, the truck coughing black fumes when he shifted gears. The highway ran in a straight line – parallel to the giant power lines that cut across the desert from Progreso up to the mines in the altiplano. The lines whined an eery sound that called up the ghosts who wandered these parts. Columba shuddered.

When they finally rounded the small plaza with its single dusty palm and a sleeping dog dressed in a stained flannel jacket, the town was just wak-ing up. It was a lazy Saturday morning and the smell of freshly baked bread summoned people out of bed, some of them still half asleep, hair uncombed, buttoning their shirts as they trudged along the side of the road, shoe laces dragging in the dust, empty plastic bag hanging off of wrists and catching gusts of wind that made them billow open like little parachutes. Other peo-ple, already with their bag of bread in hand, congregated outside the bakery, telling jokes. Columba turned her head to watch and Frozen took a sharp left towards the edge of town, leaving the bakery in the dust.

The restaurant workers slumped lazily across sacks of rice outside the back door, not paying Frozen any mind. He grumbled and jumped out to start unloading. Anxious to get back onto the highway, Columba helped and she shot the workers nasty glares but they just looked at her absently. When they finished, the cook offered them a bowl of chicken broth and bread. She was annoyed when Frozen accepted and even more annoyed as he lingered to banter with the cook's helper, making jokes as though he had all the time in the world.

Finally, they were back in the truck, driving west towards the sea and Columba saw several plumes of black smoke scratched into the blue sky ahead of them. She decided not to make an issue of it with Frozen. She knew he probably contributed his fair share to this travesty. He'd only blame her boss, "Why don't you take it up with him?" The Bullfighter boasted about how he was at the forefront, "...along with all of the environmentalists, saving the desert and the sea," he'd say. His business helped reduce garbage and it contributed to a cleaner earth, he'd say. She thought about that as she jostled along trying to block out the constant chatter coming from the driver's seat. Frozen talked non-stop about god-knows-what.

It was early afternoon by the time they reached the piles again, half-burned rags tumbling helter-skelter along the open desert. Vultures circled and oc-casionally dove at sharp angles, out of reach of the human scavengers.

"Stop here," she told Frozen.

"Okay." He turned off the engine, "But don't take all day." He slid down in his seat and pulled his hat over his eyes.

Columba approached one of the piles cautiously, uncertain if the scavengers claimed areas, and if so, if they would threaten to beat her away. But no one paid her any notice. She yanked out a couple of t-shirts and a pair of light trousers to examine them more closely.

Although she didn't recognize the clothes, they had obviously been discarded by the likes of herself. And rightly so. The t-shirts were stained and the back seam of the trousers was ripped in three places. She dropped them back down and dusted off her hands.

The large woman she'd seen stumbling over the rags that morning rounded the pile. She was unsteady on her feet, out of breath and her forehead was shiny with perspiration. She frowned when she saw Columba.

"This is all just garbage," she said. "The pickings are slim today."

"Do you come out often?" asked Columba.

"More often than I want to," she said. "I've got mouths to feed."

"Yeah."

"The gringos are sending more and more garbage," The fat woman's hand trembled as she indicated the mounds. "Most of this stuff should be filling their own dumps. Don't know why they don't send something better. Something we can get a few pesos for."

Columba said, "So who brings this out here?"

The fat lady pointed to Frozen, who was asleep in the truck. "Guys like him," she said.

"You mean, actually HIM?"

"Hell, I don't know, guys like him, that's all. The trucks just keep coming. And it's piling up faster. And the selection is worse every week." She signaled towards the smoking rubble. "Most of it deserves to be burned."

Columba didn't comment. Best not to start an argument. The woman was just trying to survive. She had no control over the deals The Bullfighter made with foreign companies. The Bullfighter, on the other hand, had no excuse. Columba felt sick from the stench of burning. How could these people stand to be out here all day? Didn't anyone know what was going on? She shielded her eyes against the sun and looked out over the desert. Mounds of garbage, burned and half-burned, lay scattered on either side of the highway. Several loads of old clothes had blown and snagged on a discarded fridge and a couple of rusted bed frames. Low towers of rubber tires and what appeared to be random car parts lay not far behind. One load of garbage was an invitation for the next.

"Who sets it on fire?"

The lady pointed towards Frozen again.

"Do you want a ride back to town?"

"Are you kidding me? Sure."

Columba yanked open the driver's door and Frozen bolted awake. With a nod of her head, Columba indicated the other woman. "She's coming with us. "Shove over."

CHAPTER 27

GAVIN

Pinpoints of light suddenly appear and expand, one after the other as if on a timer. It's as though, from the shadows, a director raises his arm and chops the air, 'Action!' The first light goes on. Then the next and the next until the path is illuminated and finally the whole scene comes into view. Some people are gifted. They see the dots and they know how to connect them.

Gavin had lain awake half the night listening to the dark. Gravel shifted and ground under the wheels of the occasional passing car, beams from the headlights bled through the curtains and ran silent patterns across the ceiling, a dog barked from over on the flats, small gusts of wind tapped at the bamboo chimes hanging by the back door, and the grandfather clock at the base of the stairs steadily ticked away the seconds. He'd spent his whole life in this town and now he was trying to read its mind. Would his new idea work? Could the town sustain a new shop for teens?

If his attendance at the Toronto fashion show taught him anything, it was that he was tired of the same old. And probably this town was too. His current line of men's and boys' wear was basic. It included shoes, trousers and shirts for school and work, and a limited selection of casual clothes and a standard line of suits. The store also carried well-known jean brands – Levis and Lees and Wranglers and a few simple t-shirt options but none of the brands that today's youngsters were hounding their parents to buy. For the coolest brands, families had to make the hour-long trip into Grant Falls, which made him believe that he should offer Burgeon something a little more radical. Make it easier to please the kids, and more convenient for parents to spend their money. He should branch out a bit. Be bolder. But with Burgeon's population of less than 19,000, maybe he was being unrealistic.

He could hear his Mom say, "Don't be impetuous. Hold your horses. Don't run wild with the first idea that enters your head." His Dad would have stood silently, nodding in agreement. He felt compelled to prove them wrong. Is that what this was about? To prove something to his parents? Maybe. He shrugged it off. What good does that sort of analysis do? He was going to do what he felt like doing because of, or regardless of deep-seated psychological reasons, which, by the way, he didn't have.

He imagined the headlines: Local businessman steps out of line and marches into the future.

He decided to do a quick market study, which consisted of sending Mark over to the two junior high schools while Gavin covered the senior students and then went over to rack up a few balls at Ernie's pool hall, where he casually turned the conversation to fashion. He was surprised to find that the young guys cared.

Mark was all for expanded fashion options and assumed Gavin was going to renovate the boys' wear section. Anticipating the move, he was already brimming with plans for the space, couldn't wait to explain them to Gavin. When Gavin announced that he would open a new shop altogether, something a little funkier, with prices at the higher end, Mark was taken by surprise. But more than anything, he was delighted. He jumped at the opportunity to design the store.

"We're going trendy, Mark. We're going cool. I'm renting half of that old basement warehouse beside the community hall and it's going to be grunge. And something else, Mark. We're going unisex."

Mark breathed in sharply. "Be still my beating heart." He fluttered his fingers lightly against his breast. "See this, Gavin, see this? It's leaping out of my ribs. Check. Just check this out." He grabbed Gavin's hand and placed it on his chest. His pulse was throbbing rapidly and his ears turned red. He folded under the weight of his own excitement and collapsed onto the wooden chair behind the till, his eyes glistening as he fanned his face with his fingers.

What to do with a crying employee? "Pull yourself together, Mark."

"I'm in heaven. I swear I've died and gone to..." he pointed with his index finger and rolled his eyes.

Mark did a fabulous job of designing the new store. He recycled an old warehouse door for the entrance, above which swung a large distressed wooden sign with a big old-fashioned painted hand pointing towards it. The sign said, "Funky Town", and in smaller letters, "Unisex Brand Name Vestments." 'Vestments' was Mark's idea. "You've got to make a impression. You'll see, pretty soon all the teenagers will be talking about their 'vestments." And he was right. Soon they were wearing oversized and ripped and grunge vestments that cost their parents a fortune.

Large 'be bold', 'be original' cut-out figures were tacked at angles along the walls on either side of the stairs that led down to the sales floor. Graffiti was scrawled across the faceless cut-outs, attributing to them, thoughts so indecipherable that surely, they must be cool. Racks crammed the sales floor, the shelves on top of which were littered with Doc Martens boots and felt fedoras and boxes brimming with heavy chain necklaces with silver skulls. There were brightly painted scarves – paisley, patchwork, big plaid. There were heavy leather bags and faded jean backpacks. The variety of clothes was broad with minimum quantities of the same item – hand-me-down cotton skirts and shirts, oversized sweaters, Afghan pants, combat clothing, stonewashed jeans. As well as displaying the big brand names a few at a time, Gavin had scoured Vancouver's east end for the starving up-and-coming designers, eager to be discovered and willing to negotiate lower minimums. The clothing looked like it belonged to a flea market. Only it was so much better and so much pricier.

Gavin hired a couple of smart kids with pierced eyebrows who wore chains that hung out of their ripped jeans pockets and he trained them as supervisors. The place was packed every afternoon, and especially after the Wednesday flyers were dropped off at the high school and after The Weekly Post published their advertisements in the Saturday edition.

Gavin was branching out. Not himself personally, because he still wore the young gentleman's styles that Mark had guided him towards. But his world had just scaled up.

Outside of its routine fresh coat of paint, Stan's shop remained the same, running along tickety-boo, doing steady business. Gavin and Mark kept their offices at the back but had to knock out the wall of the storage room to make more space for a growing administration. Sherri, who now dressed in grunge, had her part-time hours increased to full time, doing alterations for both Stan's and Funky Town. And Gavin hired a new bookkeeper called Fern, a recent college graduate with heavy oyster-framed eyeglasses balanced on a nose so small you wondered how the glasses stayed up there. She used her index finger a lot and the bridge of her nose was red but she came highly recommended.

Gavin was ready for more.

CHAPTER 28

IRENE

A mother's compulsion is to weave her child's life into the fabric of her own, to keep the child close. It's a mother's desire to provide safety and love that will flourish in the child's own life, hopefully picking up the legacy to continue the pattern. But a good mother (dare we qualify her?) also knows where her reach ends.

At first, when she sat down to produce something for Spin a Yarn's display window, Irene agonized. She watched the worsted wool unravel and disappear, knowing that it would never again wrap itself into soft balls, never again be stored, undisturbed in its original form. Her gut turned inside out. But she forced herself to get started for Matilda's sake and mostly for the sake of her job. And when she finally did, it was as though her fingers belonged to someone else. She became detached. She watched as though someone else's fingers gathered up the yarn and forced it along the length of the needles, transforming it into shapes. She watched as it was consumed by the very product it became. She made herself concentrate on the pattern, counting stitches, winding the wool around the needles, pulling it back, twisting it, holding the tension. One row knit, one row purl, cast off. Eventually warm woolly items with a purpose fell onto her lap. They took the shape of fingers and heads, arms and backs, and there were lengths of pure wool that would drape around shoulders and wrap around necks. Eventually her anguish over the disappearing balls was replaced with satisfaction.

She lost herself in the rhythm of the work, her head nodded almost imperceptibly with each count, she tapped her right foot, her nostrils flared and she blushed when she finished a row. Breathe in. Flip. Switch. She hummed crazy sounds, like a classical pianist lost in her work, tones that were out of touch and discordant but nonetheless, expressed the harmony of her soul.

It was as though something or someone had reached in and nudged the cogs in the workings of her brain, just a fraction of a millimeter, just enough to put her off track, enough to create a new cause and effect, enough to reset her thinking patterns. The base rhythm of her mental process was transformed like musical notes across waves that led her, floating, to a formerly undiscovered sensation – that of satisfaction in productivity and accomplishment.

Matilda had nothing but praise for Irene's work. She picked up a pair of polyester/cotton gloves, turned them over, tried them on and turned them inside-out, examining the craft. "It's perfection," she'd say each time Irene brought in a new hat or scarf and then eventually a man's sweater. "Let's do a woman's hat this time, okay? Here," she reached to the shelf for the heavy unbleached cotton that was wound in a thick reel. "You choose the pattern. But it won't matter how difficult because there are no imperfections in your work and you make it look so easy. I swear each time we add something new to the window, it boosts sales tenfold." Matilda's eyes softened in a sweet smile and she placed her hand lightly on Irene's shoulder.

Matilda didn't ask what Irene did with all the wool that she purchased herself or how she found time to use it after she made the display items. She must be knitting in her sleep to use up her own supply.

And Chuck didn't need to ask where her paycheck went because he saw the growing number of bags at the foot of the armchair and the new baskets under the window. The Silver Shadow was regularly refilled too. Irene tenderly patted its canopy and the carriage responded by bouncing lightly on its perfectly engineered springs.

Sometimes she showed Chuck what was going into the next window display. They were always women's and men's sweaters and accessories. All to perfection. Nothing for children.

Just out of curiosity, he twice tiptoed into her bedroom (she had insisted on moving to the guest room after Alicia died) to see what else she might be making with the wool from her own collection because, surely by now, she must be knitting for her own pleasure. He might not know anything about knitting, but he knew something about inventory. The first time he entered, there were half a dozen little sweaters for toddlers on top of her dresser. Had she dared to enter Alicia's shrine again? He moved in for a closer look. They weren't Alicia's sweaters. They were too big for that.

When he peeked in a few months later, he saw more of them – at least two dozen. Now a woolly mound covered the top of the dresser, and other little sweaters were folded on the armchair under the window. They appeared to be organized according to the colors of the rainbow. Satisfied, he smiled and quietly closed the door on his way out. She was being productive.

He was grateful that Irene was talking to him again. They had stopped seeing the grief counselor ages ago because he told them Irene had found her way beyond her despair and could now live a normal life. "You'll always miss your child, there will always be a hole here." He held his hand over his heart to demonstrate his sympathy and understanding, even though Irene had once forced him to admit the only losses he had experienced in his life were those of his elderly grandparents who had passed away after living long, satisfying lives, plus, he was quick to add, his pet dog. "But come back if you ever need to talk. My door is always open." He smiled sadly.

Chuck felt they had opened a new chapter. They had survived their tragedy. Although there were very few jaunts out to the lake for picnics and berry-picking, he and Irene were still together. That was the main thing. Irene had replaced the outdoor activities with knitting and crocheting. He noticed she was eating again. Mostly she ate soft food. She blended vegetables and fruit, she sometimes had meat pie, or else sweetened yogurt and chocolate ice cream. Lately, she'd begun to buy jars of baby food. He wondered if her teeth were bothering her but she said they were fine and she looked at him quizzically. Sometimes she substituted the baby food for a plate of freshly mashed potatoes and turnips. Chuck never questioned aloud.

She didn't have time to cook from scratch like she used to because she said, "I'm working full time at the shop, Chuck. I can't do everything." But the truth was that after she rushed home from work, her only desire was to settle down into that big armchair and knit. Chuck ate a lot of hungry man microwave dinners and he was learning to cook.

He secretly kept an eye on the sweaters in the bedroom. Over time, she'd begun to pile them on the floor. They filled a corner and then the woolen rainbow expanded along the inside wall.

Red flags began to fly around in his head (but he consciously gathered them in) after he realized she no longer used the ensuite bathroom because wardrobe bags filled with sweaters hung along the shower rod and filled the tub.

Irene never actually showed Chuck the sweaters even though on rare occasions he dared to ask. She didn't ignore him exactly but she never gave him a straight answer. It was always an absent-minded, "Not right now, Chuck. I'll show you later." She'd be rocking back and forth, humming something under her breath, needles clicking and she'd never bother to look up at him. She never did get around to showing him what she made and he knew it was because she thought it was none of his business. It had been two years since she officially resigned from his convenience store and started at Spin a Yarn. If he had to admit it, he'd say that her relationship with wool was reason for concern. It was a world from which he was entirely excluded. Perhaps what he had interpreted as a sign of progress – going out and getting a new job, wasn't progress at all. Rather, it was Irene entering her world of wool. He realized their life was not exactly what you could call normal. "But," he rationalized, "What is normal anyway?"

The red flags about the wool were still flying. They rippled in his consciousness, popping in like unwanted guests, bumping priorities from the top of his list, interfering with daily operations. He wouldn't say that he was obsessed, it was just that he needed to clarify things. It – she – was his business after all, wasn't she? Finally one morning when Irene was at work, he returned home to take a long, hard look around her bedroom, just to satisfy his curiosity, he told himself.

As he stood at her bedroom door – his checkered newsboy cap pushed up on his forehead, his eyes magnified behind those black Diors, determined not to set a foot inside but rather to be satisfied with a view from the entrance – he gawked like a stupid tourist. He was awestruck. He might as well have been standing in front of the Taj Mahal or the Alhambra or something of that magnitude. What he saw was truly amazing. And the smell, well, there was an indescribably alluring aroma in the room, some kind of earthy warmth, which while comforting, together with the colors and the soft buzzing of the ceiling lamp (he made a mental note to look into that), added to the surreal-ity. He was standing before a jungle of sweaters. It was like a fantasy filled with a million different species. And he fell under its spell. The irresistible attraction to the bizarre environment freaked him out and he stood for he-didn't-know-how-long, the hairs on the back of his neck standing on end, while he tried to resist its pull. He was a man on the brink.

The quantity and variety of sweaters was more than he could estimate from the doorway. He told himself that it was because he was a practical man and it was because he needed to investigate the number of sweaters and examine their qualities, that he had no choice, therefore, but to trespass. The truth was that he needed to feel them and smell them and see the detail up close. He surrendered to the allure and crept in.

He was unable to admit that his own obsession was instant. And naturally, being somewhat of an inventory man, he absolutely couldn't say no. He was caught in Irene's woolly trap.

Beginning the next week, he scheduled alternate Thursday mornings while Irene was at work to secretly enter her domain and perform the task of count-ing and categorizing the sweaters. He noted the manner in which everything was stacked and if he was tempted to pull out a sweater for a closer look, he was careful to replace it exactly as it was. He was, after all, a man of precision.

Categorizing the sweaters was a much greater challenge than counting and annotating them but he persisted, and after several attempts he settled on a method. Soon the sweaters were defined amidst the columns and rows of his special ledger, which he locked in the filing cabinet of The East End Grocery's back room.

Chuck worked his way through the piles of sweaters from the bottom up, correctly assuming the ones at bottom, in the back were the earliest creations. These ones were all solid pastel colors, angoras, merinos, several synthetic yarns too. They were smaller. Then the colors changed, becoming bolder and brighter – vermilion, brilliant blues and greens, some were made of heavier sport yarns. He saw their progression, from plain pastels to patterns – stripes, diamonds, and then he noticed, starting with the ones in the bathroom, that they were taking on ethnic motifs, including Navajo, then some that looked Scandinavian. He saw sweaters that reminded him of Mexico or maybe Peru. He calculated that all of these types of sweaters would fit children between the ages of about three and six years.

Irene had started to refer to her knitting as her 'collection' and Chuck looked at her through new eyes. She was genius. Maybe she was obsessed and perhaps a bit crazy but she was brilliant and she was happy.

"I'm just going to get in a bit of knitting before I leave for work," she'd say and he'd steal glances at her from over the morning paper as he sipped his coffee. He began to fear her. Who had replaced the former Irene? Who now occupied her skin? Who had she become? What was her purpose? And most alarmingly, what was she capable of? At the same time, he marveled at her capacity to fool everyone. Obviously, she did well at the wool shop and the rare time that she stopped into the convenience store on the way home, she smiled and chatted with the staff like everything was normal. But she lived in another reality and was skilled at stepping back and forth, into and out of the mundane world in which he and the rest of the people he knew lived.

As for her own early collection of yarns – the balls and skeins she bought before she began work at the shop – he assumed they, too, were being used. The truth – that only Irene knew – was that they were barely touched. They lay still wrapped in their original paper labels, in the cedar closets in the basement. They were part of something else, something sacred that must never be disturbed.

CHAPTER 29

COLUMBA

Here is the contrast between abundance and scarcity. You have to don dark glasses because you are dazzled by the brilliance, the glitz and glam of designers and brand moguls at the beginning of the fashion cycle. But by the time you wind through the production process and finally come out at the far end, the environment is so dim that you have to remove your glasses and turn on the lights. And Columba enters beyond that, through an even darker tunnel – after the threads have become cloth and cloth has become clothing and clothing has become worn and uninteresting and outdated and unwanted and cast away. She searches for a smidgeon of leftover value that might have fallen into the shadows of the industry's discarded folds.

It is was dog-eat-dog world. No question about it. Every man, woman and child for themselves. Columba understood the desperate situation of people she'd seen up at the piles. God knows, if she wasn't careful, she could end up clamoring among them, eking a living from another continent's trash.

Columba was not shocked by poverty. How could she be? So why then had she been so alarmed by what she'd seen along that stretch of desert highway? She hadn't slept that night. She could still feel the weight of the strange woman, her hands trembling in her lap as she jostled against Columba in Frozen's truck during the ride home. The woman had an unpleasant odor, the kind that Columba could only attribute to days spent buried in tons of someone else's tossed-out, unwashed throwaways. All the smells of these strangers' lives had collected into the fibers – their cooking, their perfumes, their soap, their smoke, their body odors, their disease. Combined in haphazard bundles, the unwanted fabric masses were rolled out and finally released at their final destination atop the barren, rocky roadside. After that, the dormant smells converged with the heavy smoke that had gravitated back to them and with the odors from the poor woman's own domicile. The woman didn't talk much and Columba didn't press her. She had already said there was nothing worth keeping in the piles, that all the junk deserved to be burned. On their return journey, Columba had squinted into the rearview mirror and watched smoke curling out of countless mounds, its black fingers violating the exquisite blue silk sky. Frozen's truck trundled west and when it descended sharply towards the sea, the piles disappeared beyond the high ground of the altiplano. But the smoke continued to rise into the sky behind them. And it wrote its name there in an obscure script font. *O-u-t-c-a-s-t-s.* The script dispersed and floated nebulously over the desert.

Columba had no way of knowing about the women who slaved to feed their families at the beginning of the fashion food chain, the ones who pieced together garments that would eventually be so easily disposed of. Their hopes and their sweat too, must have entered the fibers. How could she have known about the *maquilas* of Mexico, Central America and Asia, comprised of workers like herself, many of them harassed and abused by male bosses, many of them still fighting to receive the undignified wages they had been promised? Like her, they had mouths to feed. Like her, they needed the work and accepted what they could get. They showed up day after day, week after week to sit in front of industrial machines, turning out brand name garments, brands that were owned by the very same companies who pleaded ignorance about the plight of women who produced their products in the *maquilas* of the fashion food chain.

But she was aware of her own environment. And this couldn't be right, could it? She would be the last person to call herself an environmentalist. The word was not even in her vocabulary. She didn't have the luxury to sit and think these things over. But she was aware of a dull pain in her chest, a tightening of her throat, and a deep sadness at the new reality of the altiplano. Quechua people once wove themselves across the plain as they paid homage to Pachamama with their bright garments, and their now-ancient footsteps, long ago covered by time and now littered with smoldering polyester remnants, faded cotton dresses with empty pockets, ripped stonewashed jeans, tattered branded caps and fake leather purses.

She thought about the gifts Mother Earth had bestowed on her patch of ground – the rich ores that course over the face of the Andes and cross the high plains. She, Pachamama coaxes and siphons water from glaciers that are diminishing and will soon disappear from atop the volcanic peaks of the high sierra. She constructs secret passageways for rivulets to flow under the desert floor.

But now Pachamama can only watch as the water that trickles through her canals, scarce and essential, is sold to mining companies who gulp up the bulk of the rights, squandering it and then rendering it unfit because the hunger for gold and copper is somehow so much more compelling than the thirst for water. Consequently, the small desert oases dry up, goats die, avocado plants shrivel and populations fade. These same mining companies then truck in a limited amount of water for the die-hard residents who insist this will always be their home. The residents depend on the trucks, scheduling daily and weekly activities around their arrival, which is not always timely. The people, impotent, can only express their gratitude, which these same mining companies lap up and publish in expensive brochures as evidence of corporate and social responsibility.

Ore has overtaken water as the most precious element in the desert. But the mines give back. They leave tailings. The desert's undervalued ecosystem of animals – the vultures, lizards, scorpions, snakes, foxes, pumas, condors, and further east, the llamas and flamingos try to adjust. Now they must also watch, trying in vain to comprehend as the wind silently dusts their home with another new kind of soot from dispensable fast fashion that has been sent from thousands of miles away.

People like the Bullfighter turn a blind eye. The authorities turn a blind eye. Columba's sadness turned to anger. Anger not only at the Bullfighter and the authorities but also at herself. Who was she, if not just another vulture at the bottom of the food chain, who extended her hand every week to accept a salary, meager as it was, in exchange for tossing out what would later seep into the ground along the highway or then burn and eventually rain down as soot over the golden sand?

These realizations forked into fears and disgust that threatened to plant themselves into her consciousness and take root. She would have to deny them if she was to continue to provide for her family. If not, then who? She would have to be practical, she would have to stay ahead of this new consciousness. There was always the danger that she and the kids could end up out on the piles with the likes of the scavengers. She would, therefore, see to it that the reality of the altiplano would always run parallel to her own reality. Like two railway lines across the sand, they would never ever meet. She would stay on her own train. With a wisp of a prayer to Pachamama and a humble apology, she turned her back on the woes of the desert to concentrate on her day-to-day tasks. Is this not what anyone in her situation would do?

She sat down at the table with José and Anita and served them a cup of tea and a cheese sandwich before announcing her intentions to pursue new hours.

"I heard the boss is going to start a night shift. The stuff just keeps coming and he wants to run more through the plant, faster. It's more economical for him to hire more of us peasants than it is to renovate and rent more space. Anyway, so I'm going to ask for a evening shift because they say it pays more."

José exchanged a glance with Anita that signaled something they didn't want Columba to hear. There would be no arguments, though. They both nodded.

It felt like only yesterday that Columba had walked in and been turned down for a raise. That was years ago and she hadn't dared ask again.

The next day she rapped lightly on the office door. "Señor."

He beckoned her in without looking up.

"Señor, I heard that you're going to run a night shift and I would like to apply for it."

"Why?"

"Well, I heard that it'll pay more than the day shift and I've been working here a long time without a raise. I could use the extra money."

"Who told you about this?"

"Well, everyone... I mean, you know, people gossip and after you hear it from enough people you figure it must be true."

"It is."

She waited.

He was paying attention to her now, looking at her like it was the first time he'd seen her. "So, you've been here for four years?"

"More. Six." How could he forget that she was the first one he hired?

"I don't think I've had any complaints about you."

"Nope, none. Never. I work hard and I'm trustworthy. I'm also loyal." She endeavored to keeping her gaze steady, no flinching, nothing to indicate that she might be nervous or lying.

"Okay, I'll hire you for the night shift. You'll have to work three nights a week – Monday, Wednesday and Friday and sometimes Tuesdays if we need you. The shift starts at 4pm and finishes at midnight. You're responsible to get yourself home. Go and report to Jaime. He'll set things up."

"Who's Jaime?"

"Jaime," he waved his hand in the air impatiently. "You know Jaime. Jaime. Security." Oh, so Hawkeye was Jaime.

"Thank-you, Señor. You won't be sorry."

CHAPTER 30
GAVIN

The only thing that set tonight's Chamber of Commerce meeting apart from any other was that a guy called Richard made a presentation, a plea of sorts, to encourage businesses around town to set up used clothing bins for his charity. He assured them that it wasn't only the community that would benefit, but that it was an added value. The businesses would benefit too.

"We provide the bins and we make weekly pickups. All we ask is a secure meter-square spot, preferably somewhere near your front door. Here's what the bin looks like." He passed around a photo of a beige fiberglass affair with an Avail International Charities logo, something like angel wings without an angel. He continued, "We'll certify your business as one of our official sponsors. It's a simple concept and we make it convenient for you and for your customers.

"Who doesn't want to clean out their closet and donate recycled clothes for a good cause? The advantage of having a bin (besides the fact that you don't actually have to do anything) is that you make it convenient for people to donate, and it makes them feel good about buying something new. Because the bin is so convenient – at your door – anyone who wants to donate will remember that yours is the place to go to. Really, it's an added value." It was a convincing pitch and Gavin sat up and paid attention.

Avail International Charities' mission was to employ new immigrants and help them integrate into the community. They were a recognized charity and received government funds to pay minimum wages.

The many facets of the garment industry never failed to amaze. Gavin invited Richard for a drink after the meeting.

"It's a simple business with a simple cause."

After three shots of whiskey and a couple of bottles of Molson's (gotta be Molson Blue, he said, no other beer will do), Richard was a wealth of information.

"So, we collect used clothing and send it overseas."

"How did you start out in the business?"

Richard loosened his tie and leaned into the bar. "The short story is that I met my wife, Ali, down at the coast about ten years ago. She's from Zambia. Her family was never really political but they were desperate for an opportunity for a better life and they rode the coattails of political refugees during the times of some heated political unrest. I mean, I don't understand it all, to tell you the truth. Anyway, without going into the ins and outs of the bureaucratic process, she finally got her permanent residence status and we got married and we moved up here 'cause I was offered a job to manage a recycling plant.

"After awhile, Ali wants us to visit Zambia so I can meet one of her brothers who moved back there. And when we get down to Lusaka – that was in '98 – I see all kinds of second-hand clothing being sold in shops and on the street. I mean sellers are lined up, one beside the other for blocks. And they're selling clothes from here and from Europe. I mean, I see team jerseys for the Montreal Canadiens and the New York Rangers. No one there even knows what hockey is but I guess if they like the jerseys... And you know what? In relative terms, the clothes weren't all that cheap. I mean some were. But quite honestly, you can sometimes pay less for these garments from our local thrift stores.

"Anyway, so I get Ali to ask where they get all the clothing. I mean I was really curious, you know. And they all say they buy them from wholesalers at different ports who receive them from charities in North America and Europe. At first. I didn't think much of it.

"So, we get home and take a few days to unwind in Vancouver and damned if I don't start noticing all the charity shops with used clothes. And then I saw a sign for a head office for one of them. Can't remember which one now. But so, I go upstairs and ask if I can talk to the manager.... kind of like what you're doing." He stopped to take a swig from the beer and looked Gavin straight in the eye. "I hope to hell you're not planning to set up some kind of competition."

Gavin shook his head and laughed, "No, definitely not."

"Anyway, so the manager there tells me that they sell a small percentage of the used clothing in shops in Canada, like less than 5%. And they sell the rest by the kilo – shipped in containers – to third world countries. And there you go..."

"Yeah but why say it's a charity? It's a business, right?"

"Well, yeah, it's a charity if you make donations or if you have a cause. But of course, it's a business. And a damn good one too." He took another swig of beer and wiped his mouth, leaving a dab of foam on the edge of his lips, which he cleaned up with a few swipes of his tongue. He smiled, and Gavin noted some foam still bubbling at the corner of this mouth.

Gavin straightened up. "So how is it that you set up the charity for new immigrants then?"

"Well, it was Ali's influence really, and well, I mean the government sets quotas for immigrants from here and there. Our charity is set up to help train and employ new immigrants so they can practice English on the job. The wages are paid by the government, at least initially. Most of our people come from Sub-Saharan Africa. What we do is that we put these newcomers to work sorting and selling in our little thrift shop – you know our depot and shop at the south end of town, right? We have eight employees. What we sell here is just a drop in the bucket. The majority of our donations are sold to importers in third world countries."

"So, you might be making a small fortune from local donations and overseas sales?"

"We might be."

"And you're doing this by selling discarded clothing? So, your source material is all donated."

"Yup."

"Do people who donate their clothes know the clothes are not actually given away to needy people in developing countries?"

"Probably not. But I doubt if they'd want to know anyway. I mean, all they really want is to clean out their closets, donate to a good cause, feel good about themselves, you know. And we provide that. Besides they know we do a good thing with our people here." He puffed up like a pigeon and then chugged back the last of his beer. "Gotta go, man. My wife is waiting for me."

CHAPTER 31

CHUCK

Imagine glass thrown against a wall with such force that it shatters into a million pieces but there is no gravity to pull it down, so it remains suspended in the air, tiny shards gnawing at your forehead, needles poking at your ears and stabbing at your eyes everywhere you turn. Trying to ignore it, you squeeze your eyes tight but you can still feel it. You cover your ears but it persists. It's everywhere. This is the atmosphere in Chuck and Irene's house since that fateful June morning. Mostly anyway. The days that escaped it are few and far between. Living in the harrowing derangement that oscillates between a pinpoint of light at the end of a tunnel, and all-consuming darkness has taken its toll. Chuck is easily tempted by the tiniest crumb of hope.

A niggling stream of doubt – maybe no more than a few drops if he had to quantify it – had begun to trickle into Chuck's waking brain. Deep down, he knew Irene's behavior was a sign that something was wrong but so far, he had been able to avoid naming it. He didn't want to consult anyone because it was nobody else's business. Things weren't right but what if they got worse?

He had, in one brief moment of anxiety, considered calling Irene's mother, maybe suggesting she come and visit so she could see for herself what was going on. But a visit would have to be coordinated through Irene who would refuse, and who would quite possibly turn cold and silent for weeks afterwards. She still bore a grudge against her Mom. "It's complicated," she had told him more than once. "She doesn't approve of my choices, my lifestyle even. She thinks I'm better off on a farm with a dozen runny-nosed brats." Chuck thought Irene's attitude was unfair but he stayed out of it. If he insisted, she'd get nastier. "Anyway, what do you know, Chuck? My family doesn't think beyond the fences around the property. Do you think they approve of life in town? Do you think they approve of you running a convenience store, selling over-priced canned food supplied by a middle-man? Do you think they see your investments as honest rewards? Do you think that they think your money is well-earned? Simple answer is no. Do you want me to go on?"

The last time they'd seen Irene's family was at Alicia's funeral. Of course, the whole crew showed up to offer their support and sympathy. But gingerly and mostly from a distance. Her parents might be uneducated but they could read the signs. No one, not even Chuck could get close to Irene. Once when he tried to put his arms around her, she shrugged him off and took not one but two steps back, tripping and almost falling, causing everyone to turn their heads. Irene's sisters Amber and Jocelyn, who were closest to her in age but who shared nothing else in common, approached her, cheeks wet with tears and, in turn, cautiously leaned in and whispered, "Irene, I'm so sorry," and "Irene, the whole family is here for you." She resisted their sympathy. This was *her* pain, her nightmare. How could they even pretend to fathom... how dare they assume their presence or words could possibly bring any sort of consolation?

Since the launch of his sweater inventory more than a year ago, Chuck kept an eye on the woolen piles in Irene's bedroom. He secretly looked forward to his bi-weekly ventures into her rooms – the new green sweater with perky pink cuffs was entered into the green column and the one with the red crocheted buttons over a felt wool panel into the red column, size five and size six respectively. If he was honest, he'd have to admit that he, too, derived a share of secret satisfaction. But of course, it was different. His obsession was strictly from a numbers point of view, a logic, an interest in organization and accountability. No way was he neurotic, like Irene.

Last month, she declared her sewing room out of bounds. She didn't have to tell him (and never would have anyway) that it was because she needed space for more piles. The wooliness was spreading. The whole house began to smell of it.

And Chuck's ledger was filling up.

Irene's rooms contained more than 1,720 sweaters, all sizes (according to Chuck's best guesses) were between two-three and six, perhaps going beyond. All beautifully crafted in all ways imaginable. Her latest included 232 sweaters that he had seen the beginnings of a few months ago, and for which Chuck had had to open a new column entitled 'sweaters with attachments'. They were, by far the most striking. These had three-dimensional crocheted butterflies and flowers, little armless dolls without faces but with bright hats and little shoes tacked to the sweaters like characters in fairy tales. There were crocheted daisies growing from pockets and little golden unicorns prancing across one side of the chest; monkeys swinging from one shoulder to another, stars appearing from underneath puffy collars and cuffs. Her work was incomparable, genius even. The more beauty he saw in it, the greater impotence and sadness he felt. A mere interloper in Irene's world, he began to realize the dimension of her mental disorder but he didn't know how to define it, nor could he guess if it would one day subside all by itself, nor if there were viable treatments. The one thing he did know was that she didn't consider it a problem and that outwardly, at least to other people, she was normal. So, it was their secret – a secret that she didn't know he shared.

Their relationship had lost any sense of normalcy the day after Alicia died and, although he knew deep down that after all this time, he shouldn't wish for anything more, he still watched for signs of change. There was always that slim (and getting slimmer) glimmer of hope. It was like the knife-sharp sliver of light under her bedroom door at night, a sign she was alive at least, maybe moving around, maybe thinking about him, maybe even at the point of opening her door to invite him in. Up to now, though, he just paused and walked past.

Chuck would accept the crumbs. At least as keeper of her sweater inventory he was relevant, even, he told himself, essential, to her collection, if not to her. And as the collection grew, so did his relevance. After all, who else could tell her exactly what she had and where? He knew deep down that she'd never ask because he knew that she knew exactly what she had and where. But he told himself her memory might falter.

Their relationship was distant and civil and most times it was respectful but it was still devoid of intimacy of any sort. Chuck missed the picnics, the easy conversations as they leaned back on a blanket. He missed the movies in a dark theater, their fingers touching as they reached into a shared box of popcorn, glancing at each other to laugh at the funny parts. He missed holding her in bed, spooning early in the morning, feeling the full warmth of her curled up beside him. He missed her walking through the door at the store, the bell ringing her late arrival.

He was a man in mourning, and inside he had almost but not quite, converted into one of the walking dead. But he would never desert her. He would carry on, if nothing else, for her sake. She was still the woman of his dreams, and even if she didn't know it, she needed him. She'd just taken a turn, that was all. She'd just gone off somewhere and he was waiting for her to come back.

The newest sweaters that had begun to pile up in the sewing room were bigger in size. Now they were – from what Chuck was able to estimate by visually measuring children as he slowed to drive past school playgrounds – for young children, perhaps six to eight years old.

Irene was branching out, reaching up, growing beyond. That's my girl.

CHAPTER 32
COLUMBA

Even a self-imposed, isolated island-self, cannot deny that roots follow her from birth, sprouting little tentacles that curve at the soles of her feet and around her legs and meander up her back and into her brain, sowing thoughts in her unwilling consciousness. And there, innocent as they are, they raise questions and cause conflict before they eventually retreat back to the soles of the feet and lie in wait for the next opportunity. Family. It cannot be denied.

Anita was gone.

From one day to the next, the plodding progression towards a better life at the edge of this arid place tripped, fell, regained its balance, tripped again, failed to grab hold and then slipped entirely. At its point of interruption, at this point when Columba's life was briefly halted, it could never resume at its previous velocity nor move along the same trajectory. This pivotal moment was, in the bigger picture, nothing but a flash in the pan. But for Columba it was an eternity. Either that, or time stood still, and the earth failed to rotate and the sun failed to rise.

From one day to the next, Anita's mattress was empty, her voice was absent, and the recent patronizing expression on Anita's face as she looked at Columba from over a cup of morning tea was now nothing more than a ghost. It haunted Columba day and night. She could not make sense of the disappearance of her first miracle child. She was sucked into the vacuum of the shadows in the dark days that followed.

Anita had not died. No, it wasn't that simple. She was somewhere in Progreso. Someone said she lived behind a green door next to a corner bar with a small sign that said 'The Black Cat'. Columba had gone to investigate this green weathered door with the sign that squeak as she passed underneath. It waved her on. Keep going. You're not wanted here. She persisted for days but her search came up empty as the sign clattered "Leave! Do you think someone here wants to see you? Not likely. Chao."

Tormented with the knowledge that each day, somewhere (probably behind that green door), Anita made herself a cup of tea, perhaps shared a sandwich with someone (who?), she dressed each morning – squeezing into her tight jeans and dropping a loose sweater over her shoulders, flipping her hair out from underneath and clipping it up into a loose bun at the nape of her neck – to go out for the day (where?), that she laughed with new friends and maybe drank with them (or what if they did drugs?). Dozens of questions (the list was growing) were overshadowed with the eternal question of why.

What had Columba and José done? Why had Anita abandoned them without warning?

Although Columba had no way to describe her pain, she thought maybe Anita's sudden and unexplained desertion was more heartbreaking than if Anita had died. At least if she had died, Columba rationalized, she would know where she was. She could visit her at the cemetery, take her flowers and bring her trinkets, decorate her niche for Christmas, sit across from her every Sunday and tell her the latest gossip. She could sing to her, share champagne with her on New Year's Eve. She could consult with her about José. But as it was, there would be no satisfaction, there would be no knowing.

Despite being shunned by The Black Cat sign, Columba returned again and again, hoping to see Anita on the off-chance. She stopped passersby to ask if they were her friends. Withdrawing the photo from her pocket, "Do you know this girl? She's almost 17." Sometimes on her nights off, after she tucked José under his blankets, with a promise she'd be right back, she ventured down to The Black Cat bar, ordered a glass of wine and hunched into the darkest corner to watch, spying on the young people who came and went, who shouted greetings, wrapped arms around each other, laughed, nudged one another, spilled beer and finally left, calling out goodbyes that echoed down the street. But she began to wonder if Anita even frequented the place. Or maybe she only went in on the nights when she knew Columba was working. And that maybe one of these people Columba was watching was also watching her.

Columba never contacted the police because they would tell her that Anita was old enough to leave if she wanted. Lucia confirmed that the rumors about the green door were true and that Marcelo, Anita's new boyfriend had lived there for years. Besides, Columba had never had much confidence in the police. What could they do? They wouldn't force Anita to return home. "Señora," they'd say, looking down on her blonde nest, and then glancing at her bosom, "She has every right. It's a family matter. We don't get involved in that."

Columba had questions for Lucia. Lucia, head down, rubbed the toe of her right shoe with her left and, without looking up, she shrugged and said so softly that Columba could barely hear her, "I don't hear anything from Anita anymore, Señora. The only thing I know is that she lives with Marcelo. I'm sorry Señora."

How could Columba have been so blind? How could she not have known that something was going on behind her back? When did it all start?

Columba investigated Marcelo in the same way she enquired about Anita – by standing on the corner and asking if someone could point him out. She encountered two questionable characters, one a skinny, pockmarked young man who shrunk into the wall two locales down from The Black Cat, muttering as he extended a dirty hand, palm up. The other character was a plumber (dragging his tools behind him on a two-wheeled cart). The plumber told her that Marcelo was the bartender at The Black Cat, pretty much ran the place. How old was he? Was he a good man? When asked, the beggar pushed his hand out further, until Columba dropped 100 pesos into it and then he guessed that Marcelo was around thirty or forty years old. But why did she want to know? Was she an undercover cop? Did she look like one? Not very likely, Señor! Well, anyway, that's all he could say. Did she have more spare change? What can a guy do with 100 pesos these days? She didn't.

Far too old for Anita – this man called Marcelo. And that's all Columba knew for sure. Was he good to her? Or did he keep her under his thumb, a ripe young thing that he was grooming. For what? For himself? To pass around to others? Columba shuddered. For a week afterwards, she couldn't eat. José finally convinced her to put some bread into her mouth because she needed energy to work. But she couldn't keep it down.

Instead, Columba was eating herself up inside. She continued to pound the sidewalks around the streets of The Black Cat. Sometimes she planned it. Other times she just found herself there, having hailed a collector taxi or jumping onto a microbus headed in that direction.

Finally, after several weeks she caught a glimpse of Anita. It was late afternoon just as she was paying for a bottle of water, passing coins between the iron railings that protected the convenience store owner from the 'bad milk' who frequented those streets. She heard someone call out Anita's name. Her ears pricked and she turned, dropping the bottle and she paid no mind when the store owner grabbed it and put it back on the shelf, prepared to charge again for the same bottle should the Señora want it. Possession is nine tenths of the law.

"Anita. Anita, mi pita." He was mocking the girl. She estimated the man was in his mid-thirties. He was medium-height, stocky but not fat. A red bandana imprinted with green marijuana leaves ran across his forehead and disappeared into a thick mop of curly black hair. His face was pock-marked. He waved and Anita loped into sight. She was wearing a pair of high-heeled, knee-high boots with brown fringes at the top, which swayed helter-skelter, and a mini-skirt and leather jacket that was open at the front, exposing a black, low-cut t-shirt. Her hair, which hung loosely past her shoulders was streaked with purple and Columba caught the glint of a nose ring. Anita wore heavy eyeliner and purple lipstick and she strutted to a sticky rhythm that streamed from a pair of ear buds.

"I'm coming, my prince, don't panic." She laughed. It was Anita's laugh but without the child-like ring. It was like a serious laugh. She moved like she was in control until the man with the bandana grabbed her by the elbow, wrapped his arm around her and pulled her close to him. She wobbled on the high heeled boots and leaned into his chest, her hips tight to his. He pulled her hair, lifting her head so that she looked up into his face. She smiled and he leaned down and kissed her. It was a rough kiss, a kiss of control.

In her haste, Columba caught her heel on the curb and she tumbled to the asphalt, banging her head and scraping both legs. Blood oozed around the tiny pebbles that had embedded in the skin at her knees. Her trousers were torn and the heel of her right shoe had broken right off. She lost half the contents of her bag and as she clawed them back into the purse's wide mouth, she yelled, "Anita! Anita!"

The girl looked in her direction. The man looked down at Anita with a scowl and he raised his eyebrows.

"Anita. It's me!" She yelled louder now, trying to wave as she scrambled to her feet. "It's Mom!"

Anita pushed at the man's chest, said something and then shoved him towards the green door. He fumbled with a key and they disappeared inside.

Columba ran up to the door and pounded on it. "Anita. It's Mom. Let me in. We need to talk." No answer. She continued pounding until finally the door was opened violently, knocking Columba against the rough concrete wall. The man leapt out from the dim interior and he grabbed her by the throat, forcing her into the wall, her head thudded back and she could feel her hair tearing and her scalp scraping against the rough cement. The man with the bandana smelled of stale beer and cigarettes. She could see his sweat. She could see the hard, bloodshot eyes, pupils enlarged. The smog had painted his face with thin, ragged lines that scowled around his nose and up between his brows.

"Anita doesn't know you, okay? You leave her alone. We don't ever want to see you on this corner again. Got it? You are persona non grata on this street. And I won't tell you more than once."

His thick fingers dug into her shoulders and before she knew what happened he had swiveled her around and shoved her to the edge of the sidewalk. "I mean it. Get lost. You don't know me and you don't want to." Then he was gone and although people passed by and were looking at her, she couldn't hear them. Their mouths moved, maybe some of them offered her a hand, or offered her advice or maybe they were mocking her. She didn't know. She was alone in the confusion of traffic and voices.

"Oh, but I do. But I do want to know you." At the street corner, broken shoe in hand, she turned in circles, up, down and around, up, down and around. She lost her bearings, first heading north and then turning south. She looked east and turned around to go west. Finally, she found herself back on the main drag, where she waved down a collector taxi. Still clutching her broken shoe, she squeezed into the back seat with two other passengers. The ride up the winding road to Santa Rita was interminable. She bent forward to bury her face in her big, open purse as she sobbed into its mouth, and the other passengers exchanged questioning glances. One of them patted her shoulder, "*Fuerza*," was all he said. When they reached the high ridge, Columba looked out the window and caught her reflection, her pathetic eyes looking back at her through the sad lights of Progreso and beyond. She was alone and disappearing into the infinite obscurity of the Pacific.

CHAPTER 33

GAVIN

The fragrance of White Linen trailed behind a woman who brisked past Gavin in the crisp morning air, and in an instant the scent drifted through the twisted channels of his brain to latch onto a secluded memory. There it floated leisurely in the tide of his pulse, like a small treasure that had washed up at sea to find refuge on a friendly shore. White Linen by Estée Lauder had been his mother's favorite perfume.

Every Christmas from as early as he could remember, Stan would press a few bills into Gavin's palm. "She'll like some White Linen, son." He told him the same thing every year and he'd wink, "A woman who wears White Linen won't steer you wrong."

The weather that afternoon turned cold without warning. It was as if the wind had tapped the day on its shoulder, reminding it that it was November. Nostalgia was bathing on the cold White Linen beaches of Gavin's brain.

Sales at Stan's were good. Funky Town was exceeding all expectations. They were preparing Christmas promotions. Gavin always approached the Christmas season with red and green horror. But at least he recognized it for what it was and he more or less managed to keep a lid on it, churning the repugnant red and green around in his brain until it turned to a muddy brown that eventually insulated him from the overwhelming sensation of absence that the Christmas season generated. Being in retail demanded extra Christmas effort. He managed to be convincing in his fake joviality. But today it was hard. Today more than ever, he looked forward to returning home for a quiet dinner and a glass of chilled white wine, alone and free to ramble about the kitchen, prepare some pasta, and think his own brown thoughts.

He pulled up into the driveway and walked around to the back of the house, the motion sensor triggering the light over the door. He inserted the key into the lock – it was the same key he'd used all his life. He twisted the doorknob – it was the same doorknob he had twisted since childhood. The same childhood door squeaked open with the same squeak (his mental note to oil the hinges remained just that – a mental note) and as he entered the kitchen, he paused to look around.

Maybe it was the familiar panel of stained glass on the interior door and, how at dusk, the glass lily petals mingled behind the heavy green leaves, and the translucent tips of orange butterfly wings turned red. Maybe it was the final shaft of golden light that hit the counter and pointed across the black and white tiles of the kitchen floor like a wand. Maybe it was the steady ticking of the grandfather clock through the silence of the hallway. Whatever it was, he stood there, remembering the smell of his Dad's fresh coffee and his Mom's Sunday roast that would be accompanied with gravy and brussel sprouts and mashed potatoes. He could see his Mom leaning in at the sink, a blue gingham apron with a pink rose pinned on the bib, her wavy hair combed and in place as always, yellow rubber gloves up to her elbows in warm suds. She paused to listen to CBC Cross Country Checkup radio voices as they took a call from someone in Nova Scotia – "Go ahead caller...", and his Dad sitting at the table, legs crossed, swirling coffee in his "Best Dad in the World" mug that Gavin had given him when he was still in kindergarten. His Dad would pause, "Hello son, just in time," a slight smile before raising the mug to his lips.

As a kid, whenever he walked through this same door, he walked into security and warmth, a place where good, solid decisions were made on his behalf, where his shoulders were never laden with responsibilities beyond his age, where he was tucked into bed every night with a kiss and a smile, where he never had a worry in the world. As a kid, he took it all for granted just like, he imagined, any kid would do.

He walked towards the sink, which had seemed so much higher when his Mom was alive. He looked out the window, the palm of his left hand feeling the familiar chip at the rounded enamel lip of the sink. The porch swing was still out there (the cushions removed for winter), the raised garden plot was still in the back corner although Gavin didn't use it, two fir trees still grew at the far end of the yard, much taller now, overpowering almost. He turned to glance at the place where Stan used to sit. Gavin could feel the pulse in his temples. My cup runneth over. Where did that phrase come from? The kitchen, in its quiet golden light was still full of warmth. He wished they were here so he could tell them that he understood. And that he appreciated. And that he loved them.

He switched on the radio that had been on the shelf beside the kitchen sink for as long as he could remember (the same one his Mom listened to, one of a few things that he never threw out). Classical music floated out into the room. He circled the table, letting his hand brush the polished wood. His fingers strummed the rungs of the wooden chairs as he walked past. Then he padded into the stillness of the living room and stopped at his Dad's old leather recliner (another one of the things he never got around to donating). He nudged it and watched it rock a few times before crossing over to the fireplace. So, this is what it had come to – visiting, at a relatively young age, the remains of his parents on a mantlepiece. The two urns sat touched one another (discreetly kissing, Gavin thought) in the center of the shelf directly under the clock his mother had arranged to hang on the wall above. It was a clock from the 1960s, a sun mask design. The second hand jerked at each of the 60 marks on its way around the white face, and as if in response, the long ray twitched between the urns as though reminding Stan and Marianne that time was clicking right along.

Leaning his shoulder into the mantlepiece, he said aloud, "I don't know how you did it, you guys. Built our life I mean... I just never thought... I mean, I was a kid. But I appreciate it all now, you know? I really do."

Several moments passed in silence before he opened a new topic. He straightened and rotated his shoulders a few times, loosening up, "Listen Dad, I'm thinking of starting a new business before the end of the year. I'm thinking it'll be a good idea to explore new horizons. It'll mean that we profit at both ends of the spectrum."

Cold silence from the mantlepiece. He suspected that Stan wouldn't agree with this one. "What're you thinking of doing, son? Why get involved?"

"Funky Town is doing way better than I expected. It's really filling a niche. And with Stan's Men's and Boys' Wear too, well, you know, it always turns a steady profit – I'm looking for a new challenge and, well, something just fell into my lap. Or almost, anyway."

The silence from his parents was a pinched eternity. It seemed there was really nothing to discuss.

He tapped the mantlepiece a couple of times with his middle finger, a mannerism he'd pick up from Stan when he was calling a subject to a close. He paused to glance at his Mom's urn, then he touched his fingers to his lips to transfer a kiss. Without saying more, he turned away. It was decided.

Next week he would take his first step into the recycled clothing business.

CHAPTER 34

IRENE

Irene's works of art in Spin a Yarn's window were very popular, the best display on main street, according to Matilda. She received a number of inquiries each month about one or other of the items.

"Is that for sale? Can I buy the scarf and mittens set, the ones in the window?"

"Well, the set needs to stay in the window until we change the display. Can you wait? If you can, just give me your name and phone number. I'll put you on the list."

"You mean there's a list?"

"There usually is. But you're lucky this month. You're the first to ask so they're yours to buy in about three weeks if you still want them."

Matilda attributed most of the new walk-in traffic to the crocheted handbags, table runners, knitted turtlenecks, vests, gloves and scarves that Irene had made. Irene insisted that she could only change a couple of the window samples once every three or four weeks. And she also made it clear that she did not do children's items. When Matilda asked why not, Irene replied, "Because my skills are better used on these types of things." She was referring to home decoration and adult attire and accessories. "I simply can't bring any children's wear to display."

"Well, we're both missing an opportunity here. If you can do more of anything, it'll mean extra pocket money for both of us." But Irene would not be convinced.

Pocket money was not a priority and although Irene diligently turned in new display pieces, Matilda constantly tried to tempt her. "Look what just came in. I want to feature the new four-ply wool-nylon blend. Doesn't it just make your mouth water?" Or, "How about a little scoop-neck sweater with this cashmere for a little girl?" But then, "Oh, well, okay, can you crochet a small bag with this raw silk? Add a gold chain and here's a clasp that I've been saving for something just like this."

When the display changed, Matilda called the first person on the list to come and pick up their item. If they weren't there within two days, she contacted the next in line. The routine never changed and Matilda had developed a spiel, "Well, you know that you can learn to make things like this yourself. We have all you need here, and you can sign up for my weekly class too. You're guaranteed to benefit from what you make. The class is free, you just have to buy the wool." She nodded her head energetically. "This handiwork is extremely satisfying and a great way to relieve stress. Plus, it's productive. Believe me, I've been doing it for years."

Meanwhile, back in Irene's sewing room, children's sweaters piled up. Each afternoon she opened the door and stood to survey her kingdom. But she didn't, as you might expect, take a breath of satisfaction and congratulate herself on such creative productivity. She was unable to derive that sort of pleasure. No, instead she was overcome with an intense drive to do more. The need tortured her. The more she created, the more she was called upon to create. She didn't stop to ask why, she simply surrendered to the compulsion. Sometimes, when Chuck was out at the coffee shop and she didn't have to guard against intrusion, she pulled out several sweaters at random, and laid them carefully on the floor beside the big armchair. She arranged them in a circle, the little sleeves touching one another, sweaters hand in hand – ring around the rosie, pocket full of posie – united in a colorful mandala that she gazed upon in a more or less meditative state. It wasn't, as you might expect, calming but rather the sight poked and prodded at her until she prickled with urgency.

Her entire sweater inventory was piled neatly in the back of her mind. She knew exactly where to find the orange sweater with the falling leaf pattern, and the cute little blue one with the sunny face and three-dimensional bluebirds – 'there's a bluebird on your windowsill, there's a rainbow in the sky.' Unlike Chuck's inventory (the one she would never discover), hers was categorized not only by size and color but by which tune she had hummed in the making of it. She associated snippets of children's songs, lullabies, Donavon ditties, "Everything runs in a circular motion, love is a little boat upon the sea..." the mystical sounds of 'Atlantis', even lyrics from Leonard Cohen songs, "Dance me through the panic 'till I'm gathered safely in," and lines like, "I love you in the morning and in the afternoon, I love you in the evening underneath the moon..."

She handled each sweater with love and attention. Even in her compulsion to fill the space, she knew that it could not just be filled with any old sweater. There could to be no repeats. No clones, no imposters allowed. Each one had to be original, had to carry its own tune. It needed to reflect growth, to blossom, to come of age. Each length of yarn was the thread of the story of a life never lived.

CHAPTER 35

COLUMBA

In spite of one's impotence and cracked, damaged life, one refuses to surrender one's hope. Hope for intercessions, for prayers from someone who understands and is on your side. Hope that yearning will be satisfied. But how can you trust pledges that are made and not fulfilled, strings of promises that are never kept? And how long can you remain patient in the silent gaps between responses? How long can you remain passive in your misery? The answer is 'for as long as it keeps you down.'

The recycled clothing business was fine. In fact, it was booming. When the Bullfighter did well, Columba did well. The Nescafe can was full to overflowing and she started a new can that she stashed in the far corner under her bed, just for paper bills. Something unthinkable less than a year ago.

Last Sunday Maria, the president of the Neighborhood Junta paid cash for two skirts and a sweater and she brought three other women who said they could pay for their dresses next week. The sidewalk sales were going well too. Columba sold three or four items each Tuesday, Thursday and Saturday. And she couldn't complain about work at the depot either. Hawkeye still let her pass at the end of each shift with no more than a quick pat on top of her bag. Between what fit in her bag and what she could stuff into her oversized skirt pockets, she left the dock with no less than three items, and up to six if they were light. Her steady inventory came and went.

She could almost sort through the piles on the floor of the depot with her eyes closed. It was nothing. But building up her Sunday morning exclusives – now that was something. And her sidewalk sales – those were something too. She had become a successful business woman. She even dressed the part. She was in command of her own life and she was victorious.

But it was an empty victory because she was a mother without a daughter.

She spent almost every waking moment (consciously and unconsciously) seeking new angles from which to explain Anita's sudden estrangement. Was it all her fault? Had she pushed her too hard? Had she asked too much of her? Were the clandestine garment pickups too much to expect of a girl who was fast becoming a woman? Did Columba even notice that Anita had become a young woman? Did she give her enough credit for it? Does a teenaged girl need credit for her natural evolution?

Although the answers to her questions changed at dawn and again at dusk, she began to think the true answer must lie in the fact that Anita's newly-seeded conscience was stronger than her loyalty to her mother. Perhaps, with the help of the priest, Anita had begun to reject the wrongs – no matter how justified or how rational – that were committed by her mother. Perhaps Anita had decided that poverty was no excuse, that Columba had crossed the line, that she was a disgrace.

Columba remembered those many late evenings when Anita still used to return home. Just before José fell asleep, they both heard the key in the lock followed by the sound of Father Cortés's old Volkswagen Beetle shifting into gear and sputtering away down the hill. After that, José would let himself settle into a sound sleep and Columba would pull the covers over her head, disturbed by the late hour but thankful that Anita had been delivered home safe and sound.

One night after José was snug in his mattress, feigning sleep, Columba tiptoed outside to sit in the shadows of the front patio and wait for Anita's return. It was nearly two a.m. when Anita walked up the sidewalk and stumbled to the gate, head down, fumbling with the key. When Columba moved out of the shadows, Anita yelped.

"Mom. You scared me. What are you doing out here?"

"Waiting for you." She pulled Anita inside. "You need to explain yourself."

"No, I don't." She elbowed her way past Columba and into the house. She stripped off her clothes, threw a t-shirt over her shoulders and threw her mattress down beside José. She poked at him needlessly, mumbling that he was nothing but a useless, snot-nosed pest. And he definitely wasn't a miracle. "Neither of us are, miracles." she snorted. And then in a much louder voice, "And Mom is crazy. And she's just as useless as you are. No, she's worse!"

Columba marched over and yanked Anita out of bed and dragged her to her bedroom. She shoved her into the corner, and did her best to loom over her. "What's going on with you?" Anita gritted her teeth, glaring coldly into Columba's eyes. She spit the words into Columba's face. "I'm your miracle child but you're not much of a miracle Mom. Are you? Are you?" Anita leaned into Columba, nose-to-nose, daring her to react. Columba stood for a moment, unsure but when José, who now stood stiffly at the door, begged for some peace, she released Anita and retreated to the bathroom.

The next morning, Anita was petulant and she refused to look at Columba. She didn't want breakfast, she just wanted to get the hell out of this place. And if she had her way, she'd never return.

But she did return. She returned exactly four more times when Columba was at work. Columba knew this because José told her. After that, Anita was lost to them.

Columba had gone to the school and was told that Anita had skipped classes almost every day for the last month. Why hadn't Columba returned the school's calls? "What calls?" They had been calling the new mobile number that Anita had given them three months ago and each time they had had to leave a message. Columba was just like every other unfit parent and she was lucky they didn't report her to social services. Columba pressed them for the number and when she called, it rang and then cut off.

These days the only thing Columba knew for sure was that Anita spent too much time with the Youth Group down in Progreso.

She skipped her afternoon sidewalk sale and hopped onto a microbus to find Father Cortés at The Most Pure Blood of Jesus Church. The church was crouched on the east side of town at the feet of the Andes, protected in the shadows of the powers that be. Constructed more than 500 years ago, it was one of Progreso's oldest landmarks, a colonial structure with an overly tall steeple and bells that called out on Sundays, "Repent! We're expecting you. Repent." Here in Progresso, the Catholic Church, having done the heavy work centuries ago, was generally passive and didn't meddle in local affairs.

The church was in a picturesque setting – several tall palm trees swayed lazily in front of the church proper. Its crimson façade was trimmed with dusty beige cornices and balustrades. Wide stone steps led up to its over-sized wooden doors. Pilgrims crawled on hands and knees up these steps at least once a year, their blood smudged into the stone as they fulfilled their bargain with the Virgin. A marble statue of St. Michael with outstretched wings cast a shadow over a span of carefully manicured lawn, which was edged with hibiscus and birds of paradise in full bloom. Bedraggled women were pandering saint cards and medals. Beggars waited for church patrons to ascend the steps before suddenly appearing at their sides to thrust an amputated limb in front of their faces, swiftly followed by the good hand, empty palm facing up.

The rectory building was an afterthought at the north side of the church and beyond that but still in sight from the street corner was a grotto for Santa Sara, the black Virgin of the Gypsies. All around Santa Sara, charcoal wicks spiked up from melted wax pools. The Virgin's downturned eyes bemoaned her chipped and stained sandaled feet that were anchored in the midst of her wax kingdom.

Columba entered the church through the human-sized cut-out door. Its ancient hinges whimpered and she hesitated before stepping over the sill. Once inside, the years closed around her. The scurrying tic-tic-tic of mice at the walls, the pervasive mildew and stale incense, the light that fought its way past the tenebrous stained glass of the high windows, seeking out the dust that might well have been suspended for centuries in the stale air – it was all eternally the same. The ceiling's cracked and peeling chorus of saints and angels still sang out in voiceless glory.

Obscure alcoves lined both sides of the nave. Larger than life saints suddenly appeared from the shadows as you passed by, their sad eyes glancing down at the small glass cups, which were lined up like the open hands of beggars. The saints held their breath and waited for coins to drop through the slots of the little cups, and sometimes light flickered to their pained faces to illuminate fleeting smiles of gratitude.

Eyes down, hoping he wouldn't notice, Columba tiptoed past Saint Christopher. She'd passed by Saint Christopher in 1982 when she was 16 years old and pregnant with Anita. She had been looking for St. Gerard Majella but she could feel Saint Christopher eyeing her back all the while. She found St. Gerard Majella in the fifth alcove along the way and she quietly turned and knelt before him. He looked down at her, and she felt that his carved, handsome face held an abundance of sympathy and she hoped he would be equally as kind in granting an intercession. A rosary hung from the waistband of his priestly robe, and his hands were folded one over the other at his chest. She had been disappointed that there was no sign of the miracle handkerchief that, as the story goes, had helped a woman in childbirth. The story was vague in her mind and all she really knew was that he was the go-to saint for pregnant women and unborn babies even though it would have made more sense for the saint to be a woman. But a pregnant 16-year-old was not in a position to question Church authority, especially when she was in search of counsel. The patron saint, being a man, although a kindly in appearance, told her what she already knew deep down – that she'd made her bed and now she had to lie in it. She was on her own, and St. Gerard Majella would not be able to locate the father. When she glanced at him a final time, his sympathy was replaced by empty, plaster eyes. She reached into the little cup and retrieved her 100 peso coin. She wasn't paying for nothing.

She had been a teenager in love with a handsome sailor from the south and several weeks later, she was a desperate young woman, pregnant with his child. She had met him one afternoon on the beach. She was frolicking in the waves with two friends and when she shyly glanced in his direction, she unexpectedly caught his eye and then he began his pursuit, at first cautiously and then with more vigor. His ship would be there for four days he said. Why not spend some time together?

He courted her. He bought her ice cream, looked into her eyes, ran his fingers through her hair and flattered her. She was an easy conquest. And after the second night he was gone. She waited for him on the third day but his ship had already left the harbor. Later, after the hurt and anger subsided, she realized she had been infatuated but not enamored and she did not yearn for him. Her heart was not, after all, broken and she would never be so foolish again. When she realized she was pregnant, it became an immediate practical, if not a moral, problem.

Columba lived at home with her parents and four siblings, two of whom were older sisters who had become single mothers one year after the next (very likely under the same circumstances as hers, although no one ever spoke of that). They weren't going to be able to make space for a third single mother and child. So Columba's mother arranged for her to move into her cousin's garage where a broken-down car had been parked for years. The cousin's husband had hauled it in there and it had become a permanent fixture long after his ambition and search for parts waned.

"It'll be so much nicer to see a baby here than this piece of junk," her Mom's cousin said as she kicked the fender. "He's needed this kind of incentive for ages." And she forced her husband to sell the old car for scrap. They wove cardboard sheets between the rungs of the rusted iron fence that bordered the sidewalk, "For now, at least it's some protection and privacy. We can make it more permanent when we find materials." She swept the packed dirt and covered the oil stains with heavy plastic. She dragged in a second-hand single mattress for Columba and the new baby to sleep on. This, a cardboard box, a spare kitchen chair and the garage became Columba's home.

Later Columba dragged found treasures into the space, including a battered stove with propane tank. After months of cajoling, the cousin's husband cleaned the old stove and got it working. Meanwhile, Columba saved pesos to fill the tank. She found sturdy boxes and turned them into furniture and she gave the plastic Saint Expedito and Virgin icons a high spot on a shelf.

The space was cramped and inconvenient but it was home.

Two years later, as a result of a somewhat more promising relationship with a miner, José was born. Although the miner stayed with them for a week or two here and there between shifts at the mine, he never lived with them. Columba later discovered he already had a wife and family up in the altiplano. She kicked herself again. Of course he already had a wife. Why hadn't she bothered to find out earlier? The next time he showed up, she kicked him back from the gate without a word. He knew why. He finally stopped trying to excuse himself and he disappeared. For years, as her heart ached, she played the part of an independent woman without need for a man. One day she woke up and realized it was true – she was an independent woman and didn't need a man. Her children and their survival were her sole purpose in life. When the opportunity (which was nothing short of a miracle) arose for them to own a house in Santa Rita, they were already a tight little family. Columba never questioned her fate.

She shivered and continued towards the altar.

Sunlight filtered through the stained glass to light up the Virgin Mary, who stood on the left. A few candles flickered around her feet. The sanctuary smelled righteous, surely it was the smell of the Savior's gentle death. The huge cross on which Christ hung, his limp, larger-than-life figure off-kilter and dripping with blood, cast its shadow across the gold-plated relief carvings on the back wall of the nave. Columba had an urge to run and straighten out Christ's lank skeleton, to make him more comfortable. But she supposed that was the point. He died in pain.

Other than three people on their knees in front of the Virgin, the church was empty.

Back outside, Columba gasped for air and she realized she'd been suffocating in there. Why did she bother to go inside? But now was not the time for idle reflection. She turned towards the side of the church, passing two more large palms and pondered briefly what they might have witnessed in their long years as stalwart acolytes. A plaster-over-brick addition sprawled out from the side of the rectory, housing a couple of dormitories and a few classrooms. A stone path flanked by simple vine-covered columns wound its way to the rectory door.

Father Cortés was in the middle of a catechism lesson he said, and could she wait? No, she couldn't and she was sorry to interrupt but it was important. He turned to the class (mostly teenaged girls) and in a soft voice, instructed them to read the assigned passage and pay attention to the points he had mentioned. Placing his hand firmly under her elbow, he led Columba outside as a pastor leads a lost lamb, closing the door softly behind them. She noticed his old red Volkswagen Beetle parked between the rectory and a long wooden bench that stretched out under one of the palms, three brown fronds dusting the red fender.

"Father Cortés, I need you to tell me about Anita."

"How can I help?" he gestured for her to sit on the bench and he sat beside her, allowing a polite distance between them. Then he said, "She hasn't been here for weeks. "

"I know Father, I didn't think she was coming here anymore. But she's not coming home either."

He flinched and raised an eyebrow. "Since when?"

"Well, for more than a month now." Her lips twisted, her brows angled down into the bridge of her nose as she fought for composure. She knew he could see her anguish but she tried not to cry. "She stays with a man in downtown Progreso. And not in a very good part of town either. They live beside a bar called The Black Cat. Have you heard of it?" He shook his head.

She resented that Father was such a sympathetic listener because sympathetic listeners make you lower her defenses and then what? You turn into a blubbering basket case. And that's exactly what happened. He slid along the bench and put one arm around her. Her sobs racking her shoulders, she leaned in, dropped her head and let him gently stroke her hair.

"We all love Anita," Father said. "Every one of us has our soft spots and she was one of mine. She had... she has a lot of potential. If there's anything I can do... I mean I can find my way to the bar if you want. What did you say it's called, 'The Black Cat'?"

"Father, can you?"

But Columba never heard what came of his visit to The Black Cat and in the following weeks and months she knew that her trip to the Church had been just another fruitless effort. She faded and sunk in her deepening sea of depression.

CHAPTER 36
GAVIN

Gavin has never been one to seek deeper meaning. Some people are simply lucky that way. Gavin's purpose (not that he feels the need to define one) is to pass through whichever door opens next. We should not, therefore, mistake his decisive actions as steps towards a purposeful or righteous goal. In some things Gavin is as innocent as the morning dew and if we look back on his childhood, we see a young man, who, before tragedy struck (not once but twice) was much loved and protected. However, is being a victim all that is required to excuse bad decisions or to determine that you are innocent and will always fall on the side of right?

"So, Mark, what's next?" Gavin was leaning back in his chair, feet on the desk, rotating his ankles as he examined the shine on his new Bruno Magli shoes. He reached for his coffee and sipped it, pinky finger raised.

"Well, what else is there, Gavin? Seems to me we have to move into the children's market. I mean, then we'll really have all the bases covered."

There was silence as they inhaled success. Now established as the town's retail guru, Gavin contemplated how he had progressed beyond the up-and-comer stage. How had he became a man of means and influence, and how was it that people tipped their caps at him on the street, extended a hand and pulled out a chair at the networking breakfasts, some even approaching him about becoming a mentor (something he politely declined)? Who was he to mentor someone? Even with a business degree, one required common sense. Common sense was the only thing he had to offer. And he could do that in 30 seconds, no reason to draw it out in some lame mentoring program. Beneath the Bruno Magli shoes and Lacoste sweaters still lurked the young man who had certified himself as a private detective. Not that there's anything really wrong with that, he reminded himself.

"The town doesn't have a decent kids' store, nothing to compete with except for Kreske's. And how hard would that be?"

But Gavin wasn't receptive.

A couple of days later he lay in bed, having pressed the snooze button of his alarm three times, watching the morning breeze claw at the edge of the curtain until it finally yanked it by its toes and pulled it out the window. He felt irritated, sulky even, entirely dissatisfied, and for no reason that he could put his finger on. After they'd returned from their last buying trip, he felt empty. Was he irked by his own success? Had it all come too easily? Watch your ego, he heard his Mom say. Sure, they'd ordered all the right lines, negotiated the best prices, and had been assured of the delivery schedule but it all felt bland, routine, boring. Life as a private detective would have been more exciting if it had gotten off the ground. Why had he followed his Dad into retail? It meant he was bogged down with contracts and documentation. Administration. And buying shows that he didn't like. He had told Mark that he'd know when he saw the right garments and that he'd buy them. But in the end, nothing really struck him and he left it up to Mark. The magic was gone.

The fun had blown itself out like the last candle on a birthday cake. Although he knew that the birthday boy always wins in the end and that last candle never has a chance, he still felt beaten. He couldn't even think what to wish for.

This morning he had scheduled meetings with realtors and lawyers and he had promised Fern that he'd crunch some numbers with her before noon.

He rolled out of bed and sat on the edge, feet apart, noticing the dry skin on his knees, briefly questioning why that was, and then observing his manicured toenails and wondering why he bothered. He grumbled at the grey morning sky as he gathered the curtains back inside, and closed the window. He slipped into his robe and wandered downstairs, barefoot.

This morning everything in his life – his stores, his friendships, his things – was meaningless. He had no ambition, no desire to see anyone. What were his days if not just filled with empty ritual? Shower, dress, make coffee, go to work, make small talk, maybe eat out, come home, watch a little TV, pay the cleaning lady, maybe dream up next month's promotion. Climb into bed and turn out the light and start all over again. The inertia.

How did ants carry on? Where did they find the strength and motivation to haul all those big crumbs back to home base? Why did they care? As he waited for the coffee to finish dripping, he tried to muster a feeling of anticipation. But when he sat down at the table, he rested on his elbows and stared into space while his coffee got cold.

Gravity got the better of him and he remained slumped on the chair until well past nine a.m., the radio playing softly from the shelf beside the kitchen sink.

The phone rang. Who cares? What if it's an emergency? I doubt it. Emergencies don't happen to me. But what if it is? The phone stopped ringing. Two minutes later it started again and this time, after several rings he pushed back his chair, shuffled over to answer it, his voice low. It was Mark.

"Gavin, we have a meeting with the lawyer this morning. Where are you?"

"Cancel it, will you? I won't be coming in today."

"You okay?"

"Yeah, I'm fine. Just reschedule the meeting for next week, will you?"

The meeting didn't matter, the lawyers could wait, they could die for all he cared. Isn't that the best thing that could ever happen to lawyers anyway? He snorted. The stores could fade away and he'd be fine without them. He dropped down onto a chair again, staring at a stain on the cupboard beside the sink, for who-knows-how long before finally pushing himself up and creaking across the floors, without finding a place to stop.

Maybe he should go out onto the porch, breathe in fresh air. He opened the door and closed it again, the cool air not making any difference. Maybe he was hungry. He opened the fridge but nothing was appealing. He walked over to his Dad's old recliner, kicked back in it but couldn't settle, so he pulled himself up. He paced around some more, looking down at the floor boards, noticing how the wax had accumulated at the base of the walls and registering that he didn't care. He circled around to the kitchen, through the dining room, into the living room and around again, before finally flopping onto the sofa. He laid on his back, elbows bent, forearms covering his eyes, his weight settling heavily into the leather, noting how it squeaked when he moved, hearing the radio announcer laughing at his own joke and a dog barking from a couple of houses away. He began to cry and he was too tired to question why. He let the tears go. They rolled down his neck and soaked into the collar of his robe. He didn't try to stop. He didn't have the strength. Maybe he cried about his lack of desire for a partner – of any gender, about James's questions about his sexual identity, about the nondescript buying trips, maybe he cried about his routine, about the ease with which the stores ran without him these days. Maybe he cried because he felt useless. He fell asleep and the tears dried on his face. When he awoke, sunlight was streaming into the living room, he heard the mailman open and close the mailbox, and he heard him whistle as he retreated. He turned to look at his parents' urns. There was an ambient blue light and a faint orange aura around them. Maybe he just missed Stan and Marianne. A pain tracked across his chest and his throat tightened. He swallowed hard. Does it take years to grieve?

Gavin wasn't one for therapists. No sir. No need to dig into his past and discuss his worries with some stranger who would lean back in a velour chair with a notepad, and push a big box of tissues towards him. He was his own master and he'd figure things out himself. But at the moment, he felt too worn down and listless.

He slept for two days. On the morning of the third day, he awoke energized and refreshed. Must have been how Jesus felt. He showered, shaved, slipped on a crisp shirt and new vest and stepped into his brown brogues. He made a fresh cup of coffee, and turned up the radio "Good morning Burgeon-town!" He scoffed at someone who called in to complain about the weather. Everything was great. He concluded what had hit him was nothing more than exhaustion. Easily solved with a few extra hours of sleep.

He walked into the office, sharp and ready to face the challenges.

"How're the numbers looking, Fern?"

IRENE

Do coincidences count? Are they part of destiny? In this case, is it dark or light? A good sign or bad?

Irene would remember very well that crisp morning in March. The door of Spin a Yarn creaked open – the fading needlepoint *We are Open* sign tapped against the glass, and like some kind of prophecy "...and there will be a sister coming into your life and she will take things that don't belong to her" – and her sister Amber entered. Amber stepped inside, casually observing the colorful yarn-packed shelves and the huge, wool-stuffed baskets that warmed the corners. Like a leaf on an autumn day, she picked up momentum and fluttered around the shop. Matilda, as usual, was standing behind the counter, poring over a pattern book, glasses dangling from the end of the chain around her neck. She touched them lightly as was her habit, and she looked up with a big smile, her eyes shrinking behind her cheeks.

"Can I help you?"

"Yes." Amber twisted around to point to the long purple cowl-neck sweater on the headless mannequin in the window. "I'm interested in that sweater."

"Count yourself number..." Matilda paused to consult a list that was taped on the counter beside the cash register, "Let me see... 11. You'd be number 11." She smiled sweetly and prepared to recite her do-it-yourself spiel.

"Eleven. What do you mean?" Amber tilted her head.

Irene was in the back room. Her ears twitched at the sound of Amber's voice. She froze, wet teabag suspended in her hand just east of the little china cup, drips staining the cutout lace runner on the table.

She heard Matilda say, "Well, the sweater is for display only and it needs to stay in the window for another two weeks or so. It's caught the eye of a lot of people, you see, and so I made a list. It's first-come-first served. Unfortunately, at this point, you'd be at the end of a very long list and chances are that you won't be the lucky one." She cocked her head, and smiled her crinkly, sympathetic smile.

Irene tiptoed to the little window that separated the back room from the shop proper. Matilda used the window as a bulletin board and it was now almost completely covered with colorful sticky notes. "I'm going to remember to get one of those – what-do-you-call-it? a cork board – one day," Matilda had promised. But she still hadn't. Now the note-covered window was a convenient camouflage. Irene watched between the yellow, blue and pink squares as Amber stepped sideways along the length of the west wall. She crossed over to the skeins of heavy lamb's wool on the other side and reached into the basket for a fat New Zealand ball and tossed it up a couple of times.

"You can always learn to make one of those sweaters yourself." It was the beginning of Matilda's standard sales pitch. But Amber cut her short.

"No, that's okay. I was just curious." She turned, and with a little smile and her hand raised in salute said, "Thanks very much. Lovely shop." And she walked out, latching the door, the sign clattering its goodbye.

Irene put the teabag in the sink and covered the stain on the table cloth with a saucer before wandering casually out to the front.

"Did I hear voices?"

"Yes, someone was after the sweater."

"Oh. Well, I guess I better make another one."

"No, not yet. At least... well, if you want, you can start on something but let's not change it yet. We're getting a lot of traffic in here because of that one. In fact, let's leave it even longer. I think we should just add something to it."

Irene went to peer out the front window. Amber had disappeared and she relaxed. When was the last time she had talked to anyone in her family? She had refused to take their phone calls. "I'm not home," she would mouth the words to Chuck and wave them off. And on the rare occasion that one of them showed up at their door unannounced (usually Amber), she would run off to the bedroom, locking herself in and Chuck would say, "She's sleeping now. She's not feeling well." Or, "She's really tired today. Why don't you come back later? Or if you want, I can make you a cup of tea."

Normally, Amber didn't accept his offer. But twice, she had accepted the invitation and Irene had had to wait it out in the bedroom, listening to the muffled voices and forced laughter. What did they have to laugh about? Afterwards Chuck would brush off the whole thing as small talk. "I have to be polite, you know. She *is* your sister after all." And then, "Irene, I don't understand why you can't visit with her. She cares about you."

"No, she doesn't. She's just snooping. They're all snooping. They're trying to invade my privacy."

"Look," he got firm. "If you feel invaded, that's your fault. No one is invading anyone here. Just grow up and let's try to be at least a little more normal for once. Did you ever think that they might miss you and that's all there is to it?"

Without warning, Amber had appeared back in front of the store window and she was looking directly up at Irene. Irene gasped and stared back at her, hands hanging at her side, caught in a trap, roadkill, as Amber's expression changed from surprise to delight.

The door opened, the sign again slapped merrily against the glass and Amber blew in, walking directly up to Irene and wrapping her in a hug.

"Sis! How are you? What're you doing here?"

Irene didn't trust that this was a coincidence. Amber knew she worked here. And how did she know? Because Chuck told her. That's how.

Irene stood, arms at her sides, at first resisting. But Amber hung on and something came over her, something like warm, something like home, something like nice, like comfort. And she reached around Amber and held her close.

CHAPTER 38

JOSÉ

Time crawls when you're not having fun. Memories creep in and loiter in the corners and against cracked walls. Desire and vitality wane and you sleep until noon. What is there to live for? Oh yes, hope. That's it then. But sometimes our hopes are too grand and we should be satisfied that things might simply return to their former state.

To José, his Mom was the tough nut, the thick-skinned, the hard-head, the upper hand. Nothing beat her down. Until now. Until her grief. It arrived one very dark day and it outstayed its welcome. José had watched it building like an afternoon dust storm kicking up its heels on the horizon. Now it was upon them, blocking out the sun. He knew his Mom wasn't prepared. She turned her back and collapsed under the onslaught of incessantly pelting pebbles of self pity, the dust whirling around her, her silhouette shaping in and out until she was finally consumed by the dark and she let it digest her on the spot. All without so much as a wag of her finger. And then there was silence. A slinking, quiet surrender.

After the storm had run through Columba, José discovered he had inherited his mother's character (or rather, her former character... she would return to her current state, wouldn't she?) and he took command of the situation.

But before that, Columba had put José on the defensive. She had been looking for someone to blame. José had insisted for more than two weeks that he didn't know any more than she did about Anita's boyfriend. None of Anita's friends confided in him either.

"I don't even know half of them, Mom. I mean, you know. Most of her friends are the ones that go to the Church youth group. What do I have to do with them? Nothing. And we both know Lucia, and I've talked to her too, Mom. Believe me. She hasn't told me anything that you don't already know."

Columba had turned away, snarly. "Cook your own dinner tonight. I'm going out." This had been her attitude. Grumpy, annoyed and impatient.

Now five months after Anita's disappearance, Columba gazed absently across the table at Anita's vacant chair. José noticed that each morning, out of habit (or perhaps out of blind hope), Columba pulled down a third mug, paused, and then returned it to the shelf. The conversations he tried to start with her were stilted because she didn't pay attention. And if she did answer, she didn't make sense, as though she was in a daze or a kind of waking nightmare, uttering nonsense responses out of a dream state. But José was patient, and he promised himself he would never desert her. Unlike Anita, he would never have deserted his family. So what if he was just the kid brother and what does a kid brother really know? But he felt the loss too. Anita's stubborn absence was beginning to feel more like betrayal and he resented her for it. He stopped mentioning her by name, he stuffed her left-over belongings into the hollow table pedestal so he wouldn't have to be reminded. It was just him and his Mom now and he would protect her.

When Columba wasn't working nights, he knew she was stalking the streets around The Black Cat. He'd heard the rumors about that bar and he, too had passed under its squeaky wooden sign, rubbing shoulders with the drug addicts and homeless alcoholics, and often just down-right desperate human beings who frequented the neighborhood. The difference was that José had a sixth sense and he knew when not to push his luck. This was not a place for him or his Mom – or Anita. But if Anita was there, his gut told him that interfering would only make things worse. She'd run away to somewhere even darker. If such a place existed.

How long had it been since his Mom had laughed with him, even smiled at him? Lately, her attempts at a smile were vague and preoccupied, just a quick upturn of her lips that her eyes didn't agree with. Her expression was drawn, her lips permanently pursed, her complexion had a grey undertone that she didn't bother to try to improve with makeup. She neglected to style her hair, pulling it back into a loose bun at the nape of her neck, the grey roots pushing out into the greasy strands that escaped and hung limply around her shoulders. José was convinced that if she didn't see reason soon, she would just lie in bed, she'd refuse to go to work, she'd forget about her Sunday morning exclusives, she'd abandon her place on the sidewalk, the only thing she would muster energy for would be to haunt The Black Cat. He would not allow her to kill herself with this madness.

And tonight, he knew she was prowling down there. It was almost 11pm when the small circle of light from the naked bulb on the street corner illuminated his mother's shape as she shifted her bottom out of the collector taxi. José sighed and wriggled back under his blankets.

They had made it through one more day. But José decided it was time to sit her down for a serious talk. What he hadn't yet decided was whether or not to show his Mom the notebook he'd found among Anita's old clothes.

CHAPTER 39

GAVIN

Time keeps no ledger, it does not attempt to balance out the moments in one's life, weighing the gains against the losses. It has no fine blue grid to add and subtract the events that mark one's existence, one's actions and re-actions. Some people are fortunate while others are not. Some say that life is coincidence and some say it is destiny but one thing it is not, is a balance sheet. And only people who believe it is, will pay for their crimes. Otherwise there is no debt.

Gavin flows along with a certain flexibility and a 'n'er may care' for the deeper workings of the universe. His shadow is a short one but it's dark and you can feel the cold. Don't get me wrong. Gavin's not evil. He's not even bad. The thing with Gavin is that he's shamelessly immediate and people admire him for his strength of spirit and decisiveness.

Setting up the charitable society wasn't as complicated as Gavin had an-ticipated. The charity required a board and members who would agree to be dedicated to the cause, which meant he had to find a cause in the first place. Given that he wasn't much of a social activist, he was neither creative nor knowledgeable in this area. So he used Avail International Charities as a model. Almost identical, in fact. In addition to the practical issues such as insurance, methods of funding etc., there were straightforward govern-ment regulations requiring that the charitable society have a mission, charter members, bylaws, formal address etc.. Establishing the charity was, as his lawyer assured him, a piece of cake.

While admittedly lacking originality, his cause was legitimate and popular. He knew it would work because it worked for Avail. The charity's purpose would be to provide cultural and practical language training for new im-migrants, in the course of meaningful, albeit unskilled, and low-paying positions. Obtaining a job here would serve as a foot in the door to their new country, a springboard to more highly skilled and better paying posi-tions. People who would work here might have been doctors or professors in their old countries. But the move to Canada meant that many professionals had their university degrees challenged or not recognized at all. For those in his program, it started with on-the-job language-training. Other charities providing work skills served a different client base, perhaps for people over-coming mental illnesses or learning to live with physical disabilities. They ran greenhouses, others ran mailing houses, others ran technology recycling services. Like Richard's Avail International, Gavin's would run used clothing sorting and distribution services.

Outside of the board, which was required to meet only twice a year, and onto which he had invited James and Mark and Mark's teacher friend, the venture was basically autonomous.

He registered it as the White Linen Charity, a nod to Marianne, whom he hoped (but was not sure) would have approved. And in order not make waves with Richard's Avail International, he established the White Linen Charity in Grant Falls, rather than in Burgeon. He rationalized that between the two centers there was ample room for both groups. And anyway, the government agency in charge had assured him that the regional market was not saturated.

Gavin got the ball rolling well before the ink was dry on the federal gov-ernment jobs training contract. The better man in him told him to contact Richard before Richard got wind of it from someone else. But the better man in him failed to win out over the man who didn't want to make waves, who thought the less Richard knew at the outset, the better. He told himself that once his business was up and running, Richard would see that it wouldn't impact on Avail International. But Richard found out through a government bulletin and he got all bent of shape over it. Later, they met by chance at a Chamber of Commerce meeting, where Richard pulled Gavin aside and told him that Gavin's intrusion into the local market limited Avail's possibilities for expansion, not to mention how it competed for newcomers. It was the last time Richard spoke to Gavin. One bridge burned.

CHAPTER 40

IRENE

A minor incident – it could be something as insignificant as a stranger bumping your arm or you glancing in the wrong direction at the wrong time, and then, wham! You are twisted and jarred about, dangling and tossing at the end of your own thin thread, the fabric having unraveled. How do you find your way back into the story after everything has changed? Where is the entrance back to your old life? It's gone. Just loose threads now. Terribly sad being removed from your pattern against your will, forced to leave the familiar.

"Mom doesn't leave the farm much these days, Irene. I'm worried about her." Amber told Irene over coffee.

"You're worried about everyone." Irene said.

"Yes, but it's quite sudden. It was like, from one day to the next. I mean, I took her to the doctor for a checkup less than two weeks ago and he said she was fine. Nothing wrong physically and she doesn't act like she's depressed or anything. But she really fought against going. You should have seen the struggle I had to get her there. Dad had to shove her in the car and hold the door closed and I just drove off. Anyway..." she picked up the mug and sipped her coffee and gazed at the table.

Irene got up to offer more. They were in her kitchen, a new experience for both of them. The visit had been unexpectedly pleasant.

"No. thanks," Amber said. "I should get going. But it's really been nice to see you, Irene. Honestly, I have to say that I was starting to worry about you. Every time I came to visit, which was once in a blue moon, Chuck said you weren't feeling well. I was beginning to wonder if he had you locked in the basement. Seriously."

Amber's eyes were wet and she batted away tears.

Irene pretended not to notice. "No, I'm fine. I mean, there was a time, for quite a while, I think..." Irene stopped abruptly. "Anyway, I found the wool shop and now I have this job there. And I've been so busy with that and knitting and crocheting. I spend every evening and every weekend doing that.

Every spare moment, actually. So yeah, sometimes, I get over-tired and just need to rest. It's just been a coincidence that that's when you stopped by, I guess."

"So, you make all the stuff in the display window?"

"Yeah, I do. It's the best part of my job."

"Wow, Irene, it's really impressive. Why didn't I know you were so good?"

"I don't know. Maybe 'cause I wasn't."

They chuckled.

"Well, I better let you get back to it then. Where's Chuck? I should say good-bye to him too."

They found him in the garage, bent into the car, vacuuming the driver's side. He pulled himself out and turned off the vacuum. "You're off then, Amber?"

"Yup. Back home. I picked up a few things for Mom and need to get back to her. You know how it is."

"Yeah." He winked at her and smiled.

"Nice to see you, Amber. Come on by again."

Irene let Chuck show Amber to the door and she headed straight for the armchair, picking up her needles even before she sat down. Chuck whistled as he put away the vacuum cleaner and locked up for the night. It had almost been a normal evening.

The next day was Chuck's inventory Thursday. He opened Irene's bedroom door for a quick glance. No surprises. He walked into the sewing room and was met with five new sweaters. Did she ever sleep? He noted that she'd been more productive than usual during the last couple of weeks. Every time he looked at what she made, he was pulled into an emotional tug of war. On one hand, he ached for her sadness and for her unnatural way of dealing with the trauma from more than six years ago. And on the other hand, he burst with pride at her extraordinary creativity and skill. He wanted to be able to talk to her about it, to praise her, to shout it to the world.

The question of whether to try to put a stop to it, though, nagged at him constantly. He didn't have the answer. And he didn't know if he wanted to change anything anyway. They still had a life together. He heard her laugh sometimes, they ate together, they sometimes had quiet conversations after dinner and sometimes they shared a joke or two before she rushed off to sit in the armchair, leaving him to clean up. Sometimes he peered around the corner to watch as she fell under the spell of her wool. She snuggled back into the chair, pulling colorful balls onto her lap, holding them up to her cheeks, smelling them, a preamble to the yarn passing through her fingers and out from under the needles. She hummed her peculiar, discordant sounds, her needles clicking, the yarn weaving over and around, as Irene gently rocking herself into her woolly oblivion.

CHAPTER 41

COLUMBA

In a fit of aggressive misery, Columba walked up to the Nescafe can on the shelf, her nose almost touching it, "You!" she half spat at the can, her voice was pitched and she poked at it until it slid backwards, "You have been more useful to me than anyone else here. And that's not saying much."

She turned and glared at San Expedito, who stood dully at his usual post to the left of the can. He cringed sheepishly, shrinking into his plastic robe. With a sudden swipe of her hand, she sent him reeling from the shelf and without pause, she raised her other hand to the Virgin who stood coyly on the right side of the can and she swiftly banished her from there too. The little plastic icons rocked for a second on the floor, hollow faces up, painted eyes pleading to the roof. Now it was their turn to entreat Jesus to rescue them in their hour of need. Let's see how they like it. With her grey face and red-rimmed eyes, Columba towered over them.

"Useless!" she admonished them. "You're both worth zero." Forming a circle with her thumb and forefinger, she bent down and shook her hand just above their hollow noses. "Even less than zero."

She fixed her gaze on the two of them and like a couple of guilty dogs, they laid there looking up. She blinked a few times. For a second, she thought maybe she was being too hard on them. Perhaps they were innocent. Should she forgive them their incompetence? Maybe she should pick them up, dust them off and return them to the shelf. It wasn't that she hated them. But they were useless, weren't they? Yes, they were useless. They hadn't done anything for her. Why had she put so much faith in them for so long? She knew that short of deliberately stomping on them or hacking at them with a hammer, the little plastic idols were almost indestructible. So, no, she thought. They can remain right where they were for a while, think things over, see for themselves if prayers get answered. Get a little taste of their own medicine.

For five days, fine desert sand blew in through the cracks around the windows and door and derisively dusted the Virgin and San Expedito. Columba stepped around them. Finally, José, having kicked them unintentionally more times than he cared to count, and feeling twinges of remorse each time, rescued them. He stuffed them into the table's hollow pedestal. Maybe they could do their work from there. Maybe even help Anita. Discreetly.

Knowing Anita's whereabouts did nothing to ease Columba's torment because she was still helpless to make contact. She sometimes made an effort to be more outwardly calm, she pretended to dote more on José. But he could tell a distracted pat on the head when he felt one and a preoccupied response when he heard one.

Columba was vacant. Even Hawkeye found himself almost pining for her small flirtations, and he sent silent threats in the form of concentrated glares towards her packsack. She would need to give him his due or he'd turn on her. When this dawned on her, she forced a smile, and a wink and deliberately put more swing in her hips. The efforts were half-hearted but they paid off with Hawkeye. Forcing behaviors – feigning interest, flashing smiles, nodding now and then, mumbling responses (not only with Hawkeye but with everyone) – was the only way she got through each day.

More than a year had passed without a word from Anita. José showed no outward signs of missing her. But no matter what, their life was not normal. Their family was broken. Maybe if she went to the church again. No, something more practical was needed. Maybe she could talk to Lucia again, find out something new. Anything.

She climbed onto the bus one afternoon and let it take her to The Most Pure Blood of Jesus Church where she knew she'd find Lucia at the annex.

"I told you Señora Columba that I'm not in touch with Anita anymore."

"Yes, but I don't believe you."

Lucia shook her head. "She's deserted all of us. Not just you, Señora. She doesn't come to Father Cortés's classes anymore. Nobody has seen her for, like what? A year? I mean some kids still talk about her and ask about her but no one knows what she's doing or where she is." Lucia hesitated. "I did hear a rumor that she was working, though. They said she has a job working in The Black Cat."

"That's not news, Lucia. I saw her there myself."

This was all going nowhere. Why did she bother? Why didn't she just stay home? She was suddenly war-weary. Her heart was too heavy, her head was too light, her joints were too weak and for all of these reasons she was too tired to carry on living. She was disintegrating. Luckily, this sensation was fleeting and she managed to maintain her composure in front of Lucia.

"There is something, Señora." Lucia seemed to agonize. She kicked at a pebble on the sidewalk, and with her head lowered, she said, "After one of Father Cortés's classes, I saw Anita crying. This was, well, way last year. She was on the bench, you know, over near where Father parks his car." Lucia pointed her chin in the direction of the old Volkswagen. "First she was all by herself and I was going to go and ask what was wrong. But then Father Cortés came outside and he looked worried. He sat down beside her and he put his arm around her. She said something and pushed back from him. She actually pushed him in his chest, really hard. I thought that was weird. Then she jumped up. She didn't know I was there. And she shouted at Father. She swore at him, Señora. She cursed him! Then she started coming towards me. When she saw me, she stopped for a second and then just marched right past. She put her hands in front of her face to block me out and she didn't say anything. Not a word, Señora. That was the last time I saw her."

Lucia kept her head lowered, trying to avoid the sad eyes that were boring into her.

"Are you telling me the absolute truth? Are there any rumors you're not telling me about?"

Lucia looked up from under her brows, "No, Señora."

Columba didn't know what to make of Anita cursing Father. She contemplated it during the whole journey. Why would Anita be angry with him? That implied a closer relationship than a student-teacher, which is supposed to maintain a healthy wall of respect. Where were these kinds of thoughts leading? No. She wouldn't go there. She wouldn't entertain this kind of notion. Father was good to those kids and to her too.

The depot was depressing, what with its piles of rubbish, which were like monstrous grimacing heads rising up from the concrete, and scavenger-workers (herself among them) desperate to steal away with something, to dupe the boss one way or the other, to make him pay their due (if he wouldn't pay it, they would take it) and the stupid, sleazy security guard with his too-tight blue trousers and his manicured fingernails. What had this world come to? Why did she even care? Why not just give up?

CHAPTER 42

GAVIN

Where, along the way, did he get on the direct path to success? When was it that he began to make all the right decisions and gain such unbridled (and unwanted) admiration among peers? What if he had turned right instead of left at the crux of opportunity, or if he had declined the request from a stranger to light his cigarette, or if he had crushed a beetle on the sidewalk instead of leaving the energy in its beetle form? Who knew which seemingly inconsequential detail might have tipped destiny's balance? How did he achieve with such ease what so many people struggled unsuccessfully to do? He was familiar with his business success but not necessarily comfortable with it. Or with anything else for that matter.

A man who gets lost in his own thoughts in the midst of a room full of vocal wheelers and dealers is a man who is a danger to himself and to others. He is out of step and should be locked up. At least that's what occurred to Gavin as he leaned on the back wall at the annual Chamber of Commerce networking event – his casual stance, signal of easy success, one that others would naturally drift towards. He observed the conservative rituals of doing business.

He watched hands straightening ties, tugging at jacket fronts, patting shoulders, reaching across tables to shake other hands, he watched the nodding heads, he saw the hard smiles raking across faces and freezing momentarily, the congenial lips pronouncing formal, rote phrases, he noticed the eyes darting in all directions, distracted, scanning the room for the bigger fish, the guy with more connections, more money, the one who offered more status and opportunities than the one at hand.

Gavin slipped down the hall, pretending to head for the men's room and the voices droned on. By the time he reached the exit they had diminished to a monotone buzz. He knew they'd continue for a couple more hours. He found his way out to his car, inserted the key in the ignition, and satisfied with the perfect purr of the motor, he looked up at the window for a few seconds to watch the business silhouettes mingle, he smiled, pulled onto the quiet street and drove away.

The fallen leaves were still dry on the ground and as he cruised past, he glanced into the rear view mirror to see them kick up and swirl around, fluttering signs of the arctic winter making its way south. At seven in the afternoon, it had already been dark for nearly two hours, warm yellow lights glowing from inside a few offices where people had neglected to turn them off. Or perhaps cleaners were at work, their vacuum cleaners whirring, radios blaring. He pulled up outside of Funky Town, shut off the engine, and sat for a minute watching the hand-painted sign as it twitched slightly in the breeze – a wooden hand pointing to his success. Then he clicked open the car door and stepped out onto the damp pavement. Except for the intermittent buzz of a street light that threatened to burn out, it was silent. Aware that his footsteps clapped loudly across the sidewalk, he instinctively tiptoed the last few steps. He felt like a thief at his own door.

Even after he switched on the light, the stairway was dim. This initial semi-obscurity was an important part of the Funky Town ambience. He squinted to make out the graffiti and posters that Mark had arranged to look like they'd been slapped up there in a hurry, casual and cool, just happening to stick at exactly the right angle. Although Funky Town was his brainchild, he felt foreign amidst the displays and as he brushed past the racks, he could feel the sleeves from oversized shirts and retro jackets touch the back of his hands. His skin prickled and the hairs on the back of his neck stood on end. He glanced around to ensure he was the only one there. He and Mark had created a creepy place. He felt much more comfortable at Stan's Men's and Boys' Wear. Maybe it was because he had been born into it. But maybe it was because he was more like his Dad than he realized. He'd been questioning that a lot lately.

He wasn't sure why he'd driven to Funky Town after escaping the schmooze of the year but it had something to do with needing to overcome uncertainties. He wasn't sure yet what he was looking for nor why he felt lifted above the rituals of tonight's meeting where the businessmen and women were like paper cut-outs on the pages in the middle of a book. They were waiting to be chosen, punched out of the die-cut shapes where they would come alive and gain the power to look back with pride at the empty spaces they'd left behind, the outlines of their humble origins. Look how far we've come, they'd boast in their newly cutout designer outfits. But in reality, they were still just paper, once removed.

Gavin didn't want to look back at anything. Granted, he occasionally reminisced about his efforts to be a private detective but now it was with humor.

He smiled into the dark.

These days he was well beyond what would have been his Dad's comfort zone and he was at the edges of his own. Still, he felt compelled to keep pushing on. The recycled clothing business was proof of that. Right now it needed more attention than both Stan's and Funky Town put together and he had already begun to spend more time on it, anxious to see where it would lead, as though in spite of his plans, it could possibly have a life of its own.

The White Linen Charity had a good group of employees. He trusted all of them to turn up to work and do their job. One in particular named Irma, was a real find. She was a lively, middle-aged woman from Bosnia. She said that before the war, she had been a shop owner herself. She knew the garment business.

"I was owner of an exclusive high-end fashion shop for women. Leather and furs from Italy..." she had told him at her interview. Her accent and constant search for the right words and trying to pronounce them in the right order made conversation slow. "They took it all from me at gunpoint." She didn't mean to reveal that, it just slipped out and she immediately dropped her gaze to her hands, where her fingers constantly twisted, trying to capture the memories before they ran amuck. He caught the pain. She might as well have been stabbed in the eye.

Gavin jumped in. "Well, we can really use someone like yourself then. You know you're overqualified. But until you are more accomplished with the language, I hope this will do."

She beamed, flushing all the way to her ears, her eyes glistening, and in her heavy accent she pronounced, "You will not be sorry, Mr. Reid. Thank-you."

It was Irma who set an example for the other employees. She never missed a day, she was happy. She arrived each morning to repeat a new phrase she'd heard on the news the night before, asking everyone if they'd seen the story and then searching for the English words to describe what it was about. She was the glue of the social fabric in the depot, the go-to person, the one who was not afraid to ask questions and raise concerns. And she wasn't afraid to stand up to Gavin.

Gavin started making the hour's drive to the White Linen Charity warehouse in Grant Falls on a daily basis. He had set up a call center to solicit used clothing from local residents. Through contacts in Burgeon, he had made the rounds at Grant Falls' Chamber of Commerce and had successfully built relationships with small businesses who were willing to support his recycling organization.

"It's a damn good cause. I applaud your efforts. And I have no problem making space for one of your clothing donation bins. Just make sure it's emptied regularly because I'm telling you, I can attract lots of donations. And you need to be sure it's clean too. If we have to wash it, then it's time for it to go."

Gavin appointed one of the young men to make weekly rounds to 'service' the fiberglass bins. Without fail, they all had something in them, even if just a few items in a bottom corner. "It's like harvesting," the young man had told him. "I like it."

Among other things, Gavin charged Irma with sorting the donations that people dropped off at the small dock at the back door every night. Weekends was always great for drop-offs and on Monday mornings she was especially busy sorting through the bags and boxes.

"I know quality when I see it, Mr. Reid." And it wasn't long before it was Irma and not Gavin who set the prices in the White Linen Charity shop. He focused his energy on the real money-making end of things, garments for export.

IRENE

It takes years to build a fortress. But all it takes are a few malevolent minutes for it to tumble down. And what's inside the fortress? Perhaps treasures, perhaps forgotten, castaway threads, or maybe, just maybe it's full of polyester/woolen shapes that have been carefully, oh so carefully hoarded.

It was unexpected and unwelcome but there was nothing Irene could do when Chuck ushered her Mom in the front door that evening with Amber just steps behind, hand lightly on her mother's back, guiding her in like an aging ewe.

Irene was caught unaware. It was too late to dash down the hall and hide away in her bedroom. They had already seen her through the window, both waving and grinning like excited monkeys as Amber shuffled her Mom along the sidewalk. Irene could hear them murmuring.

Amber kicked off her shoes at the door and glided across the room in sock feet, bending down to kiss Irene who sat there, needles frozen in her hands, a ball of yarn having fallen to the floor. "There was nothing I could do," Amber whispered. "She insisted on coming, and on coming now. Tonight. I was so surprised that she was suggesting – I mean she was suggesting that we come and visit you – that I grabbed her coat and got her out of there before she could change her mind." She said louder, for her Mom's sake, "So here we are." She turned and smiled back at their Mom who was still seated politely at the front door in her shoes and coat, waiting for an official invitation before venturing any further.

Amber gently removed the knitting needles from Irene's hands, setting them in the basket. "Come on."

Amber's hand tight around Irene's wrist, she leaned her shoulder into Irene's and inclined her head towards her as they padded their way towards the foyer. They looked like two little girls getting into mischief. All they needed were the pigtails.

Their mother got to her feet, slowly unbuttoning her coat, her fingers trembling a little. Irene wondered if it was because of the cold or if she had developed one of those old folk's 'conditions'. The coat was the same dark green quilted one that Irene had bought her when she and Chuck were first married. She had insisted that her Mom accept the gift. "You can't run around all winter in this light thing." She had said, as she held up the worn jacket with threadbare cuffs that her Mom had used for god-knows-how-many winters. Now, somehow the memory of her Mom's staunch resistance to wearing 'such an expensive' coat reached in and melted Irene's heart.

She momentarily forgot her own deeply-worn pain and was overcome instead with a cloud of nostalgia. She wanted to protect her Mom and at the same time to have her Mom protect her. She wanted to be wrapped in the same maternal warmth and that she had rejected these last many years and she yearned for comfort and to be absolved of all responsibility. In this fleeting moment, she wanted to be her Mom's little girl again, to forget the years beyond carefree childhood and especially the year she had let her own little girl go.

She wriggled free of Amber and stood directly in front of her Mom, arms hanging at her sides. "Mom! Welcome." Surely, her Mom would declare Irene's innocence, tell her that she hadn't done anything wrong.

Her Mom stepped forward and gently stroked Irene's hair and patted her face and she drew her thin fingers up and around her cheeks, leaving her skin tingling. Irene stood still, reddened with tears as her Mom studied her, searching for the little girl in her face. When her eyes lit with recognition, she wrapped her arms around her and pulled her close.

They clung, rocking gently. Her Mom said, "It's okay Irene. It's all good." And she caressed her hair.

Amber stood back, tears rolling down her cheeks. Chuck was two steps behind, winding his fingers into knots. He finally turned around and walked out of the room to hide his own twisted emotion.

They settled in the living room. Amber noted the baskets of wool. "My, you bring a lot of work home with you." Her Mom turned her head to look at the baskets and she nodded with approval.

Irene just smiled. "Yes, it's what I do. It's all I do, actually."

Chuck offered to serve tea and he bustled into the kitchen and found some outdated shortbread cookies that he'd brought home from the store last week. He dropped several of them on a plate and set them down with an embarrassed smile. No one noticed.

Conversation didn't flow. It was stilted and uncomfortable. All three women studied one another's faces, alternately smiling and looking down, politely sipping tea and biting into the cookies, brushing away crumbs. There was really nothing to talk about.

"How's Dad?" Irene was surprised to hear her own question.

"Oh, Dad's fine. Just fine. Right, Mom?"

Their Mom nodded and sipped, and the sound of tea murmuring its way down her throat was the only sound in the room, and she smiled.

Amber excused herself, motioning towards the bathroom. She would leave her Mom and Irene on their own, maybe they'd find some words – if there were any to be found.

Chuck was perched on the edge of a kitchen chair, his ears stretched around the corner, trying to understand why the three of them were so quiet. He was unsettled, tortured about whether or not to tell Amber about Irene's pastime. Now was his chance. But should he show her the rooms filled with sweaters, ask her opinion? The question had rattled around in his brain for longer than he cared to remember. Was it right to interfere in Irene's only obvious source of comfort? Was Irene really causing any harm? To herself, to him? Did he really want to see it come to an end? But would it ever end? Where would it lead? Would confronting her and maybe removing all of it, help her to finally, truly move on?

He hadn't completely thought it through and he didn't know why he did it. Maybe he was just tired of keeping secrets. And tired of trying to decide what was right. Maybe he just wanted some help. Anyway, on impulse, he jumped up to intercept Amber in the hallway, out of sight of Irene and her Mom. His hands were shaking and he clasped them behind his back. "Amber, I need to show you something." His heart was pounding in his ears. Would he regret this? Why was he doing this?

They stood for a moment, hushed, as Amber looked at him, questioning. Chuck feared that Irene might sense something. Then he heard their voices, one raised in a question, the other a muffled response.

"Here. In here." His throat was dry. He twisted the door knob, urgently ushered Amber into the spare room, closed the door and turned on the light. They stood for several eternal seconds facing stacks of colorful, woolen sweaters. Finally, Chuck whispered, "And this isn't even half of it."

Amber gasped and grabbed at her throat. She reached back for the door, miscalculated and fell to the floor. From her low angle, the sweater stacks loomed tall. She didn't see the work, the design or the craftsmanship. All she saw was insanity. She was dwarfed by piles of madness. Threatened even. The atmosphere was all wrong, sharp and crazy, an intense other-worldliness that bulged into the space. For several seconds she sat there, blinking and taking deep breaths. "How long has this been going on?"

He stuttered. "I… I'm not sure. Maybe about three years."

She turned to look squarely in his face. "Why didn't you say something?"

If ever there was a time to be honest, now was it. God knows he couldn't lie about this. He had nothing else, no one else to turn to, no other opportunity might ever present itself. "I mean, Amber…" He stuttered. "I.. I.. I mean, at first I didn't realize it was happening. I mean, she wanted to sleep in separate rooms and so, you know, I had no reason to set foot in her bedroom. And when I did, I saw a few piles. I mean, she was knitting every night. And I don't know what I thought she did with everything. She wouldn't talk about it." He was choking back tears. "Maybe I just wanted to believe… I mean, maybe she was giving it away to kids who needed it or she'd found a charity somewhere. I don't know. I just left it. But then pretty soon there was no more space in the bedroom and she started using this room. And, well, you can see, it's almost full here now and I don't know what she'll fill up next."

Amber slumped back, thumping her head softly against the wall, like it helped her think.

Chuck was spilling his guts. "And another thing. Did you notice the baby carriage in the living room? Do you know what's in it?"

She lifted her gaze and slowly closed her eyes, then squeezed them tightly, holding her breath, waiting for the answer she knew was coming.

"It's full of sweaters, newborn size. She knits new ones every once in a while and exchanges the new ones for the ones she made months ago. Then she piles the older ones (the smaller ones) into a big cedar chest at the end of her bed and eventually puts them in here somewhere."

She looked up at him, frowning. "How well are you keeping track of all this?"

He slid down the wall to sit beside her and whispered, "Well, I actually started a proper inventory. I have spread sheets."

Her mouth fell open. She raised both hands, fingers spread out stiffly in front of her face as though if she could block out the scene, it simply wouldn't exist. "Okay, this whole thing is insane. It's sick."

"I know. Well, I mean... I don't know. That's why I'm telling you."

Chuck was trembling. His chin began to quiver. Magnified by his Diors, tears welled up and he blinked them away. "I don't know what to do. Part of me is really proud of what she's capable of. I mean, look what she can produce!" He crawled over to a small pile and he pulled out a sample, holding it up, his face red and distorted as he tried not to cry. "But what is she doing with them? I don't get it." He choked.

They sat for several moments in silence, breathing heavily, staring straight ahead into the soft piles until Amber realized she needed to get back to the living room before Irene came looking. She scrambled to her feet and pulled Chuck towards her in a clumsy, self-conscious hug. She released him almost as quickly as she had taken hold of him. But it was too late for Chuck. The walls he had built around himself crumbled in front of a willing, empathetic soul. His shoulders shook and he clutched the beautiful yellow sweater with purple butterflies that he'd pulled from the stacks, buried his face and sobbed into it.

This was too much. Amber couldn't deal with it all at one time, not right here. Desperate to escape, she left Chuck crying into the purple butterflies and she tiptoed away, gently closing the door.

When she returned to the living room, Irene and her Mom were both looking at the floor. "Where've you been?" Irene asked.

"Stomach problems." She turned to her Mom. "We should go, Mom. It's getting late."

None of them was sure what the visit had been about, if it was meant to accomplish something. But each of them felt it had been the start of something, probably not a fresh start but something that pointed them on a path to where they really should be going. For Amber it meant more than she could ever have imagined.

COLUMBA

The day that Juana gave Columba the doll was the very same day that José made his first visit to The Black Cat.

It had begun like any other day but for both Columba and José – who had each woken up feeling driven, albeit for distinct reasons – the day was pivotal. It was as if they'd stepped out of bed, pointed their feet in a slightly different direction than was their habit and they each headed off at a new angle. As a result, in the following days as they walked further and further in the altered direction, which meant they were veering exponentially off their habitual path, they each arrived at a new destination.

Columba crawled into the back seat of the taxi collector. She heard her own voice ask the driver to drop her off at The Diagonal, a block from Juana's house. She didn't know what had compelled her to dress in the plain black wool dress that hung to mid-calf. If she'd been in her right mind, she would have known the day was too hot for such a dress. The too-tight, three-quarter length sleeves and the high neck added to the discomfort. She had to keep running her finger around the neckline to alleviate the itch. The itch, she thought briefly, was an outward manifestation of how piqued and uncomfortable she felt inside. It occurred to her that perhaps she should accessorize the dress with something, a string of bright red beads and the red bauble earrings to match. But she waved them off at the last minute. Her appearance had become the least of her concerns.

José had left for school before she emerged from her bedroom. If she'd gotten up earlier maybe she would have had time to pack him a sandwich and she would have walked with him to the corner and they would have shared a few moments, maybe even laughed. But they didn't do that and hadn't done it for ages. She cursed herself under her breath from the back seat of the taxi.

"What did you say, Señora?"

"Nothing." She didn't care to participate in niceties.

When the taxi pulled up at the corner, "The Diagonal with Mar Este, Señora", she dropped a few coins in his hand and shifted her heavy bottom across the cracked leather seat and stepped out to the curb. The sun was blinding and its heat immediately penetrated her dress. She was going to melt today.

"Juana. Juana!" she leaned into the grilled fence and yelled into the open front door.

Sunlight from the window at the far end of the house described Juana's approaching shape as she rocked back and forth on her bad hips. As usual, her eyes were smiling. "What a nice surprise. Come in. Come in." Columba was the only one there at this early hour.

They walked arm in arm towards the kitchen, tucking into each other's soft shoulders. Juana gave Columba a squeeze before Columba collapsed into a kitchen chair.

"How have you been?" Juana pulled up a chair and leaned in.

"It's a long story."

"I'll make us some tea."

Juana knew her words of comfort were like grains of sand falling into a huge pit. They would never help fill the space nor close the wound. But she had nothing else to offer.

"I miss her presence, you know, Juana? Anita was my best friend. I counted on her and she counted on me. I don't understand why she turned her back on us without a word. Why would she abandon both José and I, Juana? I don't understand." There were days, she admitted, sometimes even several days, perhaps even an entire week that passed in which Anita's absence seemed normal. But then without warning, it blew in again like a cold, bitter wind, turning Columba around, almost knocking her off her feet. On those days, she circled around in a stupor.

"And, Juana..." she looked up, anguished, her face contorted, "Lucia told me that she never hears from Anita anymore. She's cut herself off from everyone. Why is she doing this?" She dropped her head onto the table, covered her face with her arms and sobbed. Juana just leaned over and hugged her and waited.

Well, maybe one day it would feel normal, maybe time would make it so. But at the end of day, there would always be a ghost. She told Juana that just when she thought she had it under control, the pain would rise up and punch a hole in her gut. It would start churning and she would be sick to her stomach, rushing to puke around the corner somewhere. And the tightness around her head would return, the weight of her limbs would increase, the nausea would send her running. These physical reactions always took her by surprise. She'd be down at the depot sorting, you know, just concentrating on the work at hand, and suddenly she was unable to control the bile that rose in her throat. Or else she'd be in the back seat of a taxi, listening to the banter between the driver and the other three passengers and without warning, she'd begin to cry. Then the questions would re-emerge. Did I put too much responsibility on her? Did she hate being my accomplice so much that she began to hate me too? Did she resent our poverty? Did she think I could do better? Did she think I was too uneducated and stupid and that she was too smart for me… and what about José? What did she think of him? Why abandon him too?

"I remember that sometimes first thing in the morning, Anita would be terribly sad and I hugged her and tried to joke, to lighten her mood, you know? And then other times, she woke up angry, and she said cruel things to me and José, like she hated us but she never explained anything. She just wanted to be angry. Sometimes I think education is a bad thing. It teaches your kids to think they are better than their parents. Did she learn that at school? I don't know…. José's still in school and he's still with me. Did she learn it from Father Cortés and the catechism classes? I don't know, Juana. I don't know where it came from. I wonder if José will turn against me one day too?" And with that she collapsed into another fit of sobs. Juana leaned closer, and foreheads touching, she caressed Columba's arms through the black woolen sleeves and repeatedly kissed the nest on her head.

Maybe Columba's tortured heart was not visible to every naked eye but Juana saw how she had obviously let herself go, that her skin was blotchy, her fingernails cracked and dirty, her hair undone, even her dress was loose fitting. She had lost a lot of weight. And why this black dress? Was she in mourning now? No, this was unhealthy. This was not good.

"I have something for you Columba. It's not a substitute for Anita but … well, maybe she'll help. My Mom, God rest her soul, gave her to me. And now I'm giving her to you. She'll make you feel better. I promise." She scraped her chair back and left Columba gazing down into her empty lap. When Juana returned, she was holding a plastic doll the size of a toddler. The doll had shoulder-length straw-colored hair and bright blue eyes that closed when she was tilted back. The doll's stiff plastic arms rotated 360 degrees from the shoulders and the legs were hinged at the hips. Juana adjusted the legs and she sat the doll down onto the chair directly in front of Columba. "I call her

Magdalena but you can call her whatever you want." The doll wore a short-sleeved green paisley dress with yellowed lace at the collar and she had a pair of thin white socks inside white plastic shoes. "This is the only dress she has but you'll probably find something nicer at the depot."

Columba stared at the doll for a moment before looking up at Juana, and unable to control it, her face twisted, and she sobbed again. She rocked back and forth on the chair and heard herself wail. Her head dropped to her chest, and her arms fell limp. She was hollow, like the doll. They both echoed inside.

But she took Magdalena home and set her on her bedroom floor at the edge of her semi-organized pile of garments. If it had been a gift from someone other than Juana, she would have tossed it into the dumpster on her way home.

The doll watched her, shiny blue plastic eyes tracking her every move. It was creepy. The doll knew everything. Columba thought about turning her around but it occurred to her that the doll's head would spin 360 degrees, like the little girl in The Exorcist. That was the last thing she wanted to see so she left her where she was.

She toyed again with the idea of carrying this hollow, molded plastic outside and tossing her in the dumpster but maybe Columba would be cursed if she did that. Who knew what this doll was capable of? No, it would be best to make friends with her. And anyway, she came from Juana and Juana's Mom before that. Columba would get used to her.

Meanwhile, José had just left The Black Cat, confused and shaken.

CHAPTER 45

IRENE

After the whole nightmare was over, Irene could barely bring herself to imagine how it must have all developed. The stealth, the planning, the audacious execution! How they had schemed to break in and steal her sweaters, her very reason for being, her life. How they had violated her! How they had dared to rummage through her private world. She shuddered at the thought of their hands, unworthy of the sweaters, their predacious fingers clawing and pinching, their hurried breaths as they huffed and puffed, one trip after another down the hallway, probably dropping and maybe stepping on them in their haste to fill up whatever vehicle they were filling up. A truck probably. Maybe two. How they evacuated her house that afternoon, their cruel satisfaction spreading like poison over an unsuspecting Sunday as they drove through town. How they had betrayed her. And with Chuck at the helm.

It was true, some of it had been easy. On the drive towards the White Linen Charity with Amber and Jocelyn crowded into the front of their Dad's truck, all the traffic lights had turned green, opening the way, parting the sea, expediting the escape from Irene's world (all of which they had managed to stuff into tight plastic bundles that bounced and shifted against the back of the half-ton). They'd left Chuck standing alone in the driveway. No time for mercy. His head was down, he was trembling but they pulled out swiftly and they didn't see his knees buckle just before he folded and flattened onto the asphalt. Twenty minutes later, they arrived at the back dock of the White Linen Charity. They were the only ones there. That part had been easy. The urgency was over. Chuck was the worst part. Shaking like a leaf, he was close to breaking down, according to Jocelyn.

When all was said and done and by the time they reached the outskirts, the street lights were just coming on. They twinkled and faded into the background as the old truck raced away. Amber was grateful for the thin gauze of anonymity that dusk provided. They escaped onto the familiar country roads that were bordered by serene fields, the distant pink skies giving into violet, silhouettes of the farm houses set back in the distance, their porch lights beaming out small yellow circles, dogs running down the driveways, horses frolicking along the fence lines.

When Amber had seen Irene those weeks ago at Spin a Yarn, she'd seemed so normal, almost happy – at the very least, grounded and content with her job. In some ways, she appeared childlike, the tilt of her head when she laughed, her habit of flicking of her hair (which was shoulder length again) behind her ears. Life had not passed her by but rather she seemed to have embraced it, made a new path for herself. And last week, when Amber set off with her Mom to visit, she had expected a pleasant couple of hours – just Irene, her Mom and her and maybe, but not likely, Chuck. She'd imagined banter and laughter over childhood memories. She'd even expected tears, but good tears, unselfconscious ones, the kind that families share. She'd envisioned Irene leaning in to whisper funny stories about Chuck, the things they'd seen on their travels those years ago, how Chuck had been so regimented that he hardly relaxed, even on holiday.

But instead she was in for that shock. Chuck had ushered her into another world. She was still trying to make sense of it. Had her Mom noticed anything? She hadn't remarked except to say how lovely it was to see Irene again. The ride home that night had been mostly silent and Amber didn't know if her Mom's was a contented silence or a worried one.

"Something has to be done." It was Amber informing – no demanding – that Jocelyn take it seriously.

"You're the big therapist," Amber told her sister. "You're the one who should know how to handle this."

"Hey, a secretary in the office of the school counselor hardly qualifies."

"Yeah, well, you're the closest we've got."

"What does Mom think?"

"I didn't tell her."

Jocelyn nodded. "Yeah, probably best that way. But you know what, we might have to let Dad know because I'm thinking we'll need his help.

"Dad, we're going to need to borrow your baling plastic." It was Amber. "We need to package up some cargo for shipping and we thought maybe you could give us some. We'll need strapping too."

Old man McArthur couldn't fathom it. No, not this weird hoarding stuff. Not one of his kids. He'd heard about that once from old man Dickinson down on Route 341. Said he had an aunt who hoarded newspapers. Got so bad that she ended up dying in the midst of them. A housefire, he said. She didn't stand a chance. But what was this about sweaters, hundreds, maybe thousands, at Irene's place? Well, sure, he'd lend a hand. But first they'd have to clear the way.

It wasn't easy. An understatement. Chuck had to drag Irene out of the house on the pretense of a gas leak. It was the best he could think of.

"I'm taking you to the store this afternoon."

"But it's Sunday. The gas company won't come out on a Sunday."

"They will for an emergency. Get your coat. We have to leave."

He settled her in the lunch room at the store. "Make some tea." He filled the kettle and plugged it in. "Here," he handed her a few magazines, one of them was 'Fishing Tackle' but he was in a hurry. "You know where everything is. I'll only be an hour or so. Just have to let the guys in and wait for them to check it all out."

The old green Ford pickup was at the house when Chuck returned. Amber and Jocelyn were crowded in, shoulder to shoulder with old man McArthur in the front seat. They were sipping tea from his thermos cup. They jumped out when Chuck pulled up.

"Well, I'll be damned," McArthur shook his head and spit.

With nothing more than a quick nod at the old man and Irene's sisters, Chuck led the way inside and down the hall. "Here," he said. "And here." He opened the doors to the sewing room and Irene's bedroom. They stood in the hall like a line of pigeons, all staring at the piles. "This all has to go." Chuck was waving his arms, frenzied, worried about what was going to happen when Irene got home." And I know where to take it. I checked it out last week. There's a charity on the north side of town that accepts deliveries of used clothing and whatever. You'll see the sign. It's called 'White Linen Charity'. The sign on the loading bay says to leave things there. Just do it, okay? And fast. I won't be able to keep her very long at the store." He turned and then said, "I can't go with you. You know that, right? This is bad enough."

He stayed at the front door, pacing back and forth, unable to leave or go back to the bedroom. "Wait!" He pulled some paper from the narrow desk in the foyer and scribbled on it. "Give them this. Make sure it's somewhere they don't miss it, okay? It's important. And hurry up. Hurry!"

The note said, 'IMPORTANT: DO NOT SELL OR DISTRIBUTE LOCALLY,' and he pressed it into Amber's hand.

A prickly red climbed up Chuck's neck, filling his cheeks and the lining of his eyelids. His eyes burned. He raised and lowered his Diors a hundred times. His whole skinny body shaking, he charged out the back door before he could change his mind and he waited in his car. He sat in the front seat, motor running, head down, looking at, but not seeing his interlaced fingers with the white knuckles. Then he unclenched and clenched his hands into fists. He pounded them into his thighs so hard that they would be bruised. He should go back in and stop them. He should say it's all a mistake. He should save those beautiful works of art. But then. No. No, this way, someone else will appreciate them for what they are. The sweaters will warm the bodies of little children somewhere. The world will appreciate how precious they are, they'll want to preserve them, the sweaters will become keepsakes for years to come, some poor family's grandchildren will wonder at them. He pictured them in a distant closet, wrapped in tissue under little packets of potpourri. Little did he know of foreign closets. And what of Irene? Well, Irene would at last realize that all of this wasn't going to bring back Alicia. She would leave her world of make-believe and find comfort in the memories of Alicia (like he'd learned to do) and she would discover that they can love each other again.

This whole thing was taking much longer than he had anticipated and he was wound up like a spring, shaking like a leaf from head to toe. At last Amber tapped on his window and gave him the thumbs up. Maybe there was still time to change his mind before they drove off. After all, maybe the sweaters were better keepsakes in Irene's bedroom than in someone else's. He got out of the car but his body was wooden. He took two steps and stopped, his muscles not responding. He stood there trembling as he watched them pull out. He couldn't make himself go back inside and check. He couldn't make himself step back into the car. He was trapped in a no-man's land on his driveway. Then he fell down and he didn't know how long he laid there. And he couldn't remember getting back into the car and turning on the engine and driving back to the store. But he did remember that when he walked into the store to get Irene, she had her coat buttoned right to the top, her collar pulled up to her ears as though she was freezing and she was standing, nose pressed against the window, leaving a foggy mark from her breath that he'd have to remember to clean off tomorrow before opening.

"Sorry," he told her. "They needed a bit more time."

IRENE

Imminent and destructive. How else do you describe such foreboding? To Irene it is a niggling, growing fear. Nothing concrete. But the greatest power and destruction begins as a spark, a thought, sometimes a premonition. It is ethereal, the thing of gods and spirits, it is just potential, just ideas. But you must pay attention to the niggling pressure on the back of your neck that climbs and twists around to tap you on your forehead. It is in front of your eyes. Interlopers. Pay attention.

Cranky for being stuck in the back room of the store and having had a couple of fishing magazines tossed at her for entertainment, she complained, "Chuck, this has to have been the worst afternoon of my life. What a bore and a waste of a Sunday afternoon. Don't ever schedule gas emergencies again."

Normally he would have remarked, "That's a dumb thing to say… you can't schedule emergencies." But he looked straight ahead, slamming on the brakes too hard at a red light.

She was fidgety the entire drive back home and Chuck was in a strange mood. He had assumed a really mousy kind of attitude. He was skittish, and he wouldn't look at her.

"What's wrong with you, Chuck? I'm the one who was holed up with nothing to do all day. Plus, the tea at the store is really bad. Speaking of that, I have to pee badly. Can't you go any faster?"

She was relieved when they pulled in at the house and waited for the garage door to open. Why was it so slow today? Chuck took his time parking the car (even longer than normal, she thought), lining up the middle of the windshield exactly as he always did, with the stupid little plumb line with the tennis ball at the end that he'd hung from the ceiling (more for her, he had said, than for him. But she didn't believe that). She sighed heavily and glared at Chuck as she stepped out of the car and slammed the door.

She kicked off her shoes and walked down the hall to the bathroom, so far, so good. Chuck was hanging back.

She had expected to walk in and find an official form from the gas company in plain sight on the kitchen counter, something about how they'd success-fully made some adjustments and that the house was, after all, safe to inhabit. But what she actually walked into was a house of horrors, an unimaginable nightmare.

Chuck could hear her talking to herself in the bathroom. He was trembling beside the fridge. Couldn't even sit down. Too nervous. Maybe he should jet out of here, just bolt. But he was inert, muscles frozen, ears piqued, eyes wide and as terrified as a deer who knows he's in your sights. He waited until she walked out of the bathroom and into her bedroom and he heard a shriek that brought back that morning from six years ago. Only this time he didn't run to her rescue. This time, he shriveled up like the coward he was and huddled into the corner beside the fridge, pushing his back into it, trying in vain to extract a little comfort from the hum of the motor.

Irene collapsed on the floor beside her bedroom door, looking at exactly nothing. The walls closed in and then they disappeared. In and out, in and out they went, the sick rhythm of someone else's breath, in and out, until she lost her bearings and spiraled down. She didn't know if her arms were moving (probably not) but she was reaching out, trying to touch something, anything, a guide, a rope, a thread, something to rescue her from this sudden and profound nothingness.

She was lost in a barren, infertile desert of hollow, echoing space, spirits slashed and burned, her emptiness raw, exposed and rampant. Her refuge had been converted, just like that – from a few rooms that she had packed full of warmth and love – to the meaningless wasteland of her former life with Chuck. The old life, its former self made its presence felt like black dust, like a vacuum ready to suck her into its unhappy sing-along tune of conform-ity and limited satisfaction.

She wailed. She got to her knees and crept along the carpet, creeping into the closets, her fingers clawing for traces of the sweaters.

Eventually, she was struck by how this must have unfolded and she stormed down the hall and into the kitchen where the lily-livered pussy was crouched on the floor. She leaned down and slapped him across the ear, then again, then across his cheek. Then the other cheek, then his head. And she didn't stop until he rolled over and covered himself with his arms. "We had to do it, we had to do something," he was whining.

"Who?"

"Well, me."

"You and who else?" She kicked him in his ribs.

"Me and Amber and Jocelyn and your Dad." He squeaked the confession. He wouldn't come out from under his arms. His voice still muffled, he whimpered, "We had to, Irene. I mean it's for your own good. I know it doesn't seem like it now. But you'll see. It's for the best. And the sweaters are being sent to needy children in a foreign land where they'll be appreciated. They'll love them. You know it's right. Your Dad bundled them up properly. You know how he does? You don't have to worry."

She kicked him again and saw him sputter, his slimy spittle landing at her feet. She stepped over him, pelting him with more open-handed slaps and then turned to leave him alone.

In her wildest dreams, Irene couldn't have imagined how the geniuses could have justified this theft – stealing all that she held dear, cutting her down at the knees, tearing out her heart, stuffing and suffocating her soul in industrial plastic, cinching it with baling cord and shipping it half way around the world to some foreign country – how could such a brazen, hostile act of betrayal possibly end well?

That day, she would shut down and it would be eons before Chuck would hear her voice again. He would pay for his sins. She would refuse to answer the telephone and in order to avoid seeing Amber or Jocelyn or god forbid, either of her parents, she would stop showing up at Spin a Yarn. Mildred would figure it out on her own.

And she did. Irene was dead to the world.

CHAPTER 47

GAVIN

Irma said the sweaters had been delivered as if on the wings of little angels. She was sure it was God's will and it was because the White Linen Charity was deserving of precious gifts.

"These," she said, as she lifted one after the other and placed them gently on Gavin's desk, displaying their fronts and backs, opening out the sleeves, turning collars, touching buttons, lifting fine little crocheted flowers that were attached here and there. "These, cannot be shipped away. These have to stay here. We have to sell them here. Maybe I can just keep them myself." Her cheeks were flushed, her eyes sparkling.

But Gavin didn't have time. His nose was in a file folder, his chair swiveled so that his back was to her, and he responded from there. "Well, Irma. I trust you. What's the problem?" Preoccupied with a new second-hand clothes buyer in South America, he didn't want to be interrupted. He was thinking about a company in Chile. Who to trust and how to know? He'd heard rumors.

"The problem, Mr. Reid, is this note."

She passed it to him.

He glanced at it and passed it back, again without looking at her. It said that the sweaters must not, under any circumstances be sold locally. "Well, then it means we won't sell any here, Irma. It's easy. We'll export them."

"No, Mr. Reid. It's not that easy. Look at these sweaters. Did you look at them?" She clucked. "You didn't. We can't ship these away to God knows where! We can't."

Still not paying attention, "We have to respect the wishes of the donor."

"Mr. Reid. You haven't looked at them. If you ship them away, Mr. Reid, then I'm going away too."

Now she had his attention. He closed the folder and swiveled around. She stood across from him, her back stiff, lips pursed, her complexion a bright red, transparent so that he could see little purple veins just under the surface. And she refused to look at him. She stretched out her right arm, her index finger stiff as she swiped her arm above the sweaters that she had laid out. "Look."

Gavin glanced down and his mouth dropped open.

He gazed at the selection for several minutes in silence, mesmerized, forgetting that Irma was waiting for a response. In all the fashion shows he's attended, he'd never seen such a striking collection. It was a tribute to youthful vitality, and it shouted with joy. A child's story was knitted into each and every one. One sweater described a lonely butterfly that was gliding on the wind across a meadow towards cloud-covered mountains in the distant horizon. Another told the story of three raspberries that were at once berries and buttons, climbing up the front of a brown band that would be its cane, bending to the wind, a lone lady bug smiling down at them. Another, sang out its story in a happy tune of treble clefs and musical notes bouncing up and around, tickling under the arms and over the shoulders and back down to hit low notes at the bottom.

And then there was the craft. He lifted a few sweaters, and ran his fingers along the rows of stitches, feeling the joins, surveying the fine, mostly invisible stitches around the sleeves and lifting the crocheted attachments. Each sweater was exquisite not only in creative design but in its skillful construction.

Finally, he looked up. "Are there more?"

"Yes, but I haven't counted them yet. There have to be hundreds and hundreds!"

"I'm coming."

They walked to the warehouse where the workers were about to open a second bale of sweaters. They'd been wrapped in heavy plastic. The final strap was cut and the bundle exploded in a bomb of color.

"Gently, gently," Gavin said. The workers were not oblivious to the beauty and they lifted them one by one to the shelves Irma had cleaned. She was prepared to do a proper inventory.

Gavin instructed that all sweaters be sorted according to size and then color and then yarn type. Irma performed the task expertly. She took her time, handling each little garment for longer than necessary, re-examining, holding them close, just for the joy of it. "Please let me take my time," she had told Gavin. These deserve attention. Trust me."

He was tempted to stay and oversee the rest of work but he was being pulled back to the question of exports to a Chilean company that he had just become aware of. Up to now, the White Linen Charity had done business with larger groups who exported to Africa. This would be his first connection to South America and he had already decided that he wanted to do it. The new market would be lucrative. The challenge was in collecting enough clothing to keep the Chilean importer satisfied. According to his information, they were going through mountains of the stuff down there and he needed to source more used clothes. The bundles of sweaters should be shipped away. There was no question about it, given the Charity's standard operating practice and now, especially with the note from the donor.

But the price could never come near the value that one should pay for these little works of art. He'd never be able to negotiate anything other than a standard price per kilo. Besides, like Irma, he couldn't see himself letting go of them. First of all, he'd stand to lose a lot of money. Secondly, he cringed to think of the sweaters wasting away, being mishandled in a street market somewhere. It would be a serious disservice. And there was also the *if* – if, wherever they landed, the importer paid attention to what he had on his hands, he'd surely make a huge profit, all of which, by rights, should go into White Linen coffers. No, the White Linen Charity was going to be the one pulling in this cash and distributing these little treasures.

Maybe he could pretend he didn't see the note. Irma would go along with him. Maybe it had gotten lost under the bales and was stepped on, kicked aside, become muddied and illegible after a night of rain (even though he remembered very well that it had not rained the night before). The note was merely a request, a hope on the part of the donor, nothing legal. What would the charity really be risking (besides a boatload of profit)?

CHAPTER 48

THE SWEATER

"Bless this place, the reason for being here, bless the coincidence. Bless the timing that put us both here... Bless God for finding us on this road.... on the path of my destiny."

(Translation of "Bendita Tu Luz," Maná)

Bless the demure, young worker at the White Linen Charity who absent-mindedly dropped this fine little sweater into a pile where it didn't belong, where it was mistakenly bundled between used garments destined for South America. Bless the coincidence, bless the timing, bless the moon above and bless the soft, dark comfort of this crowded heap in which the little sweater now found herself.

Bless the fact that energy flows through objects and is picked up on the other side. What do we know or care about inanimate objects? We normally assign souls only to animal beings. But in art, there is soul. Its very creation transmits the artist's energy, through which the soul is infused. To share ownership in an artist's soul is so much more meaningful than to own her signature.

Herself a believer in destiny and a true adventurer, the celestial blue sweater with the joyous pink clouds and yellow stars was delighted to be sent out with the dozens of old suits, colorful rayon and polyester track pants, jeans, Hawaiian shirts, t-shirts, pajamas, blouses, evening dresses and large number of polyester-blend machine knitted sweaters that found their way down to Chile as part of the White Linen Charity's maiden shipment.

Initially the sweater was too excited to settle down and she prickled the suits above and below in the bale. In a childish effort to calm down, she repeated a little tune, "You are my destiny, you share my reverie, you are my happiness, that's what you are..." The suits were annoyed and they complained about the disruptive antics of the young sweater. But there was nothing to be done, no one was in charge. In this anarchy everyone was in the same boat. Luckily for all concerned, it didn't take long before the rocking motion from dock to ship, and then from shore to shore, lulled the little sweater to sleep, and she cuddled in, content and quiet for the duration of the journey.

Outside of the fact that she sought a different life than the one she was born into, the little sweater never considered herself especially distinct from those around her, never attributed to herself qualities that she could not see in others.

But she knew she had been suffocating in the closet of her creator. She was the first to raise a silent cheer when she felt herself moving out. She could hardly contain her joy when, once her bale reached its destination and was dumped onto a dock and untied, she and the other garments sprung free, and she found herself looking up into the blinding desert sun of the northern Chilean clime and shortly thereafter, directly into the shining eyes of an ardent admirer named Columba.

Little sweaters are the last things to be in control of their own destiny. And as it turned out, rather than warming the body of a flesh and blood child in a cold climate, she found herself hugging the shoulders (and down to the toes) of a toddler-size plastic doll. As dolls go, this one was the type who was defined by her wardrobe. Clothes make the doll.

CHAPTER 49

COLUMBA

On the docks of Progreso, Columba was being held hostage by her worries. She kicked idly at the mound of old suits and dress shirts and faded blue jeans that sprawled before her on the stained depot floor. They mocked her. "Come on, pick through us if you will. You know where it'll get you, right? Exactly ten minutes further along. That's where. Or maybe you'd rather just lie down amongst us and, hey! How about we wrap our skinny legs around you and choke you to death?"

Perhaps their wrath was just what she needed. She stepped back to look down upon them. You dare to challenge me? She stiffened and took three steps, a hop, skip and a jump, and heaved herself onto the ugly, wretched denim, balancing briefly on her wide haunches before flopping sideways and sliding to the floor. She grabbed onto a few pairs and pulled them down with her. Hardly a dent. They were right – the pile still loomed. She sat, legs splayed, and sighed. Gertrudis, the enthusiastic new hire with rosy cheeks and darting black eyes was amused. Columba waved her off with a scowl and Gertrudis looked away.

Considering it best to avoid a run-in with Hawkeye tonight, Columba rallied herself and stepped over to a new mound, tossing stained t-shirts into the growing pile of rejects. It was still hours before the end of her shift. Worries about Anita, this crummy job, the constant scrounging, José's strange behavior, the entire bloody situation, all of it, bore into her until her lungs were being wrung out and left to dry. She was suffocating on the floor of the depot, the evening heat still beating through its metal ceilings. How could it be that these days she also felt suffocated in the wide-open spaces of the desert ridge? That even there she couldn't breathe? It was her life that suffocated her, her very existence was drying up. But today she still had tears. They brimmed and rolled down her cheeks. She kept her head lowered and swiped the tears away with the back of her hand. She was heartsick and was sure that she would die of it, and die soon.

It was at that moment, as she was poised at the edge of a pile of lumpy old suits surrounded by Hawaiian shirts, when she was about to drop backwards into an infinite gorge of self-pity that she came across an exquisite little sweater.

Squatting over it, she wiped her eyes and bent down, raising the little sweater just enough to touch it to her cheek before lowering it again quickly so that it was hers alone to see. There was no label on the sweater, it had been knitted by hand. The sweater was celestial blue with fluffy pink and white clouds that floated across the chest and rose up to the yellow stars on the shoulders, where the celestial blue blended into midnight blue. The clouds floated around on their woolly breeze to the sweater back. On the front, there were three little purple crocheted birds, and a bright red one that held a single green leaf in its beak. The birds glided along under the clouds on the left chest. Tiny buttons that looked like daisies, poked their yellow heads through perfectly stitched button holes at exact intervals up the right band. Yellow and red tulips bobbed out of wispy green fields that grew up around the entire base of the sweater.

Columba glanced over at Gertrudis, whose back was to her as she fumbled with a giant overcoat. Columba slyly scanned the floor for Hawkeye and saw him striding towards the end of the adjacent row, pumping along as though he was someone's hero. She watched as he held out his hands and examined his fingernails. Such vanity for an ordinary man. She turned her back to him and raised the little sweater to her face again. It was soft, almost as soft as alpaca wool. It smelled of baby powder. How, amidst all of these degenerate garments, was that possible? Even if Columba had a conscience, even if she was the most loyal, trustworthy worker on the planet, she would have been compelled to steal this sweater. She had no choice. She could not leave it. It was her destiny.

Hawkeye, over-playing the role of supervisor, was pointing a manicured finger at Sara, and with two loud claps of his hands, he commanded her attention. Columba didn't have to worry about him, Hawkeye was entirely self-absorbed. She pushed the little sweater into her skirt pocket, the deep one that she had cleverly stitched so that it hung between her legs. She tightened her thighs around it, feeling the bulge between her knees and then she leaned on it with both hands, patting the shape safely inside her skirt. She could feel the warmth of the beautiful little 'jersey,' as she would call it. The woolen treasure, energy sparking through its fibers, made her thighs tingle.

That night, after dancing past Hawkeye with a smile and a wink, she boarded the collector taxi for Santa Rita and, unable to wait until she got home to examine the jersey, she wriggled and shifted, pushed her hand deep inside her pocket and she pulled it out just enough to see the collar. It was like an innocent little bunny cautiously peering out from its hole, or perhaps more like a baby crowning. She carefully fingered the fine edges before gently forcing it back down into the safety of her makeshift womb. Columba had no doubt that this jersey had been created by a kindred spirit. She closed her eyes and whispered into the stale air in the back seat of the taxi, "Thank you," to whomever and wherever this creator might be.

José was asleep when she got home. She bent down to kiss him on the top of his head and he mumbled something before rolling over and tucking a notebook further under his pillow. She stood for a minute to watch him breathe. Her innocent son, her second miracle. She bent down to plant one more kiss before venturing off to draw the jersey out from between her thighs. She held it high, trying to see the details under the dusty, low wattage bulb that dangled at the end of a stiff black wire on the bedroom ceiling.

She examined the jersey inside and out, running her fingers across the rows, letting her hands drift into the soft tunnels of the sleeves and very gently adjusting the birds on the chest so she could see them from every angle. Why would a woman (surely it had to have been a woman) discard a sweater as precious as this? Even she, Columba, a poor uneducated mother who lived on the edge of a dry cliff in northern Chile, could see the value in such design, not to mention the craftsmanship. The little garment triggered indescribable delight. Did the woman who made this have so many beautiful sweaters that she could spare this one? What folly. But perhaps it was different in *Gringolandia*. Of course, they all had more than they could use and yet, she was told that they continued to buy more. Columba had heard they had so much money that they could shop all day, every day. It was a hobby. What should we do today? Oh, let's shop. An abundance of everything – both money and things to choose from. They just kept inventing and producing and consuming. Multitudes of many things, both useful and useless, disappeared off store shelves as fast as they could stock them. *Gringolandia* must be a glut of stuff, much unwanted, and that's why it was coming to Chile now. It made her dizzy and she shook her head. It was beyond comprehension.

She gently laid out the sweater on the bed, unfolding the sleeves so she could appreciate it in its fullness. Such a small chest, such a little opening for the neck, and such short little sleeves. Yet she felt they were more than capable of embracing the whole world.

She slowly undressed and tiptoed away, not wanting to disturb the jersey, laying there so brave and vulnerable. It glowed with a warm yellow aura and all the other garments in the room faded into their forgettable pasts. Columba would shower, wash her hair, scrub her hands and face. One must be worthy of laying down with something so exquisite.

Refreshed, she snuggled up and folded one of the sleeves across her cheek, the fine fibers, like small fingers caressing her nose. She was enraptured by its softness and that lingering scent of baby powder that any mother anywhere would recognize. She cried for Anita, turning her face so as not to offend the little jersey, which, like an innocent child was stretching out her little sleeve to embrace her, to quell a pain that she could not comprehend. When Columba had no more tears to cry, she turned back towards the jersey, and adjusted the sleeve so it lay lightly over her shoulder.

She whispered, "Gracias," and for the first time in months, the darkness of her room was merciful. She whispered, "Thank you," and to the sweater, "You won't slip away, not like Anita."

CHAPTER 50
JOSÉ

It's true you must be wary of evil creatures, and it's true that some are indistinguishable from the gentle, well-meaning types. These crafty souls come to you in the guise of goodness, gaining your trust and love, nurturing and ripening you up before they devour your innocence. This is the most egregious sin of all.

It was José who discovered the truth about Father Cortés. Or at least it was José who dared to question after he read and re-read Anita's notebook, trying to make sense of the entries. It was a sort of diary and he had no business between its covers. But it wasn't locked, was it? Not like a proper, private diary. Anyway, Anita was gone, she'd left it behind. Besides, it held clues. And they all pointed to The Most Pure Blood of Jesus, specifically to Father Cortés.

The most recent entries were short, incomplete, sort of cryptic, as though Anita was unable to bring herself to finish a thought or perhaps she needed to push it away. But the first pages of her diary (he assumed they went in chronological order, making these the earliest entries) expounded the qualities of Father Cortés. "He is so knowledgeable and just. He understands things that us kids question, knows what we are searching for. He says that we are all products of our parents but we are children of God. Lucia agrees that Father is the coolest." The diary focused almost exclusively on events surrounding the catechism or even just the teachings that she found most satisfying. "Jesus talked in parables." She wrote one day. Two exclamation marks. Nothing more.

He wondered, as he slowly turned the pages, whether Anita deliberately stuffed the little book into her pillow case, like maybe she wanted him or Columba to discover what had been going on – both inside, and outside of her head. If not, then why didn't she take it or burn it? He pictured her huddled in the bathroom, notebook on her lap, scribbling, thinking about – or trying not to think about – things she couldn't bring herself to say aloud. Maybe if they found out by accident, she would not be guilty of breaking her vow of silence. "Some Holy Orders vow never to speak…." She had written at the top of one page and she had ripped off the bottom. He imagined her fingers tense as she ground her pen into other pages that were heavily scribbled.

Several pages had been violently separated from the binding. He cringed and felt a little nauseous for a reason he could not explain.

José pondered over the notes, some of the words indecipherable. Anita's last dozen or so pages were full of whole lines that had been crossed out. Hard 'X's cutting through the paper. He found himself filling in the blanks.

"Father wants me to help him up at shanty town again. I know what that means. But how can I say no?"

"Father said I need to be grateful for the gifts God gave me, for the special qualities, for my youth and beauty."

"Father and I have shared the secret for too long. I don't want..."

"I tried to tell Lucia but I couldn't. I know she saw me and Father the other day."

"Why does God want this for me?"

"Does God really want this?"

"Is God really here?"

The only place she mentioned Columba was on one of the last pages, "Mom is happy and it's all her fault anyway. I hate her for it." He didn't see his name anywhere but maybe she had ripped it out.

Half a century ago, the Spanish had constructed their church amidst some palms at the foot of the Andes. These same mountains and these same palms had witnessed events that went beyond pastoral tradition, righteousness and humility. The powers-that-be baptized the building The Most Pure Blood of Jesus Church, an illustrious name that, as it turned out, was too ambitious to live up to. Back then, the Spanish imported their priests to predicate. They installed their icons for worship, and gripped the people with their torment-ed Savior who understood their plight and who bled with them and for them. And the people became enchanted by the priests' religion and they adopted it as their own. Ignorant of the Church's corruption, if anyone even suspected something was not right with the Church, the followers blamed themselves because they were just lowly sinners, and what did they know? Today most don't want to be reminded of the cruelties that rained down from on high. Instead they choose to recall the acts of kindness of the humble priests on the front lines. Their good deeds were like fertilizer, growing the faith and nur-turing hope in the pueblo. The Church hierarchy harvested the fruits of their labors and made it possible for Progreso's clergy of today to live in comfort and security.

Perhaps the centuries of arrogance distanced the Church from the very people the priests in the upper echelons pretended to live amongst, perhaps they simply felt empowered by their privileged status as the peoples' confessors, perhaps it was a simple weakness of character amidst an unnatural culture of celibacy, but probably it was all of the aforementioned. And their insidious crimes became institutionalized and they were offered impunity, fostering a vile network that silently approved acts of indecency and violence against innocent members of their flock. All the while, the well-nourished faces of the priests and bishops smiled sweetly over their struggling and starving little lambs, shepherding them in with arms that were raised in loving, Jesus-like gestures at Sunday mass and during Wednesday afternoon catechisms, which were attended by delicious young innocents with so much potential.

José may have been innocent but he wasn't naive and he wasn't blind and he knew Anita was one of the abused. And there were others. There was no shortage of rumors but there were no clear paths to confirmation of these things, and certainly none leading to responsibility and abolition.

He heard about how Miguel, tortured by it, unable to put it right, had died.

Miguel had been one of the school's most esteemed student political leaders, an avid member of the debate team and president of the school history club. A little more than half way through the year, he resigned from extracurricular activities, he fell silent in class and he removed himself from groups at lunch time, declining invitations and preferring to brood in the far corner of the yard. Up to then Miguel had been a fervent acolyte at The Most Pure Blood of Jesus. Miguel showed so much promise that the local bishop took him under his wing. Other young teenaged boys either looked up to Miguel or envied him for his intelligence, humanity and favored position. Thus, it was not surprising to hear some of them spreading rumors about Miguel and what had led to his unexpected death.

One morning, Miguel's father paid a visit to the school director. He was barely able to walk in on his own two legs, so weak was he from the pain of his son's sudden, tragic passing. Miguel, always the good son, had offered to clean his father's prized handgun, an heirloom from his own father. Miguel's father had trained him well in the care and handling of the pistol but something had gone terribly, terribly wrong that day. They found Miguel with a shot to the head, his body slumped against the far wall of their patio.

Marco whispered to other boys about Miguel's suicide and at first José disregarded it as jealousy because Marco used to discredit Miguel at any opportunity. But then the whispers grew like mushrooms and stories multiplied about other boys who had attended The Pure Blood of Jesus. The name of the bishop came up more than once in this dark cultivation. Stories blew around like spores, and landed on ready ears. It's true that several of the bishop's young disciples had, over the years, dropped out of school never to be seen again, some apparently moving to Santiago where they ended up in trouble with the law and yet others who had moved away to study at a seminary. Miguel had been a favorite disciple of the bishop for several years and Marco had, at first spread nasty rumors about how Miguel enjoyed the lurid attention of the bishop and how they had participated in gay orgies. When he was found shot in the head, Marco changed the end of his story but the root remained the same – Miguel just couldn't endure the abuse and inner torture of not being able to say No.

Other stories grew – not only about the bishop, who had an appetite for boys, but also about Father Cortés who, word had it, was attracted to girls. He liked the more developed ones, they said, girls with ripe breasts, long legs and deep, innocent eyes. He liked intelligent ones. These details were not missed by students who were vigilant, especially envious ones, who for their own purposes (perhaps only to discredit someone) were eager to spread the gossip.

The rumors were transmitted in excited whispers from a set of moving lips and received by a set of ears that piqued in delighted disgust. And when the whispering paused for a moment, both sets of eyes were wide, both mouths agape in horror. Then they turned their heads and looked for someone else to whisper to.

Eventually Anita's name appeared like bait on a fishing line, and José got hooked and was reeled in. He tried to follow the line to its source but it was hopelessly entangled, one story with another and then another. Although every story diverged, each one had a common ending and it had to do with Father Cortés and teenaged girls.

CHAPTER 51

GAVIN

Gavin decided to play a risky hand. The White Linen Charity was based in Grant Falls and after considering the options, in spite of the instructions on the anonymous note, he decided to sell the sweaters in Grant Falls. He knew there would be no argument from Irma, even if she still struggled with her conscience. Besides, Gavin had his own reasons for wanting to sell them in Grant Falls rather than shipping them to Chile – number one, the profit he'd make on just five of the sweaters was about equal to the return he'd get for exporting half a bale of them; number two, he liked – correction, he was enamored of – the sweaters and number three, he could smell a new business opportunity. It wasn't clear yet what, but something.

The only other option was to sell them from Stan's or elsewhere in Burgeon. Was Burgeon still considered local? He could argue that it was. So what if he opened a section for toddlers and children in Funky Town, perhaps just temporarily to promote the sweaters? There was no hurry. He could let them sit for a few months while he developed promotions. The idea of some delay eased the little bit of conscience that had not already been smothered by the prospect of the sweaters. The hard truth was that parents of little darlings would not be drawn to a toddlers' section of Funky Town, with all of its chains and piercings. Funky Town wouldn't be on their radar for several years to come, probably too soon for their liking, even though it would be inevitable once their little innocents came of age.

The other drawback was that Burgeon had a small population and these sweaters needed – no, they deserved – a wider reach. He would need to sell them from Grant Falls.

Then he hit on the idea of an independent, seasonal store – a pop up – for toddlers and young children. It wouldn't require a large investment – a fall and winter shop that he could get on a short-term lease. He figured that if he opened and closed the shop in time, the sweaters would probably sell before the donor noticed that the shop had even existed. He could plan for the Christmas season.

Mark was the one who solved the location problem. "A mom 'n pop shoe repair shop shut down in Grant Falls last month. I think the old man died. It's a really narrow space, not much good for retail, really. Not much frontage. But guess where it is? Right on the main street. I heard the owner is desperate to rent the space. So you're in a good position."

Gavin finessed a short lease, only four months (unheard of according to Mark, who gave him the high-five). It was across the street from a place called 'Spin a Yarn.' And this, he proclaimed to Mark, was called destiny, kismet, providence. It was perfect in every way. In spite of the note requesting no local sales, Gavin was determined that the sweaters were destined for Grant Falls, and he was sure that he was really doing them all a favor, whomever the donors were.

His assumption was that the sweaters had come from a cottage industry that had gone belly up. Or perhaps the owner had died, and her children, not knowing what to do with the merchandise, were simply anxious to clean up the place and sell the estate. He even pictured a funeral and a wake attended by doleful mourners, mostly grey-haired ladies with sad, heavy eyes, all draped in black woolen shawls with butterfly pins, all of them sympathetically supporting a grieving son who wore a striped grey and black woolen vest over his sunken chest and fallen shoulders. It was probably just that the son couldn't bare to have the sweaters as reminders. Nothing more than that. Gavin convinced himself he was satisfied with this scenario.

He erected a sign that said "Little Imps. Sweaters of the World. Available until December 24th or until Stock Lasts."

He ordered some labels to give the sweaters credibility, which, at the same time, made him appear to be their creator, becoming, in this act, something of a god. He hired Cindi, a high-performing yuppie type with a supply of 'grandé' home-made granola cookies, who said, between bites, that she was looking for something short term. Her full name was Cindi Crawford. Unfortunate coincidence, she admitted with a snort. More kismet and providence. Cindi took initiative (talking up the sweaters to her friends, adjusting window displays, loitering at the door of the shop charming passersby with her granola happiness) and the sweaters almost flew out the door. The results were spectacular. They sold everything well before mid-December, and Gavin let Cindi take her time dismantling little props and she ended up tootling around the place until Christmas Eve, reading, dusting and eating cookies.

Even though Cindi had posted a sign that said the Little Imps stock was all sold out, hopeful mothers popped by anyway, "Surely you must have one tucked away in the back somewhere. I'm willing to pay the price. Everyone in Suzy's kindergarten class has one. Apparently, I found out about them too late." Finally, after Cindi convinced them she was telling the truth. "I know. I feel your pain. But these things are like cabbage patch dolls. Once word got out, they were gone." Adding with a toothy smile, "And we're the exclusive distributors."

Gavin fell into a mid-grade depression when they ran out of Little Imps sweaters. It was either that, or the Christmas blues. Since Stan died but probably more accurately, since his Mom died, Christmas was a dreaded season. He knew he wasn't the only one who felt that way. But there was no escape. To make things worse, Mark was a huge fan of Christmas, and he competed with himself from one year to the next. Stan's had the sleigh bells and all the baubles in the front window, Christmas muzak floated around, red and green ribbons and bows tied around empty boxes that sat atop floor racks, snowflakes hung from the ceiling, golden lights twinkled amidst garlands around the windows. Mark even spritzed the counter area with cinnamon and pine spray. He insisted that the staff at Stan's wear an elf hat because Stan, himself used to wear one every year. Gavin might have appeared to be jolly but he never felt jolly. He was numb to the whole Christmas buzz. Except, of course, for the sales it produced.

And now, after the swift appearance and disappearance of the angel sweaters as Irma called them, and the impending closure of the Little Imps shop in Grant Falls, everything in Burgeon felt ordinary – flat, colorless, and utterly deadpan. Sure, Stan's and Funky Town purred through their seasonal success, as they had last year. But maybe that was the problem. In comparison, the amazing product and immediate success of Little Imps once again reminded him of the monotony of the day-to-day of Stan's and Funky town. Little Imps was like flying the Concord while Stan's and Funky Town was a lot like an Air Canada flight over the prairies. It's not that he took the stores for granted. No, he knew what it took to keep them greased and humming. The problem was that it was no longer challenging. He wanted to build something else. Was this a sickness he had – a compulsion for business start-ups? Was there a name for it? No matter.

He was reluctant to surrender the Little Imps shop space. He struggled when it came close to December 31, the date he was scheduled to return the keys to the owner.

That morning he woke up with a solution. It must have come to him in a dream without images – just a feeling of certainty. The kind of certainty that only comes to you once, maybe twice in a lifetime, if you're lucky.

"I'm using it for promotional purposes," he told Mark. "It'll be a teaser space. We'll display the best samples from Funky Town and Stan's. If we do it right, we'll attract shoppers to Burgeon from Grant Falls instead of the other way around."

The space was cheap and it was a write-off. And the best thing was that it worked. He also negotiated co-op dollars from the town of Burgeon, got the Chamber of Commerce on board, hung posters and set up brochure racks by the front door. From there, he saw an opportunity to print postcard ads and he rented rack space for Burgeon restaurants, 'the region's best kept gourmet hideaways,' even if it wasn't true. Ernie's Pool Hall even got in on the action, attracting some of Grant Falls' teenaged crowd who wanted to escape town for a night. Burgeon's small tourist industry, which normally consisted of a few fishing lodges and two other companies who competed for kayak rentals in the summer and cross-country ski and ski-doo rentals during the winter, began to see new opportunities.

"That Gavin, what a guy. Always thinking of something to make a buck." He accepted the nickname Midas without a grudge.

CHAPTER 52

IRENE

Wrapped in her snagged and stained dusty pink robe, Irene had installed herself in the armchair by the fireplace. She and the China rose damask chair were an ominous union of upholstered bodies – modular furniture that no one dared modify.

For several months, she had been fiercely knitting the mounds of wool and other yarns that she had stashed in the cedar-lined storage room downstairs. She did it defiantly, right out there in the open, right under Chuck's big nose. Chuck had either never considered her old wool stash a threat or else he hadn't known about it. Probably he thought she had used it all. She had had to move it downstairs eons ago to make space for the sweaters. With a pay-check every two weeks, she had managed to buy and stash wool far faster than she could knit it. Not that she had planned to do anything with it back then. She had simply wanted it and now she was glad for that.

Stupid, heartless Chuck and clueless Amber hadn't stolen her unfinished self, the self still very much in progress, the deep, secret self, the self that was still rolled into balls. Those detestable ignorant thieves, in their naive underestimation, had failed to steal her potential. She laughed aloud and the sound was nasty.

Her sweaters rebelled. They became bolder, with broad, bright stripes ripping across the chests and clawing their way over the shoulders and slithering down the backs, pompoms attached to sweater bottoms swaying belligerently whenever she lifted them up and turned them around. She made them thick, she made them tough. There was outrageous polyester-blend padding on the shoulders and elbows, some with oblong patches stretching across the left chest, like jagged clown smiles running across the zippered front with wool like matted hair fringing the collars.

She became a mother bear who refused to leave her chair-den. She warned Chuck off with cold stares and snarls, her eyes enlarged and enraged, her needles like sharp claws at the ready, preparing to end his life should he dare to venture, should he screw up the courage to creep or crawl towards her, should one of his bony, thinly-socked toes so much as brush the living room carpet, should he even be so bold as to utter a sound from those thin, quivering lips, should he even dare to attempt to meet her eye.

He had wanted to change her life – their life. Well, it was changed all right. Chuck always got what he wanted.

Irene fell asleep in the chair every night with half-finished sweaters on her lap, needles dangling onto the floor at the ends of her arms, yarn grinning up at her from the foot of the chair, from inside the agape and yawning basket mouths. She was the queen bee, the baskets were her drones. All she had to do was look at them and they knew what she wanted. She tiptoed between them after Chuck had gone to work or when he went out again in the evening to have a beer with the poor sods who had to listen to him go on and on about his day at the store. Half of them probably thought he was single or gay because, of course, he never mentioned a wife. Why would he?

She left her modular throne only to take care of her 'necessities', things like food, bathroom, and on rare occasions, a shower and change of clothes. She spoke to the sweaters in the corner and to the ones that covered the sofa and chair. The new ones were hung on the living room window curtain rod, inside the drapes, which were always drawn. The room was always in darkness, like a womb, protecting whatever was growing in there. Like developing cells, the 'newborns', as she called them, replaced the sweaters on the curtain rod. She removed the ones from the rod and folded them neatly along the sofa. She cooed to them, fussed over them, caressed them. She sang to them and laughed with them, her voice lilting and warbling.

The new sweaters were not newborn size but had grown as a child grows with the years. They were preserved in order – toddlers came before young children and those ones came before school age children, and they were spreading beyond the furniture and into the corners of the room.

This went on for exactly thirteen months. At that point, she ran out of wool and crept into Chuck's room to steal his sweaters and his scarves and mittens. She unraveled them (her childhood pastime had not been for nothing), she gave them a new life and continued her cloistered existence.

CHAPTER 53
JOSÉ

At what point in his life does a boy become wise to the world? Well, sometimes never. But José is not a coddled child, and he is perceptive and bold. The way he sees it, people either push on with their lives or they find themselves in a ditch, covered with wishful thinking.

When José returned home from The Black Cat, he was several years wiser.

His plan had been to confront Anita. She owed him an explanation as much as she owed one to their Mom. He and Anita had shared hundreds of secrets over the years, secrets that their Mom would never discover. Most of the secrets were kids' stuff and of no consequence (jumping from the roof onto piles of sand when the house had been under construction, stealing coins to buy ice cream, stealing sunglasses, sneaking out to meet a girl or a boy with a bad reputation) but just the same, secrets were secrets and part of their bond. Did Anita plan to go through life denying their sacred trust, having suddenly reduced its value to nothing? Ignoring him? Whatever her reason for abandoning Columba, she had no reason to desert him too. He felt righteous and bitter.

As it turned out, Marcelo was much older, much bigger and stronger and probably much more bitter than was José. And if José thought that being righteous meant that the wind would always be at his back, the sun would always shine on his face and he'd get whatever he set out to get, he would soon discover just how naïve he really was.

José did his best to amble casually into The Black Cat like any other patron. He chose a table at the back, ordered a Coca-Cola and looked around. The rafters were yellowed with smoke and thick cobwebs hung down from exposed beams. Grimy electrical cords drooped where they had escaped their flimsy staples and José had to duck to avoid some of them. Paint had peeled and several autographed photos of washed-up celebrities dangled at angles behind smudged glass on the far wall. The place was neglected, it had succumbed to decay, its better days having been about five decades ago. It survived because it was on a corner, it was established and it was cheap.

The bar began to fill with people and noise. José didn't recognize anyone.

Unlike at night, when it was a lair for dubious characters from the docks, on weekday afternoons, it was a hangout for university students, most of them modern-day Bohemians. There was also a small group of toughs – probably small-time drug dealers – who had crawled up from the beach just in time for the university traffic. The patrons were rowdy, and in between arguing over politics and badgering each other to cough up some coins for the next round, they barked orders at the bartender. José was not inclined to get involved in politics but their conversation was alluring (if not very enlightening) and he was drawn in. A diversion while he hung around waiting for Anita.

"This government is shit. What do the ministers know about the middle class, let alone the lower class? They all pretend to have been in our shoes just for a few votes but when it comes down to it, they can't relate and don't care."

"I don't wanna engage in such pedestrian topics."

"Who are you calling pedestrian? Just because I'm stating a basic fact."

"Yeah, well we all know the basic facts. It's all about maintaining power so they can continue to line their pockets. You have to do better than that."

"So what about the new pensions reform bill?"

"Don't get me started. What about the new labor reform bill?"

"Is anyone here planning to run for office? If so, leave now!"

There was a roar of laughter and thumping on tables.

"Hey, but speaking of politics, did anyone hear about the bishop?"

"Oh, come on. That's too easy. Did someone say something about lining pockets?"

"No, but hey. I'm serious here." There was silence as a young clean-shaven man who, with his open-collared pinstriped shirt, looked more like a stock broker than a student, raised his hand for attention. "They're talking about investigating our bishop."

"Where did you hear that?"

"I have a cousin who works for the office of the prosecutor. He let it slip last weekend at a barbecue."

"Okay, well, that's not hard to believe, is it? Did any of you happen to attend Father Cortés's after school catechism classes? Come on… someone here must've gone."

"Who'd want to admit that? It's like admitting you're part of the sex club."

Another eruption of laughter and table thumping.

"But he's only after the young plump chicks. The bishop likes boys."

"Yeah, well a pedophile is a pedophile is a pedophile."

"You got that right."

José's ears piqued at Father Cortés's name and he was tempted to go over and try to have a private conversation with pinstripe shirt but he was too intimidated by the group. A beer might give him courage but he had no more money. And anyway, they changed the subject and started talking about the guest lecturer in a law class and he lost interest.

It was getting late. Columba would have expected him to have prepared and eaten something for dinner and if he wanted to avoid the inquisition, he'd need to catch the next microbus up the hill. He made a move to slink out of the bar but stopped and slowly back-tracked when he saw Anita walk in, followed by a tall guy with a bandana and black curly hair. Together they made their way towards the bar and José watched as the tall guy unlatched the gate at the end and pushed Anita in front of him. She turned and looked up into his face with an expression that was partly adoring and partly something that José couldn't interpret. Anita's face was puffy and she probably wanted to look older than she was. He felt for her. Anita wasn't tough, all that dark eye makeup and purple lipstick was an attempt to look hard. If she thought her new look served as armor, she would soon find out that it was not impenetrable. Her hair was sleek and hung loosely down her back. Front fringes separated in strands across her forehead and partially covered her eyes like a frayed curtain. She wore a tight translucent t-shirt and a mini skirt. Oddly, it looked like she had gained some weight. How could she even eat in this place? Her high leather boots had long fringes at the top that swooshed around her legs like dozens of soft whips.

When the big guy went into the back room, José sidled up to the bar and whistled softly to get her attention. Anita swung her hips to the end of the bar and stopped short when she recognized José.

"Get out of here. Now!" She pointed a hand with fingernails that glittered black and blue, towards the door and then quickly glanced back to see if the big guy was returning. "Get out before Marcelo comes back." Her eyes were big and they glistened. José thought it was fear but he couldn't be certain.

She blinked hard as tears threatened to brim over and streak through the black makeup around her eyes. She turned away and busied herself rinsing glasses. Her hands were trembling. Without looking at him, she waved him off discreetly with one hand.

Marcelo suddenly strode in from the back room and he leaned into Anita from behind, nuzzling her neck. He pushed her tight to the counter, his hips behind hers, and whispered something, laughed and grabbed her buttocks before looking up to see José glaring at him.

"What are you looking at? You're too interested in my little woman, here."

"That's because she's my sister." José blurted out the words, bit his tongue too late.

Marcelo glanced down at Anita and stepped towards José. He leaned into the bar and grabbed José by the collar, pulling him so close that their noses almost touched. His whisper was harsh, his breath smelled like stale whiskey. "You're too young to be in here, little brother. I suggest you mind your own business and leave before you get yourself into trouble." He shook José a few times to rattle him but José spoke up, his voice cracking.

"I want to talk to my sister."

"Well, your sister doesn't want to talk to you. Especially not on my time." He turned to Anita. "Right, big sister?"

She nodded.

"She has something she needs to say to me." José knew he wouldn't be able to stand his ground against this guy.

"Do you, big sister? Do you have something to say to this little piss-ass?" He was smirking at her as he rattled José again.

"No, Marcelo. We don't have anything to say to each other." She refused to look at José.

"Well, then little brother. It's time for you to go." He grabbed José by the hair. "Or do you want to stay here all night?" He forced his face into the bar and held him there with his cheek flattened into the old wood.

José bit into the varnish, and he could taste the splinters. Marcelo held him down for a few seconds longer. Then he was suddenly around the other side of the bar, pulling José up by his ear. He hauled him to the door, and shoved him with such force that José stumbled and fell across the sidewalk.

"Tell that bitch of a mother to leave us alone too. This is the only warning you'll get."

José collapsed into the back of a microbus and he trembled all the way home. Once there, he managed to make a cheese sandwich and tea but he couldn't bring himself to eat. He sat there, mouth hanging open, staring down at the hole in the toe of the running shoe on his right foot. He wished he could have raised it high enough to kick the bastard in the teeth. But he couldn't. He was helpless. When it came to fighting, he was nothing but a shallow, weak, waste of skin. Finally, he dumped the tea and hid the sandwich under his pillow and climbed under his blankets only minutes before he heard Columba turn the key in the lock.

CHAPTER 54

GAVIN

Surely, Gavin was not born to be a fashion guru, nor was he meant to be wise to the ways of people from Sub-Saharan Africa. But look where he finds himself now. There are times when he sees his reflection as he passes a shop window and he questions the identity of the confident man in the latest Dockers and the chic sophomore sweater who promenades down the sidewalk and looks back at himself with a debonair smile.

Gavin was not the kind of guy to let a little guilt ruin his plans. No, sir, he did something about it. He moved on. He crushed guilt like a bug into dirt, leaving nothing but the shadow of his heel to mark a greasy little tomb. With time, the note that was left with the sweaters from heaven became a thing of the past. No one approached The White Linen Charity with a complaint or wrote a letter to the editor (Irma checked every edition). So, he didn't regret selling the sweaters in Grant Falls. No, not one bit. The only thing he did regret was not having more of them because they had sold like hotcakes.

The sweaters and the absence of, instigated a renewed interest in developing the White Linen Charity. Mostly he focused on the business end but in order not to ruin a good thing, he carefully managed the training and development of language skills, meeting and exceeding government targets even if it meant doctoring the stats (just a bit, rationalizing that some government goals were unrealistic) to demonstrate success, and this resulted in extended contracts and continued wage subsidies. In spite of that, there was no doubt about Gavin treating his newly arrived employees well. Open to learning from foreign points of view and acknowledging transferrable skills, he could honestly say that he did well by them.

And they did well by him. If one of the newcomers knew how to cut corners, Gavin was not above learning from him, picking up from the practical, foreign mentality, spiking the day with a new twist. If someone dared try to take advantage of him, he figured that out too. Any way you looked at it, there was no discrimination in his shop, he could say that for sure. No cheating on hours or sick days. No stealing from the bales (Irma did a pretty good job of keeping that in check). If a newcomer had him pegged as soft, Gavin was also swift to correct that impression.

Irma was his poster girl, a brilliant success story, which he told and retold at Chamber of Commerce and Rotary Club meetings and documented in government reports. He even managed to include her story as a human-interest piece in the local paper, a clipping from which he hung on a bulletin board just inside the front door.

Gavin attended a couple of seminars on garment recycling but he found practice and experience to be more valuable. Besides, he figured that his years as a buyer and a merchant gave him a leg up and that he was well ahead of the curve.

Entrenched in the cycle of garment consumption, which was growing steadily, the shops and the recycling business meant that he profited at both ends of the fashion stream. Production and distribution of new, low-cost garments from Asia fed the hungry North American markets. Garments disappeared off the shelves of Stan's and Funky Town and later they reappeared in the fibreglass bins of the White Linen Charity. He sold lots of stuff twice but he didn't brag about it.

Gavin continued to be the man for every occasion. He was the chameleon of high fashion and the altruistic master of training and recycling. He was sustainable energy. He was a local icon.

Perhaps his success could be attributed to a deliberate and carefully honed reputation but perhaps it was the case that he was sufficiently awake enough to take advantage of things that fell at his feet. In the end, it all stacked up to the same thing.

It was either because of his reputation (which was the story they would tell him) or it was just another lucky day but either way, it was the sudden appearance of a couple of old hippies that helped advance Gavin even further along his Midas trajectory.

CHAPTER 55

CHUCK

For the invasion of her soul, for the violation to her core, she was making him pay.

The living room was now half-filled with beautiful sweaters, and they were in Chuck's face. "There," Irene was saying to him (without actually speaking to him), "You don't want sweaters packed into my rooms? Okay, then here, let's display them right out here in the open, right under your nose. ...And you wouldn't dare!"

Chuck's ears became hypersensitive, especially at night. He tried everything to drown out the sound of the clicking needles. They bore into his brain – she might as well have been knitting the hair in his ears. He wore ear plugs but he could hear the needles anyway, their constant ticking and tacking. And then there was the disgusting gurgling sound from Irene's throat. It wasn't like a nice gurgle, not like the purring of a cat or the lilting coo of a dove but rather the rising up of deep guttural sounds interspersed with low voice tones. What happened to her lovely singing voice? Anyway, the ear plugs prodded at him, didn't let him rest. And maybe it wasn't his ears at all. Maybe he was just going crazy. He tried Sleep-eze. But he woke up with a grogginess that stayed with him until noon. So he tossed out the Sleep-eze. How about some soothing, new-age music, coupled with a self-hypnosis technique delivered via a cassette tape he'd borrowed from the library? Nothing, zip, nada. Before long, he turned into a walking zombie.

Therefore, he felt compelled to bring it all to an end. Again. But this time it was for his own sanity and, he told himself, Irene's too. He reminded himself of the inventory he'd set up and then destroyed along with her sweaters. That had pained him.

Back then, he'd taken his inventory records to the store and incinerated them, hoping it would destroy the dirty deed associated with them. He stood over the old barrel at the back of the store, smoke rising up from the grill, cutting a grey vapor grid into the sky. Mea culpa, mea culpa, mea maxima culpa. But the guilt dug in its heels. He tried to wrestle it to the ground and stomp on it. But he was weak.

Back then, the day before he and Amber and Jocelyn and old man McArthur had raided Irene's rooms and gathered the sweaters that were destined for the White Linen Charity, he had pulled out his inventory books and scanned the numbers. He had considered including the inventory with the donation. It would have been a thoughtful add-on, a sign for whomever would receive the gifts that this categorizing and accounting of sweaters had been an extremely arduous task, to say nothing of the conception and production of the sweaters themselves. Including the inventory would have made it a joint gift from him and his wife, who sadly, had fallen ill. It would have been their polite request to please donate the sweaters wisely, to children who truly deserved and would appreciate them. But at the last minute he repented because no one would truly understand the heartache and sacrifices that had gone into the making of the inventory (not to mention what he could not begin to fathom – Irene's end of things). So he burned the books. The guilt remained, though.

These days, rather than an inventory (because Irene had made it impossible to produce one), he became obsessed by his pages of lists. They were lists of all of the positives and negatives of Irene knitting their lives into oblivion. Obviously, it weighed heavily on the negative side. After several months of agonizing over the decision, knowing all along what the answer was going to be but tormented by the numerous possible scenarios that would result, he decided he needed to take action. Again. After all, he had to live too. He was dying here. And whether Irene knew it or not, she was also dying, sinking further into her sweater fantasy world. He had no choice but to save them both.

He enlisted the sisters and old man McArthur once more. "It'll be the last time, I promise." He had to beg them, especially the old man. He finally bribed him with $500, told him to use the money to take his wife away for a night somewhere, give her something she deserved for a change, show her how much he loved her. "Spend the money however you want but please, first just do this for me... and for Irene."

After the money changed hands, the plot was designed and carried out.

Irene had always preferred her tea extra sweet and Chuck had noticed that as the years passed, she was making it increasingly sweeter and lately she dumped no less than four big teaspoons full of sugar into her mug and stirred, clinking annoyingly against the porcelain edges for up to a full minute before she finally slurped some back and swallowed so loudly he could hear her in the garage. The most obvious (to him, at least) and least harmful way to get Irene out of the way for a few hours would be to put her to sleep.

So Chuck dusted the sugar bowl with crushed sleeping pills. He had obtained them on the grounds of severe anxiety and insomnia. And it wasn't a pretext because the situation was real enough. He did his research and he knew how much medication to add to the amount of sugar in the bowl and how it would knock her out for hours but not kill her. God knows sometimes he wanted her to die just so he could get some sleep. But no, deep down, he still loved her and he wanted to protect her, even if it was against herself.

He thought he'd given up on her a long time ago – given up on them. But one day a couple of weeks ago, he realized that he still lived for the day when things would change. It was all the fault of the little bell over the door at the store. Every time it jingled, he looked up with anxious anticipation. But then, always disappointed, he returned his attention to the work at hand. Why should he feel disappointed when a customer came in? He did some self-talk. 'You should be happy to have the opportunity to serve this person. To sell them something, to keep this business making money. Offer them more. Up-sell them. Smile.' The disappointment at the end of each bell had nothing to do with customers. No, it was because he wished it was Irene who was walking in, even if it meant she was late for work. He remembered how he used to upbraid her for her tardiness. Now, he would be grateful for her to walk in at any time, not matter how late. Just to have her back.

Once he recognized the hope that he still so foolishly and helplessly harbored, he couldn't shake it. He was like a Pavlov puppy. Although he knew better, an idiotic, happy bubble filled his throat each time the bell over the door sang out its hopeful ring.

Now, finally, if he wasn't going to drive himself crazy, he'd have to make a move, one last desperate attempt to set things right. He'd have to find a way to reawaken his former Irene, his young butterfly, the one who had flitted across meadows and danced through tall flowers and sang up at the sky and reached for, and smiled at the moon, the one who had turned to him and charmed him with her eyes, the eyes that reflected the stars, the gleeful ones that sometimes flickered with humor. While there was, he told himself, the tiniest glimmer of hope, he had to act.

Once again, the plan was realized on a Sunday. It was a warm summer morning when the streets were quiet, and after Irene had drained her second mug of tea (she always had two cups of tea).

It didn't take long before she nodded off in the armchair. Her head fell back and she snored lightly as the sweaters were stolen out from under her nose. The family of thieves hushed each other as they reached up and quietly removed sweaters from hangers, carried out armful upon armful of the beautiful garments and tiptoed out to drop them into the plastic bale wrap that was spread out in the garage. At one point, Irene jerked and gasped, and her lip curled in a spasm, her left leg jerking out from the knee, and it sent Amber and Jocelyn running to huddle around the corner in the foyer. But her body relaxed again, and she slumped deeper into the chair, slumbering long after they finished clearing everything out.

After the job was done, all sweaters removed, the McArthurs piled into the truck and left. The White Linen Charity's drop-off point was still around the back of the building. It was still always open, although not attended on Sundays. There was a new sign that said, "Thank you for your generous donation" and a bit smaller below, "Thank you for considering the environment." They forced the plastic bundles through an over-sized trap door that resembled a gaping mouth, and its wide throat swallowed the gifts down into its bin.

Meanwhile, Chuck edged up to Irene and gently touched the pulse on her throat. He leaned in to feel her breath on his cheek. It was the first time in almost two years that he had gotten this close. He collapsed on his knees at her side, and buried his face in her lap. Her head back, she slumbered, short gentle breaths reminding him of how she used to sleep so peacefully at his side.

He sobbed, his bony shoulders heaving like those of a small child. His knees were weak and he was slow to get back up. He tenderly kissed her twice on each cheek. Had he really had a choice? Had Irene had a choice? He wiped his brow with his sleeve, swallowed his tears and went to the kitchen. He double-checked the food in the fridge. Fresh milk? Check. Yoghurt? Check. Freezer full of microwave dinners? Check. Enough fresh and frozen vegetables? Check. What about canned goods? All in order. She'd be okay. He headed straight down the hall and into his bedroom to pack a couple of bags and he sneaked out – like the bad boy he was.

When Irene awoke in the morning, Chuck was gone and the living room was empty. She must be a dreaming. This had to be a nightmare. Or she had died and this was hell. She blinked a hundred times and rubbed her eyes. She raised herself to standing in front of the chair but she couldn't take a step forward. She stood there for several minutes just plucking at her eyelids because she didn't know what else to do. The scene in front of her was blurred but no matter. Blurred or not, the room was still empty. She pulled her hair until her eyes watered. She patted the chair because, surely she must be blind, then turned and plunged her hands into the empty baskets, feeling for wool or sweaters, for anything. But it was all gone. Everything was gone. Chuck was gone. She'd been abandoned.

She didn't know how long she turned circles in the living room before she began to rage around the house, slamming doors, stomping up and down the basement stairs, screaming at the top of her lungs. Her throat hurt, her eyes burned, her ears rang and her body ached. She rammed her shoulders into Chuck's bedroom door but he had locked it. It was his fortress. She pounded on it, kicked at it, ranted into the thick air, sharp arrows of rage launching through the windows and vaulting beyond the roof. She smashed dishes and used the broken porcelain to slash curtains, she swiped her arms across the kitchen counter sending a series of Chuck's precious small appliances smashing to the floor, she stormed around the living room, overturning shelves. Pictures were struck down and, like bones through flesh, they broke free of their frames. Books thudded onto the carpet. She picked them up and tore them, chomping at them like a wild dog, biting pages from the binding, flinging them at the fireplace. Then she turned on herself, wrenching strands of hair, scratching at her arms, clawing at her throat, trying and failing to whip herself with nothing but her own fingers, finally pummeling her thighs, leaving bruises that would take weeks to heal. At last, she fell exhausted onto the floor beside the fireplace, head at an unnatural angle on top of a pile of ravaged books and empty wooden picture frames, her arms askew, legs twisted like they'd been broken, and she lay almost catatonic, tortured by the quiet.

The tranquil neighborhood was patronizing in its measured response, 'There, there, that was quite a rage. Do you feel better now that you got it out? You'll settle down. Just give yourself time.' The neighborhood gave her a collaborative pat her on the head, and nodded knowingly to itself – this poor, sullen, wayward woman will surely one day find her way back to civility. The trees outside, their lush green umbrella foliage first absorbing and then waving off her anguish (this is what we do, we filter and clean the atmosphere), their branches casting feathery shadows of solace over soft green lawns, like nothing was really happening. 'It will all balance out, you'll see.' The streets were empty, the carefully edged lawns and manicured hedges and low white picket fences like arms around rose bushes, all of it, unable or unwilling to fathom Irene's wretchedness, all stoic, silent witnesses of their own determined ignorance.

CHAPTER 56
COLUMBA

The workings of the mind, especially in times of stress and confusion is truly marvelous. Have you noticed how, depending on temperament, one can manage to scratch and crawl one's way up and over mounds of worry, rising to tread over it, without noticing how sore and bruised one's feet have become?

José didn't tell Columba about his visit to The Black Cat. But then she hadn't told him about hers either.

Columba had stopped talking about Anita but José couldn't pinpoint when exactly that had happened. Nor could he remember when she had removed anything that might remind her of Anita. He supposed that Anita's things must have been removed slowly, one flimsy remnant at a time. But her ghost remained. José didn't know if Columba had tossed Anita's belongings in the bin or if she had hidden them out of sight, waiting for the day that she would return, when, like small ornaments that are stored away and called upon at Christmas time, they would be revived and Anita exulted. He assumed that until then it was best not to be remind his mother what they both knew (at least what was certain up to now) – that Anita had no plans to return.

He'd seen a plastic doll the size of a small toddler on Columba's bedroom floor. Its vacant blue eyes followed him when he walked in and out of the bathroom. Maybe his Mom had 'rescued' it from the depot. He thought it was creepy but one morning when he had finally screwed up enough courage to ask Columba about it, the doll had disappeared and he thought no more of it.

However, early one morning a couple of weeks later, he realized the doll was still there, the circumstances of which put a scare into him. He heard Columba talking with someone in her bedroom. It was too early for visitors. For a few seconds, his heart leapt and he was filled with hope. Maybe Anita had come home! How had she slipped past him? Ah, it was too good to be true. He stayed put, ears perked up, sharp and pointed, sniffing the air like two pink antennae. He heard only Columba's voice. Who else was there? What if it wasn't Anita? Who was whispering in his Mom's ear? Who had sneaked by him in the night? What if a man was there? In their house. In her bedroom. A strange man. The back of his neck prickled and a cloak of foul dread dropped over his shoulders. His stomach knotted. He crept off the mattress, sneaked up to her door to bend around and listen.

Columba was cooing like a mother dove. Surely, she wouldn't talk to a lover like that. He cringed, and thought he might need to vomit. No, there couldn't be a strange man in Columba's bed. His shoulders relaxed as he exhaled, shakily releasing the air through his lips. Never once in José's life had Columba invited a man to her bed. She had told him that many really good women had no need for a man. Men were good for one thing, and one thing only and that was to help make babies. Keep in mind, she said, that even for that they needed a woman. And look how disproportionate their contribution was. Even so, she shamelessly held to her tale that Anita and José were miracle children, born of her virgin womb, with no help whatsoever from a man. She was careful to remind José that although she had to admit that he was of the male gender, he was different than normal men, because she was his mother and she raised him to consider his place among women.

He rapped on the wall before venturing around the corner and into her bedroom. She apparently didn't hear him and she didn't respond but he stepped forward anyway.

She was hunched on the far edge of the bed, the mattress drooping under her weight, making it look like a slow valley in the midst of a knobby plain. She was facing the opposite wall. The absurd plastic doll had been propped on a wooden crate directly in front of her. The crate was covered with a woven blanket (the northern Andino kind with brightly colored stripes) and the doll sat stiffly on top of the blanket in front of Columba's favorite embroidered cushion. Why would she prop up this ridiculous doll that way? Then he realized that the doll was seated like some kind of saint on an altar. And she was adorned like a little saint too. A colorful knitted sweater that was far too big for the doll, was buttoned up around her. The doll's head with its stiff, straw-yellow hair and round blue eyes stared up from inside the collar like a freaky blonde lizard, peering out at the bedroom landscape. The sweater's bottom edge looked like a woolen field, grassy green, dotted with tulips and daisies. Above the green, spanned celestial blue with puffy clouds that floated up around the shoulders. Bright birds hung beneath the clouds. The bottoms of the sleeves were folded back several times so that Columba could hold the doll's little plastic fingers. Columba was painting the doll's fingernails a fluorescent pink.

She was whispering to the doll in what almost sounded like a prayer. Was this plastic prop a replacement for San Expedito and the Virgin? José was horrified. He stopped, muscles taut, fearing that Columba would sense him there and discover that he was a pea-brained oaf eavesdropping on his mother and her fantasies.

She'd been droning and cooing for several minutes. He strained to hear. "It's been so lonely without her," she was whining in a kind of breathy voice. "And I've taken a long time to accept her decision, even though I still don't understand it." She clucked, dusted her hands, sat up straight and her tone changed from one of desolation to something like clear vitality. "Change of subject. This sweater is perfect for you. And do you see what a little nail polish can do?"

Are you kidding me? Jose wanted to unroll the sleeves of the sweater and use them to slap the doll across the face, make her shut her freaky eyes. He wanted to insist that Columba see this for what it was – an ill-fitting fantasy, a garish sweater on a plastic monster.

Wasn't he, José enough? Couldn't she just talk to him? Was she out of her mind? He crouched a little, turned quietly, padded back to his mattress, laid down and rolled his eyes at the ceiling. Who had his mother become?

CHAPTER 57

GAVIN

Nature surrounds us not in silence but with the gentle quiet of someone who knows her place. We aren't talking about her fury and sudden rages, against which we have no hope but rather we are referring to her genius, her creativity, and her skill in making us believe in our own wisdom. We congratulate ourselves for so cleverly copying her design and Mother Nature smiles into the wind at her own craftiness.

One day in the late spring, just like a pair of old birds who'd been shaken from their nest, an elderly hippie couple ventured out of the woods and into Stan's Men's and Boys' Wear.

The couple had lived for years out of view, around the bend at the far edge of the lake that Gavin could see from his front window. They had squatted in an abandoned cabin nearly two decades ago and now it was considered theirs. If rumors were true, they had converted the place into a stylish log dwelling that included fine art, home-made weavings, birch carvings and cedar furniture. They were a couple of eccentric do-it-yourselfers. They had a few sheep and rumor had it that they kept them in the house in the winter. It was also said that they were both fine artists, had degrees from California College of Arts or somewhere similar. How they found their way to Burgeon was still a mystery. No one seemed to have the answer to that.

Now, as it turned out, they had plans to enter the world of fashion design.

When they breezed casually through Stan's front door, they caught Gavin on his way out. They paused to look around without much interest and without venturing more than a few steps inside. "Mr. Reid?"

"Yes, that's me."

The man said "We understand you're the person to talk to. You have a rep as a fashion industry guru." The man, who appeared to be in his mid 60s, spoke confidently, with a slight California accent. "But more importantly, they say you're a master with a conscience, with a real sense of social justice." The old guy's eyes were drilling him, probably his fingers were crossed behind his back.

Gavin wasn't sure what that was supposed to mean but he smiled, nodded and extended his hand. The man returned the smile. He reminded Gavin of Willie Nelson, what with his fiery, sharp eyes. "Astute," thought Gavin. The man's handshake was firm.

"My name is Frankie and this is Yolanda." He gestured towards the small woman at his side who was wearing a long, batik skirt with an elephant pattern, and a scarf that she tied in a knot atop her head, which looked so heavy it must have been a strain on her neck. She extended a bony hand and flashed a broad smile. "Nice to meet you Mr. Reid." She also had a California accent, more pronounced than Frankie's.

"Please, call me Gavin."

Fitted up in their sturdy Doc Martens (Gavin tried to picture them wandering deep into the belly of Funky Town to acquire them, no doubt the purchase of their lifetime), the two of them looked like they'd just made the trek from Woodstock. Frankie's heavy linen trousers were tied at the waist with a darker linen sash, into which was tucked a tie-dyed 'Save the Whales' t-shirt with a purple silhouette of a whale diving into his nether parts. It flattered his firm gut and trim waistline. Gavin noticed the muscular arms and assumed those had developed from years of chopping firewood and trudging through the bush, maybe even trapping. Yolanda, on the other hand looked brittle. But she too, had eyes that sparked with vitality.

"We're recycling." Yolanda grinned and patted a burlap sack that was slung across her left shoulder. It bulged under her arm and hung heavily towards her front. How such a frail-looking woman managed to lug anything at all, let alone a bag that had to weigh at least 15 kilos was a question. But she seemed unphased. Frankie helped her lower the bag to the ground and she took her time to untie it. She reached in and felt around before pulling out a small garment. She held it up for Gavin to examine. "Here, take it. What do you think?" She pushed it at him and watched his face.

He accepted the little dress and held it up. All eyes on him, alert for a turn of his lips, a squint, a frown, and hopefully a smile, with eyebrows raised in amazement. But he didn't give himself away.

What he held in his hands was a simple patchwork dress. From what he could tell it was made of squares of bleached burlap, with patches of wool felt, the dye leeching into its soft fibers to stain it with pastel flowers. There were green pockets (one above each hip), supple, something like dyed suede, they had little peace signs etched into them.

She pointed to the pockets first. "These are made of birch bark." She was smiling, eyebrows lifted as though this fact surprised even herself.

"Amazing, eh man?" Frankie rested his hand on Yolanda's shoulder. "She came up with this. We have more." He motioned to Yolanda. "Show him the others."

The bag was full of tricks. Ecological ones. Garments made with treated reeds that were woven in and out of fat wool across the shoulders, again with patches of pastel dyes in wool felt, the misty texture of which disappeared like lace into the edges. The work was genius.

"And nothing is destroyed, man. We either recycle or we harvest whatever can stand to be thinned out in the forest around our place." He grinned broadly, "We don't clear cut, I can guarantee you that."

Gavin laughed.

Frankie was the shoe specialist. He made shoes from recycled tires – not that this was a new concept. But it was the manner in which he combined it with leather and the style with which he designed uppers, using deceptive, and even unidentifiable materials. "This is from a bulrush, man. Oh, and check this out... see this here? I carved this buckle from an elk antler." The detail was stunning. Diamond shapes skillfully engraved into leather, some shoes had leather laces, some had clever combinations of thick and thin straps, others were loafers with leather cut-out uppers or treated reeds woven into durable and flexible tops. The styles were unconventional. Not like anything Gavin had seen in Vancouver or Toronto or beyond, where fashion designers, even at the fringes of the industry were too eager to follow seasonal trends.

These two individuals, isolated in the backwoods of Burgeon conceptualized works of art that were created from within their ecological habitat, and now they had arrived to introduce it to the rest of the world. They were like innocent children smiling into the faces of wolves.

Was Burgeon a market for such products? No. What about Grant Falls? Probably not.

"That's why we've come to you, Gavin," Frankie was saying. "We know we can't sell this stuff here. We don't know much about selling things anyway but you know how to get stuff out there, right? I mean, we aren't so much about the money. Although, yeah, it would be nice to have some extra cash sometimes but we think our stuff is good for the planet."

"Have you heard of the internet?" Gavin asked.

"Well, yeah, man, of course. I mean, we live out in the backwoods but we're not totally ignorant." He flashed a smile. "It's just that we don't have a connection to that, both literally and figuratively. Besides, we're not the selling type, really. It's not our gig."

"These products need to go beyond my market area." Gavin said. He picked up a pair of shoes. "Well, maybe I can sell one or two pairs. But the clothing, well that'd be risky. I mean this kind of thing is untested, especially around here."

"Well, it's not like we're asking for money up front. When you sell, you pay."

"Consignment."

"Yeah, if that's what it's called. That's our thought."

"And I can sell eco-fabric too. Just by itself. By the meter. I've been weaving recycled fabric. So, keep an open mind." Yolanda looked up and touched Gavin's elbow, a gentle prod, no hard sell.

He looked down at her. This little woman sparked with ideas and commitment to her cause. "Eco-fabric," He said. "I like that." He thought of Cindi Crawford and smiled. Maybe there was more of a local market than he knew. How many Cindis lived in Grant Falls?

IRENE

Inaction, some say, is the quiet time during which the best ideas are born. In Irene's case, this was partly true. When she was finally sufficiently recovered from her trauma, she recognized the stubborn boredom that floated up to the surface of her current reality. Irene was proof that in sickness, you tend not to pay attention to boredom. But in health – well, in health – it becomes your enemy and you must move on.

Pitiful, forsaken Chuck had stayed away for almost two months. Irene knew he was hiding out at the store. It was his only refuge. He would have made a bed for himself under the table in the staff room and he'd lie there on his back, looking up at the table. The last thing he would see before going to sleep would be the graffiti she knew one of the part-time student staffers had scratched there. "Mankind is lost in a sea of consumerism." He'd make a note to repaint the underside of the table one day. He probably had his bedsheet tucked in tight around the mattress, hopefully so tightly, that he'd choke in his pin-neat little sleep. That stupid store had been his baby, his family, his life for years now. She had always known it was his real reason for living.

Irene had a growing desire for revenge. At first it pricked at the nape of her neck, and then she felt it tingling and burning up to her ears. It grew on her. Her jaw stiffened and she ground her teeth. She steeled her back, pushed out her shoulders, and felt herself expand into the space around her. She felt imposing, sharp where it counted and brutishly blunt. Yes, she decided, revenge was the thing. What better target than Chuck's god-forsaken metal shelves full of outdated canned goods, and sticky-sweet outdated candy, and fluff-filled cereal boxes, and sugary beverages and processed breads and cookies in his orderly, good-for-nothing stupid convenience store? She should have done something about it years ago. The place was like a black hole, sucking in all of his attention and now here he was running to it for solace, like a spoiled baby. Chuck and the store – the store and Chuck – always grasping at each other like mother and child, nurturing each other in their sick, co-dependency, where she had always been the outsider.

Chuck with his store, his baby, the one that matured, grew up, came of age, and did him proud. The store, whose little bell rang customers through its door. It was Chuck who fed it – at his touch, the store opening its petulant little mouth of a cash register to eat and grow fat on dollar bills. It ate all day long, week after week, year after year. She had always hated it and now, yes, she was jealous of his relationship with it. His baby, the store didn't die. His baby would always be there for him.

Two months was a long time to sleep on a mattress in the store's back room. Chuck's self-exile couldn't last forever. He would probably return any day now. In anticipation, she began to sit all night in her wingback chair in the living room. She waited for the garage door to squeak open, for Chuck to tip-toe down the hall, shoes in hand, like the despicable criminal he was. She was prepared to stay there for weeks if that's what it took but just before dawn on the fourth morning of her vigil, she gave in and retreated to her bed. Revenge, as it turned out, took more than a small measure of energy.

Lights out to avoid her bedroom's barren reality, she stripped naked, trampling on the stained old housecoat she'd worn for weeks and she yanked back the covers to slip in between the sheets. She adjusted the quilt, tucked it around her shoulders and pulled it around her knees, conscious of its feathered generosity and warmth. The white noise protected her from her own thoughts and she felt her head sink into the pillow. She released a long sigh and for the first time in months, she fell into a delicious, heavy sleep. She slept the whole day and was still there, drifting in and out of consciousness as her little spot on the earth rotated into darkness once more.

She awoke suddenly, eyes and ears alert when she heard him bump into the table in the hallway. He muttered something under his breath. She waited, staring into the dark, as he creaked across the floor in his sock feet. She heard him unlock his bedroom door and slink inside, closing the latch with a soft click. Then the sound of two locks turning in their tumblers. It must have been nearly midnight.

Irene stayed in bed until Chuck left for work the next morning and for every morning after that. She made sure she was back in her bedroom before he returned each night. There was nothing to say to him. Her rage had cooled and now her heart was in a deep freeze. She craved revenge. Someone once told her that sharks needed to keep swimming in order to survive. Surely, until recently, she had been a shark, circling without purpose. Now, though, her purpose would be to exact revenge. She began to forge her plan for retribution. Let the war begin.

Unfortunately, being a woman with only minor aptitude for, and no true interest in planning, her thoughts wandered and revenge was lost in loose ideas that wound in and out of themselves. Although Irene had assumed that a hunger for revenge would make her so, she was not, by nature, a very ambitious shark. Several months passed and the lazy shark floated about the house in her stained housecoat, pacing the hallway, sitting at the kitchen table, staring off into space over cold cups of tea, flopping on the sofa, remote control in hand but never changing channels, staring blankly for hours at reruns of This Old House, watching Bob Vila's mouth move, watching his fingers run across the fine edges of long timbers, watching his hands manipulate tools. She passed way too much time with this erudite constructor. But what did it matter? She had nothing but time. Nothing. Finally, she realized Bob was boring her to death and she moved on to a shopping channel. That too, became a bore and she decided that perhaps full-on revenge was too ambitious. So she settled on a series of mini-revenges, something more immediate. A warm-up before the real thing. In her less than full-on vengeful state, she was at least capable of destroying a few of Chuck things.

She had already slashed his dark green jacket as it hung, forgotten, on a hook beside the back door. Chuck's first mistake was abandoning anything that wasn't locked in his room. Afterwards, she almost felt pity for it but then, not quite. She ripped the soles off his favorite walking shoes with a screwdriver. She ripped from the short wall in the entrance, an old family photograph – the one where Chuck was standing between his Dad and uncle, showing off a big salmon, grinning from ear to ear and she walked it down the hall and into the garage. Holding the frame between thumb and index finger, she swung it back and forth for a few seconds, then she dropped it, picked up a hammer and smashed it with such ferocity that the glass shattered into a million pieces and shot from one end of the garage to the other. Chuck's face still smiled out from the photograph so she pounded it with the hammer, until it was nothing but a messy stain on his otherwise pristine garage floor.

Chuck walked into the damage and destruction. But what could he say? Nothing. The house was a naked cavern, in the depths of which lurked an evil, vengeful, somewhat lazy shark.

CHAPTER 59

HAWKEYE

Disharmony sooner or later shrugs itself loose and shifts lazily through the obstacles until it finds a place of balance. There, it will lose its edge and morph itself into the new normal, crowding out the painful memories of the past and lowering the bar for happiness.

The Bullfighter loomed over Hawkeye whose uniform was unable to offer him a single thread of protection against such a formidable adversary. His blue suit, which in all other occasions, charged him with authority and bravado, now just made him feel ridiculous. He shrunk inside of it. He could feel beads of perspiration rolling down his back, leeching into his waistband. His brain, having shriveled in the heat of his boss's steely glare, was on fire, burning the thoughts before they were completely formed, confirming that he was an idiot. Unable to think clearly but aware that his pants were now too loose, he instinctively hoisted them by his belt, making him look very much like a nervous, inexperienced and bumbling criminal. He suddenly felt itchy all over and he began to twitch. There was a cold space between his baggy trousers and his knees. His knees turned to jelly, and he was helpless without their support so he folded and crumbled like a small dog at the Bullfighter's feet.

"It's been you all along, you skinny, no good scoundrel piece of shit!"

Hawkeye was, in this position, entirely exposed and shamefully impotent. The Bullfighter could see the blood pumping from Hawkeye's feeble heart to the trembling tips of his pointy red ears. He could see his eyes clouding over with fear, he could see the piss running down his legs, leaving a puddle on the floor around his skinny, sorry rump.

There was no doubt that by the end of this conversation, which Hawkeye hoped would not last all night, he would have to give his life over to the man in the tight suit, whose long, dark shadow was consuming him. If he had had a child, he would surely have had to sacrifice him. Luckily, Hawkeye thought of Columba. If he was to save his own skin, she would be the sacrificial lamb. In the midst of the fear and roaring confusion, he knew what was coming.

Cool and controlled as always, the Bullfighter said, "Let's pour a drink, shall we? Let's talk." He poured himself some expensive whiskey from the cabinet behind his desk, and he swirled it, watching its liquid legs settle around the glass. He took a slow sip, and then easily, gracefully and with the tip of his snake-leather boot, he played with Hawkeye, who was cowering on the floor beside the desk. The Bullfighter's lapis lazuli ring glinted in its golden setting. He twisted it lazily with his thumb and forefinger, pinkie finger raised. He leaned back to look up at the warped ceiling in the office of the used clothing depot. Outside in the main part of the plant the women were bantering. Occasionally, laughter rang out. Hawkeye could picture them combing through the piles faster than normal, rushing to get their own before he returned. He knew that at least three of them worked together to steal the best items for themselves. He should be out there, he wanted to say, preventing internal theft. But here he was soaking up his own urine at the foot of the Bullfighter's desk.

"So, this is what we're going to do." The Bullfighter's chair squeaked under his weight as he leaned forward.

Hawkeye dared slowly raise his eyes in the hope of a deal that might save his skin. He had 'stuff' on the Bullfighter that could absolutely destroy his mayoralty campaign. What about polluting the environment? What about undercutting the wages of the women who worked here, cheating them out of several hours per month? What about unpaid bills? What about bribes to environmental authorities? But he knew he'd never be able to use any of it before the Bullfighter used what he had against him. The mayoralty candidate versus the lowly security guard? No chance. They would have him thrown in jail before he could change his trousers.

The Bullfighter had a taste for blood. So, Hawkeye gave him Columba. "I've suspected her for a long time but haven't been able to figure out how she does it. If anyone's guilty of walking out with any of your merchandise, it's her." Hawkeye looked up from under his eyebrows, hoping the Bullfighter would be satisfied.

He wasn't. "And, I can say with 50% certainty that she's the one who vandalized your car too." Actually, Hawkeye had never suspected Columba of that but given his current circumstances it was convenient to blame her. Win him some slack.

The Bullfighter twitched his pinky finger and raised the glass to his lips. "You get rid of her... whichever one she is," he waved Hawkeye off. "I know, I know but I can't remember everyone's face. And do it tonight. Or it's going to be your neck on the line."

The Bullfighter would keep Hawkeye in check until he found a replacement but for now he would make him suffer.

Columba heard the Bullfighter bellowing for Hawkeye to get the hell into his office. He'd been in there an unusually long time. She knew others were taking advantage of his absence but she had a bad feeling. She'd be cautious this shift. Best not take any merchandise tonight. She could make it up later.

The bag inspection at the end of the shift was excruciatingly slow and Hawkeye, his dark expression locked in a serious scowl, didn't once glance down the queue at her. She noticed he was not wearing his uniform but had changed into a pair of used khaki trousers that were far too long and they bunched at his ankles. When it was Columba's turn, she unzipped her bag all the way and was not surprised when Hawkeye did a deep dive with his hand and a thorough search. He mumbled something to her. She leaned in, "What?" He repeated it, his mouth twisted to one side as though he'd just suffered a stroke. "Meet me out by my van." It was an order, not an invitation.

By the time Hawkeye locked up the place and finally kicked his way around the corner to his van, Columba was worried. "Get in. I'm giving you a ride home," he said.

She was concerned that the overly-long trouser legs might get wound around the gas pedal and cause an accident and she kept her eyes on them for the duration of the journey. Hawkeye wasn't talking.

It well past one a.m. when they pulled up across the street from Columba's door. The house was dark, José was asleep. The neighborhood was quiet except for a gang of dogs that roamed up and down, tangling with each other now and then, growling and yelping. One of the streetlights flickered and one went out, followed by another. It was a sign. It was looking dark. Hawkeye actually squeaked when he turned to look at her and he kept a grip on the wheel.

"The Bullfighter knows you've been stealing."

"What are you talking about? You no-good asshole, what have you done? You don't know that and neither does he."

"Well, he's the boss and he knows."

Hawkeye tried to appear calm but it was apparent by his twitching and scratching that he was anything but. And was this new cologne or did he smell of stale urine.? "He called me into the office. I was cool, though, Columba. I never flinched. "

She sunk from him, groping for the door handle. She didn't believe him for a second but she listened.

"Someone turned you in." He was careful to point only at her.

"What do you mean, turned me in? Who would do that?"

"Someone who you've used and abused, I suppose."

It's easy to replace the smallest affection with disgust when fear and cowardice come rolling in to suffocate the last glimmer of hope at the end of a bad day. When she looked at him, she saw him for the scrawny rat he was. Nothing but an overblown, know-it-all, waste of greasy skin, bald-faced liarloser. Why hadn't she just admitted it to herself years ago?

She was slipping into a deep black hole. She was desperate, holding on by her claws, like a cat. But she pulled herself tall, breathing in, filling her chest and opening her shoulders. She yelled at him, "And you? What becomes of you? You're the one who plays favorites and lets the merchandise slip out the door piece by piece. I can get you in a lot of trouble too."

"No. No, you can't." He looked squarely at her now, feeling for the first time in several hours that he was in control of something. He was the one who had the conversation with the Bullfighter and he's the one who set things right. He was the one who would end this, all of it. On his way over tonight, he had thought he'd break it all gently but now he saw that it needed a firm hand, 'a la Bullfighter'. He'd have to cut her down and leave her with nothing, which was the only choice that he had anyway.

"Listen, it was me who had to stand up for you. He was grilling me. I was backed into a corner, Columba. And I had no way out. He knew everything." Hawkeye took a page out of the Bullfighter's playbook and managed to control his voice, adding power to it by forming the words slowly as though she was deaf, or like she spoke another language.

She sensed Hawkeye's growing stature and she could feel herself shrinking beside it. The balance had tipped.

Hawkeye made his case. "I told him. I said 'I know all about how you pay the workers less than minimum wage and about all the money that slides under the table, money to keep the union at bay, how the union bosses are all in your pocket. And I know the poor conditions here... the toilets that don't flush, the sinks that have no running water, that there is no place for workers to take a break, that you don't even give them the minimum time required by law. And that their complaints to the fake union only end up on your desk and then in the trash. But most of all...' and this is the kicker, 'most of all,' I told him, 'I know about the discard bin and I know about the trucks full of unwanted clothing and shoes and makeup and perfume and plastic hats and purses that get hauled out and dumped on the flats on the way up to the altiplano. I know how you instruct the truckers to burn them and how what doesn't go up in smoke just settles into the floor of the desert to get tossed around by the wind. This fact will ruin your reputation. Your hopes for national recognition will go up in smoke, just like your discards do.'

"You told him that?" Incredible. She forgot herself for a moment.

"I did."

"What did he say?"

"He said 'you goddamn son of a bitch.'

"And what did you say?"

"I just sat there, didn't say any more. I just waited. He started pacing back and forth behind his desk. Then he sat down again and he said, 'Okay, we'll make a deal.'"

"What deal?"

"Well, not a deal, really. I was put in charge of dismissing you. Tonight. Here and now. You no longer work at the depot." Hawkeye started the engine and stared straight ahead, "So you better get out, Columba. That's it."

No apologies, nothing. That was it. End of her depot days.

CHAPTER 60

GAVIN

The unbridled delight at an unexpected, happy turn of events, the subtle tingling of nerves, the latent tickle that lingers just beneath the surface, making you smile or even laugh aloud...

Irma bustled into Gavin's office, breathless. "You'll never guess what arrived!" Her eyes were wide, incredulous, and she was nodding non-stop as though her head was on a spring, and she panted like an over-excited puppy. It was from more than the exertion of running down the hallway.

She beamed. "Yup," as though answering the question he hadn't asked. "More angel sweaters!"

"What? You're kidding me."

"Nope, come and see for yourself."

Irma was bursting with excitement. Gavin followed her, as she skipped like a schoolgirl, playfully tapped one wall and then the other all the way down the hall.

When they reached the warehouse, they stood side by side in front of a bale that had just been cut open, its contents still settling over the floor. They gazed in silence at the sweaters.

Irma choked with excitement. "See? Another blessing from heaven." She was smiling through happy tears, so near the point of crying that her voice broke.

Gavin walked around the mound and reached down to examine a sweater, then another and a third. Yes, they were the original sweaters, from the same source. This time they were for bigger children, as though the sweaters had matured during the last years. And the designs were bolder. My, how you've grown, he was tempted to say.

"Irma, it's time to rejig the shop on high street. And don't forget to order more labels."

There should have been more questions about the origin of the sweaters. Two times in a row, two years apart. It was too good to be true. You might say it was destiny. Destiny was an excuse you used when you were either forced to accept a situation over which you had no control – or when you really wanted something, knowing all along in the back of your head that it wasn't yours to have.

Once again, the shop would feature the sweaters, easily upstaging the Burgeon restaurants and tourist brochure racks and replacing the slow-selling consignment clothes from the backwoods hippies. Those recycled garments were gathering so much dust that Gavin could feel the store sinking under the weight of it. Up to now, even though he hadn't dedicated much energy to the exclusive eco-garments and fabric, he knew they were going to be a hard sell. The fact that they were in the 'pop-up' location, now locally known as 'Little Imps' probably didn't help sales. In fairness to Yolanda and Frankie, in a bare minimum effort to promote their products, he should have at least given the locale a different name, something more fitting. But they seemed to be off on other projects and they didn't pester him other than with an occasional call from Frankie, "How's it goin', man? Anything moving off the shelves yet?" Gavin had never quite gotten around to giving them his full attention.

As Gavin had figured, not enough Cindi Crawfords lived in Grant Falls to create a market. Cindi's friends bought a few of the eco-garments and she found a pair of eco-shoes that fit. Having convinced him that a healthy discount on the shoes would pay off big time, she clopped around in them everywhere. Unfortunately, hers was a mobile promotion that went nowhere. Gavin advised Frankie when he saw him in town one day that they would have to lower the prices. Frankie was fine with it. "Anything so that people buy them and recognize how good the garments are, both for themselves and for the planet. Right man? Go ahead, lower the price. It's not all about the money." Gavin figured it would take another generation before the eco-garments would take hold. Or maybe never. Frankie and Yolanda were both a blast from the past and a couple before their time. Gavin kept the eco-garments on display, albeit moving them further and further to the back of the narrow store. In the excitement about the angel sweaters, he all but forgot what Yolanda and Frankie had brought into the world.

Irma quickly itemized the newly-arrived assortment and, following the success of the first batch, she had 'Little Imps' labels attached to the inside back collars. The poster on the window said, "Little Imps. They won't last long! Sizes 6 to 10." And Cindi got to watch them fly out the door. They didn't even have to run ads in the newspaper. Word of mouth set the young mothers on fire and soon their little Janes and Johnnies were sporting original sweater stories at kindergartens and schools.

One of the most enthusiastic mothers in Grant Falls told Cindi that she had started a Little Imps Sweater club. "Everyone can see that there's a story in each one. It's kind of like a book club, you know? But you have to be a knitter to join. The lady from Spin a Yarn is totally into it and has offered her workshop space.

CHAPTER 61

IRENE

As it turned out, the simple answer wasn't in dying. Oddly enough, these weeks since the robbery (the second most painful heist of the century), Irene had never once contemplated ending her own life. But today it occurred to her that she could stop circling on the spot and let the current take her where it would. As she sunk down in the bathtub, she imagined her arms limp at her sides, her legs, weightless. If she so desired, she could surrender her body and sail peacefully away. She imagined floating up and mingling with cumulus clouds, overlooking green valleys and turquoise lakes. With the simple command of her index finger, she would separate the mist and send strands of golden sunlight over the fields to play across the landscape like strings of a violin. She would levitate on a breath of the wind, blue mist dampening her eyelids like so many melting stars. Why not? That would be a million times more pleasant than sharking around (what was it that she was hunting for again? she forgot) in the rooms of this ungodly house. She could exchange this shrill emptiness with the harmony of loitering among gentle clouds, dewy valleys and tranquil lakes.

With that thought still in mind, she stumbled out of the tub and turned to look back down at it, trying to picture what Chuck might see at first glance, how he would collapse at the sight of her lifeless body in blood tinted water. Try as she might, she couldn't really imagine it. She turned on her heel, the thought of her death trailing into oblivion as she knocked around the house in her housecoat and slippers for a couple of hours. Who was it who told her that fish had such a short memory that each turn around the fish bowl was a whole new experience?

How does one identify a life-changing moment? Is there a warning before you come upon it? or before it comes upon you? Does someone pull a trigger, shooting you off from a starting gate? Perhaps later when you think back, it all becomes clear. Or perhaps not. Maybe you are pushed – or you venture, or you are guided – onto a new path, completely unaware, all the loose thoughts tumbling around in the unconscious, none of them ever coming forward to take the blame or the credit. Maybe there is power beyond one's self, an energy, a god, who taps you on the shoulder and guides you towards your destiny.

Suddenly, like that fish (or shark) who turned the corner to do another rotation in its bowl, she saw everything like she'd never seen it before. These were Irene's feet, plodding along, one in front of the other. These were her toes, nails dry and cracked. These were her hands, fingers splayed out in front of her, knuckles swollen and red. What happened to Irene? Who had she become? And what about this place? What about the dust floating around in the sunlight that filtered through the blinds? How long had that wide crack in the hardwood floor along the baseboard been there? She noticed the perfect octagonal groupings of the kitchen linoleum that were broken by tiny dark gouges near the fridge where jars had fallen too many times. When had all that happened? As she passed the far end of the kitchen counter, she saw her reflection, speckled and distorted on the side of the toaster.

She crouched down, and parting the hair from in front of her eyes, she studied her reflection. Her eyes peered back from between the scattering of toasted crumbs and fine scratches over the smudged surface and she straightened again, feeling a spark of something like pain, something she had been avoiding for months. No, for years. The exhaustion and torment of her life was reflected on a dirty kitchen toaster.

It made the sad truth apparent, the boredom of sitting silently and sipping cold tea, of looking blankly at Bob Vila and the shopping channel for hours on end, of walking the rooms of this house, one corner to the next, brooding and searching, hunting for something. Satisfaction. Closure. Comfort. Love. What?

How many times had she cringed, backing away from the edge of the black abyss, the place in her head where flashing red danger signs shrieked at her, "Stop. Don't go here. You'll fall, sink in and never emerge." Finally, today, now, her defenses wore down.

She dragged a chair to the edge of the kitchen counter and sat down to stare at the toaster. Perhaps she would find an answer. One never knows.

In her mind, she tiptoed up to the black hole, approaching the red and yellow striped barriers, the ones her imagination had erected, the 'Do Not Cross' ribbons that were really too flimsy to prevent anyone from passing. She skirted around the dark cavity, talking to herself, convincing and cajoling. "Go ahead. It won't hurt you. Have a look." She bent forward and discovered that she could see herself in the watery surface of the black hole. The black hole, it seems, was full of liquid. It was moonlight blue and still as glass. She dipped one toe into it and then waded up to her knees, then to her waist. She held her breath and slowly, carefully, immersed herself, the water swirling around her legs, gliding gently up to her hips. She laid back and let it swim through her hair, let it bubble around her face. She let go, floating up and looking at nothing.

"There is nothing to see here," a voice told her. "But there is nothing to make you move on, either."

She felt she was floating out into the universe, her fears, her guilt, her regrets, her self-loathing – mostly her guilt – dissipating into millions of molecules, being absorbed into realms where they would quite possibly be understood or at least forgotten and otherwise forgiven. She thought she might see Alicia, might feel the tender touch of chubby fingers on her cheek, a whispered coo. But she didn't. Alicia was gone. She was safe somewhere else. She had released Irene or Irene had released her, the two of them agreeing to a congenial, guilt-free departure, just a sweet kiss goodbye into the air. Forgiveness. Mostly.

Irene sat in front of the toaster in this docile, meditative state for many minutes, maybe even hours. When she finally turned away, she felt transformed, renewed, energized. Who needs a counselor, a priest, a confessional when a dirty toaster will do?

She didn't feel like hunting any more, her hunger had been satisfied. She didn't try to claw it back.

Now, though, she needed purpose. First, she would find it in her hands. She would use them for mundane tasks like washing stacks of dirty dishes, scrubbing weeks of grime from bathroom tiles, vacuuming layers of dust from the floors.

The house was still a hollow cave. But instead of feeling imprisoned here, she felt free. Free to think about her lost child. But what is freedom without purpose and without hope? Her purpose, surely, was to be a mother and what is a mother without a child?

That question raked her through and through until she was nothing but blood red fingers of pain. And she kept on scrubbing, trying to figure it out.

CHAPTER 62

IRENE

There is no digital passing of time. No, the universe prefers analogue, the kind of time that ticks around a circular, finite space rather than the kind that blinks out its seconds on the spot. The seconds pass, one after the next, through their orbit that rounds them up to the top of the hour and then to the bottom, taking life full circle.

The way it was, Chuck and Irene hadn't run into each other for several weeks. And anyway, he was afraid to see her. So you can imagine his shock – or you could say terror – when, one fresh spring morning, just as he finished locking the two extra locks on his bedroom door, he heard the light tapping of her slippered feet in the kitchen. His hairs stood on end, adrenaline sent him into fight or flight mode. He chose flight. He quickly shrunk back into the safety of the bathroom.

After all those nights of lying awake on the cot in the back room of the store, listening to mice scurry up and down in the insides of the walls, counting cars that rolled down the alley, worrying about Irene, Chuck had decided to go back home because he needed to sleep in his own bed. How long had he been sneaking in and out of his own home? Too long. He always arrived late and left early so they wouldn't have to see each other. But at least, he thought, if he was there he could assess the situation. How bad was it? He never found out. Perhaps she needed him and the tell-tale signs were not apparent. Perhaps she had been sitting in her chair, that old fawning expression in her eyes, waiting for him to sense her need. But she never actually let him see her there.

God knows he deserved to be banished from the house, probably even from life itself for what he'd done. But still, he rationalized, there was always hope that the necessary crisis (as he had come to refer to it) would eventually make her see what she had become and it would be the first step towards shaking off her woolly sickness. Up to now, although the house was in shambles, he didn't sense anything life-threatening. Signs of her survival, low level as it was, were everywhere because she never tidied anything – dishes all over the counter, dusty smudges on door jambs, hand prints on walls, garbage bin overflowing, soiled bathrobes (that was all that she wore) dropped on the floor in the laundry room. He noticed the details when he returned home at night (microwave plastic on the counter beside a dirty fork, used tea bags on the saucer that he had cleaned the night before, candy wrappers on the table) and he knew she was still alive – wretched but still there.

So what had changed this morning? Here sat Irene just after the crack of dawn, wearing what looked like a clean bathrobe, a pair of clean slippers, her hair still wet from a shower. Even more surprising was that she had laid the table for two – placemats, napkins, plates and mugs, there were even eggs boiling on the stove, and he could smell coffee and toast.

He readied himself and advanced gingerly down the hallway, like a cat ready to spring back into the safety of his bedroom should there be any sudden moves. But she looked up at him with a slow smile. She smiled! Chuck approached the kitchen and made a wide circle around Irene, casing the joint in case she was hiding a weapon.

"Good morning, Chuck."

It was the first time he'd heard her voice in ages, the first time she had uttered a word, a single vowel. He cupped his ears to capture and preserve the sound.

He hovered over the edge of the chair for several seconds before letting himself sit down, hands tight against his thighs, his body taut. "Good morning, Irene." He didn't think it would be a good idea to ask what was going on. It wouldn't be a good idea to speak at all, unless spoken to.

Irene carefully (he thought) stood up to serve coffee and she passed him some toast and a boiled egg. The bathrobe she was wearing was one that he bought her years ago but that she had never worn. She looked small in it, it was bulked and folded around her back. He thought she must have lost weight. But her complexion looked rosy, her eyes were clear, her hair was shiny. He waited.

She didn't say anything. They ate in silence. All the way through breakfast, there was only the sound of munching toast, the brushing of crumbs, clinking of spoons and slurping of coffee. When he finished, Chuck sat with hands folded on his lap, like a school boy waiting for permission to speak or stand.

Finally, Irene said, "Chuck, I'm going out."

"Oh, that's great Irene." He didn't dare look her in the eye. Nor did he dare ask where or why or for how long. "It's lovely weather. You'll enjoy an outing."

She smiled and looked down at her lap.

"Well, okay then. Thanks very much for breakfast. I really enjoyed it. I better get to work."

He paused and waited for her to say something else but she didn't.

"So do you need me to take you anywhere or do you want me to bring back anything special for dinner... or anything?" He dared pose the questions, then immediately regretted it in case it would curse whatever was going on here.

"Thank you, Chuck. Bring home whatever you want. I'm fine."

After he left for work, Irene busied herself, clattering dishes in the sink, rinsing them and leaving them to dry. She padded to the living room and sank back into the knitting chair, sipping another half cup of coffee, relishing the full, rich taste that had escaped her attention for so many months, maybe years. She gazed out the window, the morning air still crisp and new, green buds just starting to open on the trees, a young boy on a bicycle, his wheels crunching the fine gravel beyond the driveway, two little girls, each with pompoms bouncing from the bottoms of pink backpacks, giggling on the way past. Yes, she would go out.

She dressed in the designer camel hair jacket that Chuck bought her just after Alicia was born. She wanted to prove that she could move on. She had sworn she'd never wear it again but Chuck insisted on hanging it in her closet because he said it was valuable. For years after Alicia was taken from them, Irene recalled every detail that led up to that terrible morning. Nothing escaped her. Everything played a role in what happened – from what they ate for breakfast the day before (Captain Crunch was now banned from the house forever) to what program was on TV the night before (a rerun of Cheers – the theme music now made her to rush to the bathroom to vomit), to the weather that week (she hated days when dull stratus clouds painted themselves across the blue) to the terry cloth robe she'd thrown on that morning (she never wore anything similar since), to 'My Girl' that Chuck had been humming to Alicia as they danced around the garden the night before (after that, she had prohibited him humming anything at all in her presence), to the nightgown Alicia had gone to sleep in forever.

The only thing – and she didn't try to justify it – that did not rip out Irene's heart was the Silver Shadow baby carriage.

So she pranced out the front door with it, camel hair coat comfortably around her shoulders, leather gloves snugly around her fingers and mauve angora tam angled perfectly on her carefully groomed hair, Kate Spade handbag hanging at her elbow. When she pushed the Silver Shadow out the front door, the pair of them resembled an elegant horse and carriage leaving a stable whose door had finally been flung open.

She set off in the direction of downtown. Her purpose: to go shopping at Chuck's convenience store. With a vengeance.

CHAPTER 63

COLUMBA

This week, and for the first time in months, Columba saw the bottom of the Nescafe can. She stared at its rusted rim. Today and for the foreseeable future there was no hope of having a spare peso to drop into it. Perhaps she had been too hasty getting rid of the Virgin and San Expedito. After all, saints worked in mysterious ways. Perhaps they had performed miracles that had gone unnoticed. Perhaps things could have been even worse. Well, now the two of them were gone and she was doubly cursed.

It had been several weeks since she had been fired. And it was from the mouth of the cowardly, no-good, stinking son of a bitch, so-called security expert. Her inventory of discarded garments wasn't going to last forever. She would have to become more resourceful. She would have to gamble something. But what? Other than the garments and a few ashtrays and a dozen ballpoint pens, she had nothing. She had Magdalena and the beautiful jersey but she would never relinquish those.

It turned out that Magdalena was a sympathetic listener, a trustworthy confidant. And Columba was 100% certain that the jersey had transformed her plastic form into something spiritual. She was convinced the jersey possessed magical powers. If only it had dropped from heaven when Anita was a toddler. Perhaps the jersey had really been destined for Anita but things being as they were in Chile, always arriving late, sometimes years later (she remembered that her friend Marta once received a letter that had been posted two years earlier, and even so, the postman refused to hand it over until Marta dropped a 100-peso tip into his palm), things were misplaced, things were stolen, and often things never arrived at all. Surely the case of the jersey was destiny arriving late. Columba was very fortunate to have intercepted it at all. She had been in the right place in the right time and this fact surely proved the case for destiny corrected.

Each time she walked into her bedroom and saw the over-sized sweater draped around Magdalena, she was filled with pure joy, all else forgotten. Sometimes she considered that but for the grace of god or the Virgin or San Expedito (who knew which?), the jersey might have been tossed into the junk pile by the likes of Jessica (who couldn't tell a quality garment if her life depended on it), and it would have bounced along amidst the tattered and the torn and dumped in the desert. And who knows? It might have immediately been set on fire. Impatient flames would have consumed it, the little jersey would have slowly melted, becoming gnarled and misshapen beyond recognition as the flames licked through it, and its misshapen remains would have melded with the other discarded junk. She shuddered at such dark thoughts and pushed them out of her mind.

Lately, she'd been haunted by the memories of her trip out to the piles. Sometimes she woke up at night smelling smoldering plastic and scorched fibers and she panicked, jumping out of bed to check on José. She dreamed of men's leather loafers and women's spiked heels walking in pairs along the desert highway, initially enjoying a jaunt on a clear day but suddenly a silent flame would shoot up from the tarmac to lick at their heels. They would run, clapping along the highway, straps snapping, buckles glancing back. But their demise was inevitable and the flames would curl into a sinister smile as they devoured the innocent shoes, their unwilling smoke darkening the sky.

In another recurring nightmare, a huge charcoal hand rose up from the side of the road and scribbled her name across the clear blue with its jagged index finger. 'C-o-l-u-m-b-a' – black, feathered letters floated above the horizon. It was like someone had hired a skywriter and now he was telling the whole world what she was guilty of. She woke up crying.

She feared that she'd end up scrounging out at the piles and end up sick, like the poor woman she and Frozen had driven back to town that day. She wondered if the woman was still alive.

Columba stopped selling down in Progreso because her selection of garments had diminished to the point where no one even looked at them anymore. The same clothes had been there for weeks. And no one wanted them. She discounted them to the point of almost giving them away and still, people moved over to the next table and she watched jealously as they opened their wallets for another vendor.

One morning, she woke from a one of her fiery nightmares and she couldn't make herself get out of bed. She was still there when the sun was high in the sky and the afternoon heat beat down through the tin roof.

Finally she forced herself to sit up. Her shoulders drooped, her hands were heavy on her lap. The mattress sagged under her weight and she glanced over at Magdalena in her magic jersey. Today, the little doll with her Mona

Lisa smile and bright blue eyes who, in the past, had offered eternal hope, lacked a certain spark. But Columba sat quietly, waiting as always for the doll to speak first. Maybe a positive, motivational greeting would be forthcoming? Something to help her get on with this godforsaken day? Of course, Magdalena never spoke first. She was a listener-type.

So Columba got to it. "I don't want to go out to the piles, Magdalena. I know what's there and it's probably even worse now. I can't bear it. My stomach churns at the thought."

The doll stared back. Well, you can't just sit here forever, waiting for someone to knock on your door and hand you a miracle. It's not going to happen.

Why did Magdalena have to be so practical?

"No, of course not. I'm realistic enough to accept that. The question is... what? What will I take up? What will save me? How will I feed José?"

The doll's steadfast, blue eyes met Columba's. Why not ask him? You've left him out for a long time and he's growing into a fine young man, and you know that he has not yet been corrupted by drugs or bad girls. You need to appreciate him more.

Columba sighed. "Yes, you're right. José's been taking care of himself for a long time now. Maybe I've let him down recently."

The doll would have leaned forward if she could. She would have used body language to convey urgency. But this was beyond her. Well, do something about it then. At least take him into your confidence.

"Yes, yes, I will." Columba promised.

Magdalena knew a half-hearted promise when she heard one. And she could see that Columba was going to begin barking up the same old tree.

Sure enough.

"Magdalena, what am I going to do about Anita?" Columba dove right into her wave of self-pity. She was vulnerable, her confidence crumbling. "Will she talk to me now?"

The doll's Mona Lisa smile remained eternally ambiguous, and didn't give anything away. Her eyes were locked on Columba's. I don't know. I doubt it though. Why do you agonize over her? She's gone from your life. She doesn't need you and certainly doesn't want you. Why do you miss that? Why would you ask to be kicked away to the curb over and over again? She rejects you without reason. Or, at least for reasons she's keeping from you. It's obvious that she doesn't want to remedy anything. Otherwise she'd confront you, right? She'd accuse you or she'd demand answers from you. And if she really wanted to hear what you had to say, she'd listen. But she doesn't. You are just an easy target for her anger. My advice is that you leave things as they are.

The soft, sad mound that was Columba shifted slightly on the sagging mattress and self-pity trickled from the high ground down to the low-lying parts, the swollen ankles, the calloused soles. The pain that constantly stalked her suddenly woke up and struck her heart with precision and Columba blurted out. "But she's my daughter. I bore her. I can still feel her inside of me. I raised her. I can still hear her little girl laughter and feel her little hands in mine. I love her. She is part of me and I can't separate the two of us."

The doll was aggravated. If she could have, she would have flapped those long woolen sleeves and slapped Columba across the face a few times. Wake up and smell the coffee. It takes two to make a relationship. Anita broke it. She trampled on it. She burned it. She doesn't want it. It's over. Live with it.

"I don't like it when you talk to me like this. What gives you the right?" Columba said through her tears. "I'm coming to you for support and guidance, not for criticism and hopelessness. You're so negative this morning."

But just the same, Magdalena insisted that she was being realistic.

"Who is being realistic? I know that you're really made of plastic. I know you really can't see and probably can't hear. Yet I insist with you too. What would you do if I were to give up on you?"

The doll acquiesced. You've got me there.

CHAPTER 64

IRENE

It's amazing how, after forcing yourself to take that first reluctant step, it leads to another and then another, and how, when you keep your eye on the horizon, you manage to propel yourself forward, one step at a time, until one day you notice that the end of the rainbow is within reach. You stop and try to peer into that huge pot of gold.

Irene didn't make it to Chuck's convenience store that morning. She was side-tracked in the midst of her jaunt. Sharp. Stunning. What? It happened just as she passed the window of a shop right across the street from Spin a Yarn.

Before that point, she had been feeling great, trotting along like a little filly, her lungs bursting with fresh morning air, invigorated after having been in-doors for so long. How long? She hadn't been counting. The sun was shining, there wasn't a cloud in the sky, the universe had cleared a path for her, green lights all the way to Chuck's store. She peered down into the Silver Shadow. It contained only a mauve blanket that was folded back and tucked under an ecru cut-out lace pillow case. She smiled into it like a mother fawning over her precious newborn. It was exhilarating to be on the main street accom-panied by the carriage. Why hadn't she thought of it before? Too much stale air is bad for the soul. Well, she'd learned her lesson. Granted, she had been a slow learner. But, well, here she was now, taking delight in a long overdue and well-deserved outing.

She hummed under her breath as she strolled the quiet street, stores not yet open for business, her head high, the finely engineered revolutions of the carriage wheels advancing the Silver Shadow along, in and out of the morn-ing shadows that were stretching awake along the sidewalk.

But suddenly – she might as well have been struck by a bolt of lightning. They say lightning can either kill you or cause you to simultaneously combust and whisk you away into an eternity. Or else, in that fraction of a second, it gifts you with extraordinary power and insight. In Irene's case, the effect was a manifestation of the latter – to be realized in the near future.

Irene's lightning was something she caught out of the corner of her eye, something that momentarily stopped her heart and caused her to freeze on the spot. It was like she died and came to life again in a fraction of a second. She had been strafed with such force that she gasped, her limbs locked and her back arched. She resembled a terrified cat suspended in mid-jump. The carriage continued rolling on its precise, single-minded trajectory towards Chuck's store but Irene instinctively reined it in just before it was out of reach, stumbling as she did so and coming to a stop on the tips of her toes, head cranked at ninety degrees as she stared into the shop window. She remained there, numbed by the sight.

Her sweaters were there. Not many. But some. Enough. There was no mistaking her own work. She remembered every tune she had hummed to herself as her needles had clicked in time like an imaginary metronome, one stitch after another, row after row, side over side, song after song.

The sweater at the forefront of the window was her Skinny-me-rinka-dink sweater. The sweater would have fit a seven-year-old Alicia. It was bright red with a heavy, padded rainbow that began at the back and rounded over the left shoulder, reaching into the little pocket on the front onto which she had stitched a bright yellow crocheted star.

Someone had strung up another sweater, one she had knitted even earlier. It was suspended by a transparent thread from the back of its neck and it was flying over a wooden toy trunk. It looked like it belonged to an angel. This sweater would have fit Alicia at six years old. It was full of flowers and there was a bold, oversized robin perched on a thick branch with three leaves, and there was a happy red dahlia, whose very center was a huge yellow button, the second from top. This was her 'It's Spring, it's spring, the robins sing...' sweater.

The memories pounded down in a heavy torrent. So clear were they that she could see her fingers manipulating the needles, feel the soft wool as she knitted, the yarn diving over and coming back up, gently playing around the needles and dropping down again. Purl one, knit one. She was humming the tunes, the lyrics weaving in and out of the garments as she counted off the rows and tied in new colors.

Oh, now she needed to sit down. This was too much to believe. Too good to be true. But where had the sun gone... the blue skies? The Silver Shadow was out of focus, she couldn't see her own feet and her knees were like rubber. But she pressed on through the light fog that had gathered in her head. She leaned into the handle of the carriage and let it bounce her up and down as its springs compensated for her weight. Somehow, she found herself at a small park, one that the yuppies had rallied for, protesting that green space was important for everyone's health. The park was mostly empty at this time of the morning. Swings were suspended in the early morning air, one of them creaked lazily as she brushed by it. She pushed the carriage across a sand pit, its posh wheels protesting as they sunk in the crystal grains.

Finally, almost tripping over a bench at the far end, she collapsed onto it, dropping her head onto her chest. She descended, confused and defeated, into piles of woolen memories as her mind picked at them like a vulture coming to rest on the spoils. Like buzzards, her own thoughts swooped down, poking and prodding, threatening to eat her alive. Then she saw Alicia half-buried under hundreds of sweaters, all of them were unable to keep her warm. They shifted and covered Alicia until finally she was no longer visible. The vultures pecked and rearranged the sweaters, trying to get at her. The giraffe sweater raised its arm in protest, a kitten one lunged across her, clouds sweaters floated over top, robins chirped their spring-song around collars, puppies frolicked unawares 'So your ears hang low', nudged by 'bows and flows of angel hair', 'only you and you alone can thrill me like you do'... and 'fill my heart with love for only you.' 'You are my destiny... you are my happiness...'

Eventually, perhaps triggered by a child's shriek, Irene climbed back out of her nightmare, her arms thrashing the air, her throat restricted. She blinked hard and looked around to see a young mother grab a toddler by his shoulders and rush him out of the park. "We'll play another day." Through her fog, Irene was sure the little boy was wearing her 'little house on the hill' sweater.

Somehow she arrived back home, eyes swimming in tears, face burning and she leaned in to whisper to the lace pillow that was tucked inside the Silver Shadow. "Are we okay? Will we be okay?" The lace on the pillow blinked and the quilt sighed. Its billowy little voice cooed, "Oh sure, we're okay. Carry on."

Leaning into the sturdy handle of the Silver Shadow, she rose to her feet, adjusted the angle of her tam, tugged lightly at her mauve, gloves and brushed off her coat. She would venture out again immediately to the little store that so unabashedly – and miraculously – dared to display her sweaters for sale.

As soon as the door was unlocked and the sign was flipped to "We're Open," Irene entered with the carriage.

A young red-haired woman greeted her with a smile. "Good morning." Then the smile turned sour and she said, pointing to the carriage. "You can't bring that in here, I'm afraid."

"Well, I can't leave it outside." Ignoring the young woman's instruction, Irene maneuvered it through the door frame and into the middle of the narrow shop floor.

"How many of these sweaters do you have?" She waved her arms at the display.

"Let me check." The red-haired woman's fingers clacked importantly and for a long time along a keyboard and she squinted at the screen. "We have, 75. Wait, no, we have 77 of them in the store right now, counting the two in the window. What size are you interested in?"

"All of them. I'll take them all."

"All?"

"Yes, please."

And that's how the unexpected run on Little Imps sweater began and that's how Irene's collection of sweaters was reborn. After she removed the foreign, and most inappropriate "Little Imps" tags (who put those there? and when?) the sweaters were 100% hers again.

She cleverly stuffed them into baskets and slid them to the back of her bedroom closet. She selected the two sweaters that she'd seen in the store window (she had insisted she could wait while the young woman reluctantly climbed into the window to free them from their pins and nylon threads) and she tucked them under her pillow. Chuck would not check her closets, nor would he check under her pillow – a ridiculous idea, were it even to occur to him. He would trust those days were well behind them. He would think he had solved that 'problem' once and for all.

At the end of the month, Chuck was puzzled by the credit card statement that included a hefty charge from a numbered holding company. But the fact that Irene had started to wander out in the mornings filled him with such hope that he preferred to ignore the cost. It was better not to rock the boat. At least not right now, not this soon, not after his heart had begun to beat with renewed faith.

CHAPTER 65
JOSÉ

It occurred to José that Columba should have named him 'Jesus' because not only was he born of a virgin but lately he felt that he was born to be a savior. Of course, he would never presume to be the Jesus. No, he'd be satisfied as the much smaller, locally-grown and less on-demand version.

He had awakened one morning with a realization, well, perhaps more precisely, an epiphany. It was almost as though an angel had visited him in a dream, instructing him to wake up and smell the coffee – or the lack of it, and the lack of tea and lack of everything else in their cupboards. If their stagnant situation was going to change, it certainly wasn't going to be because he'd managed to talk some sense into his Mom. No, Señor. It was obvious that he was going to have to be the catalyst for any sort of family transformation.

In her almost constant, dreary state of listlessness, Columba was neither aware of, nor capable of preventing herself from drowning in her own ocean of sorrow. She almost dragged José along with her. He felt the threat of this sad ocean with its advancing and retreating tide. It was preceded by a gentle spray, a meek warning (but warning just the same) and he paid attention.

Recently, José dreamed that some powerful watery hands had clutched at his ankles and dragged him out to sea feet-first, where he scraped his head across the rocky bottom, mouth open, gasping for breath, and he swallowed salty water and pebbles, his eyes closed tight in blind and desperate prayer. His prayer was answered by a voiceless and faceless angel, who had pronounced José a visionary and actuary, and who showed him the way past his mother's dangerous tide. The answer lay in following Anita's path from school to the Church. The Black Cat, alone, would not provide answers to the reason for her exodus. That came after.

Since he was already familiar with the school, he set off on the path towards the Church of The Most Pure Blood of Jesus. It was easy to enroll in the classes, they were always looking for young people who wanted to join the fold.

He began to attend weekly after-school catechism classes with Father Cortés. In spite of himself, he found that the teachings aroused curiosity. Genuinely interested, he stood out from the class with his pointed questions, beginning with the paradox of the Holy Trinity. Initially Father Cortés was impressed by this boy, who, as it turned out, was Anita's younger brother. But after several weeks of interruptions and questions that he was afraid might lead less faithful students to challenge the faith rather than to grow in it, Father took José aside for a little chat. They sat outside on the wooden bench under the old palm trees in front of the rectory (the very same bench where Anita and Columba had sat with Father). Father leaned back, casually resting his arms on the back of the bench, stretching out and crossing his lanky legs. José watched as Father rotated his ankles and he noted that Father wore expensive Guantes shoes and stylish Argyll socks. It brought to mind the Pope's red designer slippers. Those slippers had always raised questions for José. But no matter. Now he was having a private conversation with Father.

"José, I'm impressed with your enthusiasm and your thoughtful questions, and for some time now I have prayed that you will be satisfied with my answers. But I fear I can't offer what you seek here. This class is a regular catechism class designed for boys and girls who will always be satisfied with a modest understanding of what our Lord teaches us."

José remained silent, watching the sun glint off of Father's black patent leather shoes.

"I'm telling you this for your own good, son. You have potential to go far and I feel you have outgrown my class."

"Are you telling me I can't come any more?" José glanced up at him and then, wanting to avoid Father's eyes, he focused on the shoes. He wasn't hurt exactly but he was taken aback and he preferred to appear cool in Father's presence, to be the kind of kid who is never surprised, who naturally rolls with the punches.

"Well, yes but no, not at all. I was about to say that I think you should attend the more advanced classes offered by the bishop."

Now José looked over to meet Father's eyes. "What are his classes about?"

"Well, he teaches theology classes that pose deeper questions, more philosophical if you like, and that help explain what Jesus predicated. I think you will benefit from a more profound investigation. I have already arranged for you to meet the Bishop tomorrow afternoon. Can you be here?"

José wasn't sure about this move because it wasn't the path that Anita took. Still, he couldn't see how he could refuse if he wanted to remain in the good graces down here at The Most Pure Blood of Jesus. He had to admit that they provided tasty snacks, something that he looked forward to since bread had become scarce at home and he and Columba had had to regress to their old custom of rationing.

Two days later Father Cortés ushered José into the Bishop's study. The meeting was not what José had expected. They met alone. José had expected to sneak into the back of an intimate classroom, populated by attentive young people sitting around in arm chairs and maybe three to a sofa, all enthralled with the day's lesson. He had been anxious about not fitting in. Now he didn't have to worry about that but he had not been prepared for a private interview.

The bishop explained, "I arranged this one-on-one as a chance to get to know you before I introduce you to the group."

It's an all-male group, he said because it just worked out best that way, especially since some of the young men had a calling for the priesthood. He punctuated this last statement with a sweet smile. As though he had been solely responsible for their calling. He emphasized that the particular group, which he was suggesting José join, were given special privileges because of their natural inclination towards higher Catholic studies.

After about 15 minutes, Father Cortés interrupted them with a light rap at the door, and the bishop motioned for him to enter. "Your Excellency." He nodded respectfully at the bishop and then at José. "I stopped by to see if you needed anything further from me."

José smiled self-consciously. His Excellency smiled too. "No, we're getting along just as I had hoped, Father Cortés. You've introduced me to a fine young man, someone with plenty of potential."

Father Cortés, nodded and retreated without another word.

"Have you ever thought of joining the priesthood?"

José shook his head. The bishop smiled his sweet smile again. "Patience, my son. Patience and education."

The following couple of weeks passed without any kind of novelty. José attended school, leaving Columba as she pretended to clean the kitchen and pretended to sort through the same pile of garments for another pretend sales event.

He knew what she did all day. It didn't take much imagination. She would flop onto her bed, lean on her elbow and talk to Magdalena for hours. Like they were old friends or something. Then she lolled around in the front pa-tio, squinting down towards the sea and looking up at the sky, thinking who knows what, talking to herself, her sad head moving slowly from side to side, like she'd really lost the plot.

Lately she had stopped visiting friends, including Juana, and he suspected she didn't leave the house. This generous vibrant mother who used to glint sparkle was now hidden under a cloud. Her inner light was snuffed out. Her complexion had a definite grey aspect, and there was no attempt to cover it, no more heavy rouge over her round cheeks, no more lipstick. Her hair hung limp, there was no more backcombed nest atop her crown and her grey roots had pretty much taken over. The 'signature' Columba no longer existed.

José considered quitting school so he could get a part-time job gutting fish down at the dock but Columba begged him not to do that. She would take charge. She promised. But nothing really changed except that once in a while, they had cheese instead of jam in their sandwiches. She must have picked herself up and gone out to steal and then sell something. Probably at the travelling market. The point was that they survived and she hadn't yet been forced to make her way out to the piles, something he knew she dreaded more than anything.

A good feeling had breezed in from somewhere (on the wings of an unseen angel, perhaps) and José knew that one way or another, he was destined to save them.

CHAPTER 66

GAVIN

Cindi Crawford remembered just as clear as the water of a fresh mountain stream how the lady in the camel hair coat had appeared that brisk April morning and cleaned out every single Little Imps sweater. How could she forget? "I didn't have a chance," she defended herself to Gavin. "She was manic. Possessed even." Cindi's eyes were wide, Gavin thought they were in danger of rolling right back in their sockets and that he'd be left staring at the whites. My God, a granola exorcist. He'd never seen her so undone and thought he'd better calm her down before her head starting spinning on her shoulders. He took a few steps back and listened patiently.

"Well, it was like... yeah, like, she was super insistent, Gavin. And I was, like, really surprised by her attitude, you know? She was sort of passive, aggressive. She kind of just stood there like a steel post. Like maybe she was going to turn into one of those, you know, one of those robot monsters or something. I mean, it was kind of wild.... well, in a surreal sort of way. But I knew there was no way I was going to get rid of her without giving her what she wanted. For a while there, I kind of feared for my life. Plus, you know what? She wheeled into the shop with a big, fancy baby carriage and to tell you the truth I don't even know if there was a baby in there. I told her she couldn't bring that inside but she just ignored me."

Cindi finally stopped and then blinked several times before she squinted up at him. "I mean, what did you expect me to do? How was I to know she'd clean out all the inventory?"

Gavin stood in silence.

He was annoyed because he assumed the sweaters would keep customers coming in for a few weeks at least and that Cindi would gently lead those same customers towards the eco-friendly garments from Yolanda and Frankie, as he had instructed.

Gavin returned to the White Linen warehouse to tell Irma she was going to have to give up the rest of the sweaters right away. "One woman bought all of them."

"What?" She didn't have to say that she was disappointed. "They should have lasted longer. More people should have had a chance. It's not right that one woman bought them all. Does she have enough kids to wear them? What does one woman do with so many sweaters? We should limit how many sweaters one person can buy. Don't you think?" She looked accusingly at Gavin for not having thought of that in the first place.

She shook her head, "No more angel sweater stories" she said. Or something to that effect. Maybe it was a language problem, he didn't know.

"Angel sweater stories?" he asked.

"Yes, Mr. Reid. It's become kind of… how do they say? A cult thing. Yes, a cult thing."

"What's a cult thing?"

"The sweaters."

"What? What are you talking about?"

She didn't respond.

"Irma. I'm serious. Get the rest of these sweaters over to the shop."

She turned on her heels and walked back to the sorting room.

Gavin was relieved to pass on the good news to Cindi.

"Well, lucky for you, Cindi, we still have dozens of them at the depot. Irma's been hoarding them like a squirrel. She doesn't want to give them up. What's wrong with everyone?"

"The sweaters have a certain attraction," she said matter-of-factly.

"I know they're a real find, but are they that attractive?"

"Gavin, you should know," and Cindi giggled. "The sweaters have a kind of cult following."

The cult thing again. He waved it off. "Don't give me that. Irma's sending over the rest."

But Irma procrastinated, using every excuse in the book. She even toyed with the idea of stealing one but the inventory had already been sent to Mr. Reid's office and he would know. And he already said that staff wasn't allowed to buy any. So the better part of her celebrated the joy the angel sweaters would bring to the children whose little bodies would be wrapped in the woolen stories.

CHAPTER 67

JOSÉ

Each morning Columba sweeps her pain under the rug. The rug is heavy but she manages. Truth lies under the pain and she naively steps all over it.

José's self-assigned savior ranking had nothing to do with the Bishop's religion classes nor the influence of the boys in the Bishop's select group. It had to do with his modest ambition (under the circumstances maybe it was not all that modest) to find a way out for his mother. He was sad and angry but this wasn't about him. His own mother was putrefying before his eyes. He'd tried to talk sense into her but she'd just wave him off, swear under her breath and turn to caress the little sweater on the doll from hell.

Although José was aware that he had veered off of Anita's exact path, he was convinced the answer lay somewhere nearby and he continued attending the Bishop's classes.

However, it happened that the key piece of the puzzle fell into place elsewhere – at school. One morning he had escaped class with the excuse that he felt nauseous (the truth was that he was weak with hunger) and he made his way to the washroom where he squatted on the edge of a seatless toilet behind a patched cubicle door and leaned his head against the wall. Later he thanked the saint who had put him in the right place at the right time. He peered through the cracks when two boys breezed in to share a cigarette. They settled down below the window and between exaggerated tugs on the roll-your-own smoke, they whispered.

"It was my sister Sofia who told me. She's a friend of Rodrigo, the guy from the rich family across town... you know he used to go to the Bishop's classes, upstairs at The Most Pure Blood of Jesus. But he stopped going about two years ago."

"Yeah," the other kid exhaled his smoke towards the window and leaned in. "And, what?"

"Well, Rodrigo told Sofia that the Bishop and Father Cortés are in cahoots."

"What are you talking about?"

"She said that Rodrigo told her the Bishop likes to take young boys out to cabins at the retreat."

"Well, I've heard of it but I've never been there."

"Yeah, and you don't want to, either."

"Yeah, and..?"

"Well..." and he gestured with his hand. "They encourage the boys to pleasure them. And the Bishop too." José's eyes grew wide behind the crack of the cubicle door.

"What? Do you mean...?" and the other boy repeated the gesture.

"Yeah. So what do you think about that?"

"I think," he chuckled and exhaled forcefully, "We better stay away from the Bishop."

"Yeah, but the other thing, the big thing... I mean the *big* thing, is that apparently Father Cortés knows all about it. And the Bishop knows what Father Cortés gets up to, too. They cooperate. They each have their own preference and they support each other."

"What?"

"Yeah. But Father Cortés doesn't like boys, he prefers girls."

"Oh." He snickered. So they've got all the bases covered."

"So to speak."

"Well, and this is the thing – Sofia said that Rodrigo's so depressed that he tries to off himself. So his parents take him to a psychologist and that's when this all comes out. He tells the psychologist and the psychologist tells him that he needs to explain this to his parents. Anyway, so Rodrigo finally tells his Dad what's going on and his Dad goes to the Church and threatens to report them."

"Yeah, and...?"

"The bishop denies everything but he says that he doesn't want these rumors getting out and well, I guess they end up agreeing that the Church will pay Rodrigo's Dad a lot of money to keep things quiet."

"Like how much?"

"I don't know. But a lot! And Sofia says that Rodrigo is still not right in the head."

"So you think Father Cortés knows about this?"

"No doubt. And I bet the Church has covered for him too."

That night José dared to enter The Black Cat again. He'd panhandled enough pesos for a Coca-Cola and he settled into the same dark corner as before. A small, mousy-looking bartender who didn't pay him any mind was attending customers. He'd wait and talk to Anita if he had to wait all night.

After what seemed an eternity (he had been playing with his empty glass for ages), Anita and the boyfriend walked in the front door. They looked serious, discussing something in whispers. The boyfriend said something to her, pushed her towards the bar and he rushed back out the front door.

José slipped onto a stool at the far end of the bar and waited again.

Finally, head down, Anita approached him as she gathered empty bottles and dragged a cloth across the counter. She was caught up with the small quick circles she was making with the cloth. When she neared the end of the bar, she said, like she was talking to a stranger, "What can I get for you?"

"A few minutes of your time."

She started and looked up. Her eyes grew big and she glanced back over her shoulder. "You shouldn't be here, José!"

"I know you're by yourself."

"Yeah, but I can't talk to you. I don't want to talk to you."

"But Anita, this isn't right. Just give me a few minutes."

She paused, close to tears and pushed the cloth in smaller, harder circles over the counter. But she didn't move away.

"What do you want?"

"Anita, I know what happened to you. I know why you left home."

She almost spit at him and then through her teeth, "You know nothing of the sort. You don't have a clue."

"Yes, I do. Yes, I know."

"So what do you know then?" She stopped and stared at him.

"I know about Father Cortés."

Her face turned white, her chin dropped, she squeezed her eyes shut. José didn't say anything. Neither of them moved for a long time. Then he dared reached across the counter and he lightly covered her hand. He felt her tears drip onto his fingers, the dim light from above the ceiling fan illuminating each one as they rolled off to soak into the cloth, which she clutched tightly between her fingers.

She swallowed hard. "So then do you know about Mom too?"

"What about Mom?"

"Yeah, exactly." She snatched her hand back. "Exactly. Where was she?"

"What do you mean?"

"I mean, where was our great protector, our performer of miracles, our savior, our virgin?"

"What are you talking about, Anita?" José was scared now. What did Columba have to do with Father Cortés? His gut churned and the hairs on the back of his neck prickled. He knew Columba was capable of stealing but Columba was small-time. She did petty things. Besides, she'd never hurt Anita.

"When Father Cortés was 'teaching me catechism'..." she scoffed, her lips curled. "When Father Cortés was teaching me catechism, where was Mom? Why didn't she stop him?"

"Anita, Mom didn't know anything. She still doesn't. Only I know."

"And why not?" Didn't she always say she was in charge, that she knew when the smallest leaf fell from a tree? Couldn't she tell something was wrong?"

Anita stood stiffly on the other side of the counter. She was bent forward in a rage, glaring at him. A customer called to her and she yelled without looking at him. "Wait your turn, you prick! Can't you see I'm busy here?"

She spit out, "That man, that holy man took me for more than a few rides in his car. Do you know that? And he did whatever he wanted. Do you know that? And do you know why he could do whatever he wanted? Because he said that Mom knew and that she thought this was a good way for me to learn what life was all about. Mom told Father Cortés it would be our little secret. Like we were the trinity... father, daughter and holy spirit." Tears were streaming now, snot was bubbling out of her nostrils, saliva building up at the corners of her lips. She was inside-out now. Out of control. "So guess who was the holy spirit? And guess who probably wasn't being the holy spirit for nothing? Since when does Mom ever do anything for free?"

Someone bellowed for more beer and she threw the cloth behind her without taking aim. It landed on the floor.

"And you know what else? I can't stand the sight of her. She's dead as far as I'm concerned. I'm better off with Marcelo."

"No." José said. "No, Anita. You're wrong." Father Cortés is like that. He takes advantage of young girls and he does it without parental consent. He just does it. And so does the Bishop."

"Well, I don't believe you. She's our Mom. She's supposed to protect us. What good is she, playing the role of a pimp?"

"No Anita. No, you've got it wrong. If you could see our place now, you'd know she didn't sell anything, especially to Father Cortés."

"Just get out, okay? I told you. Now you know. Just be careful, little brother, that she doesn't sell you to the highest bidder too. 'Just trying to survive,' she'll tell you."

He caught the last microbus up the hill, ignoring passengers getting on and off, not paying attention to the familiar landmarks, the broken lights on the posts a block from home, dogs snarling at one another, ripping at the up-turned garbage bin on the corner. They passed the forgotten pile of rocks, abandoned for years after a minor road excavation. He missed his stop and got off at the end of the line when the bus driver yelled at him to move on. "This isn't a hostel you know. Get out." The driver shoved him out the back door. José had to backtrack several blocks down the hill.

If Anita would only come home to see the state of things, she'd understand that Columba was innocent and she'd see that they weren't living off ill-gotten gains, like she'd accused Columba of.

By the time José got in the door, Columba was sleeping like a baby. She was on the sofa, probably waiting up for him but it got the better of her. She was snoring. He bent down and kissed her on the cheek, she inhaled sharply, smiled and touched his cheek and fell back to sleep.

Columba was innocent.

Tomorrow José would make his move.

CHAPTER 68

IRENE

Joy is reborn. You must gather it into your arms all at once, fragile and bloated as it may be, and carry it with you so that you never lose sight of it again.

After the sweaters had arisen from the dead, Irene raised herself above the layers of the half-baked sabotage plans she had in mind for Chuck's store. In fact, she put them aside indefinitely. No longer interested, no longer in need of purpose.

With the revival of the sweaters, she negotiated a truce between herself and the store, which had never even sensed it was in danger. She held up her hand to halt a storm that only she knew was on the horizon. Essentially, it was her playing against herself. And she won.

After she had metaphorically kicked Chuck's store into the gutter, she obsessed over the sweater shop, that brilliant little jewel called Little Imps, amidst the ore slag down on main street.

At nine o'clock each morning, ever since that amazing day in April when Irene had discovered the mother lode, the Silver Shadow nosed its way through the front door of Little Imps, Irene's gloved hands gripping its sleek handle like a queen holding the reins of a thoroughbred. There was no need for her to utter a single word. Each morning after she strode in, the red-haired woman pronounced through pursed lips, "There are no more sweaters." And Irene, already anticipating the answer, nodded, pushed down on the handle, the Silver Shadow kicked up its front wheels, did an about-turn, and pranced out of the store. Cindi Crawford knew she'd be back tomorrow.

After her umpteenth visit, Cindi gave her reason for hope, "Last time you were here, you managed to snap up the last of our sweaters. You were just lucky. Whenever we're lucky enough to get any, they sell just like that." She snapped her fingers. Who was this woman, so desperately infatuated with the sweaters? Cindi Crawford had to admit that the sweaters were extremely attractive, uniquely creative and superbly crafted but even their most avid customers had never been quite so obsessed. She would never tell Gavin but she felt genuine pity for this woman. So she spilled the beans. "Listen, I can tell you that we definitely have more coming in. And no one else knows about that. I'm just telling you. Okay?"

On the third day, Irene was born again. She walked in feeling elated, accompanied by the Silver Shadow, which was so much more than a prop, gleaming like the star it was, fine spokes glinting above the wooden floor. Irene's cheeks were flushed, her enlarged pupils rimmed the bright blue of her irises, her eyes darted around the shop before the door closed behind her. The visit would be short. She needed to get the sweaters out and back to safety. She had glimpsed a sweater in the display window (When had they updated the display? How long had that sweater been strung up like that? It must have been only since yesterday afternoon. Too long, in any case.) Its left sleeve was held up in greeting, the right one tucked sassily into the patch pocket. It was the 'You are my Sunshine' sweater that would have fit a seven-year-old Alicia. Peacock blue with a little greystone cottage in the background, and a huge orange sun rising over the top right shoulder, its gradient orange-yellow rays extending all the way to the bottom of the sweater back and front. A ginger three-dimensional crocheted kitten was chasing a small round ball of yarn on the patch pocket.

Cindi Crawford greeted her. "See? I told you, right? They're here," and her arm cut across the air in a generous swoosh towards the shelves.

"Do you have any more in stock or just what are here?"

"No, these are the only ones we have. I promise. They've become quite a fad." Cindi beamed as though she was responsible for their success. Irene decided she didn't like her toothy smile and she frowned at her and turned towards the window.

"I'll take all of these," she indicated the sweaters on the shelves. "And I want the one in the window too."

"All of them? Are you sure? The one in the window? You'll be cleaning us out again."

"My money's good." Irene felt attacked by the girl's accusatory tone and she reached instinctively for the Silver Shadow, which had rolled a bit, nosing its way towards the clerk. Cindi Crawford frowned as she watched Irene claw the thin air a couple of times before the tips of her gloves reached the Silver Shadow's handle and she reined it in. She glared back at Cindi and waited.

"Just let me climb into the window. I'll get it."

Irene was humming as she floated along behind the Silver Shadow, which was stuffed with several bags. Strings of light splayed through the spoked wheels as it dashed along the sidewalk, a victorious Irene with five oversized bags hanging from her wrists, directing the troops back home.

She didn't count her sweaters as she folded them into their baskets and slid them into the closets. She didn't have to. She was deeply saddened to think that these were the very last of the store's sweater inventory because this was really just the tip of the iceberg. And then it struck her that many sweaters – hundreds more sweaters must have been sold out of that little shop. That meant they were here somewhere.

They were on the backs of little imps around town. And she knew exactly where to find little imps. They frequented playgrounds. They went to kindergartens and parks and schools. So she too, would frequent playgrounds. She would wander the halls of schools and kindergartens. She would venture into cloakrooms, and she would slip sweaters from hooks on the walls where they hung above dozens of miniature running shoes and Disney lunch boxes.

CHAPTER 69

COLUMBA

The sun rises each morning from behind the cordillera and begins the task of sweeping shadows into the Pacific Ocean. The slopes below the ridges glitter golden and red but at the end of the day, tired, they devolve to their mundane brown and fade into grey. Lights out. Start again tomorrow.

They had cheese for breakfast. Cheese with fresh bread and hot tea. Columba had already been to the bakery. José woke up to see her smiling down at him.

"I had a good day yesterday," she said. "Come have some breakfast."

She sat across the table, beaming. She was wearing makeup this morning and her hair, although its grey roots had not yet been dyed, topped her head in a proud beehive of backcombing that he hadn't seen for months. Her cheeks were exaggerated dollops of pink and her lips were ruby red, sketched beyond their natural shape to something larger. She had a constant, oversized pucker.

"Mom, you look pretty this morning."

"Thank you, son. Like I said, yesterday was a good day. I waited up for you last night. Where were you? Why were you so late?"

"I met some friends downtown. No big deal, the time ran away with us. That's all."

José was lucky she was too excited about her own news to drill him or chastise. "I got another cleaning job!" Her eyes were bright. "Almost the same as the bank. But this time, I'm doing two mornings a week at the supermarket."

So that's where the cheese had come from. She must have a friend in the deli section.

"That's great Mom." Maybe he was even more relieved than she was. "What're you going to do about the doll?" He couldn't bring himself to call her by a name, give her a personality, acknowledge her importance. He wanted to get rid of the thing. "I mean, she'll be by herself all day."

"She's just a doll, you know. She'll manage."

"Yeah, I know that Mom." When did she put her feet back down on the ground? "But you know…"

"Actually, I have to credit Magdalena for the idea of the supermarket job."

His heart sunk but he pretended this was all normal. "Oh, how's that?"

Columba was breaking the buns and serving the tea and she paused to recount the moments leading up to her revelation. "Well, actually, I shouldn't have said that. She is more than a doll. You know, son, she doesn't really talk much, she just listens. And the other day I have to admit that I was complaining about our situation and she was all ears as usual. And I said, 'It's always me who does the talking. Why don't you offer something to the conversation?' I guess she interpreted that as a complaint, which it was. And I swear her eyes glazed over. You know that she has her special way of communicating. She just closed up."

Columba sat back, slurped her tea, ceremoniously placed a thick slice of cheese on her bun and then chewed intently for a minute. José waited for more but Columba seemed to be satisfied that this would explain how the stupid doll had contributed to her getting a job.

"But how, by just closing up, did she get you the job?"

"Well, because I was offended by her lack of attention." Columba said it like it was so obvious. "I can laugh about it now but it made me angry then. So when she refuses to look at me, I stand up, put on my sweater, borrow a few pesos from Jorge… he's just going by with his newspapers, and I get on a bus and go to the supermarket. I mean, Magdalena must be some sort of psychologist or motivational expert of something. I mean, she knew I was going to get mad and get moving. So anyway, when I walk into the supermarket, who's the first person I see? The Devil's Doll. Who knew she worked there? But there she is behind the deli counter. Her eye still twitches, by the way." Columba paused to look over at José. "You know who she is, right? Anyway… she beckons me over to the counter. I haven't seen her for months. I mean, I don't know for how long. And she says that I look like shit."

"I tell her that I lost my job at the depot and things aren't very good lately. And she says, 'Well, this must be the day your luck changes. Thank whoever sent you down here because Ada, who cleans the floors on Tuesdays and Thursdays died of a heart attack yesterday and they're looking for a replacement.'"

"So that's how you got the job?"

"Yup, just like that. The Devil's Doll vouched for me and I was hired just like that. I start tomorrow, Thursday."

José raised his mug of tea. "Salud!"

"Cheers." She responded with a wide smile.

José got up and gave her a hug. He'd wait until another day to tell Columba what he found out from Anita. Let her bask in the happiness of her own making for a few days at least. No need to bring Anita back into the picture on a day like this. Or send his Mom spinning with Father Cortés' lies. There was no saying how'd she'd react to that. Chances are all hell would break loose and nothing would ever be normal again. He'd handle things his way.

Five days later, when she returned home from her second shift on the new job, tired but content, he still couldn't bring it up with her. Why risk breaking this happy streak? He noticed the doll was now seated in the corner by the front door, still draped in the sweater (which he had to admit was much more impressive than the doll herself). Where on earth did his mother come up with these things?

CHAPTER 70

GAVIN

If people are determined to be greedy, then let it be for something of value. But who defines value?

For Gavin, the value is not just the accumulation of the printed certificates and minted minerals (although that's how you keep score). For him it is more about playing the game, always being ready to advance around the board. He doesn't care where the other players are.

The sweaters were gone now, and that was that. Now he turned his attention to the eco-garments. In search of the right hook from which to sell Frankie and Yolanda's eco-goods, Gavin decided to make a visit to their cabin out by the lake. Maybe if he saw them in their surroundings, maybe if they led him through their processes, maybe if he became familiar with their lives, he could create a narrative that would drive the sales forward and into the right niche. He savored the challenge and he wasn't sure why it had taken him so long to pick up on it.

Gavin didn't do this out of desperation. No sir. Gavin did this because it was a spin-off from the game. A game he couldn't bring himself to stop playing. Stan's was being run properly and it would never go out of business. Funky Town had found its legs long ago and was outperforming even his highest expectations. Mark had commented recently that the two of them could go fishing every day and sales would still exceed projections. Gavin rarely accompanied Mark on buying shows now. Mark was still as enthusiastic as a kid at a circus. He never tired of them. Before the last show, he asked Gavin if it would be all right if Mr. Jones accompanied him. He wanted to share the experience. Mr. Jones was the bike-riding math teacher, the fashion addict who had come to the store for advice from Mark more than a year ago. Gavin suspected that some of Mark's newest purchases were made exclusively with Mr. Jones in mind because who else in town wanted, for instance, a paisley ascot tie and fingerless gloves? Each afternoon at about the same time, Mark rushed out to stand at the front door to greet Mr. Jones, who pedaled past, saluting Mark and unable to do anything about that enthusiastic smile. After a brief exchange, Mark would return to stand behind the counter, all lovesick and bleary-eyed. Gavin thanked his lucky stars that he, himself was a man without needs, a man for whom such banal desires never surfaced, and whose behavior was not, therefore, unbecoming.

The businesses still needed both of them at the helm to give a steer if one of the shops veered off course. But that was rare. If you hired the right people, respected them and paid them well, they would carry the business forward without many hiccups. Gavin was still disappointed with Little Imps, as the locale continued to be called, because without the sweaters, which were no more than a few flashes in the pan, the shop was nothing but a half-empty space manned (or maybe he should say 'womaned') by a red-headed yuppie who was named after a super-model. He never figured out how hippie parents (he assumed her parents must have once been hippies) would name a child after a model who represented unbridled consumption. Their child now dropped crumbs of granola into her lap as she counted stitches under her breath, her knitting needles clacking rather clumsily. "It's a new hobby", she had said yesterday when she looked up to greet him, all smiles.

He pushed thoughts of Cindi aside. It was fall and the morning air was crisp, the grass in the shadows was still wet with dew, thin clouds drifted beyond the treed hills around the lake where Frankie and Yolanda lived. He inhaled, filling his chest with rich mountain air. He suddenly felt incredibly lucky, like the giant who possesses the goose who lays the golden eggs. He could sense a good thing coming on. Like maybe he was heading to the foot of the bean stock.

Smoke curled lazily from the old stone chimney of Frankie and Yolanda's cabin. Twigs cracked under his boots. He had deliberately laced on his Doc Martens for the wander across the meadow, pretending to put their durability to the test. He didn't truly intend to give them a rugged workout, the gentle meadow was much too tame for that and anyway, he wasn't your rugged outdoorsman. It was all about appearances. He breathed evenly, making an effort to lengthen his stride, one, two, one, two, along the path that led to the beanstalk that led to the goose that laid the golden eggs.

He was within 30 meters of the cabin when, out of the corner of his eye, he spotted a swatch of bright color bounding through the high grass. A small animal, maybe a rabbit. He stopped and waited. The rabbit or whatever it was, stopped too. Both of them froze for several seconds, eyeing each other. Suddenly, the grass rustled and he saw that it was a brown hare, a bit of winter white still visible on its back. It bounded towards the cabin. It had something attached to it, perhaps an item of clothing had fallen from the clothes line and the hare had become entangled in it. It hopped away and disappeared. Gavin reached the house and paused at the foot of the wide wooden steps. The steps were made of logs that had been sawn in half lengthwise. They were fitted like perfect stones of an ancient ruin, ready to withstand centuries.

"Hello?" He called out. His voice cut through the crisp morning air. He took one step up and waited, the Doc Marten on his right foot posed impressively on the log stair. He closed one eye and framed it with his fingers, a perfect promo shot. He watched as droplets of dew on the toe of the boot rolled off the polished leather and disappeared.

Finally, Frankie swept open the front door. "Gavin! What a nice surprise." He paused for a second in all of his bare-chested, well-maintained 60-plus glory, "What are you doing here?" He bounded down the stairs and wrapped Gavin in a bear hug. Gavin pushed away from the hairy torso and held out his hand. Frankie smelled like he slept in a cedar chest.

Frankie grabbed Gavin by the elbow and pulled him up the stairs. "Come on in, my friend. How good to see you."

Gavin clomped up the thick steps, trying to keep stride. Yolanda was at the door now, barefoot, hair hanging loosely past her shoulders. She was wrapped in an ankle-length patchwork robe. It looked like she'd just pulled a quilt off the bed and it had sprung sleeves. All of this contributed to the feeling that Gavin had indeed just stepped into a fairy tale.

Their house was warm – logs smoldered in the stone fireplace, a few small flames still licking up around them, an old dog lay at the hearth, so old that he didn't care who had just walked in. He was under a fleece blanket, just his head exposed, his eyes barely open under the soppy lids. "Gordon's too old to be much of a guard dog now," said Frankie. "But he had his day. He earned his keep long ago."

"Here, take a seat." Frankie pulled out a chair from the kitchen table. The table and chairs were carved out of a tree, all single pieces, all with a matte shine from natural oils. Thick cushions, each a different color (obviously Yolanda's natural dyes), were fastened with heavy yarn that ran through precisely drilled holes at the backs of each chair. A pastel green table runner with brilliant zig-zagging red and yellow threads ran the length of the table. A heavy wicker basket that was filled with dried flowers that looked like they'd just been dropped into place at the touch of a fairy's wand sat in the middle of the table, and a long wooden chandelier hung down, almost meeting it at the center.

"We don't get many visitors out here."

"Well, I thought it was time we got better acquainted." Gavin relaxed into the comfort of the perfectly shaped chair and looked around. The walls were decorated with paintings and charcoal sketches, some of them framed, some tacked in the corners, heavy paper, dog-eared and curling inwards. There were full nudes, macro flower details painted in watercolors, a piece that looked like a study of textured wood, cut open, bare and vulnerable, modern minimalist woodcuts of one and two colors, and a few posters announcing an annual vernissage in New York. The sofa, constructed of logs from which were slung leather pieces was at the far wall. Two stained-glass lamps on heavy bases rested on old buckled sea trunks at either end. A cowhide rug covered the center of the floor. Bookshelves ran the length and height of the opposite wall, a few wood carvings, some photos and wire sculptures interspersed with the books. The house smelled of potpourri and outdoors brought in.

A tabby cat jumped up onto the window sill and preened itself for Gavin's viewing pleasure. You can watch but don't touch. It was wearing a multicolored vest with a tassel in the shape of a stiff cross hanging to the middle of its chest.

Gavin felt warmed to his center. The home was wholesome, raw, it pushed back into the mountain for shelter and at the same time, it reached out across the lake. The best of both worlds. Gavin felt a twinge of envy for the peaceful world these two individuals had succeeded in creating. Would his visit disrupt that? He hoped not but the feeling on his way down the path this morning told him something would change after today.

Without asking, Yolanda set down a big mug of tea and offered him milk. "We don't have sugar in the house," she said, not apologetically.

"So where are the sheep?" Gavin had just realized that he hadn't seen any on his way in.

"Oh, for now, they stick to the section out there, back in from the lake," Yolanda pointed west. "You can't see them from here."

Just then, the hare that he'd seen on the way up to the house, bounded past the low dining room window. "I think that animal ran away with something of yours."

"Oh, that," She laughed. "No. I gave it to him. That's Bob the hare. He's one of the tamer ones. I made him a jacket because he's one of the scrawnier guys and I thought he was cold."

"A jacket?"

"Yeah." She turned to Frankie. "Can you go and get Bob, Frankie?"

Gavin didn't know how easy it was to catch a hare but apparently it was not a great feat because Frankie returned in less than three minutes with the little animal in his arms, its ears twitching, eyes wide and staring. The hare's jacket was a work of art. It was one of Yolanda's recycled projects, a jean jacket with triangle leather patches edged with bright red stitching. The jacket was finished in alternating fabric prints, some with flowers, some with green stripes. "It looked better on him when he was white," Yolanda said. "I made it before Christmas, red and green, you know?"

"What else have you made for your animals?"

"Well, I made felt hats for a few of the sheep, a necklace for our budgie," she gestured towards a cage that hung inside the kitchen window, and nodding towards the cat, "Tiger, as you can see, has a jacket." She turned towards the old dog under the blanket, "And, oh, Gordon has a specially woven vest that fits around all four legs. I was inspired by those search and rescue dogs, you know? And I thought something that reflected in the light might be a good idea. It's a bit over the top I guess because Gordon is too old to rescue now. But at least he doesn't have enough energy to pull the sequins off of it." She walked over and bent down to lift the blanket around Gordon, who didn't budge.

He lay there in gold and silver sequined splendor, like a knight in a suit of armor. Gavin recognized Yolanda's handiwork in the dried reeds that wove up the sides of the vest, intertwining dark and light strands and the large felt wool section of various colors, like she'd played in the dye vat and pulled it out at a moment inspired.

Gavin was numb with amazement. While Little Imps locale languished with unwanted children's eco-garments and tired brochures from the town of Burgeon and as Frankie and Yolanda lost hope in their own inspiration for children, the answer lay right here in ecologically-friendly garments for pets.

CHAPTER 71

CHUCK

Chuck couldn't ignore the signal from his Visa statement. He called his bank, knowing that of course they wouldn't be able to alleviate his fears. His hands were shaking before he hung up the phone. It wasn't about the cost, although in years past, he would have complained that surely such an expense (whatever it might be) was unnecessary. And that at the very least, it should show itself, and be worthy.

The worry now was what the cost might mean. It was the fact that Irene had bought something again and that it was hidden from him. Granted, there had only been two purchases but they were from the same place, and for large amounts. The statement said it was from a numbered company so it could be anything. What if it was yarn again? Was it a replay of the same nightmare? His stomach churned, his head pounded and he broke out in a sweat. He rushed to the staff washroom at the back of the store, leaned into the toilet and gave up his breakfast.

How could he rest until he knew what she was up to? It occurred to him that he could search for a legal address of the numbered company through the government registry. He feared his own success. The company address led him to a lawyer's office in Burgeon. He called the office and was told by a crisp but friendly female voice "These things are always best discussed in person." What things? What had Irene done?

The next morning, he drove out to Burgeon, and easily found the lawyer's office – the only one in town, you can't miss it. Just turn left at Stan's Men's and Boys' Wear...

He recognized the youthful voice from yesterday's phone call. The legal assistant was pleasant and told him the numbered company was perfectly legitimate. In fact, it was owned by a charity in Grant Falls. The charity itself didn't accept credit cards so the purchase must have been made at its 'pop-up' location on the main street. She said it was trading as 'Little Imps' and she assured him it wasn't that difficult to find the shop. Right on main street, she repeated as she smiled and shook his hand.

What was the name of the charity where Old Man McArthur had donated the sweaters? It had to be one and the same. Did they still have sweaters? Here? What had become of his instructions? He reasoned that although the note was not legally binding, surely a legitimate charity with any kind of common sense and compassion would have cooperated and sent the sweaters somewhere else, somewhere far away (even if they didn't know the circumstance, which was none of their business anyway). The question of what a charity did and didn't do as a matter of practice faded in the face of his current problem, which was now something much more urgent. He would deal with the charity later.

On his drive back to Grant Falls, he didn't notice the pair of deer on the roadside, their kindly deer eyes observing the traffic before turning in unison to leap back into the safety of the hillside forest. Nothing to see here, folks. He ignored the crows, fluttering back and forth as they pecked at the remains of roadkill on the shoulder. They scattered and cawed at him when he approached without decelerating. He failed to notice the police radar trap and the traffic cop waving him over from beside a parked police vehicle about a kilometer down the road. He motored on. He paid no attention to the flashing red light, that winged over the rural landscape. Nor did he hear the screaming siren that pursued him for two kilometers. He didn't see the police car until it pulled up alongside him, the policeman in the passenger side, mouthing 'pull over, pull over' and gesturing for him to stop.

Suddenly aware, he panicked and pulled over, trembling and full of apologies, muttering to himself as he shut off the engine, "Christ, what have I done?" and then to the constable, his voice quivering, "I'm so sorry officer, I didn't notice. My mind was elsewhere."

"You're not supposed to be driving when your mind is elsewhere, sir. This is serious. Do you know how long we chased you? Your license and registration, please."

Chuck reached for his documents. Hands shaking, he dropped them and had to undo his seatbelt and reach down. He fumbled, his glasses sliding off his nose, which caused him even more anxiety and he apologized again for his carelessness as he bent down to retrieve the Diors.

The policeman ordered him to step out his vehicle, sir, hands on the car.

"My mind was elsewhere, officer." He repeated. He started to say, "My wife... you see, my wife..." but he stopped. They wouldn't understand. He assured them repeatedly that he'd pay the traffic fine the next day because really, he was a law-abiding man and this was the first time in his life something like this had ever happened. Really. Maybe it didn't seem like it, but it was true. Whether they believed him or not, it was hard to tell.

Finally, they let him continue on his journey. He was very lucky, they told him, that they just didn't cuff him and book him for trying to run and for something else and something else – he couldn't remember and didn't care right now. He was overly cautious as he drove into town, constantly monitoring the speedometer. He glided slowly along the main street, scanning the shops. He slowed when he saw the less than attractive sign for Little Imps. It was right across the street from Spin a Yarn and he remembered, in spite of himself, all the times he had wanted to drop in to see Irene on the off-chance of stepping out for a coffee. They'd feel like teenagers, he had told her, it'd be fun. "No, Chuck," she had said to him each time he suggested it, "I always take my breaks in the back room because I have to work on display items when I have a cup of tea. Break time is valuable for me. You, the world's best time manager, should understand that, right?"

He pulled into the curb halfway down the block and walked up to Little Imps. A young red-haired woman brandishing oversized knitting needles (he cringed at the sight of them) looked up from the behind the counter.

"I'm not actually here to buy anything," he stuttered. "I.. I..." (how to begin?) "I'm here to ask about a woman who made a couple of sizeable purchases over the last months." The young woman put down her knitting needles and she lowered the extra-long scarf she was making, folding it over itself several times and pushing the needles into it.

"What did she buy?" The red-haired woman asked.

"Well, I don't know. That's kind of why I'm here. I, I... I'm her husband and well, she is sort of, well, kind of ill at the moment. Something came over her suddenly," he lied. "And I think she might have lost her credit card and maybe someone else used it here?"

"Well, I wouldn't have any way of knowing that."

"No, of course not. But... so... I just wondered..." he produced his credit card statement and pointed at the highlighted purchases.

The young woman furrowed her brow and tugged a little at the red braid that pointed stiffly over her right shoulder. Chuck gazed at the braid, he thought it looked rude. She bit her lip as she focused on the statement. Chuck waited.

She raised her hand and rubbed her cheek thoughtfully. "Oh yes, oh yeah. Of course. Of course. I thought it was odd…." She looked at Chuck and tugged at her rude red braid. "Oh, I'm sorry, I just mean there was a lady who wore a nice camel hair coat and a pair of expensive leather gloves and she came in here pushing a big, fancy baby carriage. I told her that the carriage wasn't allowed in the store but I guess she didn't want to wake up the baby so she insisted she couldn't leave the carriage outside. So yeah, she bought some beautifully crafted sweaters. In fact, she bought everything we had. I think there must have been several dozen. She cleaned out the entire stock. And we'd only just got them in."

Chuck had no response. He adjusted his glasses. The clerk continued, "After that, the lady came in every morning without fail, always as soon as we opened. And every morning I told her that we had no more sweaters in stock. I felt bad because she really wanted more. I mean she was kind of pathetic. Sorry… I mean… Well, anyway, so I knew when they were going to send more over. So I told her when that would be. And she showed up that very day and purchased the whole lot. I didn't even have them all out on display yet. As you can see, things are pretty slow here now."

He was afraid to ask, "Are you getting more sweaters?"

She shrugged. "Who knows? I can't help you there."

By the time he got home, the house was dark but a light cast its thin yellow line from underneath Irene's bedroom door, which he dared not cross. He had no idea what she must be doing in there. Perhaps reading. He hoped it was something as innocent as that. He dared not confront her, and he was too tired anyway. Tired from worrying about what her purchases might mean, from speculating about where they would lead – yet again, and exhausted merely by the prospect of a renewed struggle.

He needed to avoid conflicts with Irene and to try to enjoy the limited amount of herself that she was willing to share.

Over the next several months, there were no unexpected purchases at Little Imps or anywhere else, for that matter, and Chuck relaxed. More than once during that time, he had planned to ransack the house but he could never find an opportune moment because if Irene left, she always managed to return before he did. And when he got there, he found her in an amicable mood, which he had no desire to ruin.

She had begun to cook dinner again and the table was always set for two when he returned from the store. Although they ate mostly in silence, sometimes he talked about the store and she looked up and nodded as though she might really be paying attention. Outside of a chance meeting with the mailman or words exchanged with the paperboy, she didn't disclose details of her day. But he was grateful for their shared dinners, which had become a pleasant routine, and once again, he looked upon them as a sign of their lives returning to normal. For now, he pushed aside the question of Irene's purchases.

CHAPTER 72

ANITA

Innocence is lost to observation, realization and experience. Stepping away from your mother's shadow is safe when she is still within reach but letting go of her hand and tiptoeing into the darkness of someone else's heart – someone who may not be worthy of your trust – is dangerous.

Being the eldest of Columba's miracle children, Anita the unsung daughter of an immaculate conception took her special circumstances for granted up until age eight, when Lucia exposed the myth for what it was. A big part of Anita's world had tumbled then. The truth made her question Columba and once a child starts to lose confidence in their mother, their world changes.

According to Lucia (and countless others who repeated the rumor behind Anita's back) her mother was not a virgin at all, but a whore who had two children in fly-by-night relationships with two different men. That was a lot for an eight-year-old to comprehend, let alone, swallow.

Anita laid awake at night for several months after the truth was revealed (in a cruel, childish way), pondering the person her mother must be. She couldn't find it in herself to be unforgiving of her mother's lie nor could she blame her for standing by it. She understood Columba was only protecting them but it occurred to the young Anita that her mother was also protecting herself. And she wondered which took precedence.

So since that early age, she regarded Columba with fresh eyes, and slowly she began to notice unsavory things about her Mom. She saw the unnatural blonde hair glued with highly-scented hairspray in a plump backcombed crown atop her head, the heavily rouged cheeks, the one freaky gold front tooth, the oversized purse with its bizarre contents. Early on, she noticed the ashtrays, pens, glue sticks, unused notebooks and folders, scissors, women's scarves, miniature ceramic dogs and cats and oversized chocolate bars that her Mom placed into the cardboard box and shoved on a low kitchen shelf. She also noticed that when the box was empty, coins jingled in the Nescafe can. Things appeared, disappeared and money jingled.

"Don't touch these things. They're not mine," her mother would say. Anita soon discovered that when she had enough things, Columba dumped them into a sack to sell them at a downtown sidewalk. Anita knew this because sometimes when she was down near the plaza, she saw Columba plying the wares and she always turned away, embarrassed. But she failed to realize this was the means by which they paid for gas, for power, and often even bread and rice.

Her mom was a petty thief, not that it was uncommon. But, perhaps as a result of being raised to believe she was a miracle, she felt righteous. And maybe that's why, at the age of about thirteen, she was drawn to after-school catechism classes at The Most Pure Blood of Jesus Church. Columba had never encouraged her miracle children to attend church. As a family they were, she told them, autonomous and self-sufficient. Although the icons on the shelf were useful allies, the family could, in a pinch get by without the help of San Expedito. Saying they could get by without the help of the Virgin, the most reverent mother of Jesus, whose arms were broad enough to ac-commodate all the children in the world, was a bit harder to swallow. The Virgin had higher standing. At the same time, Columba admitted that she wasn't well-schooled in things religious but rather, she followed the spirit of the Lord as she understood it from the believers around her. She did not strictly forbid formal schooling in religion but she advised moderation.

Anita's friend, Lucia was encouraged by her own mother (who, according to Columba was nothing but a social-climber who spread evil gossip) to attend catechism classes at the prestigious Most Pure Blood of Jesus Church. Lucia encouraged Anita to join her mostly because that she didn't want to ride the bus back and forth to Progreso by herself. From the very first class, Anita was attracted to the teachings, the purity and the kindness of Father Cortés.

She began to idolize him because he demonstrated true dedication and ad-herence to the teachings of Jesus, he was just the sort of man she knew a priest should be. He was tolerant but firm, open to ideas and suggestions that he could easily relate to Christian values and he had a particular skill for spinning them to coincide with the rules set out by the Church for the good of its followers. Most of all, he was like a father himself, maybe even the one who went missing from Anita's life the night after his seed was planted.

By the age of fifteen, she spent most of her spare time at the church, going beyond the Wednesday afternoon catechism classes. She offered to distrib-ute hymnals, she often swept the floor and tidied the annex, even did some filing if she was allowed. Maybe, she thought to herself, she was falling in love with Father. She knew such love was prohibited by the Church and she flushed, looking towards heaven to ask for forgiveness every time her heart leapt at the sight of him. Maybe she would become a nun and she would learn the ways of the Virgin and she would understand how to love a man without lusting after him.

The Bishop encouraged a variety of extra-curricular activities and Father occasionally organized short retreats for select groups of his own. The Most Pure Blood of Jesus Church had a private facility at an oasis in one of the deep valleys of the Andes. It was only about 45 minutes inland via Father's Volkswagen. The students strove to do well in class so they would be invited to these events, not so much for the recognition or even for the events themselves but because there was a swimming pool and even a tennis court. It was an unexpected luxury for any child, and especially one from the barren ridges of Santa Rita.

Lucia complained that she had never been invited on a retreat but that three of her friends from Progreso were called regularly. So Anita was full of joy when Father approached her one day as she finished collating the bulletins for next Sunday's mass.

"Anita, we are having a retreat for students who have demonstrated sincere interest and enthusiasm and I think it's high time you were invited."

She looked up and smiled. Her heart melted and she flushed. He stood so close to her that she could feel his breath on her neck. He gently caressed her back and she felt like someone's kitten. In her two years attending Father's classes she never would have dreamed that Father would suddenly and quite clearly consider her special.

"Lucia, Father invited me to a retreat."

"What? When?"

"I don't know when."

"You'll have to talk to your Mom first. Will she let you go?"

"I don't know. She thinks I spend too much time here already."

As it turned out, the retreat would be several weeks away and meantime, Father said he wanted to tutor Anita. He suggested she join him on visits to the outskirts of Santa Rita where some of the least privileged people lived in new shanty towns. The community was like a garden of sad flowers that shriveled at the edge of an oasis where water was already scarce.

Arriving just before mid-day on a Saturday afternoon, their first visit was at a dwelling made mostly of sheets of cardboard and old wine crates. Crumpled newspapers and old cement sacks were stuffed into the cracks of the wall. Anita was reminded that her own family could be worse off. A woman was bent over a fire pit outside and a barefoot little boy had toddled over the packed earth behind her. The little boy looked quizzically at Anita and Father Cortés and smiled. Father smiled and walked up to greet the mother with a cordial kiss on the cheek and a gentle handshake. She responded in kind but didn't smile at Father.

"Nothing has changed." Anita heard the mother say. "I applied for help from social services, like you told me to but no one has done anything. No one has come to visit, to check his health." She nodded towards the toddler. "I don't have money to go back down to Progreso."

Father took the young mother aside and spoke softly. Anita noticed that his hand was placed firmly on the small of the woman's back and that it roamed down onto her buttocks. The woman leaned into him. Then before they left, he blessed the air in front of her and he blessed the little boy, tousled his hair, and he passed the woman some money. Anita never knew if there was a solution to the woman's problem. Father didn't tell her. Instead, he seemed pensive as they drove further up, following one of the unpaved roads that led to an abandoned mine. He turned and parked the car so they sat overlooking the sea. They were a great distance now from the shanty town, in fact they were a great distance from any civilization at all.

She expected him to explain something about the poor family they had just visited but instead he turned, a new look in his eyes, something dark and penetrating that frightened her and made her heart pound against her ribs.

"You're a good girl, Anita."

She looked down at her hands folded on her lap, her thumbs restless, rubbing one across the other. He leaned over and rested a hand on hers. It was warm and soft. "My heart is filled with hope and admiration," he said. He shifted in his seat to face her and he began to stroke her fingers. Now his hands felt hot, and he moved a little closer, his fingers creeping slowly up her arms until he reached her cheeks and he caressed her face with the back of his hand. By now his face was close to hers and she felt his breath on her neck, as she had back at the church that day. His breath smelled of mints over something she couldn't identify, something less pleasant. This isn't what she expected. And it wasn't what she wanted at all. She had fantasized about some kind of intimacy with Father but she didn't think this was the way it was supposed to feel and she stiffened.

Father reached across her and pulled the lever of her seat, the seat thudded back and she jolted back with it. She gripped the side and looked up at a dark stain on the roof of the car. Father's face was right above hers now. He breathed loudly in her ear. She turned and looked outside at the expanse of desert. She could see a wind storm growing in the distance. She concentrated on what was happening outside of the car, the sun curving its way west where it would eventually penetrate the Pacific Ocean. En route it was forcing its heat onto the innocent golden sand, here and there veins of ore pulsed under its power – glittering, shivering, shifting. The sand was no longer still. The wind was picking it up and pulling it towards them in a consistently violent rhythm. She noticed a lizard dart under a rock for shelter. But it was too late and the force of the wind picked up the weak little creature, whipping it around and playing it roughly over the surface. Suddenly the whole world was attacking its own quiet daylight. The ground heaved, the sand was disheveled, rocks rolled out of place. She heard Father moan and she felt him slide away from her. He got out and walked around the back of the car. She watched him through the side view mirror as he zipped up his trousers and reached down into his pocket to extract a pack of cigarettes. She didn't know he smoked either.

As he stood on the edges of the sandstorm, his back to her, she watched how the cigarette smoke curled casually up into the quiet sky, and how the blue changed, how it lost its purity, how the fumes of his cigarette had dirtied it. She watched as other, much bigger plumes rose up somewhere distant before eventually dissipating into the sky and she thought about how the fumes from Father's cigarette and the smoke in the distance each had their particular brand of darkness, and how they each rose up to violate blue innocence.

Father dropped his cigarette butt and twisted it under the toe of his shoe. She supposed his smoke break was a signal for her to straighten herself up. She hastily pulled up her torn panties, pushed her skirt down, and tucked the folds tight to her knees before he opened the door and slid back into the driver's seat.

"It's okay. You're a nice girl." He said to her as he started the engine. "It was your first time. It's never quite what you expect. You'll get used to it and you'll learn to enjoy it. I'll teach you."

CHAPTER 73
CINDI

The adulation of unnatural creations and the rituals that are inspired by it are part of another game. It augments the money game but the games are unrelated, and not played together. There are roles to be assumed, norms to be followed, artificial processes to secure your place in both, and the threat of a sense of emptiness if you abandon them.

The Little Imps Sweater Club took on a life of its own. Matilda, the owner of Spin a Yarn had taken command and she attached a small sign on the bottom right of her store window, 'Home of Little Imps Sweater Club' like it was a badge of honor or special certification or something.

"Absolutely great for business," she'd said to Cindi Crawford one morning as they met on their way to opening the shops. "You know, a few years back, a woman who was an extremely skilled knitter worked for me. I'd almost say the Little Imps sweaters could have been her work except for the fact that she flatly refused to knit anything for children. Odd." She shook her head. "I ended up selling her work, down to the very last item. And now I'm back to the same old displays, using my standard treasures from years back." She leaned in to touch Cindi's arm. "Don't tell anyone about my recycled displays, though, will you, my dear? An antique knitted treasure is a treasure just the same."

Cindi nodded as she nibbled at her giant cookie, dropping a few crumbs for the pigeons who began to follow at warp pigeon speed. "You got that right, Matilda. You got that right." Herself, she couldn't see anything weird about old Matilda. She'd heard stories just like everyone else, about her Parkinson's but other than that, the old lady seemed to hold things together pretty well.

There were rumors of strange happenings in the back room of Spin a Yarn since Matilda had just sort of naturally assumed leadership of the Little Imps Sweater Club. Things like women cutting up strands of alpaca yarn and braiding them to 13-inch lengths, lighting them on fire and then blessing themselves as the yarn smoldered and went out, like it had special cleansing power or something. It was an obvious mimic of First Nations sweet grass ritual but without basis and without ancient wisdom.

There was more buzz about other outlandish practices at the Little Imps Sweater Club. Some of the born-again knitters let it slip to their friends who weren't quite as enthusiastic or quite as born-again, who then passed it on with screwed up noses and rolled-back eyes. Things like women dancing naked behind the shop on nights when there was a full moon. The most fascinating ritual was something they called 'weaving in,' where three women were chosen to undress (down to being stark naked, mind you). The other women were each given a ball of colored yarn (what kind hadn't been specified) and as the three naked ones rotated on the spot, the yarn was wrapped around them. Sort of like a cocoon, but with a transferring of energy. And then the other women who encircled them unraveled the yarn from the three women by taking up the ends and they braided the strands into a long, long braid, passing it around the circle, each woman raising their section above their head and holding it there as they chanted. No one seemed able to remember the actual chant.

No one knew for sure if the members knitted anything at all. And from what she heard, the group had only half a dozen or so original Little Imps sweaters. Nevertheless, they were enough to cultivate and spin legends. So, in reality, the sweaters seemed to be no more than a jumping off point for a cult of knitters – probably only mediocre ones, at that. Cindi Crawford had a friend who had a friend whose sister was actually a member of the Little Imps Sweater Club. And the version that reached Cindi's ear said that they had, in fact, knitted dozens and dozens of sweaters that had been 'approved' and socked away for a special day. Maybe the end of the world, who knew?

This friend told Cindi that Matilda had hired George (the handyman who, on his sober days, worked to pay for his drinking habit on the rest), to build three large cedar closets in the basement of her shop. George leaked information on his bad days and so word got all over town.

It went without saying that Matilda had become somewhat of a knitting messiah and all of the voices were in agreement that the Sweater Club was comprised of Matilda and twelve others, the same as Jesus and his disciples or a high priestess and her coven. It was open for discussion.

Speculation over the mission and goings-on at the Sweater Club far surpassed any other gossip, breaking local records. There were many diverse theories but the most prevalent was that the high priestess was building an inventory for the proverbial rainy day – or as some called it, Doomsday, or maybe it could even be called the Day without Sweaters, which, according to what had supposedly slipped from Matilda's mouth, might amount to the same thing.

Cindi said good bye to Matilda at the door of Spin a Yarn and, smiling to herself, she headed across the street to open up Little Imps, trying not to shake her head lest Matilda should turn back and see her and possibly put a curse on her granola ass.

CHAPTER 74

IRENE

Oh, the satisfaction of recovering what is rightfully yours. The joy of accumulation and mounting possession. The security and profound comfort to have and to hoard.

Life towards normalcy would prevail for several months, always with the hope that it would return entirely. Chuck suggested that as soon as the season came around, they should venture out to the Nazco Valley again and pick berries. Irene smiled as she sipped her coffee. She didn't say no, for which he was grateful.

She never talked about what she did all day but as long as she was keeping up with the housework, he knew things were on an even keel. He never lacked for clean, ironed clothes, food in the fridge and nutritious dinners. Although he longed for his former Irene – the impetuous, carefree girl he married (he realized that the characteristics he used to complain about were the very charms he missed the most), he appreciated the effort she must be making and he tried to be understanding.

What he was not aware of was that Irene had volunteered as a lunch time monitor at two different elementary schools. The monitor program was designed to give teachers a break from the children at mid-day. The teachers retreated to the staff room where Irene assumed they told jokes and played games of trivia, and perhaps expounded on clever teaching techniques that they had discovered by serendipity. No matter. The important thing was a mid-day escape.

"We're always pleased to have volunteers, Irene. Thank you for thinking of us. You'll have to be approved, you understand, so there are no concerns about the children's safety. But it's a formality and I'm sure we'll be calling you within a week."

She smiled demurely and repeated how much she enjoyed being around children. And, she added, "…and also the outdoors." She looked forward to being called in, she said.

Irene's job was to patrol the playground, hallways, bathrooms and the empty classrooms. It was an easy job that sometimes involved helping little ones make their way to the bathroom in an emergency or refereeing seven-years old who squabbled over a sandwich or isolating a bully who was compensating for being a poor soccer player.

Irene quietly moved about the premises, observant and keeping her distance from the one other supervisor who was also on duty. On her third lunch hour shift, she encountered a small boy called Thomas wearing her 'Little Lamb' sweater and although it was mostly blue with four little white lambs and one black one, and although the boy himself did not seem to be entirely unpleasant, the sweater was not intended for the likes of him. It irked her to see him in it.

"I think you should leave your sweater in the classroom. The sun is shining. Get some fresh air on your arms. It's invigorating. A child is meant to feel a cool breeze once in a while, it's good for your circulation."

The little boy called Thomas looked up at her quizzically. "What's invig... what's circulation?"

"Oh, it's just healthy, is what I mean. Do you want me to take your sweater inside and hang it up for you? Which classroom is yours?"

And that's how easy it was. Candy from a baby. If her sweaters were not already hanging on a hook, ripe for the picking, then she harvested them directly off the backs of children. She was, after all, the adult in charge. If they tried to put their sweaters on at recess, she advised them against it. As soon the little rascals were sent outside, their little shoes clapping happily down the hallway, their chubby hands waving to friends, she slipped the sweaters from their hooks and stuffed them into her own backpack, which she was careful to place out of reach of the little monsters and out of sight of other school staff. When she started work, she had requested a locker of her own. "Oh, it's fine if it isn't in the staff room. I don't mind having it in the hallway."

Irene was not stealing. After all, these were her sweaters, products of her dreams, her handicraft, hours, days and nights of her toiling and singing over these little works of love. And she had not tossed them out to the rest of the world. She had not granted permission for anyone to wear them. They had been stolen from her in cruel acts of trickery, she was simply reclaiming them in silence, not bothering anyone. This was quite simply a carrying out of justice.

Over a period of three months, and between the two schools, she had reclaimed more than six dozen sweaters. However, she felt no triumph in this because she knew that the quantity of sweaters out there still far outnumbered what she had been able to reclaim. In her mind's eye, she saw little sweater-owners – hordes of little sweatered henchmen, marching down the main street in colorful sweater droves, sometimes she pictured the minions skipping across fields, like a plague of overdressed grasshoppers, other times she imagined well-dressed children circling and landing, just like vultures, at a land fill.

Eventually, complaints trickled in about missing or – and they hated to even use the word so they whispered it – 'stolen' – sweaters. The school principals ordered the teachers and lunch time monitors to watch for strangers skulking around the school.

"Someone is walking in and making off with private property. These are small, innocent victims. And the items are oddly very specific. There have been too many incidents to call it anything other than targeted robberies. Apart from little Georgie Townsend's tall rubber boots, nothing but sweaters have been reported missing."

Undeterred by the orders for more vigilance, Irene continued lifting from cloakrooms at lunch time and she managed to pack several more sweaters home. She did, however, decide, that in order to avoid suspicion, she'd have to refrain from encouraging children to remove the sweaters from their backs.

The sweaters were thinning out at schools so she broadened her scope. She stopped in at daycares. "Oh, I just happened to be passing by and thought I would do my young friend a favor. She lives in the area and is going back to work. Do you have a brochure or other written information I can take to her?" While the willing childcare worker toddled off to look for a brochure, Irene efficiently poked about the cloakroom and slipped as many sweaters as would fit under her oversized coat and into her bag.

She also frequented playgrounds during mid-afternoons when the sun was at its hottest, when young mothers sat chatting with one another, half-watching their toddlers who hung about on the swings or cried out when they got caught in climbing apparatus. Sometimes the little stinkers fell down at the bottom of slides and their mothers ran to their defense to rub knees, kiss elbows, and dry teary eyes. Those were opportune moments. Sometimes Irene gave one of the urchins the evil eye, willing them to fall in order to divert attention. Then she sidled by the park benches and in one swift motion, she grabbed a sweater and tucked it under the hood of the Silver Shadow. On a good day in the park, she absconded with three or four sweaters. The collection was filling out. But she still had a lot of work to do.

CHAPTER 75

COLUMBA

Wealth and riches are relative. To some, the smallest joys make life complete – it could be a bee above the flowering strawberry plant or perhaps the pleasure of a new flat-screen television. The television will eventually wear out or cry to be replaced by something bigger and smarter. But the strawberry plant, with a little water and sunlight, will continue to produce strawberries. Sometimes it pays to keep your eye on the simple joys.

An excited Columba bustled out of the bathroom, having given the back-combed nest additional volume, and having taken extra care with her rouge and lipstick. She spritzed extra Cuban perfume. She wore the most elegant outfit José had ever seen on her. It was a two-piece forest green linen skirt suit and she accented it with an over-sized multi-color bauble necklace. It looked sharp, he told her. And the mauve pumps were a nice touch. She beamed and her lips stretched so far he thought her ears would have to make way. He had never seen her so happy.

José didn't tell Columba the truth about how he qualified for the extraordinarily generous donation from The Most Pure Blood of Jesus Church.

She knew that several months ago, José began attending classes with Father Cortés and he mentioned something about the Bishop, too. But she had no idea he was such an outstanding student.

"I always told you that my children were miracles. Did I not?" But to have a priest help her son open a bank account and deposit six million pesos meant that her children were even more amazing than she imagined. Perhaps she should follow their example and attend the Church. One never knows.

"No, Mom. It's not a donation like that. Actually, it's really more like a scholarship. But let's just say that I won the biggest ever bingo prize."

Well, but… she couldn't quite get her head around the scholarship because, well, a scholarship meant he'd have to go somewhere to study. And it wasn't that. So she settled on the bingo explanation. That she understood. And she would definitely be attending Church bingos in future. "My lucky boy. My little miracle." She smiled, a bit of lipstick clinging to one front tooth, and she tousled his hair.

On the way to Progreso in the back seat of the collector taxi, José pretended to listen to his Mom's excited chatter. He was relieved when the driver chimed in with some gossip about the new mayor. "What was his nickname? Oh yeah, 'The Bullfighter'. Good one. He'll fight for the community. We need someone like him." The driver grinned and gave the new mayor the thumbs up, hoping to catch Columba's eye in the rearview mirror. She wasn't paying attention.

José turned to look at the sea, they'd be stopping several blocks before that, at the downtown branch of the State Bank. He tried not to picture Anita, probably still fast asleep, probably locked in the room she shared with that brute behind the green door, beside The Black Cat, mere blocks from the bank. Probably she did drugs now, probably she didn't care about much else. What if she was suicidal? No, he couldn't say she was suicidal. But what did he know? Maybe drugs. That lout pothead of a boyfriend would have led her in that direction. José felt a great sadness for her and for their family. Columba was looking at him. She reached around his shoulder and hugged him close, pulled him tight to her ample bosom and kissed him several times on the top of his head.

Why did Anita have to choose such an animal of a boyfriend and how did she meet him in the first place? No doubt he had taken advantage of her crazy, confused state of mind. Why hadn't she just come home and told him or told Mom about Father Cortés? Why did she have to turn elsewhere? Why not her family?

Then he wondered how many times Father Cortés had beckoned his sister, 'Come and meet me after catechism, I have a lesson for you.' He hated Father Cortés. How often had she accompanied him on his charitable missions out to the shanty towns, puttering up there in the Volkswagen on his lusty pilgrimage? What about the retreats? Even Columba had been excited about those. And how often did Father say he needed Anita to help fold the weekly bulletins back in the rectory on a quiet afternoon? Did he hear her confession too?

José tried to not to imagine Anita's confusion and her guilt and her pain, the violation that penetrated even her soul, how she learned to turn on and off switches that triggered a new kind of logic, how this new logic would follow the twisted impulses from one damaged neuron to the next until the logic was so mangled that she shifted the blame to where it least belonged. This was supposed to be a happy day but he was heartsick because of how it came about.

Anita wouldn't have blamed the priest because a priest is holy and she had once loved him and he got a grip on her. She wouldn't blame the brute of a boyfriend. He was the one who saved her. He took her in, offered shelter when she didn't know where else to turn. That night he saw her bobbing dangerously, too far from the shore, inviting the waves in, higher, come higher please. Take me with you. I don't want to be here anymore. He saved her from the sea.

But the anger. The impotence? How and where do you channel such rage? To whom do you point a finger for this injustice? Someone failed along the way. Who was it? Who else? It was her mother-protector. Columba hadn't noticed. Anita thought she didn't care to see through it all. And worse, far worse, no matter what José said, Anita believed Father's assertion that Columba was complicit. Columba, her mother, her protector – the one who knew everything about her, who introduced her to the light of this world, red-faced and kicking, who suckled her, who could sense her smallest fear, glimpse her earliest joy – her mother was the rightful target for the rage and her mother would have to pay the price for the rest of her life.

José glanced over at Columba who was still chatting and bouncing along in the happy oblivion he had arranged for her. Her lips were moving and she was laughing at a joke she had just told the taxi driver. The driver again made eye contact with her through the mirror, laughed and gave her the thumbs up for something else. Columba sighed and sat back, looking out the window. Content. What was she thinking? José had been right to keep her in the dark. She didn't need the pain. He had solved one side of the problem and he'd work on the other. One thing at a time. Meanwhile it was good to see his Mom like this, like she hadn't been in ages. She was gregarious as she slid her bum in ridiculous little bounces over the seat and out the door of the taxi, still laughing with the driver.

Then she was suddenly all business. "Come on, son. We don't want to be late." Columba sprang ahead in her mauve pumps (more like a kangaroo than a gazelle), chin up, rigorously swinging her arms.

"I'm just a step behind you. Don't worry."

Maybe it would be the last lesson Anita would ever teach her younger brother. "Learn from my experience," she might say. He didn't need her advice. He had been forewarned and so when his time came, he would be prepared. Not like poor Anita who walked right into the trap set by Father Cortés. And, by the way, who was Father Cortés tutoring these days?

José was well aware that he too, was being groomed by the bishop. Had he not overheard Sofia's brother in the bathroom that day, he might have been caught in the bishop's trap. He sometimes wondered how he had fallen on the right side of destiny, especially considering how the rest of his family hadn't. Maybe his Dad, wherever in the world he might be (José mostly pictured him as a sailor from a foreign land, maybe a pirate) was a lucky man. Maybe he had inherited his father's luck.

Finding Sofia and being introduced to Rodrigo's Dad was part of that streak of luck.

It wasn't hard. He got Lucia to point out Sofia one day after school and he approached her, businesslike, no need to pretend his reasons were anything other than serious. He told her what he'd overheard in the boys' bathroom that day and she nodded, her big eyes sad. He thought she might start to cry on the spot.

"Well, listen, I want to help someone else, someone else caught in the same trap," he told her.

She straightened up and dabbed at her eyes with her pinky fingers. "Go on."

And the lucky streak only got richer when he discovered that Rodrigo's father would be happy to have his lawyer confront both Father Cortés and the bishop with Anita's case. "One child's suffering at the hand of this institution is bad enough, but two...? and who knows how many more? Let me see what I can do."

He sent José to a downtown lawyer, an imposing Don Alfredo Martinez, who said he was expecting José's visit.

His office was impressive with its oversized, polished raulí desk, dark leather armchair and thick maroon curtains that were tied at the sides of a huge window with a view across the main street to the port.

He motioned for José to sit in the leather chair and he picked up a pen to make notes on a yellow lined block.

"I don't work for free. But you won't have to pay me. They will." he nodded sideways. "I've handled more than a few of these cases and they always end the same. I know how to speed things along. Leave it with me."

José didn't need to know the ins and outs. He didn't know what negotiations had taken place and he had no idea if there was money left on the table. If there was, the lawyer folded it into his briefcase and José was none the wiser. For a boy of fifteen, six million pesos, translating to about 9,000 American dollars (he stopped at a currency exchange house to ask) was a fortune, more than he'd ever see again in his lifetime. And it was going into a new account that the lawyer had set up in Columba's name.

They would receive the money and spend it. When someone lives hand-to-mouth, never a peso to spare, there is no such thing as a budget or thinking ahead or saving for a rainy day. There is only the here and the now, the necessary. The immediate need for propane for the stove, for a little bread on the table and if you're lucky a little cheese and on a very lucky day, a little meat, and perhaps one day, enough to pay to reconnect the power that the company cut off last month. Who budgets?

CHAPTER 76
CHUCK

It's possible to live in the same house and in a different world.

Chuck leaned in, elbows on the front counter waiting for the bell to jingle in another customer. It was a slow day at the store. The volume of the radio on the shelf behind him was low. The large round clock on the side wall was ticking around to twelve noon. Cars hummed by, their wheels droning over the pavement. If he had been someone else, he thought, he might just fall asleep on the spot.

The voice on the radio announced the news at the top of the hour accompanied by the familiar instrumental jingle – snare drums and royal trumpets. The announcer rushed through some vague national news headlines and Chuck yawned.

"On the local front, we have an odd story about a serial robbery. It seems that of all things, sweaters have been stolen from children all over town. And not just any sweaters. The thief or thieves have targeted a line of sweaters called 'Little Imps' that were sold exclusively and for a limited time only through a shop called Little Imps, which is located on Main Street."

Sudden heat strobed through Chuck's chest a sharp pain pulsed at his temples. The announcer's voice continued with a lilt of incredulity, "The local manager of Little Imps, Cindi Crawford," and he paused trying to suppress an involuntary snort, "says they ran out of stock some time ago. She notes that it's been several months since they've had sweaters in stock and they are unable to locate a new source. According to Ms. Crawford, the sweaters had become a valuable collector's item and are even the theme for a local sweater society. The police are asking for anyone with knowledge of this bizarre series of robberies to contact them on the Tips Line."

Chuck slumped so far down onto the stool that his head disappeared behind the counter. He looked up at the clock, whose big hand had just ticked over to eight minutes past noon. "Murray, take over at the front, will you? I have to go out."

Breaking into Irene's bedroom was extremely unnerving. Where was she anyway? Sweat was dripping down his brow. He could feel it rolling into his collar and trickle down his spine. The act of breaking in was, itself, invasive but it was the fear of what he'd find inside that caused the most terror. Crouched outside her door, his hands were shaking so badly that he had to roll back on his haunches and lean into the wall to pause and take a few deep breaths. He sat there for several minutes, looking up at the ceiling, hyperventilating. Eventually, he was ready to try again.

He unscrewed the plate from the door and jiggled the workings until he found the trigger to release the lock. He stood up, wiping the palms of his hands on his thighs several times. Then he took a deep breath and walked in, holding his breath.

Irene's room was in order, the doilies under the heavy lamps were clean and perfectly placed. Her digital clock blinked back at him, its big green numbers displaying 12:37. Her bed was military-perfect, fat pillows tucked under the brocade bedspread, three lace-covered cushions placed at 45-degree angles, one slightly overlapping the other. Fresh tracks from the vacuum cleaner on the carpet over to the bed. She was taking care of things. He blew the air out of his cheeks and sank down onto the edge of the bed to celebrate his wife's sanity. "You're okay, Irene," he said to himself. "You're coming back to me. Why would I doubt you again after all this time? I know you've been making an extraordinary effort." But then – wait a minute. Where was she? Wasn't she usually at home to watch soap operas at this time of day? Just the other day at breakfast, after he had dared to pry, she said she routinely enjoyed a morning walk, sometimes stopped for a Tim Horton's coffee and then returned home for lunch. She had giggled when she admitted she had become addicted to the early afternoon soap. To the point – he remembered her saying very clearly –that she could never miss it, she had to drop whatever she was doing and turn on the TV at 12:30 pm. He couldn't remember the name of the soap because at the time he was half-thinking about a problem with the new delivery man. But he clearly recalled her saying this because she was giggling and he had been delighted to see this glimpse of her younger self.

She had lied to him. Boldly. To his face. And without tell-tale signs.

His shoulders dropped and he hunched back on the bed, staring across at the wardrobe. Hey – she had a new wardrobe on the east wall. It was floor-to-ceiling. It was deep, too. The room was more than two feet narrower now, he was sure of it. How had he missed that? Dread washed over him and he covered his face with his hands. He rubbed his forehead, the pressure on his shoulders was so great that for several minutes he was unable to stand.

Eventually, at first glancing towards the door and cocking his head for any sound that signaled her return, he pushed himself to his feet and plodded the four steps to the new wardrobe. He knew what was coming before he opened the door. He sunk to the carpet, and sat there staring up at floor-to-ceiling shelves of sweaters.

CHAPTER 77

GAVIN

Gavin moved swiftly.

"Do you like animals, Cindi?"

"Of course. I love animals!" She looked up from the two meter-long scarf she was knitting. It seemed that she didn't know how to end the thing. She stood up, folding the long woolen shape onto itself. "Why do you ask?"

"We're going to move into pet clothes and accessories."

"Okay, so you've got my attention." She pulled at her braid and waited.

He didn't see any point in asking her about her friends this time because she'd been wrong about them being wildly enthusiastic about eco-clothing for kids. Instead he said, "We need to revamp this space, make it pet-friendly."

"Okay. So, what do I do?" She was on her feet now, heading to look out the window as though the answer lay out there. Instead, she saw Matilda ushering a couple of young women through the front door of Spin a Yarn. Must be some kind of bewitching knitting session in the making. She turned back to Gavin and listened.

His instructions were simple. "Move all of the children's eco-clothing to the very back of the store and make space for the racks that Mark is having built. Keep the Burgeon brochure racks because we have contracts with the restaurants and municipality but move them to the sides because the front floor space is being used for shelves for the stuffed animals that Mark ordered."

Yolanda and Frankie were 'terribly enthusiastic' about Gavin's new idea. "Why didn't we see this for ourselves? It was right here in front of our eyes."

"Yeah, and that's why," Gavin said. "For you, it's nothing remarkable but for animal lovers who are also environmentalists... well, it's just what they've been looking for." Gavin had done some research and discovered that each year, more and more money was being spent on domestic animals. More and more people were acquiring pets. Even single people and young childless couples had pets. And they usually had more disposable income than parents with small children. This was a gold mine.

Within six weeks, Yolanda had whipped up a dozen cute outfits for miniature poodles and for German Shepherds. She had designer mirrors for parrots and painted rocks for lizards.

Little Imps (Gavin decided the name was worth hanging on to) advertised, "Beautiful pet apparel and accessories, all sizes, all designs, all pets." The slogan on the new sign said, "Made to measure. Just ask."

Frankie supplied little leather boots and belts. Everything from spiky headbasher collars to shoes with feathers and bells. He made leads too. The racks were full of ecologically-friendly, recycled products for every pet. If it continued as Gavin predicted, within two years, they'd be patenting everything and selling it all over North America. And who knows, maybe it could eventually be recycled abroad.

When everything was in place, and Gavin was back home leaning into the fireplace mantle of the old Reid home, he was pretty sure that he heard his Dad chuckle.

He cracked open a bottle of beer and leaned in a little. "So what, Dad? So, I'm clothing the world—some of the old standards and plenty of new trends plus a whole pile of recycled garments for Africa and South America—and now we're keeping animals warm too."

He clinked his bottle against Stan's urn and winked at Marianne's and he mimicked Stan's voice, "Cheers. Congratulations, son. You've done us both proud."

Gavin had to admit that he'd hit the nail on the head with this one. And even though he was not 'the same people' as Frankie and Yolanda, he did, in a small way, fit into their lives. Even though he was on the outside looking in, he had the best view. It was as close as he would get to living a peaceful fireside life in a house on a lakeshore. But now it was the old Reid place that might be compared to a castle at the top of the beanstalk.

All the credit to them, Frankie and Yolanda would maintain their lifestyle, albeit with a little less time for trapping and fishing. So now they would occasionally purchase processed food from town and grow a little fatter and less healthy for it. Gordon died sooner rather than later and they retired his sequinned vest behind the glass of a rather spectacularly carved (dog bone motif) wooden frame that they hung in the hallway. Two spotlights focused on it, celebrating the star he was.

CHAPTER 78

CHUCK

As the cogs twist and grind, the brain spits out its dubious logic.

Chuck called just before dinner to say that he wouldn't be home until late. He wanted to finish the inventory. His voice sounded tight but he was always stressed at inventory time.

"Okay. See you in the morning." Irene was content to have the house to herself, she could leave her bedroom door open, perhaps open the windows and the closets, and let the fresh breeze stream through. She showered and hummed around between her bedroom and the living room, settling briefly into her knitting chair, leaning in to the Silver Shadow to make small chat, "How're you enjoying the evening on our own. I think it's been a long time coming, don't you?"

The Silver Shadow issued its shimmered response. The energy in the whole house tilts unpleasantly to one side when he's here. It's pleasant to have an evening alone. Any special plans?

No special plans. Let's just knock around.

Content, she padded back to her bedroom and selected several sweaters. She ran her hands over a tiny but luxurious mohair. The sensation gave her goosebumps. Then she lingered over the merino and she bent down to taste the alpaca, her fingers tingling across the knots of crocheted cotton details. Finally, when she returned the sweaters to the closet, she pressed her face into the soft folds and breathed in the fibers. Then she methodically went about the house, closing windows before gently latching the closet doors and locking herself into her bedroom. The Silver Shadow nodded his goodnight and she planted a kiss on his hood.

About the time that Irene had just opened the windows to bask in the evening breeze, Amber was greeting Chuck at the homestead. Old man McArthur was a silhouette at the door, dull yellow light from the kitchen circling his shape, one arm holding up the door frame, the other hanging at his side.

"Something went wrong," Chuck said. "Something went terribly wrong." His voice was hoarse, like the air was too thin. He was gasping.

"Come in. You look like you could use a drink." It was the first time Chuck had seen the old man demonstrate even a hint of sympathy.

"Okay, so I don't understand. Irene's room is floor-to-ceiling sweaters again?" It was Amber. Her face squished up with the question.

"So, you're sure they're the same sweaters? You're sure they're Irene's?" It was Jocelyn.

"No question."

"But how? I thought the charity sent the sweaters somewhere far away. It's an international charity, isn't it?"

They pulled out a chair for Chuck. Once again, it was Amber, Jocelyn and the old man seated around the table. Irene's Mom was in bed, protected from this insanity.

"Yes, yes and I don't know how. It's crazy."

"Maybe they didn't see the note with your instructions. I'm sure otherwise a place like that, a charity, I mean… it would honor a donor's wishes, right?"

"Well, they didn't."

The four of them sat in silence, everyone looking down at the table. Amber was tracing a stain with her index finger. Finally, old man McArthur offered them all another drink. "We can use one. Make us all a stiff one, will you, Jos?"

"Well, so is she really hurting anyone with her sweater collection?" Jocelyn asked.

"No, I mean the collection is okay, I guess, if she keeps insisting. I mean… No, but it's more than that. It's much worse than that. The problem is that I heard a story on the radio today about some sweater thief who goes around stealing 'Little Imps' sweaters from children. She's responsible. No question. Your sister, my innocent Irene, is a thief. A sweater thief. How ridiculous is that? And to make it worse, she's stealing from children! From kids! You know?"

"Well, I'll be goddamned." Old man McArthur shook his head and thumped his fist hard on the table. "I'll be goddamned," he took a drink. "I don't know whether to laugh or cry."

"Is she in danger of being caught? I mean, do you think the thieving has stopped? Is she still at it?"

"I don't know. Probably. I know she's been lying to me. She said that she's always home to watch the early afternoon soap. But she wasn't there today. I mean, that's when I found everything. She was probably out stealing from babies."

Old man McArthur grunted and chuckled.

"It's not funny, Dad. She could be in big trouble. What if she went to jail? Do you want to see your daughter go to jail? Or maybe some kind of nut house? Do you want to have our name – 'cause sure as Jesus they'll tie her back to your family – do you want to see our name dragged through the mud? They'll be sniggering and laughing at all of us. You'll have reporters out here. And what about Mom?"

"Yeah, and it'll be pretty hard for me at work, too." Jocelyn blew out a sigh.

"Okay, so we need to do something."

"So pour us another stiff one, Jos," the old man said. He needed to think about self-preservation.

"If the whole town is on the lookout for some thief and keeping an eye on their kids and their sweaters, then pretty soon she won't be able to get her hands on any. It'll be over. But what if she carries on? I mean, what if she starts breaking and entering? I mean, that's serious. And sooner or later, she'll get caught. We have to get the sweaters that she's collected out of the house. We have to get rid of them." Amber said. "We can't leave any evidence lying around... I mean just in case it comes to that, which it won't. But my God, just in case..."

"Well, just maybe I have a solution for that." Old man McArthur tossed back the rest of his drink and plunked his glass onto the table with a kind of final authority.

CHAPTER 79

CHUCK

Gathered in a rush, dreamy story-sweaters are pushed and packed into bales of plastic. Soon afterwards, they are transformed to scorched particles and they catch the updraft and eventually, with the weight of the world, they fall back down again to settle on your soul.

Jocelyn had suggested that they shake Irene out of her fantasy world by giving her a taste of hard reality. "Get someone in to do – what's it called? – an intervention. Yeah, an intervention. It's like tough love," she said. "A necessary crisis," she said.

But Chuck disagreed. Irene had experienced enough trauma and to get some stranger to come in and expound on it all would be cruel and, he said, it could kill her. Taking the sweaters from her again would be a huge setback but she had come around before and he was confident she could do it again. The best thing would be to break into her room and clean out the closets. He'd live with the consequences because, as he saw it, it was their only choice.

They decided on old man McArthur's solution. "Look," he said. "I need to do a controlled burn on the outer fields..."

He didn't have to say any more.

For Chuck it was painful deja-vu, and his misery lasted for days, another reason to lay awake at night. His heart was tortured and aching but he could see no other solution. Finally, he gave the green light.

When he looked back on the decision and questioned the failure to contact professional help, he always came around to the same conclusion. No matter what, with or without help, the sweaters had to go. They were not the cause of her illness but rather the result of it. She had rescued herself from her anguish. But in her craziness, she solved the problem in an immoral, even damaging manner. But then who was he to judge her logic? Whose logic was correct? Whose reasoning was more sane? He sometimes wondered if she was right and the rest of the world was wrong. But who was he to fight against the rest of the world? Perhaps they could become recluses, retreat to a backwoods existence, which, he admitted, would probably suit Irene very well these days. Could they have become happy hermits?

Chuck was too entrenched in routine and couldn't pull himself away from the rest of the world, from his store, from his livelihood, from the pleasure he extracted from his mundane life in retail. Chuck needed to survive too. This was his life too, wasn't it? He wanted to live with his neighbors, connect with his customers, buy from his wholesalers. He wanted to come home at the end of each day to a house that smelled of freshly baked meatloaf and mashed potatoes and maybe even a carrot cake to have with a cup of tea. He did not want to grow his own crops and scavenge out in the forest for fresh berries and fight off rodents, clean out water wells and rebuild sewage tanks or, worse yet, heaven forbid, possibly have to use an outhouse. He was accustomed to his way of life and he liked it, present circumstances excepted, of course.

And Irene was in love with their urban existence too. Well, or at least she used to be. He thought of how she spoke disdainfully of her parents' life on the farm, how they struggled day to day and never got ahead. "What do they have to live for? What is their purpose out there? They're just trapped because they don't look any further." But would she change now and choose the solitary path into a rural life? And the knitting. It was hard to judge if she was either capable or even interested in knitting anymore. Perhaps, she had really taken to thievery, maybe it excited her. The thought made him shudder. She had definitely moved beyond the act of creating. Now she lived to possess, to hoard – again. If they didn't stop her with sweaters, maybe she'd start stealing something else.

Chuck was too tired to know the answer. So he just let it happen.

Amber and Jocelyn and old man McArthur came in one day when Irene was out prowling some playground just before lunch and they emptied her wardrobes. It almost killed Chuck when they found more sweaters in the basement.

Chuck was home when Irene returned. This time, she didn't call him hateful or a sinister son of a bitch. She didn't spit in his face. She didn't say anything. She didn't even look at him. She just turned slow circles in the middle of her bedroom for about an hour and then she shut down. Without closing her door, she crawled into bed, curled into the fetal position, covered her head and rocked ever so slightly. Chuck heard her whimpering like a small wounded puppy. He stayed outside her door that afternoon, slumped on his haunches, his head heavy, leaning into the wall, tears seeping from the corners of his oh-so-tired eyes. He let himself fall back onto the floor right there and he silently cried himself to sleep. He never returned to sleep in his own bed. Instead he settled outside Irene's door every night for the rest of his shortened life.

He died less than a week later, his assistant found him stretched out on the staff room floor, dead of an apparent heart attack. Chuck never called out, never made a sound. When it happened, he felt himself going down and he saw Irene beckoning him as she ran through a field of high grass. She was giggling and he was tugging on the sash that had unraveled from around the waist of her pastel pink crepe dress. Its full skirt brushed around the shape of her legs and the sun shone through it. He looked up at her. She had just popped a fresh strawberry into her mouth and her lips were juicy and they turned up in a generous smile. He let go of the sash when he fell. She looked beyond him and said what she had never in her life told him, "I love you." And she was holding Alicia, who had a crocheted daisy tucked behind her ear. Her chubby little hands happily clutched Irene's bosom and Chuck saw Irene lift the child, the girl's short arms wrapping around her neck, Irene's eyes shining with happy tears. Then he let go.

Irene took the news of Chuck's death in a cloud of silence. The police had had to break in the front door. There was a trail of cookie wrappers, empty baby food jars and half full juice boxes from the kitchen to the foot of her bed. The air in the house was cold and stale. It smelled rancid and they exchanged meaningful glances as they called out her name.

At first softly, "Irene? Are you here?" And then loudly. There was no answer either way. They finally found her, an immobile lump under her bed covers. When they pulled the covers back, she blinked up at them, her passive dull eyes unable to focus on the emptiness of the house.

"Irene," we need you to come with us.

She surrendered without a word and stood unaffected when Amber wrapped her arms around her at the police station.

CHAPTER 80

GAVIN

They say ignorance is bliss. If it blinds you to the dark sources of dirty deeds, it also relinquishes you of responsibility. Avoid what you might discover, and continue to profit in peace.

The night after the store in Grant Falls had its first run on eco-friendly collars and boots, and cashed in on some major sales that included a sequinned jacket for a poodle (a more refined version of Gordon's vest), and three felt wool vest-and-hat sets for terriers, Gavin drove back to James's place in Burgeon for pizza night.

He passed several farms and homesteads along the highway. Warm, yellow lights flickered behind semi-sheer curtains. Silhouettes moved around inside. He imagined quiet conversations overriding the background sound of a television or the hum of a radio. He wondered what the conversations would be. Probably tomorrow's chores or maybe a neighbor's wedding or perhaps plans for a dance at the community hall next month. Or maybe there were discussions about money, how to stay afloat with all the bills, not enough workers and too many chores. He noticed some outbuildings closer to the road, their sunken roofs in disrepair that were probably always on the to-do list but that never quite made it to the top. Too much to keep up with and not enough resources. He marveled at the perfect rows of hay bales that lined the fields.

Some poorer homesteads stuck out even in the dark, contours of their ramshackle buildings, one falling into another. They had probably been in the same rundown condition for years and years and the owners became accustomed to it, always knowing where to find those extra nails that were still stuck in two-by-fours piled up by the gate, or the faded blue bucket they used last year over at the cow shed. Things hidden in corners, things familiar to them because they lived there. Gavin could make out a few cows swishing their tails and a dog walking along the fence, head down, sniffing the grass. Stars rose up in the violet sky and twinkled above the pastoral setting. It made Gavin feel happy to be connected to the place, even as a stranger in the night.

The tranquility was interrupted when, just up the road to his left, he saw sparks shooting up from a nearby field. He slowed down so that he could keep one eye on it as he drove. Bright flames flashed up into the darkness, burning embers flying around and finally dying away. He pulled over to the side of the road and waited as his window hummed open. He knew that farmers watched out for one another and that if it was something serious, he'd see neighbors jumping onto their tractors, and motoring over to lend a hand. There was no activity yet. He waited a bit longer. He could hear popping and he could smell something like burning fibers (could it be wool? does wool burn?), which alarmed him. Farmers didn't burn their sheep, did they? Maybe there had been a serious disease and they had to do away with some of the flock. He almost felt sad.

The flames continued steadily for a long time before finally dying down and disappearing. He couldn't see the smoke in the dark but by the way it smelled, he knew if it had been daylight it would have darkened the sky. He thought of Yolanda and Frankie and how they would have been dismayed by the contamination. He heard voices now and then, faint commands and responses, from the direction of the field where the flames seemed to originate. They were deliberately burning something, perhaps it was garbage. Why in the dark of night? Who knew? Maybe it was a common practice and that's why none of the neighbors were alarmed. The wind was blowing in his direction carrying warm ash and fragments. Some landed on the hood of his car. He jumped out to brush them off and they disintegrated at his touch leaving soot on his fingers. He brought his hand up to his nose. Threads. Yes, yarn. The flames had died away almost as quickly as they'd appeared. Gone now.

Nothing more to see here. The burning had lasted no more than thirty minutes. He jumped back into the car, signaled his way onto the highway and continued down the road to Burgeon, towards James' place.

All these years James still kept his physical distance from Gavin and Gavin never knew if it was out of habit or if James was still on the alert for inappropriate touching. He had become more entrenched in the church and was still no closer to a serious heterosexual relationship (the mayor's daughter ran off with an atheist). As James saw it, he needed to maintain the right appearance because man, he was still 'in play'. Some things just never change.

"Hey Gavin," he greeted him at the front door. "How's it goin' man?"

"Things are great, James. Just great."

"So, I have to get into Grant Falls and check out your new shop. I heard it's a real goin' concern."

"Yeah, well the location is old. But the stuff in it is new... well, new in one sense of the word. We're selling things for pets now." Gavin grinned. "Got a beer? And the stuff is going like hotcakes. I mean the eco-animal people just can't get enough."

"I heard."

"I'm thinking of opening a pet store. And I was wondering, James, have you or anyone at your church ever thought about running a pet shelter? I mean for the homeless pets? Maybe I could partner with you?"

CHAPTER 81

COLUMBA

Miracles exist for those who believe.

Columba wanted to share the magic. Her first purchase was a child-size wingback chair upholstered in dusty pink damask.

She hired a handyman to construct a grotto into the iron fence of her front patio. And there, with no small measure of ceremony, she positioned the pink damask wingback chair and gently arranged her doll-sweater duo, Santa Magdalena. The doll, wearing the only one of Irene's sweaters now in existence, sat with her arms outstretched in a permanent gesture of warmth and welcome.

The beautiful sweater beguiled passersby. And the doll's blue eyes no longer had the cold plastic glare but like the wool she was dressed in, had taken on a new warmth. "Look at me. I am like you. I am worthy. I have overcome barriers and survived extinction as proof of what is possible. I have travelled continents to give you hope." No one would have believed that a sweater could speak – or sing – through a doll. Even those who knew about such things would testify that this beautiful, singing voice was that of a child – sweet, clear and innocent. "Come and sing a song of joy," the little doll sang. Irene's child's sweater did not have to throw her voice very far and her act of ventriloquism was easily accomplished.

Seated on her pink damask high up on the ridge of Santa Rita, Santa Magdalena kept constant vigil. Her kingdom extended as far as she could see – from the hills of Progreso to the distant curve of the Pacific horizon.

Columba's next two purchases were – in order of importance – a new sofa bed for José with a matching dinosaur print quilt and two matching pillows, and a 32-inch flat screen TV.

She was disappointed that José didn't share her joy in their newly found wealth. He was preoccupied, always muttering about something. He said he liked the new bed and quilt but, try as she might, there was no evidence of the delight she had anticipated.

Columba kept the new cleaning job at the store and dropped the old one at the bank – to allow more time for her social life, she said. She became a usual at Juana's again, slipping in around the table with friends of the season. She didn't see any reason to try to kick her habit of picking up anything that wasn't bolted down because bit by bit she had also retaken the small piece of real estate on the sidewalk downtown from which to sell her acquisitions.

José found that it was still easiest to explain their short-lived wealth as winnings from church bingos. The money was now long gone, some of it frittered away on whims. For instance, they took the bus up to Peru for a holiday (the very first one of their lives, very much deserved), scouted the produce and artisan markets and lolled around on the beaches, ordering drinks and food. Someone stole a lot of cash from a jacket pocket when José left it in their room so they had to cut their holiday short.

They booked a trip to Santiago, just to see 'the Capital', where they stayed in a modest *residencial* in *El Centro* and tried different restaurants along Avenue Manuel Montt. They even went to the national stadium to see *Universidad de Chile* play, something José never tired of recounting. Columba declared to the crowd at Juana's that she'd never seen anything like Santiago with its river and canals and skyscrapers and parks and crowds. But she was glad to be home.

For the first time in their lives, she took José to the cinema in Progreso. They sat right up in the front row and slurped Coca-Cola through big plastic straws and ate sugared popcorn. Among others, they saw The Matrix (Columba fell asleep halfway through) and Toy Story (they both loved it and went to see it three times). Columba told Juana that, of all the things they did, going to the movies was proof that she'd done well by her family.

Last year, José met a girl called Pilar and he moved in with her across the street from Columba's house. They bought a 'little marvel' automatic clothes washing machine, and a living room set with overstuffed blue flowered cushions. They had dinner with Columba every weekend and José often showed up during the week to visit Columba on his own.

In the mornings, José cleaned fish at the docks and in the afternoons he hitched a ride out to the piles to scavenge items for Columba's street stall. Columba had been against it but José said, "You need new acquisitions and where else are you going to get them?"

It wasn't long before Pilar left José for a man from the south. She wanted a man with money, she said. And she accused José of being nothing but false hope. So José moved back home with Columba. She was happy to take over the little marvel washing machine.

Magdalena was their star, their saint. She was the child who never grew up. She was the innocent one, the wise one in a magic jersey, who sat outside the front door ready to send up prayers.

Columba's tales of the doll and the jersey had long ago become neighborhood legend. The legends grew larger and more amazing with each telling and Magdalena's power as a saint quickly became firmly established.

"The jersey, well it almost threw itself in my arms," Columba relished the telling of the story. "And it was only days after Juana gave me Magdalena (these exaggerations added credence to the magic bit). "The jersey, as you can see, is a one-of, a singular work of art, a beautiful garment that stood head and shoulders above anything that ever, in the history of that god-forsaken depot, found its way, by whatever providence, to that particular spot." She pointed stiffly at the ground to emphasize the point. "And it chose me. Me!" She thumped her chest. "It was destiny, God's will, whatever you want to call it. I knew I needed to snatch it up because one of the other workers (less experienced than myself, of course) would have thrown it into the discard pile. And in that case, we all know where it would be today." She looked over at José and nodded towards the altiplano. "Yup, up in smoke or picked apart by the buzzards. I don't know which is worse. So that's why it was destined to be with me…. Because it was not destined to be there!"

In the end, it was José's story that was the most compelling. "And if it hadn't been for Magdalena's magic jersey, José never would have won the Church bingo." José never corrected her about that because he knew how Columba loved the story. She hijacked it at every opportunity.

In spite of his doubts, and even with his initial disdain for Magdalena and the magic jersey, the truth was that José did have something of an other-worldly experience as far as the doll was concerned. You could say it was like being born again. And although it didn't outwardly change his person or the course of his life, it marked him on the inside. He never revealed the whole truth to anyone. He simply led them to believe that Santa Magdalena had shown him a vision and it was this vision that helped him win the bingos.

The morning that he'd gone to meet the lawyer had been a bit of a turmoil. He'd accidentally knocked Magdalena from her wooden throne (at that time she was still inside the front door) and he was tempted to leave her lying there, face-down on the dusty ceramic tiles, a lesson for her to learn her place once and for all. But he knew Columba would complain, she might even cry and then who knows how long she'd sit and talk to the thing, trying to excuse her son's clumsiness. He bent down to pick up the doll and he pushed her back into the chair, carefully adjusting her arms to the correct 90 degrees, as though she never tired of reaching out.

It was when he bent in to adjust the little jersey, that he experienced, for the first time, its magic. It was this that he built his story around. But his story took a wide detour around the truth.

The truth is that he felt a shock, like lightning. It ran up his arm and at the same time a small woolly voice, like that of a child whispering in his ear, said to him, "Look at me." And when he hesitated, it insisted, "Look at me. Really look." He looked, really looked, as he ran his fingers down the front of the sweater from lapel to hem. He counted six buttons, he saw the beauty of the design, the way the rows of color blended in, and how they played across the woolen meadow. The intricate details came alive, threads of light emerged from under the woolen clouds and he swore he heard birdsongs. From within the green meadow that was knitted all along the bottom of the sweater, flowers nodded their heads in unison and he was filled with awe. He must have fallen into a trance but he wasn't sure if his eyes were open or closed. Either way, he saw a green valley where a woman was laughing as she skipped through tall grass, the wind playing with a sash that had come loose from her waist, and a small man with large black-framed eyeglasses who felt utter love for this woman, was crooning – "You are my destiny, you share my reverie, you are my happiness, that's what you are..." as the man tried in vain to catch and hold her. José couldn't interpret the vision but he knew there was magic in it.

After the money was safely in the bank, José told Columba over a cup of tea, that the doll had sent him a vision of bingo cards and that's when he had gone and won all that money. It was easier than trying to explain the visions and it was so much better than telling her the true story. And it definitely topped Columba's claims that her children were both miracle children born of a virgin.

She just smiled and said, "What did I tell you?" God works in mysterious ways. Small paper notes asking for intercession, and notes expressing gratitude were laid at the foot of Santa Magdalena's chair. They were like leaves in a meadow, papers softly tapping one against the other, sometimes flying away, the wind carrying them high into the sky above the mountains and into the hands of providence.

In spite of José's promise to himself to bring Anita back home, she remained a stranger. She never set foot in the neighborhood again. There was nothing

Santa Magdalena could do about that. It must have been providence.

The little sweater was content in her new life, she loved this land that had become her home. Together she and the doll personified hope. Always vigilant, and never complaining, she was an accidental donation of love from another time, another place, another set of circumstances. Providence. There you are.

CHAPTER 82

IRENE

The lawyer took care of everything. Irene signed all of the papers without so much as a word. Chuck was gone and he had not left her any sweaters and he had not left her a child. For the moment, nothing of importance existed.

Irene retreated to her mother's house. An empty bedroom had become available when Jamie, the very youngest in the family, moved out to live with his girlfriend whom none of the family had ever met. He told them that he was seeking a better life. His girlfriend had shown him how numerology would help guide him to it. He changed his names so that the numbers added up to a more positive score and he disappeared somewhere out of range.

Irene was listless for months but no one tried to coax her out of herself. No one dragged her into town or sat her down in front of jigsaw puzzles and encouraged her to pick up a piece, any piece. "She will come around," her Mom said. "She will come around."

Early one morning when old man McArthur stood alone scanning the fields from the kitchen window, he saw Irene out there in her bathrobe. She was walking away from the house and into the wind, which tugged at her hair and whipped her robe around. He watched as she carefully, deliberately placed one foot in front of the other as though walking in someone else's footsteps, measuring her stride and adjusting to someone else's rhythm. She became smaller in the distance until she was nothing more than a blurred white triangle. She was heading in the direction of the field that would lay fallow this year, the one where he and Amber and Jocelyn had burned the grass.

Old man McArthur turned as his wife shuffled into the kitchen. "She's out there," he said, leaving Irene's Mom to watch as she sipped her coffee.

Irene reached the outer field just as the sun spread its golden fingers over the horizon and had raked in all but the most stubborn darkness. She turned abruptly to her left along a row of wind-blown birch trees. They'd served as windbreakers for decades. She continued past them along the outer field, slowly, deliberately grunting and sighing her way over the rough, dew-covered earth, as though these sounds could replace the songs that she used to sing a lifetime ago. She turned 90 degrees again towards the center of the field. She bent down and noticed that when she looked closely, she could see new sprouts that had forged their way towards the sunlight, toppling small clumps of dirt and rolling aside tiny pebbles. She tried to avoid stepping on them but they were everywhere. Clusters of burnt grass had long since sunken into the soil and had disintegrated, offering themselves up to higher forms of energy. She looked over to the horizon and was blinded by the orange sun, the morning mist dissipating in the distant warmth of the low hills, which were still purple at this early hour.

She looked down at her feet, toes sliding out of the front of the dusty blue slippers, black dirt had collected under her toe nails, and she noticed that she was standing on the end of a short length of singed yarn. Rogue strands of burnt threads were being whipped up sporadically and then dropped by fickle little gusts of wind as though the wind itself was picking through the threads in search of something salvageable, something it could show off.

Irene crouched down to take up a handful of dirt and she let it sift through her fingers, gratified by its raw earthiness. The texture of the dirt was uneven and stringy. She squinted at the soil that was clumped in the palm of her hand and noticed varying lengths of blackened fiber, some quite thick, others like fine silk, microfibers that glistened as she let them go. She lowered herself to sit cross-legged on the cool soil, feeling the dampness through her flannel robe.

Higher now, the sun shone across the uneven field, drawing long shadows out of the rough, low-lying mounds of earth. She raised her hand to her brow, shaded her eyes to take in the view. Dew glistened off millions of little seedlings, the light shifted between green and gold and made the whole surface dance. She closed her eyes, seeing bright red and blue sun spots behind her eyelids and opened them again and examined the soil at her knees. It took a few moments to refocus, a fraction of time to see that she was seated on a mound of burnt-out fiber. It appeared to be old sweaters. What was old McArthur doing with a bunch of hand-me-downs on his outer field? It was all as black, as black can be. She dug her fingers into it and drew out a handful. Worms wriggled through strands of yarn until they managed to squirm free and fall back to the ground. She watched them slowly slither into the airy spaces between the soil.

She felt an odd affinity for the worms. They were, as she had done, weaving their way to a place of comfort and safety, back to where the fecund smell of nature supported their power to produce and reproduce, to create and recreate.

She wanted to take it with her, this sudden intense urge, this power born of affinity. She wanted to taste the dirt, to consume it, to meld it into some kind of archetypical shape that encompassed something beyond earthly senses.

She sat for a while longer, the sun now far above the horizon, its heat streaming across the landscape in warm rays, the mist having surrendered to it some time ago. She felt comfortable here, at one with this burnt-out patch of ground. How might it have felt before it burned? as it was burning? the flames licking out to the ends of the fibers and cracking into a night sky (or maybe it was a mid-day blue sky), sizzling and snapping before fizzling to nothing but embers. The smoke would have risen high into the air, the wind scattering it first in one direction and then the next, gathering it with its invisible brush and painting it in broad strokes until it merged with other, bulkier plumes that would have billowed up from beyond the curve of the earth. The resulting clouds would have loomed high in the atmosphere, these feathery ones from McArthur's outer field being swallowed into the mouths of the heavy masses from far and beyond, to an unknown desert. In that place the sky would be infinitely cloudless, offering a fresh canvas to other streams of charcoal-laden smoke. Its point of origin would have been in similar mounds, truckload after truckload of burning clothing that had been unwanted and discarded. Hundreds of piles, each cursing the earth with their small, destructive force. Each of them biding their time as their dyes leached into the ground below the sandy soil, insidiously contaminating scarce subterranean creeks that trickled through underground passageways.

The elements of the universe continue on their mission, the same sun shines over distinct and distant patches of ground. The same winds follow their habitual routes through the skies, skirting between mountains, diving into valleys, soaring above oceans, and finally weeping sorry or happy (depending on the circumstances) tears onto vulnerable landscapes. Atoms collect electrons, and molecules combine into matter that is gathered at consequential points at given times, everything relative. And it all counts.

Irene returned to see her mother watching her through the kitchen window, hugging a mug of coffee with both hands, the coffee long since gone cold. Irene waved and her mother wriggled her fingers and smiled a small smile.

Her mother always had something they could unravel and repurpose. They would start again. She and her mother would resume their old habit of combining natural with synthetic, knitting something new from something used. They would catch the atoms from embers that floated above foreign horizons. They would breathe vitality into castoffs. They would honor lives in search of renewal and art in search of home.

OTHER BOOKS BY EDIE AYALA

HARD BED HOTEL
ISBN Print: 978-0-9880032-2-4
ISBN Ebook: 978-0-9880032-3-1

SOUTH OF CENTRE
ISBN Print: 978-0-9880032-4-8
ISBN Ebook: 978-0-9880032-5-5

www.edieayala.com